OXFORD APOSTLES

CARDINAL NEWMAN
*From the painting by W. W. Ouless
in the possession of Oriel College*

OXFORD APOSTLES

A CHARACTER STUDY OF THE OXFORD MOVEMENT

BY

GEOFFREY FABER, M.A.

FELLOW OF ALL SOULS COLLEGE, OXFORD

'One gains nothing by sitting still. I am
sure the Apostles did not sit still.'
NEWMAN *to* BOWDEN
August 31, 1833

LONDON
FABER AND FABER
24 RUSSELL SQUARE

FIRST PUBLISHED IN JUNE MCMXXXIII
BY FABER AND FABER LIMITED
24 RUSSELL SQUARE LONDON W.C. I
PRINTED IN GREAT BRITAIN BY
R. MACLEHOSE AND COMPANY LIMITED
THE UNIVERSITY PRESS GLASGOW
ALL RIGHTS RESERVED

To

T. S. ELIOT

with affection and respect

PREFACE

The present volume makes no pretence to be a history of the Oxford Movement. Nor does it approach the Movement from any definite religious or theological or ecclesiastical angle. It is the result of an attempt by a middle-aged modern to grasp the working of his grandfather's mind; to understand the motives and the ideals of Tractarianism through the personalities of the Tractarians themselves.

It takes the form of a study of Newman's life and inner mind down to the year 1845, fuller and more detailed during the formative years before the Movement began than during the Movement itself. Keble, Pusey, Hurrell Froude and the lesser figures take their natural places in this story ; and I have tried to make the ideas by which the Movement was governed at least historically intelligible. In the narrative parts of the book the dates of the events related are given, for the reader's convenience, in the page headings ; but where the discussion takes a general turn dates are omitted. Since I am not a historian and have not written for historians, I have deliberately avoided the use of references, except in a very few instances for special reasons. All my quotations and statements of fact (with one or two obvious exceptions) are derived from the books named in the list of principal authorities. Of the inferences based upon these I am the only begetter.

Although my book appears in the year of the centenary celebrations, it was not undertaken as a 'centenary volume' in any sense of the phrase. I can best explain its *raison d'être* and its point of view by a brief excursion into family history.

b

In 1834, the second year of the Oxford Movement, my grandfather, the Rev. Francis Atkinson Faber, then a man of thirty, was elected a Fellow of Magdalen. His younger brother, Frederic, became a Fellow of University three or four years later. Both brothers were well-known figures in the Oxford of the late 'thirties and early 'forties. Fred was a fascinating, romantic, ardently religious young man, a poet before he became a hymn-writer, and a brilliant or a showy talker, according to the taste of the listener. Like Newman, he was brought up as an Evangelical. At Oxford he fell under Newman's spell. He followed his leader to Rome in 1845, became the head of the Brompton Oratory (an offshoot of Newman's Birmingham Oratory), and is still remembered, by Anglicans as well as Romans, as the author of many popular hymns.

Frank Faber was of a different type, a scholar rather than a poet, more cautious but more independent. His contemporaries respected his judgment as that of a moderate and sensible man, and enjoyed his company as that of an amusing and pointed conversationalist. A saving sense of humour prevented him from going all the way with the Tractarians ; but, though he was not an out-and-out Newmanite or Puseyite, he was very strongly attracted by Newman and by the revival of Catholic ideas. The Movement, he perceived, must lead somewhere. 'Such a sea' he said 'cannot stand still.' His letters show him bitterly indignant over the 'deep infamy' of Dr. Pusey's 'persecution'; though he speaks of Daily Prayers as 'one of the monstrous excrescences of Puseyism'. For Newman his admiration was profound. Writing to my grandmother, he called it 'latria'—hiding the strength of his feelings behind the Greek word for worship. In November 1843 he told her: 'If he [Newman] were to break down under the treatment of our rulers and be driven to the Romans, how bitter my sorrow would be.'

Looking through my grandfather's papers some time ago,

I found my curiosity excited by what remained of two series of letters. The first series consists of letters which he received from Newman over a long stretch of years, before and after 1845. Amongst these is the original of the letter which Newman afterwards used in Part VI of the *Apologia*, denying the charge of having been a 'concealed Romanist' during the last ten years of his career in the Church of England. The charge had been made by my grandfather's uncle, the Rev. George Stanley Faber, a learned and redoubtable antagonist of Popery in the North of England. The letter is one of a group written by Newman and his detractor, which stirred a mild desire on my part to know more about the rights and wrongs of that rather faded controversy. I was more keenly intrigued by one of the earlier letters (which are mostly short and ephemeral). This is a longish letter, undated but written from Oriel sometime about 1841. My grandfather had apparently understood Newman to say that temptation was of the nature of sin, and that persons in weak health (such as my grandfather) were especially exposed to temptation. He wrote in the greatest distress of mind to ask if this were Newman's considered opinion; and Newman, in reply, explained that the warfare with temptation, and the punishment for incidental defeat during it, were the ordained means of leading many of the saints to glory. The letter is interesting in itself; but what specially interested me was the character in which its writer spoke. What was this man, that his lightest word could so shake the minds of his contemporaries? And what was the nature of the society in which such questions as this were brought to him for his decision by men scarcely younger than himself?

The other series consists of letters written by my grandfather to my grandmother during their eight-years-long engagement. It astonished me to find how large a part of them was concerned with questions of religious doctrine—'polemical theology' my grandfather called them, himself amused to think 'how people would smile at such a lovers' topic!' I wondered still more at the gulf which divided my mind from his. The generations move slowly in some families. I was born eighty-five years after my grandfather; and in eighty-five years the spirit of civilization has changed as startlingly as its material aspect. The change is the more startling, because the forms of expression have changed so little. No century has seen less alteration in the English language. In the first decade of the twentieth century I was given much the same education as my grandfather in the second and third decades of the nineteenth. The poets of the English Romantic Revival—though they are behind a passing cloud to-day—were as exciting to me as they were to him. The smell of the old English clerical and professional tradition was in the air that I breathed from childhood. But the smell had grown musty. The tradition no longer commanded acceptance. The heart had died out of it.

In these letters of my grandfather's the accents were familiar, but the burden was strange, almost unintelligible. To take their meaning by direct assault seemed impossible. Should I surprise it in the history of the Oxford Movement? With this pious motive I embarked upon what I expected to find a dull and dreary course of reading. I did not find it so. On the contrary, to my extreme surprise, I found it absorbingly interesting.

It interested me for different, though connected, reasons. The personalities of the men who guided the Movement were remarkable. Most remarkable of all was the personality of John Henry Newman. It was very soon clear that the ineffective dreamer, the gentle artist *manqué* of Lytton Strachey's mordant essay on Cardinal Manning, had about as much likeness to the Newman of history as the Socrates of *The Clouds* has to the Socrates of the *Apology*. The Oxford half of his life—eventless as it was, by ordinary biographical standards, and played out upon a very narrow stage—had a compelling dramatic unity and drew to an intense climax. The story was moving, even if one regarded it superficially. As one looked below the surface and obtained some understanding of the ideas by which Newman and his friends were actuated, it became fascinating. I found these ideas extremely strange and often repellent. Nevertheless there could be no question that they were real. I do not mean that they seemed, or seem now, to me to be true. But they were certainly true to the men who held them. A very little first-hand knowledge blew to pieces Strachey's cynical estimate of the Movement as a game of exciting make-believe. It was evident that the Gallic method in biography purchased readability at too high a price; and that it might be worth while to try to understand the recent past, instead of treating it as an amusing period piece.

That, at any rate, is the spirit in which I have written. But while I have tried to treat the ideas of the Tractarians with sympathy and respect (which are the necessary conditions for the understanding of any idea whatsoever) I have not tried to conceal or to abandon my own point of view. The reader may define that point of view for himself if he cares to do so. I neither define nor defend it. Such as it is, it belongs not so much to me personally as to my generation, and is implicit in the whole of my book. I could not defend it, without passing a categorical judgment on the Tractarians. To do that would defeat the very object of my writing. But perhaps I may venture on one simple generalization. The Tractarians were determined to have something, which we have accustomed ourselves to do without—certainty upon the terms and the purpose of their earthly apprenticeship.

May, 1933.   GEOFFREY FABER.

ACKNOWLEDGMENTS

I have to record my grateful thanks to the following for permission to quote from books still in copyright:

Messrs. Longmans Green and Co. for permission to quote from the indispensable *Letters and Correspondence of J. H. Newman*, the *Correspondence of J. H. Newman with Keble and others*, Wilfrid Ward's *Life and Letters of Cardinal Newman*, Newman's *Verses on Various Occasions*, T. Mozley's *Reminiscences of Oriel*, Liddon's *Life of Pusey*, Isaac Williams's *Autobiography*, Palmer's *Narrative of Events*, J. B. Mozley's *Letters*, J. A. Froude's *Oxford Counter-Reformation* (*Short Studies*); Mrs. Sheed for permission to quote from Wilfrid Ward's *Life and Letters of Cardinal Newman*; Messrs. Macmillan and Co. for permission to quote from Mark Pattison's *Memoirs*; Sir John Murray for permission to quote from Tuckwell's *Reminiscences of Oxford*; Messrs Rivingtons for permission to quote from Wakeman's *Introduction to the History of the Church of England*.

I have also to record my no less grateful thanks to the Provost and Fellows of Oriel College, Oxford, the Governing Body of Christ Church, Oxford, the Warden and Council of Keble College, Oxford, and the Trustees of the National Portrait Gallery for permission to reproduce the portraits by which this book is illustrated. I am desired to state that the copyright of the originals (as distinct from the engravings) remains in the possession of their several owners, and that they may not be further reproduced wthout express permission. Finally, I wish to acknowledge my debt to my friend, Mr. F. V. Morley, for his invaluable criticisms of a great part of my manuscript.

G. C. F.

CONTENTS

ILLUSTRATIONS

PRINCIPAL AUTHORITIES

Letters and Correspondence of John Henry Newman during his life in the English Church. With a brief Autobiography. Edited, at Cardinal Newman's request, by Anne Mozley. Two vols. Longmans. 1891.

Correspondence of John Henry Newman with John Keble and Others, 1839-1845. Edited at the Birmingham Oratory. Longmans. 1917.

The Life and Letters of John Henry Cardinal Newman based on his Private Journals and Correspondence by Wilfrid Ward. Two vols. Longmans. 1912.

Apologia pro Vita Sua. The two versions of 1864 and 1865 preceded by Newman's and Kingsley's Pamphlets. With an Introduction by Wilfrid Ward. Oxford. 1913.

Contributions chiefly to the Early History of the late Cardinal Newman. With Comments. By his Brother, F. W. Newman. Kegan Paul. 1891.

Verses on Various Occasions by John Henry Cardinal Newman. Longmans. (1889.)

A Memoir of the Rev. John Keble. The Right Hon. Sir J. T. Coleridge. Parker. (1870.)

John Keble. A Biography. Walter Lock. Methuen. (1893.)

Miscellaneous Poems by the Rev. J. Keble. Parker. (1870.)

Life and Correspondence of Richard Whately, D.D. late Archbishop of Dublin. E. Jane Whately. Two vols. Longmans. 1866.

Reminiscences chiefly of Oriel and the Oxford Movement. The Rev. T. Mozley. Two vols. Longmans. 1882.

The Life of Edward Bouverie Pusey. Canon Liddon. Four vols. Longmans. 1893.

Remains of the late Reverend Richard Hurrell Froude. Two vols. Rivingtons. 1838. (Two further vols. published later.)

The Autobiography of Isaac Williams. Longmans. 1892.

Memorials of Renn Dickson Hampden, Bishop of Hereford. Edited by Henrietta Hampden. Longmans. 1871.

The Scholastic Philosophy considered in its relation to Christian Theology. Being Dr. Hampden's Bampton Lectures. Simpkin Marshall. (1848.)

Life of the Rev. Joseph Blanco White, written by himself with portions of his Correspondence. Edited by John Hamilton Thom. Three vols. London. 1845.

Memoirs. Mark Pattison. Macmillan. 1885.

The Life and Letters of Frederick William Faber. John Edward Bowden. Richardson. 1869.

W. G. Ward and the Oxford Movement. Wilfrid Ward. Macmillan. 1889.

A Narrative of Events connected with the publication of the Tracts for the Times. William Palmer. Rivingtons. 1883.

Letters of the Rev. J. B. Mozley. Edited by his Sister. Rivingtons. 1885.

The Oxford Movement. Twelve years, 1833-1845. R. W. Church. Macmillan. 1891.

The Oxford Counter-Reformation. J. A. Froude. (*Short Studies,* 4th Series.) Longmans. 1883.

Reminiscences of Oxford. The Rev. W. Tuckwell. Cassell. 1901.

Tracts for the Times. Six vols. (Collected reissue.) Rivingtons. 1838-1841.

Newman's Works *passim.*

Keble's *Christian Year.*

The *Lyra Apostolica.*

Reference has been made in the text to the following books:
The Anglican Career of Cardinal Newman. Edwin A. Abbott. Two vols. Macmillan. 1892.

A Century of Anglo-Catholicism. Professor H. L. Stewart.
Dent. 1929.

An Introduction to the History of the Church of England. H. O.
Wakeman. Eleventh edition. Rivingtons. (1927.)

Cardinal Manning. Lytton Strachey. In *Eminent Victorians*.
Chatto. 1918.

The dates printed in brackets are the dates of the
editions consulted, when these were not the first editions.

CHAPTER I

NEWMAN: THE BEGINNINGS

I. SKETCH OF A BACKGROUND

Gibbon was scarcely six years dead when Newman was born.

The division of time into centuries is an arbitrary human device. Yet the history of western civilization arranges itself irresistibly into that artificial pattern. Between the nineteenth and the eighteenth centuries the mysterious barrier runs with peculiar distinctness. The face of society changed. Art, thought, religion, were thrown into a fermentation. Individual temperaments sought to achieve a new balance. And the contrast finds one of its most significant illustrations in the difference between the leader of the Oxford Movement and the infidel historian upon whom he modelled his youthful style.

Both were men of enormous and incredible industry. Both were superb stylists. Both had the rare genius which casts its spell equally upon contemporaries and posterity. Both bent their minds to the study of the past, and of the same past. To each, standing on different sides of the watershed between the two centuries, the prospect was strangely different. To Gibbon it seemed that the clouds—including that greatest one called Christianity—lay below him. They were themselves a part of the landscape. One might say, they were the exhalations of mankind, appropriate and not unpleasing. He described and explained them with the same zest, the same dispassionate clarity, as he used upon the surge of human events which they parted ever and again to reveal. He himself, fortunate Augustan, inheritor of a finished and mannered tradition, saw them for the illusions they were, with irony indeed, but without bitterness. The spectacle, as a whole, was delightful to him. Safely removed by time from any disturbing personal contact with the events which he described, he exulted in the astounding panorama of passion and change, of the incessant and diverse manifestations of human energy, which the early centuries of the Christian era presented to him. It was, he wrote with studied moderation, 'the most agreeable occupation of his leisure hours'.

That occupation ended in 1788. But one year more, and the far-off murmur of great events, so agreeable to the philosopher's ears, swelled suddenly to a terrifying roar. The aristocratic dignity, the Augustan leisure, were shattered by the French Revolution. History was awake again. In England, it is true, the ancient forms of society, the Throne, the Nobility, the Landed Gentry, the Established Church, the Universities, remained where they were, and to all appearance as they had been. But only a few miles from London their counterparts in France had vanished, suddenly, almost without resistance beneath a sea of blood and terror. Who could prophesy that these things would not happen in England? Already, while Gibbon was composing, the American colonies had wrenched themselves free. What dreadful writing was there not now upon the wall? What more, in 1791, could be necessary, to vindicate Burke's Cassandra-like *Reflections on the French Revolution*, than the publication and ominous popularity of Tom Paine's *Rights of Man*? Such a book it was, that a generation later Newman's pupils took it as evidence of a singular strength of mind in their tutor that he was known to have read and to possess a copy. He kept it, indeed, under lock and key and let it out only to those who, he was assured, could come to no harm in consequence.

It was, therefore, in a world of which the forms only were the same that the young Newman grew up. The old sense of security had been undermined. Every department of the national life was under criticism, under test, yielding to pressure. Fortunately for the continuity of tradition in English life the French Revolution spent itself so quickly, passed so soon into Napoleonism, and challenged English nationalism so violently that the day of reckoning on the north side of the Channel was temporarily postponed. Partly for this reason, and partly also because of the slower national temperament, the processes of disillusionment and change in England prolonged themselves indefinitely, to be accentuated as the countryside sank into utter poverty after the war, and the industrial revolution fulfilled its grim course.

To Newman, with his more passionate sense of the past and his temperamental belief in a Golden Age, the world of men came to show a very different face from that which it showed to Gibbon. Looking out upon it from the Oratory at Birmingham he saw a sight which filled him with unspeakable distress. The passage in which he records the impression made upon him by the spectacle of human history has a dark splendour, unmatched by anything in Gibbon.[1] The horror which he feels is not caused by the social miseries, the poverty and the ugliness of the times. His concern was very little with these things. He relates it to the absence of God in the minds of men. His outlook is wholly different from Gibbon's. His mind has been formed in a wholly different environment, an environment of secular change and movement, hostile to his deepest instincts. And when he surveys, as Gibbon did, 'the world in its length and breadth, its various history, the many races of man', he finds in it no agreeable occupation for his leisure hours, but 'a heart-piercing, reason-bewildering fact', 'a vision to dizzy and appal', 'a profound mystery, which is absolutely beyond human solution', except on the hypothesis of 'some terrible aboriginal calamity'. The clouds which Gibbon looked down upon are thick about him

[1] *Apologia*, Part vii.

—clouds of error and of sin, rolling up and overwhelming the
heights on which he stands. Not for him the clear calm
secular view, the circumambient translucency of Gibbon's
empyrean. That light belongs to God; and when he
struggles into it, it is to stand alone with his Creator, on a
perilous eminence, with the dark vapours swirling round
his feet.

2. BOYHOOD

Newman was born in Old Broad Street, on February 21,
1801; baptized, in the Church of St. Benet Fink, close to the
Bank of England, since pulled down, by the names of John
Henry. He was the eldest of six children—there were two
brothers, Charles and Frank, and three sisters, Harriett,
Jemima and Mary—a striking disproof of the legend that the
first child of a family is never the most distinguished.

His parents had been married sixteen months before his
birth. John Newman, the father, came of a Cambridgeshire
family of small landed proprietors. There was possibly Jewish
blood in them, but the only evidence of this is the name and
(as some have thought) a Jewish look about the features of the
future Cardinal. The notion is contemptuously repudiated by
his biographer. 'The nose' says Mr. Ward 'was Roman
rather than Jewish.' His assertion is supported by James
Froude's odd comparison of Newman to Julius Caesar. 'The
forehead, the shape of the ears and nose were almost the
same. The lines of the mouth were very peculiar, and I should
say exactly the same. I have often thought of the resemblance
and believed that it extended to the temperament.' The likeness is not evident in the many portraits, nor in Westmacott's
marble bust ; and the nose varies according to the artist, becoming noticeably more hooked as he grows older and his
face more deeply carved by suffering. It is not easy to dismiss
the idea that there was Jewish blood in the Newman of some

John Henry Newman

JOHN HENRY NEWMAN
*From a drawing by Maria Giberne
in the possession of Oriel College*

of the Oxford-period portraits. Nor is it easy to understand why it should be so strongly resisted.

It is borne out—at least it is not contradicted—by his own aptitude for business and for figures, his habit of closely scrutinizing tradesmen's accounts, and by his father's profession, which was that of a banker. John Newman the elder seems to have begun life as a clerk. From about 1807 to 1816 he was partner in a Lombard Street banking firm, Ramsbottom, Newman, Ramsbottom & Co. The bank failed, just before his eldest son went up to Oxford, in the depression which followed the Napoleonic wars. All its creditors were paid in full only a month after its suspension, but the blow was one from which the family never recovered. For a few years Mr. Newman struggled to make a success as a country brewer at Alton in Hampshire. He died in 1824, a few months after his son was ordained.

John Henry had very little to say about Mr. Newman's character or opinions. He loved his father dutifully, was conscious of the 'loving ambition' centred upon himself, and sensible (afterwards if not at the time) of his good advice and sound judgment. Mr. Newman's death shook him, as he was always shaken when the shadow fell near his own path. 'That dread event has happened. Is it possible? O my Father!' And, when he looked at the dead man: 'he looked beautiful. Such calmness, sweetness, composure, and majesty were in his countenance. Can a man be a materialist who sees a dead body? I had never seen one before. His last words to me, or all but his last, were to bid me read to him the 53rd chapter of Isaiah.'

There is more to be learned of Mr. Newman from Thomas Mozley (who married Harriett Newman) and John's brother Frank. The picture forms of an intelligent, affectionate, equable man, much preoccupied with business, hating intolerance and fanaticism and self-righteousness, preferring Shakespeare to the Bible and finding himself, as time went

on, a little lost and lonely in the atmosphere of intense re-
ligiousness and high culture which prevailed in the family.
He would assert himself at times, and shock them by saying
that he was not a religious man, but a man of the world—as
became a keen Freemason and a member of the Beef Steak
Club. He thought that the Psalms and the Epistles of St.
Paul were disfigured by uncharitable language. His children
shuddered at his favourite proverb, 'Give the devil his due.'
After the failure of his business, anxiety fretted the edge of his
even temper and the opposition between himself and his
family gave rise to an occasional scene. There was one such in
1820, over the approaching trial of Queen Caroline. Mr.
Newman took the view of all sensible men; he was disgusted
by the proceedings. John took the part of the Ministry. The
debate ended in something like a quarrel, and in a bitter
sarcasm from the ex-banker: 'Well, John! I suppose I ought
to praise you for knowing how to rise in this world. Go on!
Persevere! Always stand up for men in power, and in time
you will get promotion.' It was an unwise thing to say; never
again would his son run the risk of a criticism so terribly like
an unsuspected truth. Worldly ambition was of the devil; he
would tear it by the roots out of his heart.

More painful still was a scene recorded by John himself in
his diary, in the following year. It was a Sunday towards the
end of the Long Vacation. 'After dinner to-day I was suddenly called downstairs to give an opinion whether I thought
it a sin to write a letter on a Sunday. I found dear F. had refused to copy one. A scene ensued more painful than any I
have experienced. I have been sadly deficient in meekness,
long-suffering, patience, and filial obedience. With God's
assistance I will redeem my character.' Next day: 'My Father
was reconciled to us to-day. When I think of the utter persuasion he must entertain of the justice of his views, of our
apparent disobedience, the seeming folly of our opinions, and
the way in which he is harassed by worldly cares, I think his

forgiveness of us an example of very striking candour, for-
bearance and generosity.'

One might guess that things were not made easier for
Mr. Newman after this, with the consciousness of business
failure perpetually harassing him, by Mrs. Newman's uncon-
cealed admiration for John's practical ability in comparison
with his own, and John's own readiness to assume responsibility for the affairs of the family. 'Everything will—I see it
will—be very right if only you will let me manage', the young
Fellow of Oriel writes to him at the end of 1822. But Mr. Newman was now too worn by the battle with adversity to resent
his son's tone. His wife answered for him: 'Your father for-
warded to me your delightful letter, which I know it will
gratify you to hear gave him so much pleasure, that I have
not seen anything cheer and comfort him like it a long time.
. . . I fully accord with you when you say, "Let me alone, I
shall do it all well. If you will let me manage, all will be
right." This is just the text I have preached from, whenever
your Father and I have discussed the subject. For many
months I always begin and end by saying, "I have no fear,
John will manage."'

If, as Frank said, there was nothing beyond natural pride
and affection in common between father and son except
their love of and skill in music, it was otherwise between John
and his mother, to whom he was—at least externally—an
always devoted son. Jemima Fourdrinier was of Huguenot
descent. Her great-grandfather left Caen and settled in Holland; his son came to England and there married a French-
woman of another Huguenot family. Their son, Henry Fourdrinier, Newman's grandfather, was therefore of pure French
descent. He himself was a draper, and a man of means.
When the bank and the brewery had both failed, his daughter's jointure—in spite of the reduction of interest from five to
three per cent—was still enough to support herself and her
two daughters. The name of Fourdrinier was known outside

the drapery trade. The Fourdriniers were engravers—their engravings are familiar to collectors of eighteenth-century books. They were also paper-makers. Two of John's uncles are said to have introduced from Italy a machine for making endless coils of paper, and thereby to have initiated the mechanical marvels of the modern newspaper.

Mrs. Newman was a profoundly religious woman. Her religion was of a simple, non-controversial character, broad enough to accompany John up to the threshold of his High Church period—but no further. Till then she all but idolized him. She writes to him on his twenty-fifth birthday begging him 'to accept the kindest wishes that a mother can offer to a son who has ever been her greatest consolation in affliction, and a comfort and delight at all times, and in all situations. We are daily receiving great instruction and advantage, I trust, from the course of sermons you last sent us. We all agreed that a week was much too long to wait between each; and when we have read these repeatedly I hope you will let us have more.' 'It is, my dear,' she writes a little later 'a great gift to see so clearly the truths of religion; still more to be able to impart the knowledge to others.' It cannot be doubted that it was from his mother that his mind, so plastic and so tenacious, first took the impress of the religious mould. The mould was to be broken; fresh patterns were to succeed it. But the original impress was never to be effaced; and it was the more lasting because of the quiet determination with which it had been originally made. For that was Mrs. Newman's way. Her manner was gentle, but her will was as strong as her son's, and her opinions far less subject to change.

'You see, John,' she said to him after a battle between them, when he was a very small boy, 'you did not get your own way.' 'No,' he retorted 'but I tried very hard.' Her discipline moulded, but it did not break him. Later on he took his own way—a different way from hers, though it remained a re-

ligious way. When she became aware of this, a critical attitude replaced the sympathy and praise of which, while he
conformed to her ideal of the clergyman son, she had been so
lavish. Newman was not a man who was ever happy under
criticism, unless the critic could be taken by the throat. He
was deeply wounded by the withdrawal of her confidence.
And though her death was a terribly distressing event to his
sensitive conscience he recovered from it with a rapidity
which surprised his friends and perhaps even himself.

When John was little the family lived at Ham. Though they
moved back to Old Broad Street when he was six years old,
Ham was always the home to which his thoughts went back
throughout his life—sometimes on the oddest occasions. It is
Ham of which he instantly thinks when he gazes on the
rocky island of Ithaca. It is the shrubberies of Ham which
comfort him in his nightmare at Naples. When he dreamed of
heaven as a boy, it took the form of Ham. Strange apotheosis
of a suburban garden! No other home that he shared with
his own people ever succeeded it in his imagination; in some
mysterious manner he had unlocked the riddle of existence
there to his own secret satisfaction; the rest of his life was, in
some sense, the pursuit of that half-forgotten answer, the
search for its intelligible expression in a sacred formula.
Other places drew his love: Oxford, Trinity Chapel (because, though his reason went with the Gothic, his heart was
with the Grecian—was there ever a more curious avowal?),
Oriel ('Yes! the beams in the roof were always rotten. He
had a little broken bit of one in his room now', to Scott Holland at Birmingham, when he was 76 years old), Littlemore
(where he kissed the bed and the mantelpiece and other parts
of the house, on leaving it), and finally his Oratory at Birmingham, to which he came back, a Cardinal, from his visit
in old age to the Holy City, thankful for the happiness of
being home once more. But much as he loved these later
homes of his, loving them indeed with an intensity of passion

such as other men give to persons, Ham had always for him a more peculiar magic.

There is significance in this. A man's genius does not except him from the laws which rule the formation of his mind. Obscure as these laws are, we understand something of their nature. We know that they begin their operation at birth—if not earlier—and exert their most powerful effect in the very earliest years of life. We know, also, that the way of a mother with her child is the strongest factor in the growth of personality. A trained psychologist can argue back, with a considerable degree of certainty, from the abnormal characteristics of a grown man to the decisive influences which he encountered in infancy. The eldest child of a family is often more marked by such influences than his younger brothers and sisters. It is natural that this should be so. Mothers have to experiment with their children; they learn the technique of training them by a combination of instinct with a method of trial and error. The more strong-minded a woman is, the more exacting and certain in her moral and religious opinions, the greater is the risk of distortion in the plastic structure of the child's mind.

How Mrs. Newman used her eldest son remained her own secret. But that she would have him perfect, after her own pattern, is not to be doubted. It was a moral rather than a dogmatic religious pattern. The child learned to conform to the standards of a pious Christian household, learning his Catechism and reading the Bible, but not acquiring any very definite notions of doctrine. The moral pattern sank deeply into him. He grew up with his intellect and his emotions unnaturally divorced from his body. That may, or may not, have been the necessary condition of his genius. If genius is an infinite capacity for taking pains, it is also, perhaps, an infinite necessity for taking pains: the abnormal concentration of a man's energies in the only direction left open to him. Newman's fundamental masculine instincts were cauterized. As he might never be an ordinary boy, so he was never to be a whole man, and as a leader he was to prove a broken reed. Here, certainly, Froude's facile comparison of him to Julius Caesar is hopelessly wide of the mark. An unfriendly critic (Edwin Abbott) says justly of him that 'affectionate though he was to his relations and intimate friends . . . it is impossible to say that his sympathies with men in general were wide or deep.' For controversial purposes he understood them well enough; he understood them in the rational and imaginative parts of their minds, never in the instinctive. His inner life belonged to an ideal world, in companionship with a God to whom the crude processes of His own creation were as odious as they were to Newman.

If this interpretation of Newman's character is a true one, his life becomes not, as he represented it to himself, an intellectual pilgrimage, but a difficult emotional progress. The difficulty lay, simply and naturally, in the abandonment of his prejudices, of his family ties, of his professional position, of friends to whom he was warmly attached. The intellectual processes which accompanied it were altogether secondary. One set of reasons was gradually allowed to prevail over another. That is not to say that there was no rational conflict. The rational conflict was real, but it was decided by the transfer of emotional rather than logical weight from one scale to the other. The solution of the conflict was followed by the feeling of peace which he himself took for a witness that he had indeed found ultimate truth. It meant no more, perhaps, than that he had achieved the most final harmony of which his nature was capable. Years of intense hard work and bodily mortification had killed what he would have called his baser instincts; or, if they were not completely dead, they were now so mutilated and enfeebled that they were completely subservient. It was no longer necessary for him to bury them beneath mountains of superhuman labour. Even beneath that incredible load, and after the long suppressions

of childhood and youth, they had given curious evidence of
their all but indestructible vitality in the strange repellent
'fierceness' of his Oxford campaign. That was indeed the
period when Newman was most alive, most nearly a complete
man. He said himself: 'It was, in a human point of view, the
happiest time of my life.'

But in the old-fashioned early Georgian house at Ham and
in its spacious grounds, and for long afterwards, the old
Adam was in no condition to trouble him. He was happy. It
was a bright and glorious time. He was free to enjoy his
dream of a sinless heaven upon earth. There 'God's presence
went up with him, and gave him rest.' Within doors he takes
great delight in reading the Bible. He has a perfect knowledge
of the Catechism, but as yet 'no formed religious convictions'.
He listens 'with wonder and interest to fables or tales; he has
a dim shadowy sense of what he hears about persons and
matters of this world; but he has that within him which
actually vibrates, responds, and gives a deep meaning to the
lessons of his first teachers about the will and providence of
God.' His mind runs, in his schooldays, on marvels, 'on unknown influences, on magical powers and talismans'. He is
superstitious, and crosses himself when he goes into the dark.
In the dawn of conscious thought he fancies 'life might be a
dream, or I an angel, and all this world a deception, my
fellow-angels, by a playful device, concealing themselves
from me, and deceiving me with the semblance of a material
world.' He feels himself isolated from the objects which
surround him; he 'rests in the thought of two and two only
supreme and luminously self-evident beings, myself and my
Creator.' That, at any rate, is the general direction of his
childish imaginations. The psychologist recognizes in them
the familiar symptoms of early repressions. The sense of a
deep given difference between himself and others; the devices
by which his inferiority is converted into a grand superiority;
the escape from facts into fantasies; the ecstasy of untram-

melled day-dreaming, so satisfying at the time, so poignant in recollection, so certain a forerunner of unhappiness in later life.

As if to correct the picture of a child too incredibly remote from the things of this world, other memories stayed with him in his old age. Exceptional in this as in other ways, Newman differed from most men of egocentric temperament in being sharply observant of external things. His self-absorption never blinded him to his surroundings. On the contrary it intensified his interest in them. Just because they were *his* surroundings, every detail about them remained indelibly printed on his memory. His passionate treasuring of the past was rooted in the same hypertrophied sense of his own uniqueness. So he recalled every room, every decorative detail, every tree and shrub of all the places he had lived in; and simple natural scenes returned to him out of the past and smote him with an exquisite nostalgia. How he had lain in bed as a child of five and watched the candles lit in the windows to celebrate the victory of Trafalgar. How he had lain there in summertime and listened to the sweet sound of the mower's scythe cutting the lawn. How he had gorged himself with gooseberries in the kitchen garden, and had been taught to play billiards (at six years of age!) by his father, and had soared dizzily skywards on the swing hanging from the massive branches of the large plane tree.

He was a precocious child, and his parents fostered his precocity by playing upon his vanity. When he was not yet six his father wrote him his first letter, to be read aloud to his mother and Charles to show how well he could read writing. 'But you will observe that you must learn something new every day, or you will no longer be called a clever boy.' He was only just seven when he was sent to a school, kept by Dr. Nicholas, at Ealing. It was a large school of some 200 boys, with a great reputation. 'It was conducted on Eton lines; everybody sent his sons there; they got on', said a friend

of the family. His two brothers followed him there later—
the wastrel Charles, the even more brilliant and precocious
Frank. Frank was of very different mettle from John, taking
his full share in the ordinary amusements of his schoolfellows.
Ealing was a great school for games. But John was never seen
to play any game. 'He did go to our bathing-pond, but never
swam.' His only physical accomplishment was riding, which
he learned by his father's desire.

There is a pathetic and revealing picture of the little boy in
his first term at school, drawn by Newman himself. His father
and mother came to see him, and after they had gone Dr.
Nicholas found him by himself, crying. Why didn't he go into
the big room with the other boys? 'O sir! they will say such
things! I can't help crying.' Dr. Nicholas made light of this
possibility. 'O sir! but they will; they will say all sorts of
things. Come and see for yourself!' And he caught the master
by the hand, and led him into the crowded room, where, of
course, under the circumstances, there was no teasing.

'Francis is adamant,' said his mother to him in later years,
'but you are such a sensitive being.'

Certainly he was very sensitive, but there is no sign that he
was unhappy at school. He was shy—he never lost his shyness until Whately took him in hand as a probationer Fellow
of Oriel. But he knew himself to be the superior of the young
barbarians about him, and he could easily escape from their
uncongenial society into the realm of ideas, where they could
never follow him. He raced up the school at a speed no other
boy had ever equalled. He must have had his friends and his
special friend; he was never without his worshippers at any
time, and he gave his love always to anyone who made
advances to him. ('My habitual feeling . . . that it was not I
who sought friends, but friends who sought me.') In 1875 he
refers in a letter to the approaching anniversary of the death
of his 'greatest school friend, Hans Hamilton'. In spite of his
shyness and aloofness he was looked up to and became some-

thing of a leader. Shortly before he left school he wrote and circulated two papers—*The Spy* and *The Anti-spy*—thirty numbers of the one and twenty-seven numbers of the other; and, according to Frank, he 'initiated a number of the boys into a special Order, with whom he was every week to read *The Spy*.' Frank's informant was his older brother Charles, who told him that 'there were different degrees in the Order, marked by ribbons of different colours, with J.H.N. as Grand Master.' A copybook of John's had a coloured sketch, done apparently by a friend, on one of its pages, 'of a party of boys of fifteen or sixteen sitting round a table, addressed by a member standing on his chair, whose marked features make it clear who was the leading spirit of the company'. The Order was broken up by the '*profanum vulgus* of the uninitiated'. Thirty years later, on John's becoming a Roman Catholic, Charles—the atheistical black sheep of the family—wrote to Frank that it was no more than one might have expected from that affair at Ealing.

During these schooldays John's outward character was developing as consistently as the image on a photographic plate. Each year he became more grave, considerate, philosophical, knowledgeable, fastidious and superior. But religion was as yet far from being the all-absorbing interest. He had his secular excitements and accomplishments. Music, of course, was the chief of these. His brother-in-law, Tom Mozley, declared that he would have been a second Paganini, if he had become a professional musician. He wrote a mock drama and a satire on the Prince Regent at eleven; a dramatic piece 'in which Augustus comes on'; a burlesque opera, tunes and all, at fourteen. Frank remembered in this or an earlier 'opera' of John's composition acting the part of fisherman to the lord of a Welsh castle, and the eulogy of his master put into his mouth for 'eminence in the four cardinal virtues' and above all for being so fond of fish. The three brothers and the eldest girl, Harriett, 'were all dressed out theatrically, to my father's great amusement'. It was at fourteen that John read Paine's Tracts against the Old Testament 'and found pleasure in thinking of the objections which were contained in them.' He read Hume also, and 'some French verses, perhaps Voltaire's, against the immortality of the soul' which shocked him, not unpleasurably. He acted in the plays of Terence performed annually at Ealing. He devoured *Waverley* and *Guy Mannering*, as they came out, lying in bed in the early summer mornings. He kept a diary ('1810, May 4. Heard for the first time the cuckoo. Dreamed that Mary was dead.') and wrote poetry of which he was sternly critical. To his mother and sisters he was the admirable Crichton; to his brothers the slightly insupportable corrector of their ignorance. What else stirred dangerously behind the grave façade, no one except himself ever knew. But can it have been only the extravagant language of prayer which made him, as a man of fifty-eight, 'writing on his knees and in God's sight', thank God for the wonderful grace which 'turned me right round when I was more like a devil than a wicked boy, at the age of fifteen'?

He was fifteen and his voice had broken, when the great change came to him. Staying on at school during the summer holidays he 'fell under the influence of an excellent man, the Rev. Walter Mayers.' That was in 1816, just before he went up to Oxford. Before Mr. Mayers became the means of grace to the slim, precocious, blue-eyed, dark-haired boy, with the strongly marked features, a quite different possibility had existed. 'It is difficult' wrote the aged Cardinal in 1885, in one of his innumerable and not always consistent re-traversings of the past 'to realize or imagine the identity of the boy before and after August 1816. . . . I can look back at the end of seventy years as if on another person.' Many years earlier he wrote in one of his notebooks: 'I recollect, in 1815 I believe, thinking that I should like to be virtuous, but not religious. There was something in the latter idea I did not like. Nor did I see the meaning of loving God.'

What if, at the critical moment, when his faculties were expanding and his deeply repressed nature was beginning to show signs of taking at least an intellectual revenge, he had come under the influence not of a Mr. Mayers but of, say, a Godwin? Nothing of that sort was possible at Ealing—that admirable school, where parents sent their boys because 'they got on'. But—if it had been possible? These influences were in the air, though not in the air of Ealing or of Old Broad Street. Yet Shelley had been sent down from University College not many years before. *Queen Mab* was already three years, *Alastor* a year old; and in the very year of Newman's conversion the poet of revolt was married to the daughter of the free-thinking philosopher. How different would the intellectual and moral and religious history of the last hundred years have been if Newman had broken towards Athens instead of towards Rome?

3. CONVERSION

'On my conversion how the wisdom and goodness of God is discerned! I was going from school half a year sooner than I did. My staying arose from the 8th of March. Thereby I was left at school by myself, my friends gone away.'

The reason for this change of plan was the failure, on the 8th of March, of Mr. Newman's bank. To John this was no accident. The bank must fail that he might stay on at Ealing and be converted. It was so that he interpreted everything that happened to him. In the *Apologia* he describes the event as follows:

'When I was fifteen, (in the autumn of 1816), a great change of thought took place in me. I fell under the influences of a definite Creed, and received into my intellect impressions of dogma, which, through God's mercy, have never been effaced or obscured. Above and beyond the conversations and sermons of the excellent man, long dead, the Rev.

Walter Mayers, of Pembroke College, Oxford, who was the human means of this beginning of divine faith in me, was the effect of the books which he put into my hands, all of the school of Calvin. One of the first books I read was a work of Romaine's; I neither recollect the title nor the contents, except one doctrine, which of course I do not include among those which I believe to have come from a divine source, viz. the doctrine of final perseverance. I received it at once, and believed that the inward conversion of which I was conscious, (and of which I am still more certain than that I have hands and feet), would last into the next life, and that I was elected to eternal glory. I have no consciousness that this belief had any tendency whatever to lead me to be careless about pleasing God. I retained it till the age of twenty-one, when it gradually faded away; but I believe that it had some influence on my opinions, in the direction of those childish imaginations which I have already mentioned, viz. in isolating me from the objects which surrounded me, in confirming me in my mistrust of the reality of material phenomena, and making me rest in the thought of two and two only supreme and luminously self-evident beings, myself and my Creator;—for while I considered myself predestined to salvation, I thought others simply passed over, not predestined to eternal death. I only thought of the mercy to myself.'

'The detestable doctrine last mentioned' are the opening words of the next paragraph. They do not refer, as a careless reader might think, to the doctrine that the unregenerate are predestined to eternal death. They refer to the doctrine of final perseverance—by which is simply meant the Calvinistic belief that the converted are given an assurance that they *will* persevere to the end and *cannot* fall away. Newman declares that it never really took root in his mind, though he admits that he held it for some six years after his conversion. What did take root in his mind was 'the fact of heaven and hell, divine favour and divine wrath, of the justified and the

unjustified'. There is a peculiar obscurity in his references to
the doctrine of final perseverance; for while he relates that
he accepted it, he goes on to say that it was 'simply denied
and abjured . . . by the writer who made a deeper impression
on my mind than any other, and to whom (humanly speaking) I almost owe my soul,—Thomas Scott.' It was Scott,
whose 'zealous faith in the Holy Trinity', achieved from a
Unitarian starting-point, 'first planted deep in my mind that
fundamental Truth of religion.' This also happened in the
year of his conversion, when he was but fifteen years old.

Besides Romaine and Scott, in this same late summer or
autumn, he read and was deeply impressed by Law's *Serious
Call to a Devout and Holy Life*. From that moment, he declared,
'I have given a full inward assent and belief to the doctrine
of eternal punishment, as delivered by our Lord himself, in as
true a sense as I hold that of eternal happiness; though I have
tried in various ways to make that truth less terrible to the
reason.' And he planted in himself 'the seeds of an intellectual inconsistency which disabled me for a long course of
years' by reading two other books 'each contrary to each'—
Milner's *Church History*, which fascinated him with its long
extracts from Augustine and Ambrose and the other Fathers,
and Newton *On the Prophecies*, which convinced him that the
Pope was the Antichrist predicted by Daniel, St. Paul and
St. John.

There are several very interesting features about this conversion of Newman's. In the first place it was not, in the
technical Evangelical sense, a 'conversion' at all. Several
strangers wrote and told him so, after the publication of the
Apologia. He quite agreed. 'He was sensible that he had ever
been wanting in those special Evangelical experiences which,
like the grip of the hand or other prescribed signs of a secret
society, are the sure tokens of a member.' Even when he was
still in the Evangelical fold he was forced to 'speak of conversion with great diffidence, being obliged to adopt the lan-

guage of books', never having himself experienced 'its stages
of conviction of sin, terror, despair, news of the free and full
salvation, apprehension of Christ, sense of pardon, assurance
of salvation, joy and peace, and so on to final perseverance'.
His own feelings, he wrote ten years after the event, 'were *not*
violent, but a returning to, a renewing of, principles, under
the power of the Holy Spirit, which I had already felt, and in
a measure acted on when young.' But he was more fortunate
than the hero of Dr. Jacks's story *A Philosopher among the
Saints*, for the failure of his conversion to conform to the
accepted pattern caused him no distress. His conviction that
truth was rooted in himself was too strong. 'The reality of
conversion' he noted a few months after leaving school 'as
cutting at the root of doubt, providing a chain between God
and the Soul, that is with every link complete; I know I am
right. How do you know it? I know I know.'

'Know', 'doubt', 'intellect', 'dogma'—these words are the
key to the true nature of the experience he had undergone.
Hitherto his own emotional peculiarities and limitations had
received no special intellectual support, nor had they found
any intellectual expression. The foundations of his character
had been laid in his infancy; they had never been disturbed,
they never were to be disturbed. All the sap, which might have
nourished his instincts, was diverted into the exceptionally
rapid growth of his mind. The rigid and specious logic of the
Calvinistic system was exactly suited to his requirements.
It held together, it safeguarded the sense of his own eternal
importance. Later on he came to distrust it, as he came to
distrust all 'paper logic'. He wished always 'to go by reason,
not by feeling', but he insisted that 'it is the concrete being
that reasons . . . the whole man moves; paper logic is but the
record of it.' This was a later, richer conception of reason. At
fifteen he was content to pack his faith into a series of
syllogisms with texts for premisses. The brief flicker of natural
wickedness was put out by this logical douche.

What happened to him in 1816, then, was scarcely a conversion, though it was something equally definite, startling, fatal. It was the sudden concurrence and conjunction of the two halves of his conscious self—intellect and feeling. The impressions of dogma squared exactly with his instinctive attitude. Once interlocked the two could never be separated again.

Was this Newman's good fortune or Newman's tragedy? The answer must depend on the point of view, by which the question is prompted. Certainly it meant that all hope of any further development of the non-rational side of his nature was at an end. And this not because it was fixed and clamped by his reason. He did not stay for the rest of his life in the position he took up in 1816. The union of feeling and reason was permanent, but 'the whole man moved'. What was the cause of the movement? That is the riddle of Newman's career. It was not a movement of the reason, dragging the feelings with it; it was far more a movement of the feelings, justified by reason. 'That my *sympathies* have grown towards the religion of Rome I do not deny; that my *reasons* . . . have altered it would be difficult perhaps to prove.' (1841.) But though the feelings moved, they did not develop. In his old age he was still substantially the child who walked with God at Ham and dreamed that his brother-angels were hiding themselves from him. All the resources of his intellect were employed throughout his life to protect that dream from destruction.

That was the function of dogma in his mind. It was the solidest buttress he could find to the aethereal constructions of his childhood. It was at once the impenetrable shield of those shrinking yet confident fantasies, and the means whereby they were brought into relation with the real world. Without such a hard outer covering his naked sensitiveness could not have supported social life. It was like a shell secreted by an otherwise defenceless animal, but secreted according to a chosen pattern. Given the initial direction, his final choice was beyond question the right choice. His *Via Media* satisfied, and *mutatis mutandis* satisfies, others. It could not for long satisfy him, partly because it depended too much on his own inferences and too little on external authority, and partly because its adherents were too few in number and too dependent upon himself. In the Roman Catholic system he enjoyed the maximum of protection and the maximum sense of community with his kind. Possibly this explains why as a young man he had 'not a grain in his composition of that temper of conviviality so natural to young men', but as a Roman priest he showed a special 'amiability in society' and went so far as to say astonishingly that 'if he had had to choose between social intercourse without literary pursuits and literary pursuits without social intercourse, he would, as a student, without hesitation have chosen the former.'

This intellectual reinforcement to the maldevelopment of his instincts came to Newman soon after puberty. 'With the growth of independence' says a modern medical psychologist[1] 'which comes about in the child as it begins to take its place in the world, there is an opening out of its consciousness and a readiness to absorb new ideas, which is perhaps most marked in those years immediately succeeding puberty.' It was Newman's peculiar destiny at this critical period to encounter, instead of new ideas, an impressive religious system, suited to his temperament, satisfactory to his intellect, embodying principles with which he had always been familiar, and urged upon him by the flattering interest of an older man. If he had, at this period, encountered an intellectual system of a quite different kind, presented to him by somebody whom he liked and admired, he might have undergone a real conversion, a real transformation of his inner nature. It was not, so to speak, original sin but original virtue, which held him in thrall. But no such revolution was allowed to occur.

---

[1] Dr. J. R. Rees : *The Health of the Mind.*

There was a third possibility. Had he survived the time of
his adolescence without coming under the influence either of
religious dogma or of Godwinian rationalism, he might have
been led by the restlessness of his own mind into a gradually
increasing conflict between reason and feeling. His truncated
natural instincts would have met with a less firm barrier to
their reattempted growth. How the battle would have gone,
is an idle speculation. But Newman's *Confessions* would have
had a wider circle of readers to-day than his *Apologia*.

Either of these two possibilities—a violent revolution or a
long conflict—implies that Newman's intellect might, under
different circumstances, have seized or attempted to seize
the citadel where his infantile self lay entrenched. That, it
must be admitted, is a bold supposition. In fact, keen and
tireless though his reasoning powers were, they never passed,
even for a moment, after his 'conversion', out of obedience to
that childish domination. They brilliantly performed the
tasks dictated to them from the citadel; they surveyed the
hostile country lying round it; they executed masterly ex-
peditions into the enemies' territory, and brought back
trophies of victory and clear-sighted reports of the situation.
But they never once rebelled or criticized, never once dreamed
of questioning the orders they were given or the principles on
which those orders were based. Those principles had fixed
themselves unassailably in his mind before his reason grew
up. They were not won by reason; they were not even maintained by reason. In consequence he displayed a naive
credulity, which is startling in a man of so much mental force.
It would be unbelievable, if we had not his own word for it,
that in his late thirties he conceived political movements to
be the work of a race of intermediate beings, between angels
and devils; whose existence he accounted for by supposing
that they were the offspring of amorous intercourse between
the angels who fell before the deluge and the daughters of
men. Such a being, and of such a parentage, is John Bull, 'a

spirit neither of heaven nor hell'! Or, as an example of the way in which his reason could go through a hoop to please his feelings, take his discovery, at the age of thirty-two, that 'it was not the Church [of Rome], but the old dethroned Pagan monster, still living in the ruined city, that was Antichrist'—a discovery which he can quote with approval, at the age of sixty-four, as his 'first advance in rescuing, on an intelligible, intellectual basis, the Roman Church from the designation of Antichrist'.

One conclusion, at least, is forced upon the mind by the attempt to touch the springs of action and thought in great men. The measures which apply to lesser men do not apply, without qualification, to them. We cannot, without risk of self-deception, treat a Newman as if he were a patient in the consulting-room of a psychoanalyst. The psychologist, accustomed to deal with men whose texture is not tough enough to endure long mental conflict, is not yet equipped to handle giants. His net will not hold the big fish. Doubtless the same laws hold of the big and the little. But they have, as yet, been formulated from experience of the little. They provide clues, they do not guarantee solutions. Let this stand for a warning after what has been so far written. There is an initial vigour in men of genius which separates them from the emotional and intellectual cripples who find their way into the hands of the mental doctor. They do not go to others to be healed, nor do they run away from the conflict between the world and their dreams. In one way or another, at whatever cost of suffering, they work out their own salvation. And no one who looks at a portrait of Newman in his old age—such as the beautiful head in Joseph Brown's engraving of 1873—however little sympathy he may have with ecclesiasticism and dogma, can fail to perceive that this man attained truth and expressed it in his own person.

FATHER NEWMAN
*From the engraving by Samuel Cousins
after the drawing by Lady Coleridge*

4. THE DEEP IMAGINATION

Some such note of warning needs to be clearly sounded before the other 'deep imagination' which took possession of the converted fifteen-year-old boy, namely that it was the will of God that he should lead a single life.

Newman, in 1864, refers to this 'with great reluctance', though he does not indicate what the cause of this reluctance was. All that he says of it is this:

'This anticipation, which has held its ground almost continuously ever since,—with the break of a month now and a month then, up to 1829, and, after that date, without any break at all,—was more or less connected in my mind with the notion that my calling in life would require such a sacrifice as celibacy involved; as, for instance, missionary work among the heathen, to which I had a great drawing for some years. It also strengthened my feeling of separation from the visible world, of what I have spoken above.'

Beside this may be set a passage from a letter which he wrote from Malta to his mother in January 1833, evidently in answer to some approach of hers to the topic of marriage, or of home-life, at a time when he was unwell.

'Well, I am set upon a solitary life, and therefore ought to have experience what it is; nor do I repent. But even St. Paul had his ministers. I have sent to the library and got 'Marriage' to read! Don't smile—this juxtaposition is quite accidental. You are continually in my thoughts of course. I know what kindness I should have at home; and it is no new feeling with me, only now for the first time brought out, that I do not feel this so much as I ought. Thank God, my spirits have not failed me once. They used, when I was solitary, but I am callous now. . . . I wonder how long I shall last without any friend about me. Scripture so clearly seems to mark out that we should not be literally solitary. The Apostles were sent two and two, and had their attendants, so I suppose I should soon fail.'

The reason which Newman gives for embracing a single career is very remarkably inadequate. Missionaries, if they are married to women of a similar religious temper, do their work, not worse, but better. And the prospect of a missionary career hardly came sufficiently close to Newman to exercise so great an influence upon his life. One might have expected him to put himself upon the ground that celibacy was the proper state for a priest. But this would have squared neither with his Evangelical opinions nor with the fact that he was originally destined not for the Church, but for the Bar. When he became a Roman Catholic priest he was naturally under that rule himself, and for some years previously he had certainly been in sympathy with it. But it does not appear that he ever held it with such intense and passionate conviction, and certainly not from so early a date, that it could have determined him in boyhood or early manhood to dedicate himself to the unmarried state. It was one of Kingsley's charges that, preaching as Protestant Vicar of St. Mary's, he had insinuated 'that a Church which had sacramental confession and a celibate clergy was the only true Church' and had (in the theological jargon of the day) named celibacy as one of the 'notes' of the Church. To which Newman answers: 'Define the Church by the celibacy of the clergy! Why, let him read 1 Tim. iii; there he will find that bishops and deacons are spoken of as married. How, then, could I be the dolt to say or imply that celibacy of the clergy was a part of the definition of the Church?' All that Newman had, in fact, said was that sacramental confession and the celibacy of the clergy tended to consolidate the position and influence of the priesthood—an obvious truism. He goes on, in the original *Apologia* (the passage was omitted in the revised version) to say: 'At the same time I cannot conceive why the mention . . . of Clerical Celibacy, had I made it, was inconsistent with the position of an Anglican Clergyman. For . . . though the 32nd Article says that "Bishops, priests, and deacons, are not *commanded* by

God's law either to vow the state of single life or to abstain from marriage", and "therefore it is *lawful* for them to marry", this proposition I did not dream of denying, nor is it inconsistent with St. Paul's doctrine, which I held, that it is *"good* to abide even as he", i.e. in celibacy.'

This was the view of celibacy which he held, in 1843, (when the sermon attacked by Kingsley was preached), and for some years previously. 'Clerical celibacy' says Tom Mozley 'used to be either a vulgar necessity or a heroic devotion at Oxford, where the great majority were Fellows waiting for livings. In its more exalted form it was one of the favourite ideas of the new school, which, however, had by and by to suffer a long list of cruel disappointments as one Benedick after another proved faithless to his early professions.'

Two at least of these defections touched Newman in his most vulnerable part. First there was Keble's marriage in 1835, at the age of forty-three. There is scarcely any reference to this in Newman's published correspondence. He tells Froude in May that Keble is not yet married; and in October that he was married on the 10th and told no one. There is nothing more, and no exchange of letters between himself and Keble on the subject. But he talked to Mozley and, though Mozley's recollection of dates is hopelessly inaccurate, his account of what Newman said bears the stamp of truth. He gave Mozley to understand that Keble was about to make 'a humdrum marriage'. He did not disguise his regret; but he appreciated the reasons. Keble wished 'to discourage young men from aiming at a standard above the age and possibly also above their own power to attain'. It was like Keble's humility to make such a sacrifice. The lady was understood to be the elder sister of his younger brother's wife. The union was therefore quite a 'suitable' one; there was no question of the sainted author of *The Christian Year* having been carried away by his natural passions. But, in fact, the new Mrs. John Keble was a younger and not an older sister of Mrs. Thomas Keble.

She was charming and delicate—a fact which enhanced her
attractiveness to Keble—'with beautiful brown eyes and hair,
a very delicate complexion like porcelain, and an air of extreme refinement'. Keble had known her from childhood, and
had been engaged to her for several years. Mozley, at least,
had no doubt that Keble was following the 'bent of his
inclination', as he had in another and earlier, but unsuccess-
ful, love-affair.

Henry Wilberforce's marriage in the previous year had
been a more direct shock to his leader. Writing to his friend
Frederic Rogers on January 14 1834 Newman announced
confidently: 'By-the-bye, talking of H. W., do not believe
a silly report that is in circulation that he is engaged to be
married . . . he has been staying here, and though we often
talked on the subject, he said nothing about it, which I am
sure he would have done were it a fact, for the report goes on
to say he has told other people. For myself I am spreading my
incredulity, and contradicting it in every direction, and will
not believe it, though I saw the event announced in the
papers, till he tells me. Nay, I doubt whether I ought then to
believe it, if he were to say he had really told others and not
me.'

Questioned by Rogers, Wilberforce replied:

'I have no wish whatever to deny the report in question.
Indeed, though I did not tell Neander (as who would?), yet
I did tell his sister and gave her leave to tell him. . . . Whether
Neander will cut me I don't know. I hope my other Oxford
friends will continue my friends still. . . . It is, I am sure, very
foolish of Newman on mere principles of calculation, if he
gives up all his friends on their marriage; for how can he
expect men (however well inclined) to do much in our cause
without co-operation? I suppose, however, he will cut me. I
cannot help it. . . . Nor, again, am I without a feeling of the
danger, as you know, of married priests in these days of
trouble and rebuke, but I have taken my line.'

Upon which, Rogers took on himself the task of mollifying Newman:

'Many thanks for your letter, in which, however, I must say, you do not use your judgment. How can you possibly suppose that, after your way of treating *perditum ovem* H. Wilberforce, you would be his first confidant? The fact obviously is that he came to Oxford with the intention of breaking the matter to you; but when he came near, and saw how fierce you looked, his heart failed him, and he retreated ἄπρακτος. And now at this moment he is hesitating about the best way of breaking it, and hoping that someone else will save him the pain.'

In the end Newman became godfather to Wilberforce's eldest son, and all was well.

The attitude of Newman, as the leader of the new party in the Church, to which Keble his senior and Wilberforce his junior both belonged, was that married priests were likely to be drawn away from their work by domestic cares and obligations at a specially critical time in the history of the Church. To marry, therefore, was to be a backslider from a task requiring all a man's devotion. This was so to speak the *official* attitude, and it was perfectly rational and intelligible, though the arguments against it were at least as strong as the arguments for it. But there was an entirely different attitude, encased so to speak within the official attitude, yet very much present to the consciousness of Newman and his *alter ego* Hurrell Froude. Within this again there lay a third and more intimate and secret attitude, to which Newman's language in the *Apologia* gives the clue.

The second, the intermediate attitude, the 'high severe idea of the intrinsic excellence of virginity', was probably one of Froude's gifts to Newman, as it was one of those characters in Froude which Newman most admired. But whether it came to Newman through that channel, or whether he revived it for himself by his study of the Fathers and the Saints, it was an idea which evidently took strong possession of his mind. 'Evidently', because, unlike some others, he was exceedingly reticent about the whole subject; his views upon it were implicit in his tenor of life rather than deliberately promulgated. He and Froude may have—one would say, must have —discussed it in intimate conversations. However that may have been, the idea was common property among the Tractarians. Frederic Faber, one of the Roman converts of 1845, who spoke of himself as an 'acolyth' of Newman, writes to Jack Morris in 1840, at the age of twenty-six, denying a report that he is engaged to be married. 'I am not even in love as most people would count love; and I very seldom turn my thoughts that way. I honour the celibate so highly, and regard it as so eminently the fittest way of life for a priest, that if Christ would graciously enable me to learn to live alone, I should prefer much, even with great self-denials, to live a virgin life, and to die a virgin, as God has kept me so hitherto.' And three months later, to the same correspondent : 'I may as well say that I never felt so strongly determined by God's grace to "make a venture of a lonely life", as J. H. N. says, as I do now . . . But enough: I am too weak a disciple to talk thus. I rather covet than enjoy the calm love of virginity; but it may be God will reveal even that unto me.'

But this ardent sense of a singular moral beauty in the frustration of his animal nature was not the fundamental cause of Newman's early resolve to live a single life. If it had been he would have said so, instead of connecting his resolve so lamely with the notion that he might perhaps become a missionary. He lacked sympathy with animals, and used often to speak of the brute creation as a disturbing mystery. Perhaps this was because the mating instinct had never developed in him. When the ideal of virginity became a part of the furniture of his conscious mind, there was nothing else there which needed to be painfully dislodged. Whenever he thought of marriage, he thought of it not as a means of satisfying carnal desire, but as the antithesis of solitude. Companionship he *must* have; he could not last without it. But friends and disciples could, and did, give him all that he needed.

It is, in fact, wrong to speak of any resolve on Newman's part against marriage. He uses no such expression himself. He came not to a resolve, but to a 'deep imagination', an 'anticipation' that God did not wish him to marry. The phraseology is deliberate, and its meaning is, obviously and simply, that he had made a discovery about himself, from which he concluded that he was not likely to marry. How complete that discovery was there are no means of knowing, but there can be no possible doubt of its nature. At fifteen, Newman had reached the age when a normal boy begins to be conscious of a special attraction in the opposite sex. Under the artificial conditions of our modern educational system, which keeps boys in pupilage at school to a much later age, the development of this consciousness is often unnaturally, and sometimes fatally, retarded. But Newman left school at fifteen and was an undergraduate before he was sixteen, and his contemporaries at Ealing left school even earlier than he did. It is plain that he had compared himself with them, and had realized in himself an abnormal lack of that particular sensibility.

From what did this peculiarity of his derive? No certain answer can be given. There may have been two disposing causes, one psychological the other physiological. The training which his mother gave him in early childhood, which seems to have induced in him his exaggerated sense of 'separation from the visible world', would have produced that effect by wounding his animal instincts at their first appearances. Newman himself perceived the fact of the connection, though not its nature. Certainly this is pure hypothesis. It is open to anybody to maintain that Newman's was a more unearthly spirit than those of ordinary mortals, less able and less willing to forget the glories he had known and the imperial palace whence he came. There is no evidence for the contrary view, except the evidence collected by psychologists from the analytical treatment of their patients. But the cumulative effect of that evidence is very strong; and the *a priori* probability that Newman's 'case' was not essentially different from the hundreds or thousands now on record is, at least, very high.

That there may also have been a physiological cause is suggested by his possession of what are commonly called 'feminine' characters, though perhaps 'neutral' would be a truer term. Description after description conveys the same impression. Take Tom Mozley : 'Robust and ruddy sons of the Church looked on him with condescending pity as a poor fellow whose excessive sympathy, restless energy, and general unfitness for this practical world would soon wreck him. Thin, pale, and with large lustrous eyes ever piercing through this veil of men and things, he hardly seemed made for this world.' Aubrey de Vere is still more precise: 'Early in the evening a singularly graceful figure in cap and gown glided into the room. The slight form and gracious address might have belonged either to a youthful ascetic of the middle ages or to a graceful high-bred lady of our own days. He was pale and thin almost to emaciation, swift of pace, but when not walking intensely still, with a voice sweet and pathetic, and so distinct that you could count each vowel and consonant in every word. When touching on subjects which interested him, he used gestures rapid and decisive, though not vehement.'

It is curious to contrast these descriptions of Newman, as he was in the prime of his Oxford career, with a portrait of him drawn by a temperamentally hostile critic. 'I met Newman almost daily,' writes the Rev. W. Tuckwell in his *Reminiscences of Oxford* 'striding along the Oxford Road, with large head, prominent nose, tortoiseshell spectacles, emaciated but ruddy face, spare figure whose leanness was exaggerated by the close-fitting tail-coat then worn.' There is not much trace of effeminacy there, and the epithet of 'ruddy' is in definite contradiction to Mozley's description. But Tuckwell was not always particular about the accuracy of his epithets, and he wrote his recollections, animated and vivid as they are, in extreme old age. He can hardly have remembered Newman quite so well as he thought.

Perhaps the reason why Tuckwell never thought of Newman as effeminate was because he neither knew him intimately nor admired him. For Newman's 'feminine' characteristics were closely associated, in the minds of his disciples and admirers, with his personal charm. No other description shows this so clearly, or brings Newman's manner so vividly to the imagination, as a very remarkable passage in Wilfrid Ward's *Life of Cardinal Newman.*

'The present writer's father' he says '—never one of the most intimate of the circle which surrounded Newman at Oxford—used to say that his heart would beat as he heard Newman's step on the staircase. His keen humour, his winning sweetness, his occasional wilfulness, his resentments and anger, all showed him intensely alive, and his friends loved his very faults as one may love those of a fascinating woman; at the same time many of them revered him almost as a prophet. Only a year before his death, after nearly twenty years of misunderstandings and estrangement, W. G. Ward told the present biographer of a dream he had had—how he found himself at a dinner party next to a veiled lady, who charmed him more and more as they talked. At last he exclaimed, "I have never felt such charm in any conversation since I used to talk with John Henry Newman, at Oxford." "I am John Henry Newman", the lady replied, and raising her veil showed the well-known face.'

Nor did the impression fail as he grew older. In some of the profile portraits of the Cardinal the artists seem to have tried to emphasize a sort of aged strength and ruggedness, which were the last qualities to strike those who met him. Scott

C

Holland's account of him in 1877 is a perfect corrective. 'I turned at the sound of the soft quick speech, and there he was—white, frail and wistful, for all the ruggedness of the actual features. I remembered at once the words of Furse about him, "delicate as an old lady, washed in milk". . . . So the urgent enquiries went on, in silvery whispers, keen and quick. . . . I had to fly for my train, and sped home tingling with the magic of a presence that seemed to me like the frail embodiment of a living voice. His soul was in his voice, as a bird is in its song.'

The comparison to a 'lady' recurs, with a seeming inevitability. It was indeed inevitable; just as his charm was inevitable; just as were the consequences, for himself and for his friends, of that seductive weakness in his temperament, joined to his brilliant natural gifts.

There were moments when his own conviction that he was not for any woman wavered. All that is known of these occasions is that they were few and brief, and that they ceased after 1829, the year in which, as he says, his acquaintance with Hurrell Froude ripened into 'the closest and most affectionate friendship'. Whatever they were, and whoever was concerned in them, they passed without leaving the faintest trace upon his character. No secret romance of the conventional type existed in his life. They were no more, it may be supposed, than faint visitations of a wish that he were like other men, that his sexual indifference might be disturbed. For it was indifference, not dislike. His charming description of Mary Froude, 'one of the sweetest girls I ever saw', being bullied by her brother Hurrell and worshipped by her devoted admirer Mr. B., 'receiving with equal readiness and equability the homage of the one and the playful rudeness of the other', is enough to show that there was no conscious misogyny in his composition. But all the love he gave to women was given where it could never be suspected of any gross alloy—to his mother and his sisters, and above all to his darling youngest sister Mary, 'joy of sad hearts and light of downcast eyes', who died when he was twenty-six and whose name he could not mention at the age of eighty-one without the tears coming into his eyes.

The strength and the emotional depth of his friendships with men were the natural counterpart of this indifference to women. Whether he realized this must remain uncertain. It must be remembered that passionate friendships, usually coloured by high religious aspirations, were far from uncommon a century ago. No one can understand the movement of which Newman was the central figure who is blind to the strength of the attachments which bound so many of its principal figures together, or who mistakes the nature of the personal fascination which he exercised at the very centre of the Tractarian whirlpool.

CHAPTER II

NEWMAN AT OXFORD: THE FIRST PHASE

I. MATRICULATION

Not till the last minute did Mr. Newman make up his mind whether John was to go to Oxford or to Cambridge. The postchaise was at the door, early in December 1816, and he was still undecided. A feather determined the issue of John's destiny—and not John's only. The feather was a Mr. John Mullins, not otherwise remembered, curate of St. James's, Piccadilly, 'a man of ability and learning, who had for some years taken an interest in the boy's education.' Mr. Mullins was an Exeter man, not without influence in his own college, and he was, at this moment, in Oxford and very willing to use his influence on John's behalf. Being entered at Oxford—and presumably at Cambridge too—was a serious business in those days. Fathers made it an excuse to escape from the cares of business, the exigencies of matrimony, or the tedium of country parishes, and set out by road, with their sons beside them, and their own youth temporarily renewed. Mark Pattison's entry on the books of Oriel involved the whole family in an expedition from Yorkshire to London, and a subsidiary expedition from London to Oxford, lasting for several days and requiring the employment of all his father's available means of intrigue. Even after this, the intending undergraduate must wait his turn to go into residence, until a vacancy came his way. Pattison had to wait two years. Newman was more fortunate. Mr. Mullins was unable to find a vacancy for him at Exeter but gave him an introduction to Trinity, where he was forthwith matriculated, on December 14.

Lytton Strachey has constructed a fanciful picture of the fatal consequences which Oxford inflicted upon Newman. 'At Oxford, he was doomed. He could not withstand the last enchantment of the Middle Age.' 'He might, at Cambridge, whose cloisters have ever been consecrated to poetry and common sense, have followed quietly in Gray's footsteps, and brought into flower those seeds of inspiration which now lie embedded amid the faded devotion of the *Lyra Apostolica*.' It is a picture which—as the victim might have put it— does credit to the essayist's imagination at the expense of his judgment. To suppose that Newman, being the man—or the boy—that he was, could in any circumstances have pursued an amiable artistic or literary career, is to misapprehend his character utterly. The remote idealism, the emotional sensibility, the vaulting imagination, the dialectical subtlety, which are the heads under which Strachey catalogues him, would themselves have combined with difficulty into a minor Cambridge poet—and a major poet he could never conceivably have become. Possibly the fusion might have been achieved, if Newman had been these qualities and no more. But he was very much more. For all his youth and his temperamental limitations, he was a man of will, of a will relentless to himself and to others; he was a stern moralist; he was a man of peculiar mental consistency—his opinions changed, but they changed in a set and given direction; he had unsurpassed gifts of preaching and of controversy, which could not have been permanently suppressed; he had already settled in his own mind his position in the universe, and the main characters of the universe and its Ruler. It would have taken more than Cambridge to dislocate that conception. If Newman had become a Fellow of a Cambridge College, there would have been a Cambridge Movement of some kind or another, with Newman at its centre; and it would have been a movement of a religious character.

After his matriculation John returned to London and reported, timidly, to Dr. Nicholas that he was now the member of a college, of which he had never before even heard the name. He was reassured. 'Trinity?' exclaimed the Headmaster. 'A most gentlemanlike college—I am much pleased to hear it.'

He had only six months to wait before a set of rooms fell vacant at Trinity, and he employed the time as a convert should, in consolidating his religious position. Already he had exercised his mind on the subject of recreations. He concluded they were bad and resolved to give them up—in this, as in so many other matters, making a virtue out of inclination. But, foreseeing a collision between himself and his parents, he works out the moral problem on paper. The proper course will be to present 'my scruples with humility and a due obedience to my parents; open to conviction, and ready to obey in a matter so dubious as this is, and to act against my judgment if they command, thus satisfying at once my own conscience and them.' Then he rehearses the argument he will have with them. 'The beginnings of sin are small, and is it not better, say, to be too cautious than too negligent? Besides, I know myself in some things better than you do; I have hidden faults . . . I hope I am not so enthusiastic as to treat it as a concern of high religious importance. You may think this contradicts what I said just now about the beginning of sin; if so, I am sorry I cannot express myself with greater exactness and propriety.'

Of all the strange symptoms which heralded and attended the Oxford Movement none will be so incomprehensible to the modern reader as this. It was not peculiar to Newman or to the Evangelicals. Here is Hurrell Froude, highest of Tory High Churchmen, wrestling with his evil self, on a holiday in Wales at the age of twenty-three. 'Oct. 13. I have kept a very good fast to-day, as far as eating goes; but have spoilt it all this evening, by playing at that game, instead of coming up and reading. . . . These games do not answer: I am not excited now: yet I feel the good of the day almost entirely gone; and feel no more ready for my prayers than I did in the morning. Their interest turns upon conceit; and they cease to be amusing when they become harmless.'

During these six months young Newman was busy reading, writing and corresponding with Mr. Mayers. He carried on a paper called *The Beholder*—successor to *The Spy* and *The Anti-spy*—which he had begun in February 1816. It was all in his own hand, and ran to forty numbers—160 closely written octavo pages. He wrote an essay on Fame—' there is no such thing as a *person* being famed. Let it not be thought a quibble when I say it is his name that is celebrated, and not himself.' He was deep in Bishop Beveridge's *Private Thoughts*, and already involved in the difficult questions raised by the Sacrament of Baptism. How could baptized infants dying in infancy be saved unless baptism itself were accompanied by the Holy Spirit? Sermons and 'sermonets' flowed under his pen. The topics of seven of these are recorded in a footnote to the *Letters*. Amongst them was a dissertation on everlasting punishment, another on the vanity of human life, another on the reign of sin in mortal bodies, another on fasting. And one bore the significant heading, 'Let no one despise thy youth.'

2. SKETCH OF A UNIVERSITY

Three Royal Commissions and a hundred years of reform have passed over Oxford since Newman went up to Trinity. *Plus ça change*, say the cynics, *plus c'est la même chose*. But the outward changes, at least, are great. Let us 'borrow the wings of Historic Imagination and hover lightly' over Oxford as she seemed when the nineteenth century was in its youth.

The Colleges were everything in those days, the University almost nothing. There were hardly any intercollegiate lectures. The instruction of the undergraduates in all the various branches of knowledge, upon which they would be examined for their degrees, was undertaken in each College by the tutors of that College. The system of serious examination for the granting of degrees had only been recently introduced. It was initiated by Eveleigh, the great Provost of Oriel from 1781 to 1814. In essence it was the same system which is in force to-day. That is to say, that a man might read for an honours or a pass degree. But the range of choice was extremely limited. If he read for honours he read, of course, for Classical or Mathematical Honours or both. Philosophy came into this *via* Plato and Aristotle, and ancient history *via* Herodotus, Thucydides, Livy and Tacitus. Modern history was not taught at all for the Schools, nor modern philosophy, nor natural science, nor any other language but Greek and Latin. The standard of instruction was low, the scope of examination narrow, and a favourable verdict in the Schools was no more a guarantee of a first-rate intelligence than failure was a mark of an inferior one.

Men went to Oxford, in fact, to receive the conventional education considered appropriate for a gentleman, whether they went afterwards into Parliament or resided upon their estates or took holy orders or entered the law. Even medicine had almost ceased to be a serious part of the studies of the University. The twin shadows of an established church and a self-satisfied order of society still lay thickly over the entire University. No young man was admitted unless he formally subscribed to the Thirty-nine Articles of the Church of England. Once matriculated he must attend the services of his College chapel and receive Holy Communion at least once a term. In Oriel certainly (and no doubt in other Colleges) he must attend the University Sermon on Sunday mornings and satisfy the authorities by a *précis* of its argument that he had listened to it with attention. He was governed and taught exclusively by clergymen. Any intellectual adventure outside the so-called 'humanities' and the

walled city of classical mathematics was at once difficult and
dangerous. Even theology was a post-graduate study, for it
could not be safely approached until the rash speculations of
youth had dissipated themselves into the void. Such was the
society into which Shelley had hurled *The Necessity of
Atheism* just five years before Newman became an undergraduate.

Mark Pattison's description of the way in which the Colleges recruited their Fellows in the previous century applied
generally up to the appointment of the first Royal Commission in 1850. It was 'done under conditions which left no
place for any qualification of learning, even if learning had
existed at all in the University. The fellow to be chosen must
have been born in a particular district, to which the vacancy
was appropriated; he must be in orders, or proceed to take
orders as soon as elected; he must be, and remain unmarried.
. . . Even those societies which had preserved self-respect
enough not to sink into the conditions of sots and topers preferred a "companionable" man to any acquirements or
talents.' A Fellowship was held for life, unless its holder
married; and he was not obliged to live in Oxford at all,
after his probationary year. The livings of which a College
was the patron were offered in rotation as they fell vacant to
its members; and many a man, waiting to marry but without
the means to do so, lingered on as a College tutor, year after
year, eating his heart out and weary of his office, until opportunity at last came his way.

Oriel was the first College to break through the rotten
system of close Fellowships and to elect its Fellows from the
University at large on their intellectual merits. This reform,
too, was the work of its great Provost, Eveleigh, who introduced a method of examination conducted upon the principle of ascertaining, not what a man had read, but what
he was like. The result was remarkable. From the beginning
of the century for about thirty years Oriel stood on an un-

approached eminence. In its common room there grew up
a habit of keen hard talk. Dull-witted guests and enemies
complained that it 'stunk of logic'. Its members were nick-
named 'the Noetics'. Among them were Copleston (Eveleigh's successor as Provost), Whately (Archbishop of
Dublin), Arnold of Rugby, Hampden (whose Bampton Lectures were to outrage orthodoxy)—all of them men who
began their lives, if they did not continue them, by putting
reason before authority. Yet, in Pattison's view, their origi-
nality had no sufficient roots. 'It was only in the then condition of the University, hidebound in the tradition of narrow
clerical prejudice, that the new Oriel school of the Noetics
. . . could be welcomed as a wholesome invasion of a scurfy
pond, stagnant with sameness and custom.' Reaction was
inevitable. Tractarianism, born in the same common room,
was very soon to sweep the Noetics away.

'It was soon after 1830', to quote Pattison once more, 'that
the "Tracts" desolated Oxford life, and suspended, for an
indefinite period, all science, humane letters, and the first
strivings of intellectual freedom which had moved in the
bosom of Oriel.'

The undergraduates fell into three main classes—the
Scholars, the Commoners, and the Gentlemen Commoners,
young men of birth and means, who wore silk gowns, dined
at a separate table, or with the Dons at the high table, and
'kept up a style of living such as is usual in large country
houses.' The social position of the Scholars, at the turn of the
century, was definitely inferior. They were called 'charity
boys' and formed a race apart. But their position was on the
mend. The Commoners for the most part aped the manners
of the Gentlemen Commoners, and did as little work as their
tutors permitted. There were no organized recreations. The
rich hunted, rode, and drove tandem; the lesser breeds
rambled abroad or went 'skiffing'. Magdalen is said to have
been the only College which boasted a cricket-field in the

SKETCH OF A UNIVERSITY

'thirties. Men wore their caps and gowns in the streets—the Commoner's gown had not shrunk to a mere vestigial relic. In Hall frock-coats or tails were *de rigueur*.

One is tempted, reading the lives of Newman and his associates, to suppose that introspective piety and the baffled pursuit of learning occupied the minds of all the intelligent young men. Doubtless, the typical clever youth of to-day, if he could have been ante-dated by a hundred years, would have been a devotee of the Newmania. His *credo in novum ordinem* would have been the *credo in Newmannum*, which went from mouth to mouth in those religious days. He would have fasted, prayed, and kept a diary of his spiritual advances and retrogressions. For that was the way that nearly all the young idealists were treading in the late 'thirties, and pietism, of an Evangelical brand, had been in fashion even earlier.

Yet it would be an error to divide that remote undergraduate Oxford sharply between expensive idlers and the rabble of their imitators on the one hand, and earnest religionists on the other; just as it would be an error to divide the Fellows into port-swilling sots, rut-plodding tutors, and non-resident pluralists. There was a peculiar flower which grew freely in the soil of pre-Commission Oxford; a complex bloom of wit and scholarship, useless perhaps, except as an evidence of the rich capacity of the human mind to perfect itself after its own strangely devised patterns. Useless, certainly, but how delightful! at any rate to those who have learned to appreciate its subtle scent and colour. A few late specimens survive to this day in Oxford common rooms, a little damaged by unavoidable compromise with their modern environment, but still retailing the authentic aroma. This was the pure distillation. Its essence combined freely with all the best and the worst of Oxford. It tempered the asceticism of Froude, the piety of Keble; it enshrined Newman's old tutor at Trinity, Tommy Short, in the memory of countless pupils, in spite of Isaac Williams's harsh verdict that he 'seemed almost incapable of looking on college matters in a moral or religious light'; it lay, in fact, all round Newman, and was not the least of the elements in the Oxford atmosphere which finally neutralized and dissolved the corrosive vapours of Tractarianism.

Though science was no part of the University curriculum, it was not wholly unrepresented at Oxford. There was Dr. Daubeny, of the physic garden, who lectured on Chemistry and whose demonstrations invariably went wrong. Daubeny's 'laughing gas' found its way into Oriel, where William Froude, Hurrell's younger brother, tried it, with startling consequences, on some of the senior members of the College. A more substantial figure than Daubeny was Buckland, the first Professor of Geology, whose lectures were popular and well attended. Among his pupils was Charles Lyell, who was four years Newman's senior but his contemporary at Oxford. It is curious to reflect that Lyell's great work *The Principles of Geology*, which demolished for ever the old Mosaic cosmogony, dealt a mortal blow to the chronology of Archbishop Ussher, and made Darwin's life-work possible, was published before the Tractarian movement began and made no more immediate noise in clerical Oxford than an explosion in the moon. Buckland himself reconciled faith and science. He 'endeavoured to show that the whole of the enormous superficial deposits of the globe are to be accounted for by Noah's flood.' Even that degree of rationalism was accounted dangerous. Keble and Buckland argued all the way from Oxford to Winchester on the top of a coach, and Keble, driven desperate, 'finally took his stand on the conceivability and indeed certainty of the Almighty having created all the fossils and other apparent outcomes of former existence in the six days of Creation.' Shuttleworth, the witty Warden of New College, sheltered Moses behind an epigram:

> Some doubts were once expressed about the flood,
> Buckland arose and all was clear—as mud.

Dean Gaisford, more seriously, thanked God, on Buckland's departure for Italy, that they would hear no more of his geology. Let the young men concentrate, not on the so-called sciences, but on 'the study of Greek literature, which not only elevates above the vulgar herd, but leads not infrequently to positions of considerable emolument.' Early in the 'forties Dr. Acland brought a fresh enthusiasm into scientific Oxford, and began the movement which led to the building of the Museum in the 'fifties, when clericalism was on the retreat and Newman safely out of the way.

What Newman's attitude to science would have been, had he been forced as a young man to formulate one, can only be guessed. It is true that, later in life, in his long effort to create an Irish Catholic University, he was at pains to define the relationship between religion and science. He 'planned a University in which theology and science alike should be free and flourishing.' He had no fear at all that the conclusions of science might undermine the basis of religion. Nothing, indeed, could be more dangerous to theology than that it should remain in ignorance of the rapidly advancing sciences. *Cuique in sua arte credendum.* The truths of revealed religion were not to be apprehended without long effort and training, and were not open to assault from the sciences. It was all very well to argue, in this general way, with the rock of Rome under his feet. But he seems never to have perceived, in his own mind, any direct collision between a particular scientific conclusion and a particular religious belief, hardly even the possibility of such a collision. The collision was between two different tempers of mind. Doubt, he said, was like the discrepancy between a tuned piano and the ideal scale; you cannot exclude it, but you must nevertheless tune the piano. There was never any question for him but that the revealed scale put doubt in its proper place. As a youngster he was not a little fascinated by mineralogy and chemistry. Yet this came to so little in his mind that, according to Tom Mozley, he 'would have nothing to say to physical science. He abstained from it as much as he did from material undertakings and worldly affairs generally.' Perhaps one reason for this was the sense he had of an innate tendency to scepticism. At any rate he shelved the issue between faith and science until he felt irrevocably sure of his own position; and even then his treatment of the problem cannily, if unconsciously, evaded every concrete difficulty. When he was seventy he was invited to join the Metaphysical Society, which met once a month to discuss first and last things. He refused, and thanked his stars that he had done so, when five years later he heard that Dean Church and the Archbishop of York (to say nothing of Cardinal Manning) were going to let Professor Huxley read in their presence a paper against the Resurrection.

But to return to Oxford. The city itself must be visualized. The reader must wish all the modern accretions away—Schools, Museums, New Buildings, Women's Colleges, Laboratories, modern shops, the whole of North Oxford, the railway stations, and the suburban overflow—except where the first slums were just beginning to make their appearance towards Headington. Here is a description of the approach from London as old Mr. Tuckwell remembered it in the days of his youth and as Newman trod it almost daily for more than fifteen years.

'It was said in those days that the approach to Oxford by the Henley Road was the most beautiful in the world. Soon after passing Littlemore you came in sight of, and did not lose again, the sweet city with its dreaming spires, driven along a road now crowded and obscured with dwellings, open then to cornfields on the right, to uninclosed meadows on the left, with an unbroken view of the long line of towers, rising out of foliage less high and veiling than after sixty more years of growth to-day. At once, without suburban interval you entered the finest quarter of the town, rolling under Mag-

dalen Tower, and past the Magdalen elms, then in full un-
mutilated luxuriance, till the exquisite curves of the High
Street opened on you, as you drew up at The Angel, or
passed on to the Mitre and the Star. Along that road, or into
Oxford by the St. Giles's entrance, lumbered at midnight
Pickford's vast waggons with their six musically belled horses;
sped stage-coaches all day long—Tantivy, Defiance, Rival,
Regulator, Mazeppa, Dart, Magnet, Blenheim, and some
thirty more; heaped high with ponderous luggage and with
cloaked passengers, thickly hung at Christmas time with
turkeys, with pheasants in October; their guards picked
buglers, sending before them as they passed Magdalen Bridge
the now forgotten strains of "Brignall Banks", "The Trouba-
dour", "I'd be a Butterfly", "The Maid of Llangollen" or
"Begone Dull Care"; on the box their queer old purple-
faced, many-caped drivers—Cheeseman, Steevens, Fowles,
Charles Horner, Jack Adams, and Black Will.'
  The society concentrated in that circumscribed but lovely
city was, except for 'a select few ladies, frank spinsters and
jovial matrons, who shared the conviviality of the resident
Fellows', confined to the families of the Heads of Houses, the
Canons of Christ Church, and one or two married Professors. The Heads formed a remote and tremendous oli-
garchy. 'The Heads' are the villains of the Oxford Movement. Their domestic splendours were a scandal to men of
pious inclinations. 'Expensive parties' says Isaac Williams
indignantly 'still continued, especially among the Heads of
Houses, who used to eat and drink very freely, and therefore
with them our principles made us very unpopular. . . .
Fridays in Lent were still the chief days for party-giving with
the heads of houses.' In this circle it may be easily supposed
that Newman was not a frequent or a favoured visitor. 'But,
really,' he makes Charles Reding say to Mary in his novel
Loss and Gain 'if you saw Oxford as it is! The Heads with
such large incomes; they are indeed very liberal of their

money, and their wives are often simple, self-denying persons, as everyone says, and do a great deal of good in the place; but I speak of the system. Here are ministers of Christ with large incomes, living in finely furnished houses, with wives and families, and stately butlers and servants in livery, giving dinners all in the best style, condescending and gracious, waving their hands and mincing their words, as if they were the cream of the earth, but without anything to make them clergymen but a black coat and a white tie. And then Bishops or Deans come, with women tucked under their arm; and they can't enter church but a fine powdered man runs first with a cushion for them to sit on, and a warm sheepskin to keep their feet from the stones.'

3. UNDERGRADUATE

In June 1817 Mr. Newman carried his son down and installed him in his rooms at Trinity. It was just before the end of term, the lectures were finished, and it was difficult for John to get what he most wanted—any information about the books he ought to read. Tommy Short, his tutor, paid him a visit on his first day, but John was out, complaining to the tailor about the fit of his gown. It pleased the new undergraduate to learn that Mr. Short was not at that time liked in College because he was strict—stricter than Mr. Ingram, whom he had recently succeeded. 'Thus I think', he wrote to his father, 'I have gained by the exchange, and that is a lucky thing.' His first dinner in Hall impressed him favourably. 'Fish, flesh and fowl, beautiful salmon, haunches of mutton, lamb, etc., fine strong beer; served up in old pewter plates and misshapen earthenware jugs. Tell mamma there were gooseberry, raspberry, and apricot pies.' There is no suggestion here of any ascetic disapproval. 'The wine' he adds 'has come; $8\frac{1}{3}$ per cent. is taken off for ready money.'

At the end of the first week he finds he can read without

hurting his eyes (which had been troubling him), and has
'begun to fag pretty well'. He feels lonely, had been low-
spirited at first because he couldn't read. He is 'not noticed
at all except by being silently stared at', but from what he
has seen of the others he does not think he would gain the
least advantage from their company. 'For H. the other day
asked me to take a glass of wine with two or three others, and
they drank and drank all the time I was there. I was very
glad that prayers came half an hour after I came to them, for
I am sure I was not entertained with either their drinking or
their conversation.' As he wrote of himself in his old age, he
'had not a grain in his composition of that temper of conviviality so natural to young men.'

Nearly three weeks passed, and he was still without reading
orders for the vacation. Coming back on Sunday evening
from a walk in the Parks 'he saw one of the tutors in topboots
on horseback on his way into the country. Thinking it his last
chance, he dashed into the road, and, abruptly accosting
him, asked what books he should read during the vacation.
The person addressed answered him very kindly; explained
that he was leaving Oxford for the vacation, and referred
him to one of his colleagues still in College, who would give
him the information he desired.' He acted on the hint, and
went home next day, equipped with the desired instructions.

Amongst the freshmen was a young man named John
William Bowden. He was exactly three years older than Newman; their Christian names were identical, their birthdays fell
on the same date; and both were earnest and religious. Between the youth of nineteen and the boy of sixteen sprang up
instantly the first of those warm friendships which saved
Newman from becoming a solitary. Bowden had charm and
good looks. When Frank came up to Oxford six years later
he was fascinated by his brother's friend. He saw in him a
type of beautiful manhood; perhaps 'too tall for an Apollo,
but his modest sweetness of expression seemed Christian

beauty such as I had not seen in the British Museum from any Greek.' His were the first overtures; they were accepted, and he fell completely under Newman's peculiar spell. The two friends, the old Cardinal wistfully records, 'lived simply with and for each other all through their undergraduate time . . . being recognized in college as inseparables,—taking their meals together, reading, walking, boating together—nay, visiting each other's homes in the vacations.' Their paths separated after they had taken their degrees. Bowden became a Commissioner of Stamps and Taxes, married, and had several children. But he and Newman remained intimates. He wrote for the Tracts, was closely associated with the Oxford Movement, and occupied his leisure, obedient to his friend's will, upon a history of Pope Gregory VII. He died in 1844, and his widow was one of Newman's first converts to Roman Catholicism.

It did not take the Trinity tutors long to discover that a very uncommon fish had swum into their net. Meeting his new pupil's father, on some occasion, Mr Short 'went up to him as an old friend, and holding out his hand, said, "O Mr. Newman! what have you given us in your son!"' Never was undergraduate more diligent and docile. He startled Mr. Short by his previous acquaintance with the first five books of Euclid, when all the rest of the class were still on the wrong side of the Pons Asinorum, and soon found himself leaping over the stiffest theorems in hot pursuit of the assiduous Bowden. His classics kept pace with his mathematics. At the end of his first year, when he was but seventeen, he was elected to a Trinity scholarship, in open competition against men from other Colleges. The scholarship was of the value of £60 a year, and was good for nine years.

This distinction was not gained without hard work and some damage to his health. A letter to his mother, in the October before he won his scholarship, relates how he had fainted in the University church. In fact he was one of those people who are never really well, yet seldom really ill. The trouble with his eyes was not permanent; it was apparently due to shortness of sight, and was relieved when he took to wearing spectacles for ordinary purposes. His oculist advised him to keep his head cool in bed and his feet warm, and to apply leeches to his temples once a fortnight. Toothache, and later on indigestion, were lasting torments. But his constitution must have been fundamentally tough. His industry and his powers of application were enormous. The drain upon his vital energies was exaggerated by the nervous tension with which he approached each crisis in his career. As time went on it was still further intensified by the strenuous emotionalism and the rigorous bodily discipline required of him by his religion. To some extent his practice of the religious life was an escape from the world of facts and men into a world more congenial to his cloistered spirit. He felt, at these hours, like the philosopher of Plato, released from the cave for the contemplation of absolute truth. But, until he had crossed the last bridge, he could not rest in contemplation. Wrestling in prayer takes its toll even of the saints.

The fainting-fit in St. Mary's was the first symptom of the overstrain. It was also the first evidence of the safety-valve. Newman's temperament saved itself from wreckage by frequent collapses. His recovery from these was always rapid— so rapid as to give some support to the theory that his breakdowns were induced not so much by overwork as by a suppressed fear of failure. There is certainly truth in this. But the overwork and the fatigue were real. Newman's relentless will drove him along an exhausting path. The completeness of the collapses, and the rapidity of the recoveries, scarcely prove more than that his physical organism refused to be driven right up to the real breaking-point.

His success in the scholarship examination reveals a quality in Newman which would have carried him to the summit of any secular career, once he had learned the art of husbanding his physical and nervous energy. This was an intense ambition to succeed. Before the examination he felt the tortures of suspense so much that he wished and wished he had never attempted it. 'The idea of *turpis repulsa* haunted me.' Yet he had an inner confidence that he was bound to win. As his religious opinions developed, he came to regard this ambitiousness as an odious characteristic and bent all the power of his will to tame and subdue it.

But now, in the summer of 1818, after his triumph against men much older than himself, the face of the secular world seemed bright and satisfying, and he passed an 'idle' Long Vacation. He had no thought whatever of the ministry. One of the attractions of his scholarship was that it might lead to a Trinity Fellowship which could be held 'for five years without taking orders'. He had been sent to Oxford as a preliminary to the Bar; his interest in religion, strong and deep as it was, was as yet like John Bowden's only the interest of a layman. In the Long Vacation of this year, the seventeen year old scholar was reading Gibbon and Locke and letting his mind expand in a direction away from the set curriculum of the Schools, away, too, from Bishop Beveridge and Thomas Scott and the writing of amateur sermons. Gibbon, indeed, was so much an obsession with him that his letters took on a 'very Gibbonian style'. He re-read Gibbon next year, with mounting admiration. 'Oh, who is worthy', he exclaimed to Bowden, 'to succeed our Gibbon? *Exoriare aliquis!* and may he be a better man!' Dreams of Gibbon filled his nights; his ears 'rang with the cadences of his sentences.' Many years later he ranked the unbeliever Gibbon as the only English writer who had any claim to be considered an ecclesiastical historian. One might have supposed that he would have learned to say bitter things of the infidel. But the harshest condemnation he ever permitted himself was to write of Gibbon's Five Causes of Christianity: 'We do not deny them, but only say they are not sufficient.'

Early in the next year the two friends started 'a small periodical like Addison's *Spectator*.' It was called *The Undergraduate* and was more successful than the usual run of such papers. However, the names of the editors were discovered, and it came to an abrupt ending. In the same month they published a poem, their joint composition, called *St. Bartholomew's Eve*. 'The subject'—so Newman, with a touch of humour, described the poem in his old age—' was the sequel of the unfortunate union of a Protestant gentleman with a Catholic lady, ending in the tragical death of both, through the machinations of a cruel fanatical priest, whose inappropriate name was Clement. Mr. Bowden did the historical and picturesque portions, Mr. Newman the theological. There were no love scenes, nor could there be; for, as it turned out, to the monk's surprise, the parties had been some time before the action husband and wife, by a clandestine marriage, known however to the father of the lady.'

Gibbon and Locke and his own literary adventures were far from exhausting the boy's earnest leisure. He went to Buckland's lectures on geology; read Crabbe and Sir Walter Scott; played the fiddle a great deal and joined in the formation of a musical club. His natural versatility was budding exuberantly. The infantile ruler of the citadel was not yet in deep fear for itself; his intellectual forces ran free and exulted in their liberty, unaware—except when the shadow of a mysterious gloom fell across his spirit—how unreal and brief that liberty was to be. 'When I have taken my degree,' he promised himself repeatedly 'I will do many things—compose a piece of music for instruments, experimentalize in chemistry, get up the Persian language.' To these delicious visions of intellectual and artistic freedom was joined the alluring dream of worldly success. Only two years later, when the dream had been shattered, he wrote of this period: 'In 1819 and the beginning of 1820 I hoped great things for myself. Not liking to go into the Church, but to the

Law, I attended Modern History lectures (professorial), hearing that the names were reported to the Minister.'

In an age when serious parents preached to their equally serious children on the necessity of a grand purpose in life, early embraced and rigidly pursued, 'these excursive acts' seemed like a dangerous dissipation of energy. But, Newman protested, they were 'not more than such a recreation as boating might be in the summer term.' The image of Newman's adolescence would be forbidding indeed without them, and without the occasional glimpses of romantic reverie which he rescued for us from his past. One can see the boy at the window of his room looking at the snapdragon growing on the opposite wall and dreaming into it a metaphor of his own clinging affections. One sees him there on a summer evening listening to the sound of the Oxford bells pealing, and trying to put on paper the incommunicable feelings they stirred, the 'longing after something, I know not what . . . something dear to us, and well known to us— very soothing.' Not God, nor Christ, nor the Virgin, nor the Saints; not the past years, nor the angel faces; not the 'dear earliest friend'; not the 'dear Self' with whom, under his long eclipse, he talked in private as with a friend more intimate than any other. Was it, perhaps, a dearer Self still, a Self whom he had lost in infancy, and was never to find again?

The summer term of 1819 drew on to Trinity Sunday. John was parted from his friend, who had gone home to the Isle of Wight, where his sister lay dying. The fortnight's solitude encouraged what he called *ignes suppositos cineri doloso*— the fire which always lay concealed under the deceitful ashes. The approach of the College Gaudy on Trinity Monday excited him to pour out his feelings to Mr. Mayers. 'To-morrow is our Gaudy. . . .Oh, how the angels must lament over a whole society throwing off the allegiance and service of their Maker, which they have pledged the day before at His table, and showing themselves the sons of Belial!' He had

hoped this year that there would be no subscription for wine.
A quarrel had divided the College. 'Unhappily, a day or two
before the time a reconciliation takes place; the wine party is
agreed upon, and this wicked union, to be sealed with
drunkenness, is profanely joked upon with allusions to one of
the expressions in the Athanasian Creed.' Many had secretly
hoped there would be no Gaudy. But 'all are gone, there has
been weakness and fear of ridicule. . . . Oh that the purpose
of some may be changed before the time! I know not how to
make myself of use. I am intimate with very few. The Gaudy
has done more harm to the College than the whole year can
compensate. An habitual negligence of the awfulness of the
Holy Communion is introduced. How can we prosper?'

But the Gaudy passed, and no thunderbolts fell, and John
entered on his third Long Vacation, and enjoyed 'that
soothing, quiet, unostentatious pleasure which only an
equable unvarying time of living can give.' He worked hard.
Herodotus, Thucydides, and Gibbon employed him from
morning to night. In October the tragedians—Sophocles and
Aeschylus—succeed to the historians. He and Bowden are
'reading between eleven and twelve hours a day, and have
an hour for walking and an hour for dinner.' His hopes of
success are rising; and he looks forward to the coming year
with anxiety, certainly, but with 'great delight'. The delight,
it is true, is in the prospect of another long vacation spent in
steady reading, not in the prospect of the ordeal which lies
beyond it next November. But that is his typical mood. He
can never abandon himself to the life of pure scholarship or
art or contemplation; there must be always some powerful
external compulsion, directing the use of his faculties. For the
moment the compulsion of his final Schools is sufficient for him.
After that it will be necessary to his well-being that he should
submit himself to some grander discipline. He is the schoolboy of genius, but he leaves one school only to join another.

This submissiveness to authority is one of the clearest features in Newman's character from first to last. Not to *any* authority. The yoke must fit his neck; it must be old and stately; it must be absolute. And, by a seeming paradox, he must choose it out for himself. So his submission satisfies both his humility and his pride. Each step that he takes demonstrates his superiority to the crowd and brings him nearer to the utter self-abasement which his soul desires. And because the full pleasure of abasement can only be tasted by a spirit deeply in love with itself, and poignantly aware of the greatness of its surrender, it follows that such a man as Newman will place himself at the very centre of the universe. Everything that happens to him will seem important, and will seem to have happened for his sake. Every date, every anniversary, every letter, every pencil jotting must be preserved. His path is strewn with omens. Every tiniest incident will be a moment in the unfolding of that incomparable drama, the progress of John Henry Newman from the cradle to the grave. 'Did we but see,' he writes in the *Lyra Apostolica* 'when life first opened, how our journey lay between its earliest and its closing day . . . such sight would break the youthful spirit.' And in his best-known hymn he sees himself stumbling, obedient to the Heavenly will, 'o'er moor and fen, o'er crag and torrent, till the night is gone.' Had he written so of himself as an old man, with the long sorrows and the bitter disappointments of his later life behind him; or had he written so, to borrow the phrase of Keats, in the space of life between the imagination of a boy and the mature imagination of a man, there would be no special significance in these images. But both poems were written when he was turned thirty, at the beginning of the most active, successful and happy period of his life, after a decade of quiet scholastic and parochial work. There was nothing at that time in the past or the present or the visible future to break any youthful spirit, or to explain the romantic metaphors of 'Lead, kindly Light'.

His undergraduate period could naturally, therefore, be nothing less to him than 'a picture of a whole life—of youth, of manhood, of old age—which could not be understood or felt without actual experience.' He watched the process with keen expectancy, and in his last long vacation became 'half conscious of some mental or moral change within him'. It was the presage of the returning tide of faith; the death-knell of his dreams of a secular ambition.

'Half conscious', be it observed. The shock of actual failure converted half consciousness into full consciousness; and one is tempted to think, not that coming events had cast their shadows before, but that he read back afterwards into his mind something which had not really been there until failure came. But he was right in his account of himself. Half-way through this last Long Vacation, three months before the ordeal, in August 1820, he is writing to Frank in a deeply religious mood. He is conscious of a heart too solicitous about fame and too fearful of failure. He is reading hard, but God enables him to praise Him with joyful lips when he rises, and when he lies down, and when he wakes in the night. It is his daily prayer that he may not get any honours if they are to be the least cause of sin to him. He tells his sister that he dare not think much of the schools because to do so makes him covet success; he will not therefore ask for success, but for good. Alone at Trinity, in his rooms, in the library, in the garden, overshadowed by the heavy foliage of the late summer and the obscure conflict within himself, he lifts his head from his books to brood on the inward horror and darkness of Christ's passion in another garden.

What was the cause of this creeping shadow? Was it the forerunner of dedication to high and stern service? Was it the inevitable nemesis of a too hardly driven boyhood? For more than a year now the pressure had been unrelenting, and increasing. From June to October in the previous year he was reading nine hours a day. After that the rate increased.

He was now, in this last August, working on an average more than twelve hours a day—if he read nine hours one day he read fifteen the next. He had been driving himself at this rate since the beginning of the vacation and kept it up, with hardly a break, till his examination. He had been living almost continuously in Oxford for a year and a half, terms and vacations alike, sometimes with Bowden to keep him company, often quite alone, getting up in winter and summer at five or six, and scarcely giving himself time to eat. Under this ruthless mechanical pressure the intellectual frivolities of adolescence were crushed.

And what was the power which drove the machine? Was it love of learning? Was it desire of fame? Was it hatred of failure? Was it the demon of thoroughness? Was it a kind of mental self-flagellation? Was it an assertion of spirit over body? And did it make or mar the mechanism, to be so driven?

Certainly it made the mechanism. If the human brain is left to unfold itself like a flower, it may be an ornament but it will not become an instrument. It needs to be put to tasks beyond its power. Periods of intense effort and concentration earn their reward in an increase of mental ability. The increase may not be apparent all at once. A fallow interval is often necessary. But if the immediate results of hard work are disappointing, the ultimate result is often startling. It has, however, to be paid for. It may be won at too great a cost of physical exhaustion. Or, in the pursuit of intellectual power, the other components of the human organism may be neglected and allowed to atrophy. Or, again, the concentration may be too prolonged in too narrow a field, until the mind becomes incapable of seeing value in any other form of activity. This last risk was one which Newman was to incur far more seriously in his subsequent studies. His greatest present danger—which he did not escape—was over-intellectualization.

November came at last, and with it his 'grand examination'. In those days the principal part of the examination was
not written but *viva voce*. Bowden passed through his own
ordeal and went home, leaving his friend still waiting to be
called up by the examiners. 'By the time you receive this', he
wrote to Newman, 'I conclude you will have completed your
labours in the schools and covered yourself and the college
with glory.' In the young scholar's overwrought condition
the knowledge that everyone expected him to give a brilliant
performance and that Trinity, which had not had a first
class for ten years, was counting on his success, was in itself
dangerous. He was called up a day sooner than he expected
and ignominiously collapsed before the examiners. In the
event he failed to secure mathematical honours, and on the
classical side of the examination his name appeared 'under
the line'—the equivalent of a third or a fourth class. In other
words he did just well enough to qualify for his degree—presumably by the courtesy of the examiners. Otherwise his
failure was not merely complete, it was spectacular.

It was characteristic of Newman that he could do nothing
by halves. If he could not succeed brilliantly, he must fail
utterly. He must be the leader, the hope of his people, the
admired of all beholders. But he could never sustain that
part for long, and there were only two tolerable ways of
escape; breakdown or renunciation. You cannot renounce
your belief in the desirability of a double first in the middle
of your examination. All you can do is to save your face by a
breakdown. Which was what Newman did—not, of course,
deliberately or consciously. Nothing less than a first class was
the true index to his ability and his power of reading. He
had, in fact, read himself stale. But staleness would not have
paralysed him, if he had possessed a normal temperament.
Spectacular failure saved him from the intolerable ignominy
of an undistinguished second class.

4. FAILURE AND RECOVERY

'December 1, 1820. It is all over, and I have not succeeded. The pain it gives me to be obliged to inform you and
my mother of it, I cannot express.' In these terms Newman
wrote to announce his failure to his father. Mr. and Mrs.
Newman treated the catastrophe with admirable good sense.
Their only sorrow was on his account. He insisted in his
reply that his only sorrow had been on their account. 'A man
has just left me, and his last words were, "Well, Newman, I
would rather have your philosophy than the high honours
to which you have been aspiring."'

The recovery was not much more than a matter of hours.
He had failed, but he knew, and everyone else knew, that his
failure was not 'the measure of his intellectual merits'. And
now that the tyranny of continuous reading was over he felt
'quite lightened of a load'. A few days later he went home for
the Christmas vacation.

The next year, 1821, Newman's twenty-first, was a year of
relaxation, and yet it contained the two determining points
of his career, his decision to remain at Oxford and take
orders instead of going to the bar, and his resolution to stand
for a Fellowship at Oriel.

All the contradictory features of his character flash up
and fade away in turn during these twelve months. First his
abortive interest in science. He attends Buckland's lectures
on geology. His comment is revealing: 'To tell the truth, the
science is so in its infancy that no regular system is formed.
Hence the lectures are rather an enumeration of facts from
which probabilities are deduced, than a consistent and
luminous theory of certainties, illustrated by occasional
examples. It is, however, most entertaining, and opens an
amazing field to imagination and to poetry.' He wants the
authoritative system, and would accept it, if it was there. He
is still the schoolboy. He has no interest whatever in the slow

process of establishing a system of scientific theory by the means of experiment and observation. Nor should theory stop short of certainty. *Hypotheses*, he might have said, *non fingo*. Nevertheless he dabbles in illustrative experiments, and uses his sister Harriett to steam away 'the superfluous water of the nitro-sulphate of copper'. Indeed he recorded that 'mineralogy and chemistry were his chief studies, and the composition of music.'

Side by side with this second flowering of his secular interests his religious preoccupations were deepening. The mystery of the Holy Trinity exercises, perplexes, his reason. His difficulties are eased by a dream, in which a spirit from the other world tells him that it is absolutely impossible for the reason of man to understand the mystery of the Holy Trinity and in vain to argue about it; but that everything in another world is so very, very plain that there is not the slightest difficulty. 'I thought I instantly fell on my knees overcome with gratitude to God for so kind a message. It is not idle to make a memorandum of this, for out of dreams often much good can be extracted.' So easy was it for the ruler of the citadel to quell the first beginnings of mutiny. His intelligence, turned back on the threshold of a too dangerous adventure, began to examine the articles of his Evangelical faith. Doubts of the doctrine of election and final perseverance made themselves heard.

At what precise point the idea of a legal career was abandoned, and by whose particular initiation—Newman's own, or his father's—no certain information exists. This is what Newman himself states in his *Autobiographical Memoir*:

'He had been destined by his Father's loving ambition for the Bar, and with that purpose had been sent to the University, and in 1819 had entered at Lincoln's Inn; but his failure in the schools making his prospect of rising in a difficult profession doubtful, and his religious views becoming more pronounced, he decided in the course of 1821, with his Father's full acquiescence, on taking Orders.'

Whether Newman made up his own mind or whether (as Mr. Ward suggests) his father precipitated his decision for him, it does not seem certain that the decision was as yet quite final. After his election to an Oriel Fellowship a friend and contemporary, writing to congratulate him, asks which ladder he proposes to climb—that leading to Canterbury or that leading to the Woolsack. 'You now have it in your power to decide.' Had he then *not* decided earlier?

Well, he had so decided, certainly, in the first wave of reaction, after his breakdown in the schools. But as the year went on, and his natural forces collected themselves, he began (in his own words) 'to think about retrieving his losses'. And he quotes from his novel *Loss and Gain* a passage describing how he and Bowden climbed to the top of an Oxford tower to observe the stars; and how, 'while his friend was busily engaged with the pointers, he, earthly-minded youth, had been looking down into the deep gas-lit, dark-shadowed quadrangles, and wondering if he should ever be Fellow of this or that College, which he singled out from the mass of academical buildings.'

There was one College, in particular, where Newman's record was least likely to be remembered against him and might be most spectacularly reversed. This was Oriel, now at the very height of its reputation, where men were elected to Fellowships rather upon their abilities than upon their scholarship. 'Every election to a fellowship,' wrote Bishop Copleston, Provost of Oriel when Newman was elected, to Provost Hawkins in 1843, 'which tends to discourage the narrow and almost technical routine of public examinations, I consider as an important triumph. You remember Newman himself was an example. He was not even a good classical scholar, yet in mind and power of composition, and in taste and knowledge, he was decidedly superior to some competitors who were a class above him in the schools.'

It was not until near the end of the year that Newman made up his mind to be a candidate at Oriel. This was fortunate for him, since it was useless now to prepare himself for the examination by an elaborate course of reading, and he had been happily and healthily wasting his time at mineralogy and chemistry. Otherwise he would have spoiled his own chances once more. Another distraction was the companionship of his younger brother, Frank, who came up to Oxford from Ealing in the autumn and shared his lodgings at Seale's Coffee House. The examination was to be held at the beginning of April 1822. On November 15, 1821, he notes that he has 'nearly' decided to stand. There were four months left to him. What could be done in four months, but a little sharpening of his Latin? He would stand in April, just in order to make himself known and to learn the nature of the examination. The year after he might have a better chance.

But the bare possibility of success at Oriel stimulated all his worldly ambitions to rear their shameful heads. 'How active still', he cries to himself, 'are the evil passions of vainglory, ambition, &c., within me. After my failure last November, I thought that they would never be unruly again. Alas! no sooner is any mention made of my standing for a fellowship than every barrier seems swept away; and they spread, and overflow, and deluge me.' So he upbraids himself in his private journal in November. A fortnight later his heart 'boils over with vainglorious anticipations of success.' Two months later: 'Alas, how I am changed! I am perpetually praying to get in to Oriel, and to obtain the prize for my essay. O Lord! dispose of me as will best promote Thy glory, but give me resignation and contentment.'

Queer language for a boy of twenty-one to use, but not so queer as his answer to his mother's birthday letter. 'Not that

I am sorry so great a part of life is gone—would that all were over!—but I seem now more left to myself, and when I reflect upon my own weakness I have cause to shudder.' Mrs. Newman wrote back at once in some alarm. Her adored John shuddering at *himself*! What could be more absurd? 'We fear very much, from the tone of your letter, you are depressed. . . . We fear you debar yourself a proper quantity of wine. . . . Take proper air and exercise; accept all the invitations you receive; and do not be over-anxious about anything. . . . I see one great fault in your character which alarms me, as I observe it grows upon you seriously . . . a want of self-confidence and a dissatisfaction with yourself.'

Mrs. Newman was both right and wrong in her diagnosis. Her son was a mixture of an exaggerated humility and an overweening pride. These two opposing currents in his soul were charged with a wholly abnormal energy. He spoke and wrote in the phrases of ordinary family life. But every now and then the measured conventional sentences betrayed their inadequacy to contain his emotion, and a glimpse was given of the alarming inner conflict. That was something which his mother could no more understand than cure. Had she not willed John to be perfect? And was he not perfect, if only he had the good sense to see it? It was impossible for her to realize the tragic fracture which extended, like a great geological fault, through all the strata of his spiritual being. He himself knew of its existence if not its true extent and character. It was fundamental, it conditioned his religion, it determined his career.

'As to my opinions' he answered her at once, in a letter which no study of his life can leave unquoted, 'and the sentiments I expressed in my last letter, they remain fixed in my mind, and are repeated deliberately and confidently. If it were any new set of opinions I had lately adopted, they might be said to arise from nervousness, or over-study, or ill-health; but no, my opinion has been exactly the same for

these five years. . . . The only thing is, opportunities have
occurred of late for my mentioning it more than before; but
believe me, these sentiments are neither new nor slightly
founded. If they made me melancholy, morose, austere, distant, reserved, sullen, then indeed they might with justice be
the subject of anxiety; but if, as I think is the case, I am
always cheerful, if at home I am always ready and eager to
join in any merriment, if I am not clouded with sadness, if
my meditations make me neither absent in mind nor deficient in action, then my principles may be gazed at and
puzzle the gazer, but they cannot be accused of bad practical
effects. Take me when I am most foolish at home, and extend
mirth into childishness; stop me short and ask me then what
I think of myself, whether my opinions are less gloomy; no, I
think I should seriously return the same answer, that "I
shuddered at myself." '

But henceforward, in his letters to his mother, he was
careful to make the very most of his social activities and
his rare indulgence in any form of recreation.

On the same day, or only a day or two later, he wrote to
his father, who had warned him against being the cause of
his own failure:

'I assure you that they know very little of me, and judge
very superficially of me, who think I do not put a value on
myself *relatively* to others. I think (since I am forced to speak
boastfully) few have attained the facility of comprehension
which I have arrived at from the regularity and constancy
of my reading, and the laborious and nerve-bracing and
fancy-repressing subject of mathematics, which has been my
principal subject.'

Spiritual self-hatred and intellectual self-admiration.
When these currents meet with such force as they did in
Newman, the result is a vortex into which a whole society
may easily be drawn.

5. SUCCESS

Examinations for Oriel Fellowships were held always in Easter week and lasted for four days—Monday to Thursday. The elections were made on the Friday. The candidates were shut up all day in the hall, and there they stayed until they could write no more or it became too dark to see. James Mozley was said to have written his English essay at the end of a long day's work on another paper, lying down on the floor to get the light of the fire. It consisted of only ten lines, but the ten lines, said Dean Church, 'were such as no other man in Oxford could have written.' James, however, was not elected. Latin and Greek translations and compositions, an English and a Latin essay and a paper of quasi-philosophical questions, made up the examination. At intervals the candidates were haled away to the room in the Tower where they were obliged to read and translate at sight passages of Greek and Latin before the Provost and Fellows. This ordeal, twice repeated, was the *viva voce*; it lingers still, though but a shadow of its once terrible self, in the Fellowship Examination at All Souls.

How the Fellows were able to come to a proper judgment of the work of the candidates in so short a time is something of a mystery. But if Dean Church is to be believed they did not scamp their work. 'The custom was for the whole body of Fellows to examine together each set of papers. We met in common room and sat round the table, each of us having one man's essay or translation; if a translation, one of us read a sentence of the English, etc., and the corresponding sentence of each translation went round the table in turn, till the paper had been gone through, sentence by sentence, and each sentence had been discussed and criticized. It was a tedious process, but very thorough', and rather more merciless to the fading scholarship of many of the Fellows than to the weaknesses of the candidates.

This kind of examination, searching yet informal, was much better suited to Newman's temperament than the dry rigour of the Schools; and the English Essay, which ranked with the Latin Prose as the most important paper in the examination, gave his genius its perfect opportunity. These two papers occupied the first day, Monday. Newman's performance so impressed the Provost and Fellows that three of the electors were sent over to Trinity on Wednesday morning to make the usual confidential enquiries about a promising candidate. But Newman, knowing nothing of this, came back to his lodgings in Broad Street in the early afternoon, on the brink of collapse, having made up his mind to retire from the examination. He found a summons from his tutor, Tommy Short. Mr. Short was leaving Oxford that afternoon, and was sitting down to an early dinner in his rooms, when Newman knocked at his door. There were lamb cutlets and fried parsley on the table; and perhaps—for Mr. Short was an astute man and knew his pupil—it was not by accident that there was enough for two. Those lamb cutlets were savoury still in old Dr. Newman's memory when, fifty-six years later, he was entertained at Trinity as an Honorary Fellow and replied after dinner to the toast of his health proposed by James Bryce. 'I remember how he entertained us' wrote Bryce 'by conveying indirectly and by a sort of reference that Mr. Short was lunching [sic] off lamb chops. I do not think he mentioned directly that the lunch consisted of lamb chops, but he played round the subject in such a way as to convey that lamb chops were on the table.'

And well they might be savoury in his memory, for the chops and the parsley and his tutor's encouraging manner and comments upon his own account of his work in the examination persuaded him to return to the contest. Back in Oriel Hall, he looked up at a window, and there, in a coat of arms, was a motto clearly intended for a direct message to himself. *Pie repone te*, said the motto, somewhat obscurely—

'Renew thyself (or, relax thyself), thou righteous man.' So the over-anxious youth took heart of grace, and, when his turn came for the *viva voce* in the Tower, he acquitted himself with 'great readiness and even accuracy'. All through Thursday *pie repone te* comforted him from the window as he wrote. He went to bed 'very calm' on the eve of the day, Friday, the twelfth of April, 1822, which he was ever afterwards to regard as 'the turning-point of his life, and of all days most memorable'.

The Provost of Oriel's butler was, by custom, the bearer of the good tidings, and this functionary had his own facetious way of prolonging the successful candidate's suspense. He arrived to find Newman playing the fiddle to himself. Disconcerted, he employed his formula, with something less than the usual effect. 'He had, he feared, disagreeable news to announce'—one imagines a pause, becoming more uncomfortable to the messenger than to Newman—'viz. that Mr. Newman was elected Fellow of Oriel, and that his immediate presence was required there.' The account is best continued in Newman's own words. 'The person addressed, thinking that such language savoured of impertinent familiarity, merely answered "Very well" and went on fiddling. This led the man to ask whether, perhaps, he had not mistaken the rooms and gone to the wrong person, to which Mr. Newman replied that it was all right. But, as may be imagined, no sooner had the man left, than he flung down his instrument, and dashed down stairs with all speed to Oriel College. And he recollected, after fifty years, the eloquent faces and eager bows of the tradesmen and others whom he met on his way, who had heard the news, and well understood why he was crossing from St. Mary's to the lane opposite at so extraordinary a pace.'

It was to the torture-chamber in the Tower that the successful candidate was summoned. There Newman received the felicitations of the assembled Provost and Fellows.

Amongst them was John Keble. 'I bore it till Keble took my hand,' he wrote to Bowden 'and then felt so abashed and unworthy of the honour done me, that I seemed desirous of quite sinking into the ground.' It was his first meeting with the man, whom already he revered as 'the first man in Oxford'. 'How is that hour fixed in my memory' he exclaimed in the *Apologia* 'after the changes of forty-two years, forty-two this very day on which I write!'

Back from Oriel to Trinity, half dazed at the sudden transformation of the world about him, yet sharply observant, as always, of all the events in this most wonderful of days. To Kinsey's rooms—Kinsey was Dean of Trinity. Then to the President. Excited interruptions at every point. Men dashing in and out of each other's rooms, in and out of College, eager to pass the great news on to somebody who had not yet heard it. All the bells in the three towers set pealing—at Newman's expense. The honour and credit of Trinity restored. Success, success, success!

Then back again to Oriel. His first attendance at Evensong in the chapel of his new College. The service over, one of the Junior Fellows took him by the hand and led him to the Provost's stall. The Provost, with affected surprise, asked him the traditional question '*Domine, quid petis?*' (Sir, what is that you seek?), received the traditional answer *Peto beneficium hujusce collegii in annum* (I seek the bounty of this college for a year), and conceded the request. Whereupon the new Fellow was led back to his seat, on probation for twelve months, before being admitted to a full Fellowship.

And after Chapel, at dinner, with a large party, in the common room, sitting next to Keble and finding him, as he had been told, more like an undergraduate than the first man in Oxford; so perfectly unassuming and unaffected in his manner. And at last, alone in his room, writing these things down in his diary, writing to his father, 'I am just made Fellow of Oriel, thank God! I am absolutely a member of the Common Room; am called by them "Newman", and am abashed, and find I must soon learn to call them "Keble", "Hawkins", "Tyler".' Last of all, falling on his knees and pouring out his whole soul to God in thankfulness and humble, but high, resolve.

CHAPTER III

CROSS-SECTION

I. THE PARTIES IN THE CHURCH

A haze, not thick but tantalizing, hangs over the first few years of Newman's life in his new home. The general shape is definite enough; the details waver. He was entering now upon a period of slow change, under the influence of his new associates. For the first time in his life he was thrown continually into the intimate society of other men, his intellectual equals, mostly older than himself. He drew, later on, in the *Apologia* and in his own *Autobiographical Memoir*, the broad outlines of their several influences upon his character and opinions; but a clear picture of him at this time is strangely difficult to construct. It occupies no more than a page or two of his biography; the published letters are few and meagre; the reminiscences of friends and disciples add little.

It becomes necessary to look away from Newman himself at the men who were so to influence him, and beyond these individual influences at the religious environment in which both he and they were set. The distinctions of religious party, which bulked so big less than a century ago, mean so little to many modern readers that a brief sketch of them must be attempted at this point. The Oxford Movement, even if it were studied from a purely behaviourist point of view, would be unintelligible without some knowledge of the divisions which then existed in the English Church, and of their historical pedigrees. In the account of these divisions which occupies the following pages I adopt Newman's own ter-

minology, from the appendix on the constitution and history
of the Church of England, which he wrote for the French
edition of the *Apologia*. But the description of the parties is my
own, and is at once inadequate and incorrect. Inadequate because it is impossible to do justice to any system of belief
in a few sentences; incorrect because none of the three parties
were unanimous within themselves upon their own fundamental principles, and each party was at least as much the
unconscious product of a complex series of causes, political
and psychological, as the fully conscious vehicle of consistent
doctrine.

Newman, then, writing in 1866, divided the Anglican
Communion into three great parties—the Apostolic or
Tractarian party, the Evangelical party, and the Liberal or
Latitudinarian party.

The Tractarian party, of course, in 1822 was still in the
womb of time. But it claimed, when it was born, to be the
heir of a more ancient party, dating from the reigns of James I
and Charles I, represented in the eighteenth century by the
Non jurors who refused to take the oath of allegiance to
William III by reason of their belief in the divine right of
anointed kings. Its members claimed to inherit, through the
continuity of an episcopate which derived its sacred authority
unbroken from the Apostles, the true tradition of a Catholic,
sacramental, priestly Church. They rested their faith upon a
twofold revelation: upon the Bible, as the Church and the
Councils of the Church alone knew how to interpret it, but
still more certainly upon the existence and authority of the
Church itself. They held the prestige, the independence, the
supremacy, of the Church to be more important than anything else in the world, and they resented bitterly the subordination of its affairs to the lay rulers of the State. They
were hostile to Roman pretensions, and severe towards
Roman abuses; but they claimed the same title of Catholic,
the same ecclesiastical inheritance; and they loathed the title

of Protestant only less than that of Dissenter. Their temper was the temper of passionate and proud belief in a God, whose unseen splendour was manifested on earth to the eyes and ears of the faithful in a majestic and divinely instituted society. The Church, its priesthood and its sacraments, were the ordained means of grace; and no beauty of character or purity of intention could be allowed by men to offer the hope of salvation to any soul which refused to travel by the appointed road. The Reformation had obscured, but it had not destroyed, the true tradition. It could not do so; man might reform the abuses of man's own making; to reform the Church of Christ was not in his power. All earthly dominion took its sanction, for Christians, from this sacred source. The pattern of a truly Christian society must follow the pattern of Christ's revelation. There must be men in authority, and men under authority, and over all the King, his coronation a sacrament of the Church, holding his authority from God, whose glory he and all his subjects had been created to serve.

The Evangelical party, as Newman said, derived from the Puritans. To them the Scriptures, rather than the Church, were the embodiment of the revealed truth. The Bible contained all that a man needed for salvation. The gospel had but to be preached; the sinner to be converted. Thenceforward he was in a direct personal communion with God, and in perfect assurance that he would be saved. No priest, no mystical rite, had any office or function to perform between him and his maker. There must, certainly, be order and organization. Men must meet to praise and to pray and to be wrought upon by preaching. Baptism and the Lord's Supper were symbolic and commemorative acts, enjoined by Holy Writ. The ministers of God's word were, by the sacredness of their mission, set apart from other men, yet they were, in Wakeman's phrase, 'merely the ministers of the congregation and not the stewards of the mysteries of God'. Though the

body of the faithful constituted the Church, and though the
Church, like every other human society, must have ordinances, practices, officers and a discipline of its own, it was
not the channel of God's grace to the individual soul. The
keynote of Evangelical Christianity was enthusiasm, in the
literal sense of the word. The converted sinner was filled with
God, and he carried his conviction of God's presence into
every moment of his daily life. His assurance of his own salvation did not allow him to rest idle. It could not do so, or he
had not been truly converted and his assurance was an
illusion. Loving God in this direct and personal manner he
must labour to increase the number of God's elect. Hence
the remarkable fact, which Newman notes, that it was the
Evangelical party which maintained all the Biblical Societies
and most of the associations for Protestant Missions throughout the world. He might have added that most of the great
practical philanthropists were, like Wilberforce, men of
Evangelical persuasions.

The growth of the Evangelical party in the Anglican
Church was the result of the great Evangelical movement
initiated by John Wesley eighty-six years before Newman's
election at Oriel. Though the Wesleys seceded from the
Church their influence—or, rather, the influence of George
Whitefield—worked within it, and in 1866 Newman could
still call the party by far the most important of the three
which he was trying to describe for the information of his
French readers. This was strange, because if ever the name
'the stupid party' was deserved it was deserved by the
Evangelicals. Their insistence on the literal inspiration and
understanding of the Scriptures, combined with their exaltation of feeling, atrophied their reasoning powers. Their
thought, hobbled by texts, failed to explore even the fenced
field of the Calvinistic logic. The fathers of the school made
no effort to relate their conceptions to history or to philosophy, and their successors—even the ablest of them—wasted

their minds on extravagant attempts to apply Scriptural prophecies to the events of their own times. The development of
science passed above their heads as if they were children. As
the initial fervour of the movement spent itself, piety, un-
supported by intelligence, tended towards pietism, and its
phrases, once charged with earnest force, became the stock
equipment of pretentious insincerity.

It is easier to convey a general impression of the spiritual
character of Evangelicalism than to describe its doctrines,
and Newman, writing for his French public, prudently
made no attempt at such a description. Perhaps it is right
to say that while the doctrine of human depravity has been
an essential part of Christian teaching, in all its manifestations, until the appearance of Modernism, the Evangelicals,
following in the Puritan tradition derived from Calvin and
Zwingli, erected it into the main article of their creed. Conviction of sin must come before anything else. Furthermore,
the escape from sin could only be by a full realization of
God's grace working in and transforming the sinner. There
were no magical dodges, no easy ways round; nor was there
any means of escape, however hard, open to a sinner, however determined upon his own reformation, of which he
could avail himself of his own will. He might challenge God
with God's promise of redemption to all mankind; but unless
God answered the challenge and flooded his soul with the
consciousness of salvation, he was doomed. This was the
significance of the 'new birth', the experience of conversion,
from which the saved dated their religious life. The only
alternative was eternal damnation.

For those, then, who had this conviction of safety, the
Christian religion was a religion of love. It was such to
Wesley himself. He would have denied that the central
article of his faith was belief in the total depravity of human
nature. He would have admitted that human nature was
depraved; but he would have insisted that the supreme fact

of all was the power and the willingness of the divine love to annul human sin. He saw, clearly enough, the moral dangers contained in the Calvinistic doctrines of predestination and justification by faith rather than works. He did not see (nor perhaps did many of the Evangelicals) that these doctrines were the inevitable counterpart, in a logical mind, of his own insistence upon the necessity of the new birth. But Wesley, who held that a belief in witches was an essential part of Christianity and refused to study mathematics because his faith might be weakened, kept faith securely separate from reason. Whitefield, reputed to have been the poorest of theologians, saw the weakness of Wesley's doctrinal position clearly enough, and held fast to the triple formula of corruption, election and justification by faith.

The Evangelicalism which developed within the Church of England had more in it of Whitefield than of Wesley, and it found—or thought that it found—unmistakable support for its doctrines in the Thirty-nine Articles. For the Articles say: that Holy Scripture containeth all things necessary to salvation; that the flesh deserveth God's wrath and damnation; that man is justified by faith only; that good works done before the grace of Christ have the nature of sin; and that those whom God hath predestined to life are called according to His purpose by His Spirit working in due season. It is true that the Articles say a number of other things less consonant with the Evangelical creed. But the Articles were intended from the first as a common platform, on which Protestants and Catholics might meet; and it is not surprising that each party was content to focus its attention on those declarations of doctrine which it found sympathetic and to minimize or ignore those which it found antipathetic. And this was the easier to do, because the Articles could never claim a more than legal authority; they were not divinely inspired or guaranteed. They were noto-

riously a compromise of conflicting views, dictated by
Cranmer, re-edited and re-enforced by Elizabeth.

It would seem, then, that the typical Evangelical religious
attitude was based upon fear—fear of the terrible fate which
awaited all who were not rescued by a manifest act of God,
fear of God's deafness to the supplications of those whom
He had not chosen for His own, fear of all sensual pleasures
and beauties, for these are the natural delights of the unregenerate. This fear was, of its own nature, a selfish fear.
And there is, perhaps, nothing stranger in the whole tangled
history of religious thought than the translation of so bar-
barous, even so savage, a motive into the chief principle of a
religion, which began as a message of goodwill towards men.
This was the kind of fear, which lay at the bottom of Newman's mind and was not expelled in his progress from
Evangelicalism to Catholicism—the kind of fear which
speaks again and again in his Anglican sermons, as when he
says that 'if a man is taken at unawares, an apparently small
sin leads to consequences in years and ages to come so fearful
that one can hardly dare contemplate them', and breaks
through the ordered argument of his *Apologia*, as when he
writes, '*if* there be a God, *since* there is a God, the human
race is implicated in some terrible aboriginal calamity.'

But of all states into which the human mind can fall, the
state of fear is that in which it can least endure to remain.
Every resource it possesses will be employed to dispel it. So
the religion of fear will disguise itself as the religion of confidence and of love. Like those hysterical women who conceal
their barrenness by the symptoms of child-bearing, the believer will convince himself that he, at least, is assured of
salvation. That is to say, not that the process of conversion is
necessarily an illusion, but that it must often be so. The wish
becomes father to the thought. That has always been the
peculiar weakness of Evangelical Christianity. By the sharp
line which it draws between black and white, unregenerate

and regenerate, it forces its adherents into the belief that they are of the elect. And it is not good for the average man to think himself a saint of God.

This hard general picture of Evangelicalism in the first half of the nineteenth century must not be allowed to obliterate the happier picture which could often have been painted in particular places. Such a picture is to be found in J. A. Froude's study of *The Oxford Counter-Reformation*. He describes there the family of an Evangelical clergyman in Ireland, with whom he stayed in 1842.

'There was a quiet good sense, an intellectual breadth of feeling in this household, which to me, who had been bred up to despise Evangelicals as unreal and affected, was a startling surprise. . . . In Oxford, reserve was considered a becoming feature in the religious character. The doctrines of Christianity were mysteries, and mysteries were not lightly to be spoken of. Christianity at —— was part of the atmosphere which we breathed; it was the great fact of our existence, to which everything else was subordinated. . . . The problem was to arrange all our thoughts and acquirements in harmony with the Christian revelation, and to act it out consistently in all that we said and did. The family devotions were long, but there was no formalism, and everybody took part in them. A chapter was read and talked over, and practical lessons were drawn out of it; otherwise there were no long faces or solemn affectations; the conversations were never foolish or trivial; serious subjects were lighted up as if by an ever-present spiritual sunshine. . . . More beautiful human characters than those of my Irish Evangelical friends I had never seen, and have never seen since.'

Francis Newman is similarly concerned to defend the memory of the Rev. Walter Mayers. 'Like most other Evangelicals of my youth, his Calvinism consisted in this, that he did not *explain away* the 17th Article [about predestination], but bowed under it with reverent shuddering. To give prominence to so dreadful a doctrine, and *argue* for it, was against his nature.'

The third party in the Church described by Newman was the Liberal party known, as he said, 'in previous centuries by the less honourable name of Latitudinarian'. The essential principle of Latitudinarianism was the supremacy of reason. It appeared as a recognizable party in the Church of England in the reign of Charles I, but it was not until after the Revolution of 1688 that it became dominant. Its ascendancy lasted throughout the eighteenth century, in spite of the encroachments of Evangelicalism, and received a fresh lease of life, as Liberalism, from the apparent failure of the Tractarian movement. In its third incarnation, as Modernism, it is alive and flourishing still, though the Anglo-Catholics have so far beaten it in the race that, according to Professor Stewart (himself a Presbyterian Modernist) they 'have practically captured the machine of the Establishment.'

Not mystery, but reason was the note by which the Latitudinarians distinguished religion. It was not sufficient for them, though it was essential, that the Christian revelation should be demonstrably true, that faith should be justified by reason. God's dealing with man must be reasonable and intelligible likewise. They found the Puritan conception of a capricious inner flow of grace no less distasteful and absurd than the Catholic conception of a flow of grace through the sacraments. Religion must be straightforward and aboveboard, an affair of morals and good sense and a right orientation of the whole personality. This attitude of mind was bound to make strong political and intellectual allies. The claims of the Stewarts to rule by divine right were deeply repugnant to it. Like Catholicism, and unlike Puritanism, Latitudinarianism could only flourish in an ordered, graded society; but the order to which it was first attuned was that, not of a reflected hierarchy, but of an elegant, formal, self-

sufficient civilization. Its ideal aristocracy was one designed
not to exalt the majesty of a supreme ruler, but to exhibit the
choicest talents and graces of humanity. As time advanced
and the given pattern of society began to disintegrate, this
ideal gave place easily to others. The strength of religious
Liberalism is its power of adaptation to changing social and
political conditions; if reason is free, it will create order out
of any chaos, and is not afraid to destroy in order to recon-
struct. But in its earlier period of ascendancy Latitudinarianism did not reach, because it did not need to reach, this
knowledge of its own powers. Allied with the Whigs, and
armed by its own intellectual champions, from Locke to
Butler, it helped to maintain that marvellous triumph of
manners over matter which was called the Augustan age.

By Newman's time that triumphant illusion was in shreds
and tatters. The eighteenth-century synthesis no longer
existed. Too much had been left out. The rational man was
too partial an abstraction from human nature; and the scope
of reason, before the birth of the biological and psychological
sciences, was limited by a fatal ignorance of its necessary
subject-matter. From the first the Latitudinarians distrusted,
and not without cause distrusted, 'enthusiasm'. But, by inevitable consequence, while the sap of life mounted in the
popular varieties of religion, it drained away from their own.
'Lethargy', in Wakeman's startling metaphor, 'like a
malarious fog, crept up the body of the Church of England
and laid its cold hand upon her heart.' Pluralism, the pursuit
of ecclesiastical preferment, the maintenance of a selfish and
decadent social order in the interests of a fortunate leisured
class took the place of religious zeal. But these were as far
from being the characteristics of Latitudinarianism as such,
as they were from being the characteristics of the Liberalism
which developed from similar intellectual principles. Rather,
they were the consequences of emphasizing reason at the
cost of feeling. Meanwhile, outside the charmed circle where

history sought to stand still, enthusiasm prepared a battery of revenges.

To these three parties Newman assigned their separate, distinctive principles—to the Tractarians and their predecessors the 'Catholic' principle, to the Evangelicals the 'Protestant' principle, to the Latitudinarians the 'sceptical' principle.   He went on to point out to his French readers that if the Anglican communion were composed solely of these three parties it would inevitably be split into separate sects. It was prevented from doing so, he explained, by the fact that the great mass of churchmen either did not belong to any particular theological party or, if they did, held its tenets in a very mild and unemphatic manner. What held the Church together was the Toryism, the Conservatism, of the Anglican clergy and laity alike, expressing itself in devotion to the principle of the Establishment. This ecclesiastical Toryism, symbolized by the toast of 'Church and King', was not to be confused with the theological Catholicism resurrected by the Tractarians. It had no real theological roots; it was nationalistic, rather than Catholic; it worshipped a compromise; it distrusted dialectic, as much as it disliked enthusiasm; it hated Rome because it threatened the Establishment from without, Dissent because it weakened it from within. It was, in short, the reflection, within the Church, of the typical upper-class Englishman's unthinking determination to maintain the settled order into which he had been born. But its extraordinary power was due to the fact that it provided Englishmen with an ideal object of loyalty, which transcended while it protected their individual interests. Theologians might shudder at Erastianism, cynics might smile at political jobbery, but the conception of a single national Church, solid with the political State, remained comforting to the imaginations of ordinary men.

The difficulty of giving a coherent account of the parties within the Church of England is increased by the confusion

F   F.O.A.

which has existed in the use of the terms High, Low and Broad Church, and by the variety of the explanations which have been given of their origin. Thus Professor Stewart says that the epithets 'high' and 'low' made their first definite appearance in debates about the Toleration Act of 1689. The 'high' churchmen denounced, and the 'low' churchmen defended, the concessions which the Act made to religious liberty. Newman threw the meaning of the epithet 'high' much farther back. A high churchman, he said, was one who maintained that the Church was one of the branches of the civil government; so that a Calvinist, like Archbishop Whitgift in the reign of Elizabeth, could properly be called a partisan of the High Church. In this definition there may, perhaps, be detected evidence of a desire to discredit the term with his Roman Catholic readers. However that may be, the general sense of the word 'high' was, to begin with, as much political as theological. It meant of a man that he put the claim of the Church to regulate the religious life of every citizen 'high'; that he thought of the Church as the partner, in an indissoluble partnership, of the State. And long after the word had come to have a doctrinal meaning, its political associations continued round it. The 'high and dry' ecclesiastical dignitaries of Newman's own time were 'high' because of their attachment to high politics and 'dry' because of their emptiness of any living religious faith.

Then who were the 'low' churchmen? They were the men who did not put the claims of the Church so high. They were the tolerant party. They were, to begin with, the Latitudinarians, whose successors came to be known not as 'low' but as 'broad' churchmen. Newman says that they were the party which, in opposition to Erastians like Whitgift, considered it antichristian to give the State any power whatsoever over the Church of God. This is, perhaps, the invention of his own logic. But whatever its original signification, the term came eventually to be attached, not to the

Latitudinarians, but to the Evangelicals. It is not difficult to see why; for the Evangelicals rated the importance of the Church as the vehicle of grace lower than any other party. They were, moreover, to be visualized at the lower end of the scale; they were related closely and obviously to those who had been excluded, or who had excluded themselves, altogether from the Church. And as this came to be the new meaning of the term, its contrary came to have a new meaning also. If a 'low' churchman was an Evangelical, a 'high' churchman must be his opposite, that is, a Catholic. The Latitudinarian or the Liberal took his place, not quite logically, between the two as a 'broad' churchman. But the classification, if not perfectly logical, was ingeniously close to the facts. There was a clash of dimensions. The views of the broad churchman spread out in directions not contemplated by those 'above' or 'below' him in the vertical scale of Anglican doctrine.

This, at least, seems to have been the proper significance of the term 'broad'. It came, however, as the nineteenth century wore on, to be used of people who belonged to the Church but had no well-defined doctrinal views—people who liked a certain degree of ceremonial in the Church services, but drew the line at incense and bowings to the altar, who were quite sure that they did not believe in Transubstantiation but felt that the bread and wine had undergone some other sort of change, who tolerated an anthem in place of a hymn but were uncomfortable if they were obliged to attend a choral celebration—people, in short, who had no clear grasp of principles and practised an instinctive gentlemanly compromise between the extremes of high and low, using the epithet 'broad' of themselves, without the least understanding of its theological ancestry. 'Middle' would have been, for such people, a truer epithet than 'broad'.

The gradual emptying of meaning—of theological and political meaning—was not confined to this one term. Again

as the century wore on and the theological battles of the
'thirties and 'forties sank into ancient history, attention
began to concentrate upon the superficial characteristics of
the high and the low parties within the Church, until to call
a man a high churchman was often to say no more than that
he was a ritualist, while a low churchman was one who pared
ceremony down to a minimum. This was the result of the long
series of ritual prosecutions which continued throughout the
second half of the nineteenth century. These prosecutions
centred round the growing practice of Anglo-Catholics to
celebrate the Office of the Holy Communion as if it were
the Roman Mass, with the Eucharistic vestments, incense,
acolytes and all. And this development of practice—or
rather this reversion to an ancient practice still actually prescribed, by implication, in the rubric which stands before
the Order for Morning Prayer—was a natural consequence
of Anglo-Catholic doctrine. But the high churchmen of
Newman's day were not much concerned with these things.
Newman himself was indifferent to them; Pusey hostile.
Listen to the note of amused contempt for lying rumour in
one of Newman's letters to Bowden, written in 1837: 'Truro
people told Keble that they had it from an Oxford man that
he (the Oxford man) had gone into Littlemore chapel and
found lights burning there, and was told they burn night
and day. Daman, our Fellow, was told at Ilfracombe by the
clergyman that I wore on my surplice a rich illuminated
cross.' Or, again, to Pusey, writing in 1860 to Bishop Tait:
'I am in this strange position that my name is made a byword
for that with which I never had any sympathy, that which
the writers of the Tracts . . . always deprecated,—any innovations in the way of conducting the Service, anything of
Ritualism, or especially any revival of disused Vestments.'

To think, then, of the Oxford Movement as a ritualistic
movement is a gross error. Ritualism became the mark of the
Anglo-Catholic party which grew up in the Church after the

Oxford men had done their work. The Tractarians were concerned with invisible, not visible things. In those who accepted their principles the aesthetic self-consciousness of the later nineteenth and early twentieth centuries worked, naturally, towards a supposed beautification and elaboration of the accessories of worship. It was certainly a needed re-action from the depressing conditions which prevailed in Newman's youth. They are vividly described by Wakeman.

'The interior of the churches spoke eloquently enough of the two prevailing vices of the time—apathy and exclusive-ness. The whitewashed walls, the damp stone floors, the ceiled roof, the high stiff pews with mouldy green baize cushions and faded red curtains, allotted to all the principal houses and farms in the parish; the hard benches without backs, pushed into a corner or encumbering the aisle, where the poor might sit; the mean table with a moth-eaten red cloth upon it in the chancel . . . the dirt . . . the indescrib-able dank smell of decay, are experiences of their childhood familiar enough to many now living, and almost universal to those who lived a century ago.'

In most of the churches, says the same authority, 'the doors were only open for about four hours in the course of every seven days. When they were opened the Services were performed with little attention to the directions given by the Church and scant sympathy with the spirit of liturgical worship. . . . In most parish churches the prominent position assigned to the pulpit, the arrangement of the seats round it, the ill-kept chancels and the mean and dirty appearance of the fonts and altars, pointed to the inferior position occupied by the administration of the sacraments in the mind of the people as compared to that held by the sermon.'

2. KEBLE

It was, of course, as an Evangelical, a low churchman, that Newman entered Oriel.

The society of which he was now the youngest member was the ablest collection of individuals in Oxford. But it was more than a collection of able men; it had a unity of spirit, even of religious opinion, which gave it almost the character of a school. It was a spirit, so Newman looking back defined it, 'of moderation and comprehension', neither High Church nor Low Church; offensive to 'the old unspiritual, high-and-dry—then in possession of the high places of Oxford'; disliked by lesser men of slack discipline in other colleges; more sympathetic to the Evangelicals, who recognized its sincerity and were grateful for 'that liberality of mind which was in such striking contrast with the dominant High Church.' Speaking of it in these warm terms he seems almost deliberately to be shutting his eyes to its close kinship with the Latitudinarian, Liberal school, which he so much detested. As if 'liberality' were a more honourable word than 'Liberalism'!

A free logic, rooted in a classical tradition, was the note of this society. Conversation in the Oriel common room was a hunting of first principles, an amalgam of Aristotelianism with Christianity, quick, acute, open-minded, learned, earnest and witty. To these 'Noetics' it must have seemed that the intellectual future of Oxford and of England was theirs. And so perhaps it might have been, if they had not made the fatal mistake of thinking that they were strong enough to digest such men as Keble, Newman, Pusey and Hurrell Froude.

The greatest mystery is that of Keble. He was elected a Fellow in 1811, in the same year as Whately, the future Archbishop of Dublin, eleven years before Newman's election, being nine years Newman's senior in age. Not that there was

JOHN KEBLE
From the engraving by Samuel Cousins
after the painting by George Richmond

any mystery about the election. Keble, within his own strict
limitations, was the most brilliant scholar of his day. He had
taken his double first in classics and mathematics, and in the
year after his election he won both the English and the Latin
Essays. He had, too, a charming whimsical modest way with
him; no clever young man could have filled the place of a
junior fellow with a more delightful self-effacement, a more
gracefully humorous acceptance of his station. But the Oriel
into which he was elected was far from being his spiritual
home. The mystery (which baffled even Tom Mozley) is
that, being the man he was, he could have achieved any
modus vivendi with his colleagues. The Evangelicals, said
Newman, continuing his analysis of the Oriel common
room, 'in Keble again—in spite of his maintenance of baptismal regeneration—recognized, to use their own language, a
spiritual man.' And even to the Noetics spirituality, accompanied as it was in Keble by humour and scholarship, seems
to have excused his powerlessness in debate, the closed circle
of his ideas.

John Keble was the son of the Rev. John Keble, vicar of
Coln St. Aldwyn's near Fairford in Gloucestershire. He and
his brother Tom, one year younger than himself, were
educated at home by their father, who had been a Scholar
and Fellow of Corpus. There were three sisters, Elizabeth
the eldest of the family, Sarah and Mary the two youngest.
The atmosphere of the family was one of deep and unforced
affection between all its members. Elizabeth, a lifelong
invalid, shy and saintly, was John's 'wife'; Mary, gay and
light-hearted, his 'sweetheart'. Sarah died of consumption
in 1814; his mother died in 1823; Mary followed in 1826.

John was only fourteen, when he gained an open scholarship at Corpus. At that time (1806) the College consisted of
twenty Fellows, twenty Scholars, four Exhibitioners, and
six Gentlemen Commoners. Many of the scholars had taken
their degrees; so that the number of undergraduates was very

small—not more than twenty, if so many. Consequently
Keble's contacts with the world were extraordinarily few. In
his own home at Fairford he was his father's docile willing
pupil; the ideas which he absorbed there as a boy sufficed
him throughout his whole life. He passed them on to his
pupil Hurrell Froude, and through Froude to Newman, but
he did nothing himself to develop them. He adorned them
with his own peculiar sweetness of character, preserved them
with his invincible obstinacy, shared them fervently with
pupils and friends, and popularized them by his facile lyre.
But they remained simply the ideas which his father had
taught him—devotion to the memory of King Charles the
Martyr, belief in the principles of the non-jurors, hatred of
dissent, of Erastianism, of liberal thinking, loyalty to the idea
of a priestly Apostolic Church. His mind was passionately
contented with the past. His temperament was submissive
and romantic. 'A word, even a look, from the father sufficed
to determine his decision.'

Nothing at Corpus interfered with his family traditions or
with the development of his character. His attitude to social
life had no resemblance to Newman's. It was, he told his
brother, with difficulty that he avoided 'intostication' at the
Common Room parties held at the end of each term. He
made a number of warm friendships—with Coleridge the
future Judge, Tucker who became a missionary in India,
Miller and Ellison and Cornish and Dyson, who all filled
academic posts and afterwards became country clergymen.
Not least of his friends was Thomas Arnold, of whom he
wrote in 1816, 'the more I see of Arnold the more I love him.'
For Keble, as for Newman, the language of friendship was
the language of love. His friends are 'dearest', 'very dearest',
though after the custom of the time he addresses them always
by their surnames. 'My dear Dyson,' he writes, at the age of
fifty-seven, after the death of Cornish, 'do ask for me that I
may meet *him* again. . . . Ever your most loving J.K.'

It seems a little strange that his intimacy with Arnold should
have had no effect whatever upon his opinions. Indeed it is
said that Arnold, in his youth, deferred to Keble; and it was
Keble who advised Arnold, stricken by doubts concerning
the Holy Trinity, to settle his mind, once and for all, by taking
orders. But nothing ever had the least effect upon Keble's
opinions. They were unalterable, inaccessible. If he could
avoid controversy, he avoided it; if he could not avoid it, he
lost his temper. 'There was no getting on with Keble' said
Tom Mozley 'without entire agreement, that is submission.'
'If you did not agree with him,' J. A. Froude confirmed,
'there was something morally wrong with you.' When Arnold
produced his scheme of a national church based upon the
lowest common factor of dogma, Keble broke with him.
When Arnold—not, of course, in the least modifying his position—wrote a conciliatory letter, Keble's comment was: 'I
have had an Easter letter from Arnold, so kind and mitigated
in tone, that I cannot but be comforted by it, and in time
I trust he may come nearer to Church views.' Francis Newman reports what happened to Grenfell, one of Arnold's
masters at Rugby, when he came up to Oxford to vote
against the proposal to deprive the heretical Dr. Hampden
of his vote in the choice of the Select Preachers. After the
meeting he saw Keble, whose friend he was, on the other side
of the High Street and crossed the road to shake him by the
hand. 'But he held his hand out of my reach, and, glaring at
me, said solemnly: "Grenfell! you have sacrificed at the altar
of Jupiter, and I renounce your friendship from this day."'
J. A. Froude tells another story of the same kind. Calling one
day at the house of an intimate friend and learning that a
member of the family who had adopted Liberal opinions in
theology was at home, Keble refused to enter and remained
sitting in the porch. He could not distinguish between a
man's character and his opinions, could see nothing but
wrong in opinions opposed to his own. He had a peculiar

power, too, of shutting his eyes to ability, unless it was exerted in what he considered the right cause. 'It was remarkable', wrote one of his curates, 'that *badness* always seemed to him *stupidity*, he never seemed to be able to perceive the cleverness of wickedness; of even able things written in a bad spirit he constantly remarked, "I cannot think how people can be so stupid."' The same sympathetic observer noted 'the eager youthful energy, the strong indignation and resentment at wrong, especially at anything which threatened to touch the sacred deposit of truth, that mingled with his gentleness and humility.'

Such an attitude is in itself suggestive of limited intellectual power; and indeed Keble, outside his scholastic attainments, was in many respects a rather stupid man. It is not at all difficult, even for an unfriendly critic, to appreciate the talents of Newman and Pusey. But Keble's ascendancy is a much more mysterious affair. It rested, evidently, on personality. A man so charming and boyish and unaffected, so pure and sweet and good, so humble and so devout, so learned and so elegant, so capable of indignation for the truth, must have seemed to those who shared his vision of the truth a living proof of their own rightness. His personal appearance supported and deepened this impression. He was not handsome nor distinguished. A boyish figure, of middle height, with stooping shoulders, which he had a trick of every now and then squaring and flinging back; a well-shaped head with a 'forehead and hair beautiful in all ages'; clear, brilliant, penetrating eyes of dark brown; a plainly featured face, with a large mouth; his manner often rather shy and a little awkward. These were the elements of the outward man. But the expression which gave light to them is something that can scarcely be described—now quick and gay, now tender, now fiery. There is a hint of it in the account which Newman gave to Dean Church of that pathetic last meeting between Keble and himself in 1865. 'As hours went on the *nota facies* came out upon his countenance, as if it were the soul itself showing itself in spite of the course and change of time. He always had an expression like no one else, and that sweet pleading earnestness never showed itself so piercingly to me as then, in his eyes and in his carriage.' Richmond, the painter, is said to have described his face as one of the most remarkable he had ever seen for one who had eyes to see. A man's manner of speaking has a great deal to do with the impression he makes upon his contemporaries. Keble had a singular power of making every word he used appear significant, 'brilliant or a pearl', and all the more remembered 'from there being so little of it, and from it seeming to come from a different and holier sphere'. But Tom Mozley, who so describes his conversation, adds that 'there was not much continuity'.

If one could imagine Keble deprived of his religious faith, he would have been a romantic and copious minor poet of the Lake school. Few, if any, modern critics would maintain that *The Christian Year* is good poetry. Fewer still, perhaps, would maintain that it is good religious poetry. Our standard in these matters is something different from that of J. A. Froude, who indeed criticized *The Christian Year* as poetry of a particular period, not for all time, but considered that it was excellent of its kind, especially in comparison with earlier English religious poetry which was not, he said, poetry at all! As a poet, Keble was the Ella Wheeler Wilcox of his time. There is no observation behind the images he employs; no thought behind his emotion; no emotion behind his thought, since there is no thought there, nothing but simple assertion; in Mr. T. S. Eliot's phrase, no 'mechanism of sensibility'. There is not even any great technical skill. The rhymes, the rhythms, the vocabulary are without distinction —mere 'crockery', as he himself deprecatingly described his verses to Hurrell Froude. If it had not been for the fact that *The Christian Year* was 'religious' poetry, removed from serious criticism by its hallowed associations, it would have sunk into swift oblivion. That fate would nevertheless have overtaken it, if Keble had not, as Froude perceived, made his high-church poetry a vehicle for the emotions of Evangelicalism. He pleased everybody. Was this, perhaps, the reason why he persistently refused to alter the one stanza which always gave offence to his own friends? This was the thirteenth stanza of the poem entitled *An Address to Converts from Popery*:

> O come to our Communion Feast!
> There, present in the heart,
> Not in the hands, the eternal Priest
> Will his true self impart.

It was not until he lay on his deathbed that he authorized the substitution of 'As' for 'Not' in the third line.

Of all the strange features of the Oxford Movement none is stranger than the feebleness of its poetry. Here were men long and closely trained in a sternly classical school, judging their own and their friends' poetical effusions by no canon at all except that of sentiment. 'Enough', writes Newman in the *Lyra Apostolica*, in a couplet which is surely one of the worst ever written,

> Enough, I eat His Flesh and drink His Blood,
> More is not told—to ask it is not good.

What makes such versifying by a man of genius an almost treasonable offence at the bar of criticism is not the mere technical poverty of expression, but the attempt to dispose of argument by bare assertion. Simple contradiction is not very effective in prose. In poetry it is intolerable. If poetry meets argument it must meet it either with counter-argument, sharpened and vitalized by the poetic form, or with an imaginative presentment of truth. The Tractarian poets seldom attempted either. They held the unfortunate view that the enunciation of approved sentiments, tricked out with ornament and metaphor, was an adequate recipe for religious poetry.

Newman's own poetry was a mixed product. His instinctive artistry, working almost without his own knowledge, fashioned occasional superb lines and images, to be found embedded in the lava-like flow of the *Lyra Apostolica*. Now and then he displays an inventive command of rhythm. Once and again art has her way with him and uses his romantic sentiment for a universal purpose. But most of his poetry is really bad. And it is bad because he wrote to order. Writing to order does not necessarily mean writing bad poetry, any more than painting to order means painting bad pictures. But the order must be an order for a work of art. The order to which Newman wrote was an order for a piece of religious propaganda. The *Lyra Apostolica*, to which he and Keble were the chief contributors, was conceived as 'a verse department in Rose's Magazine [the *British Magazine*] *for all right purposes*'. (The italics are mine.) It was to be 'an effective quasi-political engine'. The idea was to 'catch people when unguarded'. Verses written for such a reason are not likely to be good poetry.

Nor, indeed, did Newman suppose that the *Lyra* was good poetry. It was only 'a ballad', composed in stirring times, relying upon the general tension of men's minds for its effect, rather than upon any high quality of poetic expression. If it was poetry, it was so by accident. The art of it was rhetoric and persuasion—his own words. But his conception even of this inferior art was not very happy. 'Ten thousand obvious ideas' he told Rogers, writing to him from Rome in the spring of 1833, 'become impressive when put into a metrical shape; and many of them we should not dare to utter except metrically, for thus the responsibility (as it were) is shoved off oneself, and one speaks ὡς παιδίζων, though serious.' The obvious idea in metrical shape—there could not be a better, nor a more damning, description of the art of poetry as it was practised by Keble as well as by Newman.

The earliest poems in *The Christian Year* date from 1819,

eight years after Keble's election at Oriel. At the time of his
election he was writing the kind of verses that any romantic
and impressionable youth must have written in those early
Wordsworthian days.

> How soft, how silent has the stream of time
> Borne me unheeding on, since first I dream'd
> Of poetry and glory in thy shade,
> Scene of my earliest harpings?

These are the opening lines of the poem which he wrote *On
leaving Corpus Christi College, on his Election to a Fellowship of
Oriel*. Pleasing enough, but for the outburst of exaggerated
sentiment which follows:

> I ne'er
> Shall see thee but with such a gush of soul
> As flows from him who welcomes some dear face
> Lost in his childhood.

Love poems, stanzas addressed to the Nightingale, thoughts
on a Fine Morning—which is, of course, nothing but

> a pledge
> And precious foretaste of that cloudless day,
> Gladdening at intervals the good man's heart
> With earnest of infinitude—

thoughts on a Wet Day at Midsummer, on the First Sight of
the Sea—there is the same evidence in them all of a romantic,
earnest, uncritical mind, 'labouring inwardly with lofty and
tender thought' (if thought is a synonym for sentiment) but
never for a moment testing itself against the edge of present
fact or seeking to interpret its own experience.

For a year or two after his election Keble lived the pleasant
life of a junior Fellow with no duties, reading, taking private
pupils, falling in and out of love, cultivating his numerous
friends, carrying off University Prizes, writing occasional
verse, learning Hebrew, and accustoming his mind to the
tremendous prospect of ordination. There is a picture drawn
by his intimate friend J. T. Coleridge of a reading party
which he took to Sidmouth, where the Cornishes lived, in

1813. How he was excited by the beauties of Devonshire; how he entered into the gaieties of the little watering-place—the concerts, the dances, the morning and evening parties; how he formed an attachment to a young lady and addressed four ardent stanzas to her (*Nunquam Auditurae*) full of moonlight and roses and brooklets and amarant wreaths and eternal silent passion:

> 'and when the port of endless rest
> Receives me, may my soul be blest
> With everlasting upward gaze on you.'

'Even at this early period of his life' comments his biographer 'what might have been a mere love-song became in his way of dealing with it elevated (perhaps too elevated) and holy from the habitual holiness and elevation of all his serious thoughts.'

There followed a spell of duty as one of the Examiners in the Schools—at an age when the undergraduate of to-day is himself sitting for his final examination. In 1814 his sister, Sarah, died. He grieved, but his grief was checked by his firm faith that she was happy. In 1815 he was ordained. 'Pray for me, too,' he adjured Coleridge; 'pray earnestly, my dear, my best friend, that He would give me His grace, that I may not be altogether unworthy of the sacred office on which I am, rashly I fear, even now entering; but that some souls hereafter may have cause to bless me.' Was not the salvation of one soul 'worth more than the framing of a Magna Charta of a thousand worlds'? A mood of adolescent depression and self-analysis seems to have clouded his mind at the beginning of his ministry—'a certain humour calling itself melancholy, but, I am afraid, more truly entitled proud and fantastic, which I find very often at hand, forbidding me to enjoy the good things, and pursue the generous studies, which a kind Providence throws so richly in my way.'

His Examinership ended in 1816, when he left Oxford to be his father's curate at Coln, 'no more to return officially', sick of 'the very smell of the Schools', happy that he was 'now free to give myself up entirely to my profession—my dear delightful profession—which I grow fonder of every day.' But a year later he was offered, and accepted, a Tutorship at Oriel. 'You consider Tuition as a species of pastoral care, do you not?' he wrote to Coleridge at the beginning of 1818, justifying his return to Oxford by an argument which was later to bring disaster upon Oriel. 'Otherwise it might seem questionable, whether a clergyman ought to leave a cure of souls for it. And yet there are some people at Oxford who seem to imagine that College Tutors have nothing to do with the morale. If I thought so I would never undertake the office.'

How far, as Tutor, Keble set himself to impregnate his pupils with his own religious ideas, in accordance with this pastoral conception of his office, it is not easy to say. Years afterwards (in 1841) he wrote explicitly that even if you could silence a Catholic tutor from direct theological teaching, he was bound to teach ethics or poetry or history 'by the light which the Church throws on all'; that, in effect, he 'must either teach Catholicism or not teach at all.' But during the actual years of his tutorship there were no signs of proselytizing. His spiritual son, Hurrell Froude, was in no need of conversion when he became Keble's pupil. The glimpses of Keble's life as a tutor show him taking infinite pains over his pupils' work, enjoying their society, admitting many of them to intimate friendship. He gets up and sets to work with the best of these 'delightful fellows' at six in the morning. His way with them is charmingly informal and considerate. But those who formed their views on the pattern of Keble's must have been moved to do so rather by their love and admiration for the man than by any direct dogmatic teaching.

The best description of Keble at this period of his life was written by one of George Cornish's sisters after he had been on a visit to the Cornish family at Sidmouth.

'*Sept.* 8 1819.—Keble went away early. We are all very sorry to lose him, as he is a person that is not to be met with every day. . . . His manners are singularly simple, shy, and unpolished, though without the least rudeness or roughness, as he is the mildest and quietest person I almost ever saw. He speaks very little, but always seems interested in what is going on, and often says the cleverest and most witty things as if he was not the least aware of it. In his own family I should think he must be more missed when absent than any one else could possibly be; he seems formed for a domestic circle and all the feelings attendant on home. Without making any fuss about it, he seems so interested in every one, and has such a continual quiet cheerfulness about him, that I cannot imagine how his father and mother, brother and sisters, can do without him. But it is his religious character that has struck me more than anything else, as it is indeed that from which everything else proceeds. I never saw any one who came up so completely to my ideas of a religious man as Keble, and yet I never saw any one who made so little *display* of it (I use this word for want of a better at present); he seems to me a union of Hooker and George Herbert—the *humility* of the one with the feeling and *love* of the other. In short, altogether he is a man whom the more you see of and know, the less you must think of yourself.' [1]

Six years passed by. In 1823 Keble took the decision, which had never been far away from his mind, and resigned his tutorship at the end of the Hilary term. A month or two later, in May, his mother died and he made up his mind to live near his father. The curacy of Southrop, near Fairford, was vacant. Keble united this to the care of two other small adjacent parishes, making his own home at Southrop. There, amongst others of his pupils, he was joined by Robert Wilberforce, Isaac Williams and Hurrell Froude. And there, while

[1] Quoted by Walter Lock in his *John Keble* from *The Monthly Packet* of 1887.

Newman was slowly 'coming out of his shell' at Oriel, and in almost complete spiritual isolation taking the first steps of his strange religious progress, began the first coalition of spirits, the first spiral movement of the waters, to which Newman's genius was to communicate so great an impetus.

3. COPLESTON AND WHATELY

Though Keble was still Tutor when Newman joined Oriel in April 1822, and was resident in College throughout Newman's probationary year, there was very little intercourse between them. There are no references to Keble, of any interest, in Newman's letters until much later; and the first letter from Keble to Newman is a pleasantly jocular note written two years after he had left Oxford. In fact, the two men did not come together until 1828, through the offices of Hurrell Froude, who reckoned it the one good deed of his life that he had brought Keble and Newman to understand each other. Keble was shy of Newman, because of his Evangelical opinions; Newman shy of Keble for the same reason, as well as for the reverence he had of the elder man's academical distinctions, and his own *gaucherie* towards his seniors.

This *gaucherie* must have been disturbing to the electors. Two things had happened recently to put the nerves of the Oriel common room on edge. There had been the unfortunate affair of Hartley Coleridge, the eldest son of Samuel Taylor. Hartley was elected a Fellow in 1820, and failed lamentably to conform to the required pattern of a probationer. He reeked of tobacco smoke; he would not dress for dinner; he omitted to shave for days at a time. Worse still, he could not hold his liquor. Worse even than this, he hobnobbed with his social inferiors. Repeated admonitions by the Provost and the Dean were of no effect. The story went that he was found lying dead drunk in the gutter in Oriel

Street by the Dean. Whether this happened in fact, or was Tyler's sudden vision of what might be expected to happen, the College recorded that 'it could be no party to the degradation threatened by the behaviour of Mr. Coleridge', and deprived him of his place before his probationary year was more than half completed.

This was a disagreeable shock to the self-esteem of the electors. It was their pride to discover talent which went unrecognized in the Schools. Hartley was a second-class man. The pursuit of unclassified ability evidently had its own peculiar dangers. Nevertheless the College stood by its principles and in the year between Hartley's election and Newman's chose another second-class man, C. J. Plumer of Balliol, in preference to a brilliant first-class man, D. K. Sandford of Christ Church. In this choice the electors hardly displayed their usual acumen. It was generally felt, outside Oriel, that a mistake had been made. Sandford, confident of his own powers, angry and humiliated at his rejection, took public revenge by a pointed and malicious attack in the *Edinburgh Review* on the methods of election to open Fellowships in the English Universities.

Now, for the third year in succession, Oriel was defying the judgment of the Schools in a still more spectacular manner by electing in Newman a man who had failed even to achieve a second class. Not unnaturally the Common Room and the Provost scrutinized their latest capture with a barely concealed anxiety. How was he going to turn out? Their first impressions were not favourable. He was shy, he was tongue-tied, he was odd, he was inclined to refuse the wine. They learned with alarm that he played the fiddle in a band. The Provost indulged in one of his calculated asperities: 'We don't help sweetbread with a spoon; butler, bring a blunt knife.' The strange creature became dumb. Like many self-conscious and earnest young men unused to society he suffered from the constant dread of committing some social solecism. At the high table in Hall he sat perforce lowest of the Fellows and next to the Gentlemen Commoners, whose conversation was all of sport and scandal, of Freddy This and Johnny That. The pale spectacled youth listened to their chatter, with disgust and contempt. More than ever before he felt himself to be a solitary; and while this feeling of loneliness brought dejection into his heart it also brought a kind of exaltation. He never felt so near Heaven, he told Harriett in 1836, as when in dejection from solitude; during the first four years of his Fellowship, he added, 'I used to be very much by myself, and in anxieties of various kinds which were very harassing. I then, on the whole, had no friend near me, no one to whom I opened my mind fully or who could sympathize with me. Ever since that time I have learnt to throw myself on myself.' And he recalls this period of isolation in the *Apologia*: 'I was very much alone, and I used often to take my daily walk by myself. I recollect once meeting Dr. Copleston, then Provost, with one of the Fellows. He turned round, and with the kind courteousness which sat so well on him, made me a bow and said, "Nunquam minus solus, quam cum solus."'

The Provost, Dr. Edward Copleston, was one of the out-standing men in Oxford. Tall, handsome, stately, 'the most substantial and majestic and richly-coloured character' in the University, a good classical scholar and Latinist, with a magnificent voice and a fine formalism of manner, a man of the world to his finger tips, as much at home in London society as in Oxford, he seems almost too splendid to have been more than a figure-head. In fact, no one could have been less of a mere figure-head. He was an exceedingly hard worker, a man of business as well as a man of letters, a pioneer in the fields of education and economics, a keen controver-sialist, a far-sighted reformer. To these gifts he joined others that might easily have been lacking—humour and irony and a fundamental kindness of heart, though the third quality

EDWARD COPLESTON
PROVOST OF ORIEL 1814-1828
From the painting by Thomas Phillips
in the possession of Oriel College

was not always obvious to the victims of the second. It was
to him, first as Tutor and then as Provost, quite as much as
to his predecessor Eveleigh, that Oriel mainly owed her
pre-eminence. Even before he became Provost on Eveleigh's
death in 1814 he, together with Davison, were the rulers of
the College. Sir John Coleridge remembered dining as the
guest of the newly elected Keble 'and being struck with the
deference with which these two were treated; it was such as
somewhat to check the social pleasure of the party.' Yet
Copleston was then a young man of thirty-five; and he was
no more than forty-six when Newman came into the College.
His personality was of that marked kind which provokes
imitation. Undergraduates, and even sometimes junior
Fellows, used to mimic his manner of speaking. Mr. Joseph
Parker, the bookseller, who happened to resemble him
closely, carried imitation so far that he was often mistaken
for the Provost of Oriel and was to be seen and heard in the
streets of Oxford using the Provost's very walk, wearing the
Provost's 'suit of funeral black, with frill at the breast and
massive gold seals pendent from the fob', and talking with
the Provost's 'sustained note, measured cadence, and careful
choice of words'.

Between Copleston and Newman no intimacy ever existed.
The young man's painful shyness prevented it. Copleston had
discerned Newman's quality as a candidate; he failed entirely
to draw it out of him after his election. Perhaps, given his own
freely ranging mind and sceptical temper, and the formal
barriers of age, position and manner, the difficulties of communication between them were too great. Neither of the two
men ever adequately appreciated the other. To Newman
Copleston was always something of an enemy and a danger;
to Copleston Newman was in the end something of a traitor
to the College which had reared him. He spoke of him in the
language of the chorus in the *Agamemnon*, as the lion-cub
brought up by the fireside, gentle and harmless, playing with

the children and charming the old people, but destined to bring destruction upon the house.

Davison, who had been joint regent with Copleston, had left Oriel four years previously. His place in the College had been filled by Richard Whately; and it was Whately whom his anxious colleagues now charged with the special duty of licking Newman into shape. In point of fact, he had just ceased to be a Fellow, for he had married and was about to go off to a Suffolk rectory. But he was still living in Oxford lodgings and was delighted to spend a few months on the congenial task assigned to him.

Whately was big and powerfully built, with a strong, keen face. His manners were bluff and unconventional. His mind was vigorous, sceptical, speculative within the widest bounds set by Christian formulas. Anything but a sentimentalist or a mystic, he was concerned to produce the best possible working compromise of faith, reason and behaviour. He was a tremendous talker, witty, original, trenchant, at his best with young men who were content to be what he called his 'anvils'. They stimulated his intellect, in Newman's phrase, 'into the activity necessary for carrying him through the drudgery of composition'. Such an anvil Newman became for a time in 1822, and in spite of the deep dissimilarity of their minds and temperaments, in spite too of the contempt which Whately had for his Evangelical opinions, he accepted the older man's dominion with a peculiar pleasure.

The future Archbishop of Dublin belonged to a type new in the young man's limited experience. His methods with promising young cubs were attractively brutal. He delighted to knock them about in argument, to hold them figuratively up by one leg like 'dogs of King Charles's breed'. Newman, in that novel position, showed himself of the royal breed. He did not whimper. On the contrary, he submitted to these bracing indignities with 'affectionate abandonment'. His desire for self-surrender was satisfied in this early discipleship as it was never satisfied in any other personal relationship, never otherwise satisfied at all until his submission to Rome. Warmest admiration, gratitude, deep affection—these are the careful terms in which, fifty years later, he described his feelings for the man whom he still spoke of as his 'master'. All his references to Whately were coloured by a painful consciousness of broken friendship. How adoring, hero-worshipping, a friendship it was is nevertheless plain to read. 'There is scarcely anyone,' he wrote in a private memorandum dated 1860 'whom in memory I love more than Whately, even now.' Accused once, in his militant Tractarian days, of casting aside his friends without a thought when they differed from him, he burst out: 'Ah, Rogers, you don't understand what anguish it was to me to pass Whately in the street coldly the other day.' Writing to Whately, long before that breach, as a young man of twenty-five writing to a friend fourteen years his senior, he strove to express his devotion in language which had to be kept strictly free from sentimentalism: 'There are few things which I wish more sincerely than to be known as a friend of yours, and though I may be on the verge of propriety in the earnestness with which I am expressing myself, yet you must let me give way to feelings which never want much excitement to draw them out, and now will not be restrained. Much as I owe to Oriel in the way of mental improvement, to none, as I think, do I owe so much as to you. I know who it was that first gave me heart to look about me after my election, and taught me to think correctly, and (strange office for an instructor) to rely upon myself.'

Newman's surrenders were emotional, never intellectual surrenders. His submission to Whately was a submission of the heart, not of the mind. Nor would Whately have had the least use for a mental submission. An anvil is not a yielding object. His task with Newman was to draw him, not to flatten him, out. He succeeded brilliantly. But there was

much more in their relationship than intellectual intercourse; there was the mutual attraction of two complemen-
tary characters, the one strongly masculine and objective, the
other sensitive and introspective, and both capable of warm
feeling.

'A bright June sun tempered by a March north-easter', was
Newman's picture of his masterful friend. The north-easter
blew vigorously wherever it listed, and despised all compromise with feeble conventions. Half Oxford trembled
before it. Evangelicals and High Churchmen alike withered
in the frost of his contemptuous sarcasms. Timid dons
shuddered as they saw the great man, in his rough clothes,
striding with huge steps round Christ Church meadow,
accompanied by a horde of dogs, tossing sticks and stones for
their amusement, and shouting logic to some younger companion. Refined Oxford hostesses gasped when he came to
call, remembering the dreadful experience of 'newly married
Mrs. Powell, who had just filled her drawing-room with the
spider-legged chairs just then coming into fashion. On one
of these sat Whately, swinging, plunging, and shifting in his
seat while he talked. An ominous crack was heard; a leg of
the chair had given way; he tossed it on to the sofa without
comment, and impounded another chair.' (*Auctoritate* Tuckwell.) So much vital force needed exceptional recruitment.
At Oriel, when he dined in Hall, 'to provide against the
danger incident to those who talk and eat at the same time,
a large dish of currie, or calf's head hash, or other soft and
comminuted meat was provided', and the helping destined
for Whately was, on the servant's whispered instructions to
the Fellow serving the dish, specially adjusted to his capacity.
It would be interesting to know whether the abstemious
Newman, when it was his turn to serve the dish, catered
properly for his master's appetite.

Whately's gift to Newman was not merely the stimulation
of his reasoning powers, nor the destruction of his shyness.

He left his imprint upon the young man's opinions. He taught him, first, to think 'of the Christian Church as a Divine appointment, and as a substantive visible body, independent of the State, and endowed with rights, prerogatives and powers of its own'; and, next, he fixed in him 'those anti-Erastian views of Church polity which were one of the most prominent features of the Tractarian movement.' In other words, it was Whately who first made young Newman conscious of the Church as a historic and divine institution, and first roused in him a suspicion that the soul of man has no private right of entry into the kingdom of Heaven.

4. HAWKINS AND THE ORIEL COMMON ROOM

In spite of his affectionate intimacy with Whately, Newman's isolation remained essentially unbroken. Friends were soon to come to him. But Whately left Oxford for Suffolk soon after Newman had been committed to his care. He had succeeded in cracking the shell of the young probationer's reserve. But for at least a couple of years the shell remained unbroken, and the full process of incubation was not completed for another two years. During these four years the figures of the Oriel common room, at first so remote and awful that the idea of calling them by their surnames, without any prefix, seemed an impossible act of presumption, changed little by little into approachable and almost into criticizable human beings.

The first of the more senior Fellows whom he came to know at all intimately was Edward Hawkins. Hawkins was then Vicar of St. Mary's. Newman was to succeed him in that office, when Hawkins became Provost of Oriel. Like Whately, he was to suffer the loss of Newman's friendship through the collision of their opinions. A long life stretched ahead of Hawkins—he died in 1882 at the age of ninety-four, when Cardinal Newman was eighty-one—a life of impressive authority and influence and outward success. But by comparison with his predecessors his rule over Oriel was a commonly admitted failure. It is one of the minor ironies of history that he owed both the success and the failure to the youth whom, in Whately's absence, he began to take under his wing.

Hawkins was not a Copleston or a Whately, but he was no mean figure. Like other members of the Oriel common room he had what can only be described by that abused word 'personality'. His quality showed itself in his voice. 'Voice', said Tom Mozley (in one of the penetrating observations which give the lie to the charge that he was no more than an 'amusing rattle'), 'voice must have had no small part in Hawkins' election to the Provostship. His was a remarkable combination of sweetness with strength, sincerity, seriousness, and decision.' 'He spoke incisively, and what he said remained in the memory and seemed to come from him.' He had originally intended, like Newman, to go to the Bar. His mind certainly had a legal—or at any rate, practical and administrative—cast. But he was a thinker, as well as an administrator, though a thinker of a very different type from Whately, less freely ranging, less robust, more cautious and circumspect. In the days of his intimacy with Newman he was (in Newman's own words) 'clear-headed and independent in his opinions, candid in argument, tolerant of the views of others, honest as a religious inquirer, though not without something of self-confidence in his enunciations.' Had circumstances not forced him into resistance to a movement which he was not a big enough man to oppose effectively, Hawkins might have played a happier part in the history of his College and his University. As it was, the circumspection and the self-confidence degenerated into an obstinate conservatism. The judicious administrator became a ceremonious martinet. It is told of him, as Provost, that when an undergraduate fell into the quadrangle from an upper window and was killed, he stayed to put on his cap, gown, and bands before he came out of his lodgings to look at the boy's dead body.

But nothing of that coming deterioration of character was visible to Newman at this earlier time; and after the dust of battle had cleared away it was the early image which remained in his memory. 'I can say' he wrote in the *Apologia* 'with a full heart that I love him, and have never ceased to love him; and I thus preface what otherwise might sound rude, that in the course of the many years in which we were together he provoked me very much from time to time, though I am perfectly certain that I have provoked him a great deal more.' The affection which he felt for Hawkins was liking, perhaps, rather than love. He admired Hawkins's practical qualities, his high character, his sense of duty, his abstemiousness, his painstaking clarity of thought, his peculiarly impressive manner in the pulpit. Most of all he admired him for having 'far less than others of that secular spirit which is so rife at all times in places of intellectual eminence.' To know him, he said, was 'to esteem and revere him'. Long intimate evenings, when the young curate took the older man's advice upon his parochial duties, gave to this esteem the warmer colouring of personal friendship. But there is no sign that his heart went out towards Hawkins with the same passion as towards Whately.

As to doctrine, Hawkins 'was the means of great additions' to Newman's beliefs. As an undergraduate Newman had already been deeply impressed by his University sermon on the subject of tradition. Doctrine, said the sermon, was not to be learned from the Bible, but from the formularies of the Church, such as the Catechism and the Creeds. The Bible existed not to teach doctrine but to prove it. The impression was almost the first dent made in Newman's Evangelical opinions. Later on Hawkins gave him a copy of the sermon, and the dent grew deeper. The gift of the sermon was followed by the gift of a book—Sumner's *Apostolical Preaching* —which completed the rout of Calvinism. We shall observe the change taking place soon after Newman's ordination.

The other principal members of the Oriel common room at the date of Newman's election can be more briefly described.

The four College Tutors were Keble, Hawkins, Tyler and Jelf.

Tyler was also Dean—an important office in Oriel—and somewhat conscious of his importance. He once sent a note to Dean Gaisford, which began: 'The Dean of Oriel presents his compliments to the Dean of Christ Church.' Gaisford read it aloud in company and commented, 'Alexander the coppersmith sendeth greeting to Alexander the Great.' Tyler was a popular picturesque and florid figure, a good lecturer, fond of his pupils especially if they were sprigs of the nobility. He liked to take them down to Moreton Pinkney in Northamptonshire, where he held a perpetual curacy, and record their heights 'on the inside of a closet door'. In 1826 he left Oriel to become Rector of St. Giles-in-the-Fields, thereby losing his chance of the Provostship.

Richard Jelf was Newman's senior in the College by only one year, though he was three years older. He held the office of Tutor until 1826, when he went to Germany as tutor to Prince George of Cumberland, afterwards King of Hanover. Professor Lloyd of Christ Church had been charged with the selection of the right man for this delicate post. The only restriction was one of age—the tutor must be at least twenty-seven. Lloyd sent first for Newman. The interview was brief. 'How old are you?' 'Twenty-five.' 'Get away, boy. I don't want you.' Newman departed, mystified, and Jelf was chosen. 'Boundless' moralized Mozley 'is the vista of consequences with which this little difference in age may be credited.' Jelf came back to Oxford as a Canon of Christ

Church, to be one of the six Doctors who sat in judgment upon his old friend Pusey in 1843.

One might have expected that Newman and Jelf would have been drawn quickly together, especially as Jelf was the particular friend of Pusey, who was elected to an Oriel Fellowship the year after Newman. But this does not seem to have happened. Jelf had dropped naturally into a position of authority and influence. Newman was still shy and uncertain of his foothold.

Among the senior Fellows was William James, who earned himself a special mention in the *Apologia*. 'One of the graver tutors' in an earlier generation he was still resident in College and showed kindness to the grave young probationer, taking him for walks round Christ Church meadow and introducing him to the doctrine of Apostolical Succession. 'I recollect' wrote his pupil 'being somewhat impatient on the subject at the time.'

Henry Jenkyns, Joseph Dornford and Samuel Rickards, together with Plumer and Jelf, formed a group of younger Fellows elected between 1818 and 1821. Jenkyns figures in Newman's correspondence, but his chief claim to memory— besides being the younger brother of the great Master of Balliol—is the fact that when Pusey in a fit of despair during the Oriel Fellowship examination tore up his essay, Jenkyns picked up the bits and pieced them together. Otherwise Pusey might not have been elected. Dornford was the military expert of the common room. He had enlisted at seventeen as a rifleman in the Peninsular War, done two years of active service, and ended his subsequent career at Oxford with a Fellowship at Oriel, where he succeeded Keble as Tutor. He was a fine, swaggering fellow, with a fund of racy stories and an irresistible fascination for women. Not, one might have supposed, a type congenial to Newman. Yet Newman seems to have liked him, and he to have admired Newman. And when Dornford finally retired to his country parsonage he fitted up a room 'as an oratory, with a magnificent and costly reredos, containing the Passion in five compartments'.

Samuel Rickards married early and settled down as Vicar of Ulcombe in Kent within a few months of Newman's election. Of all the younger Fellows he was the one who could most have lightened the sense of heavy isolation which weighed upon Newman for the four years between 1822 and 1826. No one could fail to be charmed by Rickards. One of Mozley's best stories is that of a girl who, on the day before her marriage, poured out her misgivings to Mrs. Rickards. 'My dear,' said Mrs. Rickards 'the day before I married I was the happiest of women.' 'Oh, but' her friend expostulated 'you were going to marry Mr. Rickards.' Mrs. Rickards was as delightful a person as her husband. Their house at Ulcombe was a regular hostelry for their Oriel friends, and Newman and his sister Harriett came to be on terms of the most affectionate intimacy with them both. Rickards, however, had the same rigidity of opinion as Keble. His hatred of Rome was so violent that, as the current of Tractarianism set in the Romeward direction, his friends shrank from telling him what was going on. Newman's secession was a shock for which he was wholly unprepared. It put an end to all intercourse between them.

A little senior to the group of younger men just mentioned were two former Fellows of Oriel who were to come into bitter conflict with Newman in the future. These were Hampden and Arnold, elected in the same year (1815). Arnold had not yet gone to Rugby. He was already married and taking pupils in the country, and consequently was not to be seen in Oriel. He was, nevertheless, according to Mozley, 'present in spirit'—whatever that may mean. Not until 1828 did Newman and Arnold meet, in a formal disputation for their degrees of Bachelor of Divinity, dining afterwards at the Provost's table. That was the year of Arnold's installation at Rugby. But the meeting left no im-

THOMAS ARNOLD
From the painting by Thomas Phillips
in the National Portrait Gallery

pression on the mind of either. It seems almost incredible
that they met only on one other occasion, at the College
Gaudy, on February 2, 1842, four months before Arnold's
death. That was a richly comic encounter. The arch-enemy
of 'the Oxford Malignants' and the chief Malignant himself
forced to exchange polite trivialities for hours in the uneasy
presence of Provost Hawkins, who was seen to wince visibly
every time Newman opened his mouth. Newman maliciously
enjoying himself upon thin ice. Dr. Arnold somewhat less at
ease, registering the discovery that the less he saw of so
dangerously attractive an opponent the better for his own
peace of mind.

Hampden, like Arnold, was not in Oxford when Newman
became a Fellow of Oriel. Their paths did not cross until
several years later. There will be more to say of him when
that point is reached, and of his theory that the formularies
of the Church (the Creeds included) were of human and not
of divine origin. Perhaps his position was, as he stated it,
untenable, though it was a much more subtle position than
his opponents understood. It was the most definite achievement of the Noetic school, warmly defended by Copleston,
Whately, Hawkins and Arnold. At this early stage in Newman's career, Hampden's theory had not yet been formulated. But the forms of thought which led up to it were in the
air of the Oriel common room. And we may take the theory
for a clue to the quality in Newman's mind which prevented
him from succumbing to the Noetic influence.

In the last analysis, for all its subtlety, its dialectical brilli-
ance, its magical command over the means of expression,
Newman's mind was literal. A fact was a fact, a mystery a
mystery, truth and falsehood absolute. His theory of the
gradual development of religious doctrine was in accord with
this literal habit of mind. Development meant, for him, an
unfolding, not a transformation of truth. As time went on
men's minds became ready to accept a new portion of the

truth; but the portions of the truth already in their possession were not changed by the addition, were not made any less or differently true. The celebrated theory had nothing in common with the bolder speculations of the modernists, who endeavour to reconceive Christian dogma as completely as the theory of relativity has reconceived gravitation. The Noetics were reaching out after such a new conception. Hampden's assault upon the technical language of the theologians was a first move in that direction. But the attempt to restate dogma implies that dogma is a human invention. And the absoluteness of dogma, as a final revelation of truth by God through the Church, was the sheet anchor of Newman's whole faith, the tethering rope of his reason. If Hampden, Whately, Arnold and the rest had their way, a mind like Newman's must be swept on to the rocks of materialism.

The Noetics went so far, for their day, that one cannot help wondering why they did not go further. Did they perceive that they could not stand still? It was their weakness that they were ignorant of their isolation from the main stream of religious thought on the continent. Their inheritance of the settled English order—these solid Fellowships, Livings, Canonries, Bishoprics, this practical commonsensical reasonable domesticated amalgam of religion, culture and country life—blinded them to the consequences of free speculation. How could the premisses of such a society ever be called in question? So they let their logic run where it would, never fearing that it might double back and destroy clericalism at its centre. It is not the only instance of Englishmen making revolution without knowing it. But it is less common for the unconscious revolutionary to nourish the conscious reactionary in his bosom.

Hampden's Bampton Lectures were mistakenly said to have been inspired by another member of the Oriel common room, the Rev. Joseph Blanco White. Blanco White is remembered now, if at all, by his sonnet 'Mysterious Night!' But his life was strange, significant and pathetic in the highest degree. He was born at Seville, in 1775, of an Irish Roman Catholic family settled in Spain. At the age of eight he was apprenticed to his father's business. Four years of this were enough for Joseph, but his only way of escape was to discover a vocation for the priesthood, which he entered, after a long preliminary training, at the age of twenty-five. His instincts were already at war with his professions. Even at eight years old the reading of Fénelon's *Télémaque*, with its descriptions of pagan ritual, had created in his mind a picture of a sunlit religion to which the dark and morbid imaginations of Spanish Catholicism were an unwholesome contrast. The Spiritual Exercises to which he submitted himself were successful for a time in subduing his natural temper. But even as he practised them he found himself unable to overcome his dislike for 'that cloying, that mawkish devotion. Though tears flowed from my eyes, and convulsive sobs were wrung from my bosom, my natural taste recoiled from that mixture of animal affection (I do not know a more appropriate name) with spiritual matters, which is the very essence of mysticism.' He had not been a priest for more than two or three years when he came to the conclusion that Christianity was an imposture. Here was a terrible position for an ardent young man. He could not bring himself to leave Spain, because of his dread of hurting his parents. He could not relinquish the priesthood without incurring the charge of heresy, punishable with death.

From this nightmare he escaped to London in the confusion which followed Napoleon's occupation of Madrid, and there Christianity crept back upon him by degrees. He became a priest in the Church of England and settled down to study Greek and Divinity at Oxford. This was in 1814. After several wandering years, he took up his life in Oxford again in 1826, a Master of Arts by special diploma and an honorary

H   F.O.A.

member of the Oriel common room. He was on intimate
terms with Newman and Pusey. But Whately was his special
hero; and when Whately went to Dublin Blanco White went
with him as tutor to his son. His health was by then wretched,
and his religious doubts had returned. He became a Unitarian and died, a lonely and miserable old man, at Liverpool
in 1841. His autobiography was the final proof for Newman
'that there is no medium between pantheism and the Church
of Rome.'

Blanco White must have been at Oxford when Newman
was elected; for Francis Newman relates that when he came
up to Oxford in that year the Dean (Tyler) 'at once insisted
that I should have my meals from Oriel buttery; so we moved
into a lodging, still known as Palmer's, in Merton Lane,
where we found the Rev. J. Blanco White abiding.' 'He and
my brother' the account continues 'enjoyed the violin
together. I gradually heard their theological talk, which was
apt to end by Blanco's sharp warning: "Ah! Newman! if you
follow that clue it will draw you into Catholic error."'

Strange encounter of the homeward and the outward
bound!

CHAPTER IV

INCUBATION

I. PUSEY AND LLOYD

Newman's first task, when Whately had done with him by the beginning of August, was to improve his scholarship. If he had worked hard as an undergraduate, he worked even harder now that he was a Fellow. He stayed up at Oxford through the long vacation, reading, writing till his hand could not 'compose a flowing sentence', coaching a pupil, taking only four hours' sleep. But he was careful, now, to preserve a lighter tone in his letters home. '*Liber sum* (my pupil having gone),' he wrote to his mother at the end of September 'and I have been humming, whistling, and laughing aloud to myself all day.' In October Francis came up, and the two brothers shared lodgings, and John played the part of coach; reporting home that Francis was a far better Greek scholar and mathematician than himself. The year closed with a characteristic entry in his journal: 'This year past has been a scene of laborious study from the commencement to the close. Let me praise that excessive mercy which has blessed me with so strong a frame. I have sometimes quite trembled on retiring to rest at my own exertions. Quite well, indeed, am I; free from headache and every pain.'

The next year (1823) passed in very much the same way. The single pupil became four, one of them 'very docile and very *nice*'. The hours of sleep were increased a little. By November he has made it a practice (so he tells his mother) to be in bed by eleven and to get up at half past five. He draws for her a picture of the inconvenience it is to paddle to

dinner at Oriel through the slush of an early snowfall in thin
shoes and silk stockings. He takes in hand—at a distance—
the education of his sisters. He criticizes their verses; en-
courages Harriett to translate Tasso and paraphrase Gibbon, Jemima to illustrate the generation of asymptotic
curves, Mary to acquire a better understanding of English
grammar. To Harriett he writes in his most earnest manner.
She is continually in his thoughts—need he add, continually
in his prayers? Let her spend her Sunday leisure in learning
portions of Scripture by heart. 'The benefit seems to me incalculable. It imbues the mind with good and holy thoughts.
It is a resource in solitude, on a journey, and in a sleepless
night; and let me press most earnestly upon you and my
other dear sisters, as well as on myself, the frequent exhorta-
tions in Scripture to prayer.' In between whiles he occupied
himself in drawing up an argument for the strict observance
of the Christian Sabbath from the writings of St. Chrysostom
and other Fathers, and with the reading of Butler's *Analogy
of Natural and Revealed Religion*. From Butler he derived much
of his subsequent philosophy of religion—in particular the
idea that material phenomena are sacramentally related to
an invisible divine order, and the idea that probability is not
only the guide of ordinary life but the logical basis of religious
belief.

With Pusey's entry, this same year, into his life the evidence
of this preoccupation with religious matters becomes still more
definite.

Already, Pusey, dining at the high table as Jelf's guest,
had impressed himself on Newman's sensitive memory with a
peculiar distinctiveness. 'His light curly hair' wrote the old
man, more than fifty years later, recalling every detail of that
meeting as if it had been the opening moment of romance,
'was damp with the cold water which his headaches made
necessary for his comfort; he walked fast with a young
manner of carrying himself, and stood rather bowed, looking

up from under his eyebrows, his shoulders rounded, and his bachelor's gown not buttoned at the elbow, but hanging loose over his wrists. His countenance was very sweet, and he spoke little.'

The entry in his diary which recorded Pusey's election to an Oriel Fellowship (April 1823) had, as he himself said, a high patronizing—or was it a self-protective?—tone. 'Two men have succeeded this morning, who, I trust are favourably disposed to religion, or at least moral and thinking, not worldly and careless men.' The tone was not held for long. A week or so after the election he takes a walk with Pusey after church; there is 'some very pleasing conversation. He is a searching man, and seems to delight in talking on religious subjects.' Three weeks later: 'How can I doubt his serious-ness? His very eagerness to talk of the Scriptures seems to prove it. May I lead him forward, at the same time gaining good from him!' After another fortnight: 'That Pusey is Thine, O Lord, how can I doubt? . . . Yet I fear he is pre-judiced against Thy children [i.e. against the Evangelicals]. Let me never be eager to convert him to a *party* or to a form of *opinion*. . . . What am I that I should be so blest in my near associates!' The Long Vacation interrupted these earnest entries. The moment term began, they began again. Pusey was now in lodgings in the High Street, in the same house as Newman, and their intimacy was growing fast. There was 'a delightful walk' that winter; 'our subjects all religious, all devotional and practical'. The topic most discussed then and in later walks was missionary work. In March of the following year some deep confidence passed between the two youths which moved Newman as he was seldom moved again. 'We went along the lower London road, crossed to Cowley, and, coming back, just before we arrived at Magdalen Bridge turnpike, he expressed to me . . .' What it was that Pusey ex-pressed the journal did not dare to say, and its aged transcriber (alas! for the transience of the deepest emotions) could not remember. But it must have been a unique confidence to provoke the almost hysterical phrases which followed: 'Oh what words shall I use? My heart is full. How should I be humbled to the dust! What importance I think myself of! My deeds, my abilities, my writings! Whereas he is humility itself, and gentleness, and love, and zeal, and self-devotion. Bless him with Thy fullest gifts, and grant me to imitate him.'

Ten years afterwards, off the little island of Zante, he made a poem out of these meetings.

> I saw thee once, and nought discerned
>   For stranger to admire;
> A serious aspect, but it burned
>   With no unearthly fire.
>
> Again I saw, and I confessed
>   Thy speech was rare and high;
> And yet it vexed my burdened breast,
>   And scared, I knew not why.
>
> I saw once more, and awe-struck gazed
>   On face, and form, and air;
> God's living glory round thee blazed—
>   A Saint—a Saint was there!

What was it, in Pusey's conversation, which vexed and scared the young Evangelical? Partly a revelation of character, partly a revelation of mind. 'They know very little of me,' Newman had said to his father 'who think I do not put a value on myself *relatively* to others.' It was not easy for him to admit his own inferiority. His one intimate friend, John Bowden, had been Jonathan to his David. Between himself and Pusey a different relationship was forming. 'It was not I who sought friends, but friends who sought me.' This was his belief in old age, when he had grown accustomed to the devotion of Ambrose St. John. But it was not true of his friendship with Pusey; nor was it true of the still more intimate and exciting friendship with Hurrell Froude. It was he who pursued Pusey. Whatever the first verse of the poem might say, he had seen something strangely and instantly appealing in the sweet countenance and the damp curly head of hair. He was lonely, in great need of friendship, very conscious of a mission to save souls. In this delicate, charming, gifted boy love and religious zeal craved an equal, an indistinguishable fulfilment.

But the course of such a love seldom runs true to its earliest imaginings. Pusey was not in the same need of romantic affection. He had his own intimate friends. He came of good family. He had a settled place in the world. He was already deeply, though at this time hopelessly, in love with his future wife. In comparison to Newman's his temperament was simple if abnormally emotional. Intellectually he was very much more solidly equipped. His theological position was far better secured. His zeal and his piety were at least equal to the zeal and the piety of Newman. And Newman, as the extracts from his diary show, found himself abandoning the idea of converting Pusey to his own religious views and admitting Pusey to be the better man.

He would not yet admit that Pusey was right and he was wrong. He was 'always slow in deciding a question'. And Pusey's influence was not the only one. If Catholic views lay to the right, and Pusey's boyish charm beckoned in that direction, Liberalism lay to the left, and Whately's masterful north-easter blew compellingly to that quarter. Whately was out of the way for the time being. But he was soon to come back to Oxford and to take Newman under his wing again; while Pusey was to desert Oriel for Göttingen. From 1823 to 1827 Newman's mind was in transition from one set of opinions to another. The uncomfortable thing was that he did not know in which of two totally opposite directions he was going. 'The truth is,' he says in the *Apologia*, speaking of the end of this period, 'I was beginning to prefer intellectual excellence to moral; I was drifting in the direction of the liberalism of the day. I was rudely awakened from my dream at the end of 1827 by two great blows—illness and bereavement.'

Whichever of the two principles—the Catholic or the Liberal—was on balance gaining the most ground in his mind (and it is difficult to think that he was so much in danger of becoming a freethinker as he afterwards supposed), the Lutheran doctrines of his youth were being rapidly eaten away. Just before his election at Oriel he received a lecture from his father. 'Take care,'—so he reported his father's words in his diary—'you are encouraging a morbid sensibility and irritability of mind, which may be very serious. Religion, when carried too far, induces a mental softness. No one's principles can be established at twenty. Your opinion in two or three years will certainly change. I have seen many instances of the same kind. You are on dangerous ground. The temper you are encouraging may lead to something alarming. Weak minds are carried into superstition, and strong minds into infidelity; do not commit yourself, do nothing *ultra*.' To which John added his own reflections: 'How good God is to give me "the assurance of hope"! If any one had prophesied to me confidently that I should change my opinions, and I was not convinced of the impossibility, what anguish should I feel!'

Yet the thing was happening.

This first intimate contact with an unfamiliar type of religious belief was reinforced by the lectures of Dr. Charles Lloyd, the new Regius Professor of Divinity.

These lectures were a new departure in Oxford. They were attended, not by undergraduates, but by a handful of young Masters of Arts. The class consisted at first of eight: four students of Christ Church and four Fellows of Oriel—Jelf, Pusey, Newman and Churton (who was elected at the same time as Pusey).[1] Newman and Churton were the only members of the class who had not been at Christ Church. One imagines the four earnest youths, in their caps and M.A.

---

[1] *Life of Pusey*, i. 62. Newman (*Letters*, i. 111) gives Ottley instead of Churton.

gowns, crossing the road from Oriel to Canterbury Gate, in the winter term of 1823, Newman perhaps hanging back a little at his first entry into the aristocratic precincts of Peck-water Quad, and wondering what he had let himself in for, but reassured by a smiling backward glance from his new friend.

For Lloyd was the ruler of a hostile camp, and to become his pupil was to defy both Evangelicalism and Whately, as Newman related in his *Autobiographical Memoir*:

'At that time there was a not unnatural rivalry between Christ Church and Oriel; Lloyd and Whately were the respective representatives of the two societies, and of their antagonism. Sharp words passed between them; they spoke scornfully of each other, and stories about them and the relation in which they stood towards each other were circulated in the Common Rooms. Lloyd was a scholar, and Whately was not. Whately had the reputation specially of being an original thinker, of which Lloyd was not at all ambitious. Lloyd was one of the high-and-dry school, though with far larger views than were then common; while Whately looked down on both High and Low Church, calling the two parties respectively Sadducees and Pharisees. Lloyd professed to hold to theology, and laid great stress on a doctrinal standard, on authoritative and traditional teaching, and on ecclesiastical history; Whately called the Fathers "certain old divines", and after Swift or some other wit, called orthodoxy "one's own doxy", and heterodoxy "another's doxy". Lloyd made much of books and reading, and, when preacher at Lincoln's Inn, considered he was to his lawyers the official expounder of the Christian religion, and the Protestant faith, just as it was the office of his Majesty's Courts to lay down for him peremptorily the law of the land; whereas Whately's great satisfaction was to find a layman who had made a creed for himself, and he avowed that he was *prima facie* well inclined to a heretic, for his heresy at least showed that he had exercised

his mind upon its subject matter. It is obvious which of the
two men was the more Catholic in his tone of mind.'

The lectures which Lloyd was now giving were not definitely Catholic in their teaching. His subsequent lectures on
the origin of the Prayer Book, in which he showed, to the
astonishment of an ignorant University, that it was the de-
scendant of the primitive and mediaeval liturgies and the
close English cousin of the Roman service books, were a
powerful stimulus to the first Anglo-Catholics. But Newman
did not attend the Prayer Book lectures; he derived their influence through others. These earlier lectures were concerned
with the Bible, the historical accuracy and authenticity and
linguistic interpretation of the several books of the Old and, to
a lesser extent, of the New Testament. The class studied
Sumner's *Records of the Creation*, Graves on the Pentateuch,
Carpzov on the Septuagint, Prideaux's *Old and New Testament Connected*, and other learned but antiquated works. They
were obliged to digest them very thoroughly, for the lectures
largely consisted of the pupils' own answers to the Professor's
searching questions. The result of the lectures was to implant
in their minds a solid assurance that their faith was grounded
in historical fact, and a conviction that the full meaning of
any scriptural text seldom lay plainly on the surface. It is easy
to see how such a course of training strengthened Newman's
powers of resistance to sceptical enquiry on the one hand and
loosened the mortar of his Evangelical opinions on the other.

It had another, and very beneficial, effect upon him.
Answering Lloyd's questions before the class gave him a new
self-confidence. And Lloyd's methods with his pupils were
not unlike those of Whately's. 'Treat 'em rough', was the
principle upon which both teachers went. Roughness, so long
as it was the covering of kindness and understanding, was
exactly the right thing for Newman. It is true that in writing
of Lloyd he is at pains to say that Lloyd was not the man to
exert an intellectual influence over him as Whately did, and

that he always felt constrained and awkward in Lloyd's presence as he never did in Whately's. The reason for that lay in the fundamental difference of their minds—the difference between the mind of a theologian and the mind of a scholar—and in the fact that Newman, as an Evangelical, knew himself to be under suspicion, however kindly. But it is impossible to read his own account of the way in which Lloyd treated him without perceiving how well he relished it.

'It is difficult' he wrote 'to see how, into such teaching as this, purely religious questions could have found their way; but Dr. Lloyd, who took a personal interest in those he came across, and who always had his eyes about him, certainly did soon make out that Mr. Newman held what he called Evangelical views of doctrine, then generally in disrepute in Oxford; and in consequence bestowed on him a notice, expressive of vexation and impatience on the one hand, and of a liking for him personally and a good opinion of his abilities on the other. He was free and easy in his ways and a bluff talker, with a rough, lively, good-natured manner, and a pretended pomposity, relieving itself by sudden bursts of laughter, and an indulgence of what is now called *chaffing* at the expense of his auditors; and, as he moved up and down his room, large in person beyond his years, asking them questions, gathering their answers, and taking snuff as he went along, he would sometimes stop before Mr. Newman, on his speaking in his turn, fix his eyes upon him as if to look him through, with a satirical expression of countenance, and then make a feint to box his ears or kick his shins before he went on with his march to and fro.'

2. PUSEY

Pusey comes into Newman's life so suddenly and so intimately only to withdraw again to a distance. Their careers will not run again in parallel for several years. We have caught a glimpse of him, as an attractive earnest youth of twenty-three, through Newman's eyes. Let us now glance at the family and the home from which he came, and trace the simple curves of his boyhood, youth and early manhood up to his appointment, at the age of only twenty-eight, to the Regius Professorship of Hebrew.

Edward Bouverie Pusey was his full name. His ancestry was curious. His father was Philip Bouverie, a younger son of the first Viscount Folkestone. The Bouveries were an old and prolific French Walloon family. The name means 'ox-stall'; the thirteenth-century ancestors of the nineteenth-century English saint and scholar were herdsmen in the countryside of Liége and Bruges. They married above their station; became rich; produced a Mayor of Liége, a Bishop of Angers, and in 1542 a certain Laurence Bouverie, who was converted to the principles of the reformation, refused to attend Mass and ran away to Frankfort to avoid the Inquisition. He sat down to rest himself at the gate of a silk-manufactory. The owner of the factory, passing by, discovered that he was a religious refugee and took him into his employ. Eventually he married his employer's niece and inherited her uncle's fortune. Then, thinking the reformation in danger in Frankfort, he emigrated to England and settled at Canterbury. His grandson, Edouard des Bouveries, became a London Turkey merchant and was knighted by James II. The knight's son became a baronet. The baronet's son became a friend of Sir Robert Walpole and, in consequence, Viscount Folkestone of Folkestone and Baron Longford of Longford. The viscount's eldest son became Earl of Radnor. Few family histories can show a more consistent record of material advancement.

The Hon. Philip Bouverie, Edward's father, was Lord Folkestone's youngest son, by his second wife. The sun of fortune shone equally upon him. His aunt, Lord Folkestone's sister, had married into the Pusey family. For seven centuries the Puseys had ruled the estate in Berkshire from which they took their name, ever since their Norman ancestors ousted the Saxon tenant of the manor at the conquest. But the dynasty was failing. Miss Jane Pusey, last of her race, looked round for an heir. Her choice fell upon Philip, who changed his name to Pusey and in due course became the owner of Pusey House and property.

Philip's mother, the second Lady Folkestone, came from a learned and distinguished family, the Marshams, who—like the Bouveries—had made their way in the world up to the peerage. Lady Folkestone prevented her son from marrying as a young man, and lived with him at Pusey until her death. He was fifty-two, a man of stern religion and methodical charity, when he married a young widow of twenty-eight, Lady Lucy Cave (*née* Sherard), daughter of the Earl of Harborough. Edward, born on August 22, 1800, was the second son of this late marriage. His brother Philip was just a year older. A string of five sisters followed, three of whom died in infancy. Two more sons came at the tail of the family.

The various strains of this ancient pedigree all made their contribution to Edward's character. The Bouveries and the Marshams gave him his brains and his tenacity of purpose; the Sherards his emotional religious temperament. Like Newman he had a partly foreign and commercial ancestry. Unlike Newman he had the traditions of the English gentry and nobility in his blood—traditions too of scholarship and churchmanship. The seventeenth-century Egyptologist, Sir John Marsham, was among his ancestors. The Sherards of the same century were royalists and high churchmen. His grandfather, the fourth Earl of Harborough, was a beneficed clergyman, Prebendary of Southwell and Canon of Salisbury. It never occurred to Edward that he should be anything but a clergyman himself. It was the younger son's natural career. Religion was the atmosphere of the house. The cast of his religious opinions he took from his mother, who treasured the vigorous faith of her own royalist ancestors.

To this long and solid and conscious inheritance of blood Pusey House added its own silent testimony of the significant past. The dignified Georgian house, standing where manor-house had followed manor-house for a thousand years, looking over water and trees and the miles of Pusey land to the unchanging outline of the downs, house and church and tiny village keeping company together as they had done for centuries—all this spoke to the boy of a permanent, immutable, yet gracious and living order, the soul of which was the living mystery of a religion once and for ever revealed. It needed no deliberate resolution on his part to renounce the worldly ambitions which had worked for five hundred years to give him this unclouded assurance from his birth. Thwarted sensuality would take its own terrible toll. The colour and the taste would drain away from earthly things, his own nature become loathsome to himself. But no doubt of God's revelation ever raised its head in his consciousness.

Lady Lucy Pusey was a gentlewoman of the old school. 'A typical lady', so Dr. Liddon described her, 'of the days of Fox and Pitt. She was tall, slim, with long hands and tapering fingers—a feature in which all her children, and not least her second son, resembled her. She commonly wore a watered-silk dress, very plain, with large lace collars and ruffles. With a sweet but piercing expression in her blue eyes, there was still a touch of severity in her bearing; she rarely or never would lean back in her chair, and she used to say that to stoop was the mark of a degenerate age. . . . Her time was laid out by rule: a certain portion was given to reading the Bible; and another portion to some book of established literary merit—generally an historical author. She would read this book with her watch at her side; and as soon as the self-prescribed time for such reading had elapsed, she eagerly turned to the more congenial task of needlework for charitable purposes.'

She carried the habits of the eighteenth century into the

second half of the nineteenth, using a sedan chair to church in South Audley Street from the Pusey mansion in Grosvenor Square, speaking of Edward as 'Ed'ard' and herself as 'an old 'ooman' who had drunk green tea all her life and was none the worse for it. People thought her practical and unsentimental, even formidable. She made no unnecessary parade of her feelings. Hers was one of those rare natures, which are content to love and to do good by stealth, and seeking no response from others receive it in the fullest measure.

There could be no question of Edward's devotion to her, nor of the fact that, if he derived his brains from his father's side of the family, he owed his convictions to his mother. 'All that I know about religious truth', he said, 'I learned, at least in principle, from my mother,' adding: 'But then, behind my mother, though, of course, I did not know it at the time, was the Catholic Church.' And near the very end of his life he told a friend that he had learned the doctrine of the Real Presence from her explanation of the Catechism to him as a child.

He was a delicate, obedient, 'angelic' little boy (his mother's epithet), with light flaxen hair and light-blue eyes, with none of the repugnance for country pursuits that might have been inferred from his physique and temperament.'Master Edward is a better shot', said the keeper, 'than young Mr. Pusey: he do take more pains about it.' As a boy he had the reputation of being a daring rider to hounds.

The two brothers were sent away, when Edward was seven, to a school in Surrey, where boys were prepared for Eton. The headmaster was a sound scholar and a very strict disciplinarian. In those days nobody supposed that little boys could be overworked or take any harm from being beaten. At the age of eleven, Edward was at his books for more than ten hours a day. At eleven and a half he went on, with Philip, to Eton. There he was happy enough, so long as he could get off 'fagging cricket'; but he does not seem to have distinguished

himself except at playing chess. His life at school, says
his biographer, was blameless; and he never omitted the
prayers which his mother had taught him. He made a few
intimate friends, of whom Richard Jelf is the only one that
need be mentioned here. And he was once all but drowned
while bathing—an experience which he always afterwards
remembered as 'very delightful'.

When he was seventeen he left Eton and went for a year's
special tuition to Dr. Maltby, Vicar of Buckden, near Hun-
tingdon, afterwards Bishop of Durham. There he was able to
read to his heart's content; and Maltby put a finer edge to his
scholarship than Newman ever had a chance of acquiring.
Half-way through his time at Buckden, while he was spending
a few weeks at Pusey, he met his future wife, and fell instantly
and deeply in love with her. Maria Barker was the daughter
of a neighbouring landowner. To other eyes she seemed no
more than a charming, impetuous, wilful, worldly minded,
girl of seventeen. But Edward saw her differently. For nine
years, against his father's unreasoning opposition, he held to
his faith. It was more than justified. Yet, if any man was
made for a matrimonial misadventure, it was Edward Pusey
—simple, devout, learned, passionate, unworldly, and always
trusting that things would work out for the best.

In January 1819 Edward went up to Christ Church. He
found Jelf already an undergraduate of more than a year's
standing, anxious to introduce him 'to a good acquaintance'.
He made Jelf the confidant of his 'morbid feelings' about Miss
Barker—morbid, because he saw no hope of marriage and yet
could not dismiss her from his mind. The morbid feelings did
not prevent him from indulging in the enjoyments proper to
his age and station. He played at being a Whig—his father
being a Tory. He toured in Wales with Jelf; visited Paris for
the first time; hunted three days a week. But during his third
year at Oxford Mr. Pusey saw fit to bring down his autocratic
foot upon Edward's romance and 'forbade all intercourse

Much

P-S-Y   from Christ Church Oxford

EDWARD BOUVERIE PUSEY
AS AN UNDERGRADUATE
From a drawing in the possession of Christ Church

between his son and Miss Barker.' There seems to have been
no particular reason for this violent show of authority, except
that he had married late himself. Perhaps he distrusted
Edward's judgment, and thought Maria a flighty girl. The
result of his interference was very nearly disastrous. Edward's
depression of spirits deepened into a form of melancholia.
For a time he felt as if his reason was giving way. His health
broke down. He suffered from excruciating headaches. He
poured out his despair, by letters, to Jelf; and Jelf persuaded
him that 'even to think of losing his mind was to lose trust in
God'. The best thing he could do was to return to Oxford
and read hard for his degree.

He followed this prescription with such violence that Jelf
became alarmed. 'Pusey reads most desperately, and it is as
much as I can do to make him take an hour's exercise.' It
was said that he read as much as sixteen or seventeen hours
a day. Only a few months remained before his examination.
He acquitted himself brilliantly. Among the examiners was
Keble, who put him on to translate a passage of Pindar. 'I
never knew' said Keble afterwards 'how Pindar might be
put into English until I heard Pusey.'

Old Mr. Pusey, delighted as he was with his son's first class,
gave no sign of relenting towards Maria Barker. He asked
Edward to choose himself a present. The young man ordered
a complete set of the Fathers. He spent the early summer
with his folios in a shady corner of the garden at Pusey House
'with a tub of cold water close at hand, into which he plunged
his head whenever study made it ache.' In July his father
consented to a three months' tour on the continent. With
Sheffield Neave, an Eton and Christ Church friend, Edward,
pencil and notebook in hand, explored Switzerland. He
watched the evening sunlight rest on Mont Blanc, as the
lesser peaks were swallowed up by the shadow, and felt his
soul 'excited almost to tears'. Bidding farewell to the mountain, as the evening mist rose in the valley, he wrote in his

notebook: 'The chill scene struck cold on my heart . . . there was too much to remind me of my own lot not to inspire the deepest melancholy.' A tree leaning over a precipitous ravine was a type of his own desperate situation: 'It was restrained from final destruction by one single support. When that support should cease, it was destined to plunge headlong from the mountain's height deep in the roaring tide below to endless night.' Wherever he went, his melancholy fed upon the visible scene. He confided these feelings, however, only to his notebook. 'Neave, ignorant of its cause, must not share its effects, yet he occasionally excites it; and when he bade me this evening take leave of the Aiguille peak for ever, the words found a gloomy correspondence with feelings of my own. They are pressing on my soul more and more; and Heaven alone can—He will if I bear me as a Christian—lighten my burthen.'

How far were these feelings spontaneous, and how far were they induced by the romantic pessimism which Byron had popularized by *Childe Harold*? Pusey was, at this period of his life, under Byron's peculiar spell. 'The extreme force and beauty of Byron's poetry' he wrote in later life 'induced us to give our assent to, and even in a measure exult in feelings of whose full extent we were either at the time not aware, or at least against which we half, and but half, shut our eyes.' His biographer, Dr. Liddon, thought that his Byronism 'did him harm by leading him to dwell morbidly on thoughts and feelings which would have been better repressed and forgotten.' He himself, even in his Byronic period, declared that he never arose from reading Byron a better man. But poison has to be eliminated somehow from the system; and an obsessive passion, like Edward's for Maria Barker, needs some kind of outlet. A perfectly healthy normal man does not fall into a lasting melancholy or fear the loss of reason, because he is crossed in love. But Edward was neither healthy nor normal; and Byron was the kind of medicine which he needed. As for his Byronism—it did not, in the words of his biographer, 'lead him to give up habits of regular prayer; or to renounce his faith in God's loving providence; still less into moral mischiefs beyond.' It was, indeed, a very safe solution of Byronism and water.

Edward came back to England in time to be present at his elder brother Philip's wedding in the autumn to Lady Emily Herbert. The Herberts—that is to say, Lord Porchester and his brother Edward Herbert—had been Philip's and Edward's closest friends at Eton. Their father, Lord Carnarvon, was a Whig; old Mr. Pusey was an inexorable Tory. This political difference had stood for four years in the way of an engagement. Mr. Pusey had been at last persuaded to relent. But poor Edward was no nearer the fulfilment of his own heart's desire than before. However, in his sister-in-law he had gained a devoted friend and a warm champion.

He set himself now to prepare for the Fellowship examination at Oriel in the Easter of the coming year. Oriel's chief attraction for him was the fact that it was Keble's college. He had already met Keble at Fairford, where the Barkers lived, and he had conceived a great desire to know him more intimately. His friend Jelf was already a Fellow. Ill health was the great danger. Nothing except severe illness was ever able to put a stop to Pusey's reading. Nevertheless, like Newman, he all but collapsed during the examination. On the first day he tore up his essay. On the second he 'wrote a letter begging to retire from the examination and left the hall.' But the essay had been laboriously pieced together, and read. Plumer was deputed to recall him. He allowed himself to be persuaded, and was elected. 'The bells of the parish church of Pusey expressed the satisfaction of his father and family.' And Jelf wrote him a letter of congratulations which he put 'into my mother's hands, who read it with tears, and my father's, who pronounced me above measure blessed that I had such a friend.'

The way seemed plain for a year or two of quiet study, ordination, and a curacy—perhaps a joint curacy with his new, earnest and oddly attractive friend Mr. Newman. In October he settled down to writing a Latin Essay in competition for the Chancellor's prize, on a comparison between the Greek and Roman systems of colonization. The subject might seem impregnably remote from Christianity. But Pusey was not daunted. The English colonies, by spreading the Christian faith round the world, are fulfilling a higher destiny than either the Greek or the Roman. 'Silent', said the glowing contortions of his Latin peroration, as nearly as they can be rendered into English, 'silent are the arts of Greece, vanished the state of Rome, but that the faith of Christ shall grow from age to age through the everlasting centuries, is aboundingly evident from the surest testimony, up to the point when, at length, it shall have extinguished all that is vile or inhuman and encircled the ends of the earth with the single bond of love.' The Essay gained the prize. Mr. Pusey, now nearly eighty, attended the Sheldonian Theatre to hear his son recite it. The bells of Pusey Church rang again, as the family party drove home in the June evening.

But while he was composing his Essay Pusey had begun a correspondence which was destined to have a profound effect upon his career. At Eton he had made friends with a studious retiring boy, known only to the world as 'Z'. 'Z' went up to Cambridge, and in that dangerous atmosphere lost his faith. He was now living in Paris. Pusey wrote asking him to interest the Paris booksellers in some French translations of English religious books. 'Z' replied that he would do what he could; but that it would be more to the point if Pusey could refute the French antichristian philosophers. He named Voltaire, Rousseau, and in particular Dupuis. He himself was an admirer, in fact a convert, of Dupuis, who regarded Christianity as a corruption of primitive astronomy. Christ represented the Sun; the Virgin Mary the constellation Virgo; the

Cross the intersection of the equator and ecliptic. Pusey, horrified, wrote to 'Z' at enormous length. 'Z' did his best to stem the tide of apologetic. First he refused to continue the correspondence; then he tried to divert it by beseeching Pusey to compose a systematic refutation of his favourite author. The challenge was accepted. Pusey read Dupuis and set to work on a rejoinder. It was written, though never published. The writing of it revealed to Pusey the limitations of his own knowledge. He was obliged to have recourse to the work of a German apologist, Gottfried Less, on *The Truth of the Christian Religion*. But Less's book was only partly available in an English translation; and Pusey knew no German. The direct consequence was a decision to study theology in Germany, where faith and rationalism were in far more open conflict than in England.

His vain attempt to redeem 'Z' had another, still more direct, consequence. It was, he wrote at the very end of his life, 'my first real experience of the deadly breath of infidel thought upon my soul. I never forget how utterly I shrank from it. It decided me to devote my life to the Old Testament; as I saw that this was the point of attack in our defences which would be most easily breached.' The body of Christ's Church, which at Pusey House seemed so tranquil and so secure, was threatened (so his correspondence with 'Z' taught him) by unappeasable enemies in her very entrails, enemies who diverted scholarship to the poisonous uses of atheism. Very well then. Learning should be met by greater learning. He was ready to postpone his enlistment into the priesthood until he was armed *cap à pie*. It was, indeed, high time that Oxford theology should have some cognizance of the critical battles which were being waged on the continent. It was hardly safe to rely much longer on the pious wish, expressed a few years earlier by Edward Tatham, the Rector of Lincoln, that 'all the Jarman critics were at the bottom of the Jarman Ocean.'

In the Long Vacation of 1825, after his failure to carry off

the English Essay upon 'language in its copiousness and structure considered as a test of civilization'—a subject less easily
related than that of colonization to the supreme topic with
which his mind was engaged—he set off on his voyage of
discovery, with the benediction of Dr. Lloyd, who, though he
knew no German himself, realized that there ought to be more
than two men in Oxford who did.[1] 'I wish' said Lloyd one
day to Pusey 'that you would learn something about those
German critics.'

He went first to Göttingen, where he began to learn the
language systematically and attended the lectures of the
venerable Eichhorn, a German scholar of prodigious learning, on the Books of Moses. Eichhorn cared not a rap for the
'religious import of the narrative'; his satirical treatment of
the episode of Balaam's ass was a well-known annual treat.
Pusey heard this particular lecture, and was the only person
in the room who was not reduced to laughter. He was, in fact,
very much shocked. Here was a man of colossal scholarship,
Professor of Philosophy in a supposedly Christian university,
who described himself as too much given to orthodoxy yet did
not even dream of treating the supernatural stories of Holy
Writ as if they were literally true. Perhaps the Professor of
Theology would be a more trustworthy guide. But Professor
Pott was little better than Professor Eichhorn. He defended
the Resurrection, certainly; but he explained all the miracles
cheerfully away. 'This' exclaimed Pusey to himself in a
sudden panic 'will all come upon us in England; and how
utterly unprepared for it we are !'

From Göttingen he went to Berlin. Here he was more
fortunate; though perhaps, if he had not been already
inoculated at Göttingen, he would have been almost as badly
shocked by the great Schleiermacher, as by the great Eichhorn. Schleiermacher, Professor of Theology in the Univer-

[1] Dr. Cardwell, Principal of St. Alban Hall, and Mr. Mill of Magdalen.
Life of Pusey, i. 72.

sity of Berlin, was a devout rationalist, who succeeded by a
tour de force of personal genius not only in reconciling this
contradiction in his own nature but in making the reconciliation the basis of a new theological school. He did this by an
exaltation of feeling above thought. He *felt* towards the person of Christ the kind of mystical devotion which the Mor-
avians practised—the desire to dwell in imagination upon the
Five Wounds of the Lord, upon the Bloody Sweat, and the
Piercing of His Side. Piety of this type made the strongest
possible appeal to Pusey. It fulfilled a temperamental need,
a craving for emotional self-torture, of which signs had
already appeared in his slavery to 'morbid feelings' about
Miss Barker and his addiction to a diluted Byronism. In these
early years, and during his short married life, it did not take
him beyond the bounds of a reasonable asceticism and a
habit of constantly overworking. After his wife's death, as we
shall see later, he surrendered to it completely.

Schleiermacher's devotion to the person of Christ, and his
general theory of religion as 'consisting altogether in a feeling
of dependence on God', pleased Pusey so well that he could
not be very severe on the Professor's doctrinal lapses. He could
even write calmly to Lloyd that Schleiermacher's Christianity was little better than pantheism; and that his view of
the divinity of Christ consisted in thinking that, while God
displays Himself in every human being, He displays more of
Himself in Christ than in ordinary men. With Neander, the
historian of the Church, he had a closer intellectual sympathy,
though Neander's respect for the early Church was considerably less than his own. But Berlin's principal attraction for
Pusey was a young theologian named Tholuck whom he had
already met at Oxford. Tholuck's history was an inspiration,
a consolation for any number of 'Z's' and Eichhorns. At
twelve he scoffed at Christianity. On leaving school he read a
paper on the superiority of Mohammedanism. Then he was
converted, and bent his extraordinary powers to the service of

a positive theology. He was fluent in Persian, Arabic, and all the principal languages of Europe, and an Oriental scholar of distinction.

Heartened by this evidence that unbelief was not having its own way unchecked in Germany, Pusey returned to Oxford in October. His four months abroad had confirmed him in a determination to become an Old Testament scholar. The reality of the New Dispensation, he perceived, rested on the authenticity of the Old. As there was no doubt about the former in his mind, so there could be no serious flaw in the latter. But the Eichhorns could only be confounded by learning greater than their own. That learning should be his. Ordination must wait, and Newman continue alone in his large parish. Such at least was the process of conscious reasoning. He sat down at once to rub up the forgotten elements of Hebrew, and began to study Arabic, with Chaldee and Syriac looming ahead. But Oxford was no place for such an ambitious programme. Lloyd persuaded him that a second and longer visit to Germany must be undertaken. Pusey was not unwilling. His father gave his consent. In June 1826 the young man set out again for Berlin.

A few days before his departure Oriel celebrated her quincentenary. There was a great dinner, with turtle-soup. Pusey was very angry. 'What is this stuff that they are going to give us?' he said indignantly to Newman. He and Newman had already been defeated in a battle over the wine. It was proposed to add French wines—then considered a great luxury— to the usual port and sherry. 'Pusey and I' Newman remembered 'agreed to oppose the plan; and we carried our point in a Fellows' meeting. But the Provost, Copleston, forthwith said that he should give French wines on his own account. On which Pusey said to me that Oxford seemed incapable of being reformed.'

Pusey's second German visit lasted for a year, and surely so much learning was never packed into a twelvemonth before or since. After a riot of lectures and a preliminary skirmish with Chaldee and Syriac at Berlin, he settled down in the country, near Schönhausen, where Jelf was tutoring Prince George of Cumberland. Here he worked from fourteen to sixteen hours a day at Arabic. It pained him greatly to have to spend so much time on non-Christian literature, but a mastery of Arabic was, so it was then believed, necessary to a real mastery of Hebrew. During the autumn he studied Arabic and Syriac on the shores of the Baltic with the Orientalist Kosegarten. In November he came back to Berlin for a week or two, and found letters from Hawkins and Newman offering him a tutorship at Oriel. He answered, offering to undertake a theological lectureship, and the more he thought over this plan the more he liked it. A tutorship would make it impossible for him to go on with his Oriental studies; but a theological lectureship would enable him to keep his twin interests—theology and languages—going together. But the Fellows of Oriel were not in the least disposed to accept what they had not asked for, and Pusey despondently sank back into the 'practical inactivity' of fourteen hours' solid reading every day. He was now at Bonn, still working at Arabic and also at Hebrew. At Bonn he became intimate with a number of the students and professors; was more than once nearly involved in duels by his absence of mind in walking on the wrong side of the road; visited the sick and the poor; and rescued one young student from a state of indifference to religion.

Early in 1827 his youngest brother died. The shock, coming on the top of so much intense hard work, nearly caused him to break down. He slightly reduced his hours of reading, and mixed a little more Hebrew with his Arabic. By the end of June he had carried out his astonishing programme, and came back to England an accomplished Semitic scholar.

Two surprises awaited him. The first was his sister's engagement to his old school friend, Luxmore. Nothing could have been more suitable. 'Daily intercourse', he felt, 'with one so pious and rightminded as Luxmore must be a means of improvement to anyone.' The other surprise was the withdrawal of his father's opposition to his own marriage, just in time to prevent Miss Barker from forming, as his biographer puts it, 'another engagement which, in the judgment of those who knew her best, did not seem likely to ensure her happiness.' Pusey proposed to her at Cheltenham, at the end of September, and gave her a sprig of verbena. Not long before his death a pot of verbena, brought to him from Fairford by his daughter, recalled the ecstasy of that moment, and the old man burst into tears.

Overwork and the sudden loosening of the nine years' strain brought on a serious breakdown in his health. He was ordered to Brighton, where the Newmans were then living. There he 'bathed every morning at seven in the sea' (in November!) and 'allowed three hours in the day to the more immediate imbibing of sea air and exercise.' 'Dear Pusey' wrote Newman to Harriett 'lodges at 5 Eastern Terrace. My Mother will send her card and he will call. He is very unwell; his nerves very much tried. He is not well in mind or body. All of you be very dull when he calls, for he can bear nothing but dullness, such as looking out upon the sea monotonously.' But even at Brighton he did not stop working. He had conceived the stupendous task of revising unaided the Authorized Version of the Old Testament. Lloyd, now become Bishop of Oxford, warmly encouraged the scheme. Edward wrote to Maria from Brighton explaining at length what he was about, and how convenient it would be for them to live at Oxford when they were married, within the reach of books and MSS. and scholars.

But when could they be married? Mr. Pusey thought, in two years' time. Edward must be ordained; a good living would be found for him. But Edward was resolved to be a student, not a parish priest. In all other matters he might give

way to his father; in this one respect he was adamant. Mr.
Pusey came down to see him at Brighton. Alarmed by his
son's condition, and by the doctor's report, he consented to
an early marriage. It was fixed for April 17th.

Meanwhile Pusey put aside his revision of the Authorized
Version (never afterwards resumed) in order to write an
essay on the causes of unbelief in Germany. The book was
published in May, and involved him in a sharp controversy
with the Rev. Hugh James Rose of Trinity, Cambridge,
hitherto the recognized English authority on German Protestantism, and the man who was to be the actual instigator
of the Oxford Movement.

Events now moved for Pusey with a rush. His father died
suddenly four days before the date fixed for the wedding.
Fresh plans had to be made. 'Poor Pusey' wrote Newman to
Jemima from Oriel on May 10 'came here last Monday. He
is much thrown back, and his spirits very low.' He was
ordained deacon by Bishop Lloyd on Trinity Sunday, and
experienced the usual solemn reflections. That evening he
read prayers for Newman at St. Mary's. 'If you read from
your chest in that way, it will kill you' said Newman, now a
master of ecclesiastical elocution. Next Sunday he assisted
Newman at the altar by administering the chalice. 'The
person whom I am going to assist is a very valued and dear
friend', so he wrote to Maria, 'with whom I should most wish
to be joined in this holy office.'

A few days later he was married. The honeymoon lasted for
three months. They explored Derbyshire, the Lake District,
the Western Highlands, the Hebrides, visited Mrs. Southey
and Mrs. Coleridge, and stayed with Sir Walter Scott. The
tour ended at Badger Hall in Shropshire, where they stayed
with the Boddingtons, cousins of Mrs. Pusey's. There Pusey
preached his first sermon on 'holiness, without which no man
shall see the Lord.' Miss Boddington thought it beautiful, and
wept. So did a Mrs. Dorothea Whitmore. But 'Tom' and

'Reginald', whatever they thought of the sermon, considered their guest 'very stupid'.

From Badger Hall the Puseys went to Oxford, where they spent a month in the lodgings which Bishop Lloyd still retained in Christ Church, as Regius Professor of Divinity. A few days after their arrival Dr. Nicoll, the Regius Professor of Hebrew, died. Hebrew scholars were not very plentiful. Before the year was out Pusey, at the age of twenty-eight, was Professor in Nicoll's place and a Canon of Christ Church.

3. SHADOWS OF COMING EVENTS

Our narrative goes back five years to Newman in 1823.

While he was passing through his phase of tutelage to others, learning the insecurity of his own religious views and shaping his own personality in the contact with new teachers and friends, Newman was not content to be a mere pupil. We find him, for example, trying his 'prentice hand upon 'a young man of sceptical opinions'. Whatever changes might take place in his mind, he was never in the least doubt of one fundamental fact; namely that the ascertainment of religious truth was the most important thing in human life. 'We are playing with edged tools', he wrote to the sceptical young man. Errors in astronomy or chemistry 'are unattended with danger to the person who maintains them.' But errors in the faith render a man 'incapable of true moral excellence, and so exposed to the displeasure of God'. 'I should be grieved' he goes on 'if you thought I was desirous of affecting superior wisdom, or gaining converts to a set of opinions.'

Examining his own moral condition at this time he is alarmed by a tendency to censoriousness. He saw no harm, before 1821, in 'going to the play'. But now he thinks differently, and feels uncharitable towards those who frequent theatres. As an undergraduate he had profaned Sunday by reading the newspaper. But now he can 'hardly bring himself

to believe anyone to have a renewed mind who does so.' The
censoriousness is not a very surprising symptom. The harden-
ing of certain elements of opinion, just at the time when his
opinions in general were in a confused stir, is more remarkable.

Another note, of similar date, draws a distinction between
doctrine and morality. Men's doctrinal differences, he thinks,
with a flash of an insight not his own (perhaps Whately's?)
may simply be due to their different understanding of terms.
But when a man 'talks of our natural sin as an *infirmity* and I
as a *disease*, he as an imperfection and I as a poison, he as
making man imperfect, as the angels may be, I as making
him a foe of God, and an object of God's wrath, here we can
come to no argument with each other, but one or other of us
must fearfully mistake the Scriptures.'

His flux of mind, then, in these years, never touched his
deepest convictions. The sense of sin, of the fearful urgency
under which every human life is conducted, was not in any
way shaken. This was the conscious basis of his feeling of
responsibility towards others—towards his young friend of
sceptical opinions; towards Pusey, until he saw that Pusey
was in no need of salvation; towards his brothers and sisters;
towards the parishioners and pupils who were soon to be his.
Was there, perhaps, an even stronger unconscious basis? Had
his 'affectionate abandonment' of himself to his older friends
a reverse side? There was that in Newman which, from his
earliest boyhood, sought to impose itself on others.

As a party-leader he was to be a tragic failure. But the
cause of his failure was not in any actual defect of his leadership. It was in his double nature—the nature of a man who
must both lead and follow. He both craved and feared to be
the symbol of men's hopes. Yet it is not true that he was a bad
leader, nor that he had leadership thrust upon him. He protested that he never was, and never wished to be, anything
more than a leading author of a school. But, while he may

have genuinely believed this to be true, he could no more
help being the leader than he could help filling the church of
St. Mary by his sermons. If leadership was thrust upon him,
it was thrust upon him by himself—not merely by his possession of the necessary qualities, enthusiasm, energy, driving
power, controversial genius, personality of the kind that could
threaten even Arnold with its dangerous fascination—but by
the secret ambition and pride, which perpetually outran his
consciousness of them, and submitted to his repressive discipline only to reach their end by a hidden route.

In the letter to his sceptical friend, in the entries about
Pusey in his diary, the very anxiety of his disclaimers shows
what was really in his mind. 'I do not want to gain converts.'
'Let me never be eager to convert him to a party.' Why does
he say these things, unless because he *does* want to gain converts, and *is* eager to convert Pusey? The desire rises up in
him; as soon as he recognizes it he challenges it. He challenges
it, because he is afraid of spiritual pride; and he is afraid of
spiritual pride because he *is* spiritually proud. He challenges
it, again, because the first hint of uncertainty has crept into
his mind and he is too cautious a man to take his stand upon
a rotten plank. Let him be convinced of a mission, and all
doubts and fears go by the board. And here is the second
reason for his failure as the leader of the Oxford Movement.
He had not made sufficiently sure of the plank. A crude
Scriptural syllogism betrayed him. Jesus was thirty when He
began His ministry. Jesus is the pattern upon which every
man must model himself. Therefore everyone must make up
his mind finally by the time he is thirty. Childish as it may
sound, this maxim undoubtedly played a considerable part
in persuading the Newman of 1831 that he had ended his
theological pilgrimage, when in fact he was only half-way to
his destination. Small wonder that he deserted his troops!

That the desire for leadership was always latent in his heart
was shown very clearly by an incident of his old age. After

twenty years of heart-breaking drudgery, obscurity and discouragement he had once more tasted fame and success with his *Apologia pro Vita Sua*. A proposal to build a Roman Catholic Hall at Oxford, under his presidency, had been vetoed at Rome some years before. Now, in the flush of returning self-confidence, he planned a Church and a 'House of the Oratory of S. Philip Neri' in the heart of his old University. The consent of the Vatican was secured; land was bought; money poured in. At length, on April 6, 1867, Father Neville of the Birmingham Oratory packed his bag. He was to 'take over' from the old priest who had hitherto represented Rome in Oxford. His train went in the afternoon; in the morning he went for a walk with Newman.

'Newman, the sunshine on his face, talked of the prospect. "Earlier failures do not matter now," he said; "I see that I have been reserved by God for this. There are signs of a religious reaction in Oxford. . . . Such men as Mark Pattison may conceivably be won over. Although I am not young, I feel as full of life and thought as ever I did. It may prove to be the inauguration of a second Oxford Movement. . . ." Thus happily talking, they returned to the Oratory. The servant, who opened the door to admit them, at once gave Newman a long blue envelope. . . . Newman opened and read the letter, and turned to William Neville: "All is over. I am not allowed to go." No word more was spoken. The Father [Newman] covered his face with his hands, and left his friend, who went to his room and unpacked his portmanteau.'[1]

The youth who disclaimed any desire to convert his friends was the father of the man who planned a second Oxford Movement at the age of sixty-six. His time was not yet. But there was a sphere in which he already felt himself called upon to exercise his influence—his own family, and particularly his brother Francis.

Francis William Newman was four years younger than

[1] *Life of Cardinal Newman*, ii. 138.

John. He followed John at Ealing, where he, too, was 'converted'; and came up to Oxford in the autumn of the year in
which John got his Fellowship at Oriel. He was then seventeen. In 1826 Frank took, without effort, a brilliant double-
first, and was elected a Fellow of Balliol. The further John
moved in the High Church direction, the further Frank
moved in the opposite direction. For a time he helped John
in his parish at Littlemore. But by 1830 he had moved out of
the Church altogether. He resigned his Fellowship and went
off with the eccentric Lord Congleton, a Plymouth Brother,
on a missionary expedition to Persia. It was a very distressing
affair, but John tried to be charitable, and to console his
mother by pointing out that 'God is not extreme to mark what
is done amiss. He looks at the motives, and accepts and blesses
in spite of incidental errors.' In 1832 Frank returned, reaching home only a few hours before John's arrival from Sicily.
Their meeting was not a comfortable one. Frank found his
brother's 'dignity as remarkable as his stiffness'. John regarded Frank as a heretic, who had excommunicated himself. They met seldom after this, and when they did meet conversation was hard to find. Frank's Christianity grew more
and more attenuated, and finally disappeared. He became
Principal of University Hall, London, and wrote a religious
autobiography called *Phases of Faith*, which created a sensation in the middle of the century by its attack upon New
Testament morality. His career might almost have been designed as an ironical commentary upon that of the author of
the *Apologia*.

In early life the two brothers shared the unemphatic Evangelicalism of their home. But they had from boyhood taken
the opposite sides on every other possible question. Soon after
Frank came up to Oxford religion was added to their other
differences. The younger brother's position cannot have been
an easy one. He owed everything to John, who supported him
'not out of his abundance, but when he knew not whence

weekly and daily funds were to come.' John, said the third brother, the shiftless, impossible, atheist Charles, ought to have been a prince, since he spent money like a prince—upon Charles, amongst others. But gratitude could not destroy Frank's sturdy independence of mind. It seemed to him that his elder brother was developing strangely superstitious ideas. If his account is accurate, there must evidently have been a kind of premature rehearsal in John's mind of opinions which, he then put off for a while before he finally embraced them.

He began by giving Frank to read a manuscript argument against baptismal regeneration—that is, against the doctrine that baptism wipes previous sin completely off the record and gives the soul an entirely fresh start. This was all very well. But when Frank went to hear him preach on behalf of the starving silk-weavers of Spitalfields, just after he had been ordained a deacon in 1824, what was his astonishment and that of the Rev. Walter Mayers to hear him say from the pulpit that the silk-weavers deserved to be helped because they were *baptized*? This seemed ominous. But much worse was to come. Frank, in this same year, moved into a new set of rooms. Going in to arrange his furniture he was amazed to see 'a beautiful engraving of the "Blessed Virgin" fixed up'. It appeared that John had ordered it. This was more than Frank could stand. The print was taken down, and its removal was followed by a serious dispute. Protestants, said John, forgot that sacred utterance, 'Blessed art thou among women.' To which Frank retorted with Christ's answer to the woman who blessed the womb that bore Him and the paps that He had sucked— '*Yea rather*, blessed are they who hear the word of God and keep it.' 'Our Lord' he concluded 'did not approve of honouring His mother.' John made no answer. From this moment, it appears, Frank dated the unhealable breach.

Such were the amenities of fraternal debate in the Oxford of 1824. But the remarkable thing about Frank's story— which seems too circumstantial to be untrue—is that it shows

John moving, so to speak, well ahead of his scheduled time. Yet perhaps it was not so remarkable. It had happened before. Had he not crossed himself, as a child, and drawn in an early exercise-book a picture of a rosary and a crucifix? And it was to happen again, in 1839, when the thought came to him that Rome was right after all.

4. THE CURATE OF ST. CLEMENT'S

How soon hath Time, the subtle thief of youth,
Stol'n on his wing my three-and-twentieth year!

'Is it possible?' wrote Newman in his diary on February 21, 1824, with Milton's sonnet very evidently in his mind. 'Have twenty-three years gone over my head? The days and months fly past me, and I seem as if I would cling hold of them and hinder them from escaping. . . . Keep me from squandering time—it is irrevocable.' Like Milton, perhaps, he felt—though he did not confess as much even to his diary—that inward ripeness was slower to appear in him than in other more timely-happy spirits. The grave tutor of his brother and sisters, the manager of his family affairs, was drifting already from the simple convictions of his boyhood. Like Milton, again, he was given to speculating on his destiny whether mean or high. Like Milton he lived in the consciousness of his great task-master's eye ever upon him. But unlike Milton he had already determined upon his vocation. 'I quite tremble to think,' he wrote 'the age is now come when, as far as years go, the ministry is open to me.'

No such heart-searchings as Keble's are recorded of Newman on the eve or the morrow of his ordination. The great event seems to have happened with no more than the proper degree of solemn excitement. He was ordained deacon on June 13, 1824, by Dr. Legge, the Bishop of Oxford. 'It is over; at first after the hands were laid on me, my heart shuddered within me; the words "For ever" are so terrible.' So he wrote an hour afterwards in his diary; and on the following day he wrote again: 'For ever! words never to be recalled. I have the responsibility of souls on me to the day of my death.'

His ordination was the natural consequence of the offer of a curacy in the Oxford parish of St. Clement's. This came to him in May through the offices of Pusey. The Rector of the parish, John Gutch, antiquary and octogenarian, was no longer equal to the task of serving St. Clement's without assistance. In effect Newman was, from the very beginning of his career as a clergyman, his own master. The parish was poor and populous. At the beginning of the century it had contained some four hundred inhabitants; now in 1824 the population numbered two thousand and was increasing rapidly. This was partly due to the 'new canals' which, before the railway, first brought commerce to the ancient seat of learning. It was also due to the clearance of old, closely packed, houses from the centre of the city. Tuckwell, writing of the early 'thirties, after Newman's new church had been built, gives a sharp picture. 'On the three approaches to the town, the Henley, Banbury, Abingdon roads, it was cut off, clear as a walled and gated Jericho, from the adjacent country. Only St. Clement's, sordid by day, by night oil-lighted, stretched from Magdalen Bridge to Harpsichord Row at the foot of Heading-ton Hill, where had lately risen the hideous church known from its shape as the "Boiled Rabbit". The old church stood at the fork of the Headington and Iffley Roads, close to the Cape of Good Hope public-house.'

It was already designed to pull down the old church and build a new one by public subscription. What was wanted of the new curate was that he should be 'a kind of guarantee to the subscribers' that when the new church was built 'every exertion should be made to recover the parish from meeting-houses, and on the other hand ale-houses, into which they [that is, the parishioners, not the subscribers] have been driven for want of convenient Sunday worship.' To this task

Newman felt himself entirely equal. The only thing that worried him was, astonishingly enough, his weakness of voice—the voice of which Mozley, connoisseur of voices, said that it needed no description, for it had enthralled half the English world. But everybody advised him to accept the curacy—his old schoolmaster, Walter Mayers, now Vicar of Warton, eighteen miles from Oxford; the Dean of his College, Tyler; the Vice-Provost, Hawkins; his own contemporaries Jelf, Pusey and Ottley. So he accepted; and having done so 'went and subscribed to the Bible Society, thinking it better to do so before engaging in this undertaking.' He could fight the 'meeting-houses' the more easily if he had one foot, at least, planted in the Evangelical camp.

All this spring and early summer he was working at the highest pressure. There were his pupils; his efforts to improve his own scholarship; his attendance at Dr. Lloyd's lectures, with all the detailed reading which this involved. An article from his pen appeared in the May issue of the *British Review*— he had already contributed articles to the *Christian Observer*. As if these occupations were not enough, he accepted an invitation from Whately to write a full-length study of the Life and Writings of Cicero for the *Encyclopaedia Metropolitana*, in the place of a defaulting contributor, for a fee of £14. Two months were allowed him for his task, which he completed about the end of May. His allowance of sleep was reduced accordingly. Once, at least, he worked all night till four in the morning, and then walked the eighteen miles to Warton before breakfast, in order to take Mr. Mayers's pupils under his charge during his friend's absence. Cicero finished, and the ordination ceremony over, he paid a flying visit of two or three days to his father and mother, before he began his ministry.

On June 23, at Warton, not at St. Clement's, he preached his first sermon on the text 'Man goeth forth unto his work and to his labour until the evening.' This was the sermon in aid of

the starving weavers of Spitalfields, which alarmed Frank
and Mr. Mayers by its emphasis on the significance of baptism. Mrs. Newman, however, admired it very much. The
preacher himself considered that it 'implied in its tone a
denial of baptismal regeneration.' He showed it to Hawkins
who 'came down upon it at once on this score.' The conflict
of evidence is curious and significant. Newman's language
must have reflected the uneasy balance which his mind was
trying to hold between two totally different opinions—seeking still to represent baptism as a symbolic act rather than an
instrument of plenary grace, but investing the symbol with
all the importance of the thing symbolized, that is to say,
membership of the Christian brotherhood. What happened
at baptism, was the question which was now beginning to
torment Newman beyond all others. He still held that the
Christian world was divided 'into two classes, the one all
darkness, the other all light'—the elected and the damned.
His sermon was quite clear on this distinction, though
Hawkins's shrewd criticism, that it simply did not correspond
with the obvious facts, opened his eyes to its crude unreality.
He could not resist Hawkins's argument that St. Paul at one
and the same time addressed the brethren as sanctified in
Christ and rebuked them for their scandalous misbehaviour.
The world, he came very soon to understand, was not black
and white, but a world of infinite gradations. Yet this discovery only intensified the baptismal difficulty. What *did*
happen at baptism? In the black and white world of the converted and the unconverted the answer was easy. Baptism
could do no more than put the infant into a position of
advantage for the reception of God's grace when the proper
time came. It by no means followed that he *would* receive it.
But the black and white world was dissolving into various
shades of grey. Where then lay the urgency of baptism?
What did the Prayer Book say? 'We yield thee hearty thanks,
most merciful Father, that it hath pleased thee to regenerate

this infant with thy Holy Spirit.' Then, at baptism, the
child was regenerate, was promised 'the blessing of eternal
life' and a share in the everlasting kingdom. Something, in
fact, must happen in baptism, more than formal admission
into the Church. Yet the promise must evidently be, in some
sense, conditional. The wicked man could not safely rely on
the fact that he had been baptized. Was there then, after all,
a necessity for some subsequent conversion? At what point
did that necessity begin? And what happened to infants if
they died before they had been baptized?

But for the moment Newman thrust these hard questions
to the back of his mind and threw himself methodically into
the practical duties of his parish. He undertook a house-to-
house visitation 'asking the names, numbers, trades, where
they went to church, etc.', taking 'care always to speak kindly
of Mr. Hinton, the dissenting minister'. His father feared that
these uninvited clerical calls might not be so welcome as the
young curate supposed. But they were, in fact, very well
received. His parishioners called him 'a proper minister' and
'a nice young gentleman'. They flocked to hear him preach,
and had to be turned away at the doors, since the church
could only hold two hundred people. 'Those who make comfort the great subject of their preaching' he noted in his
diary 'seem to mistake the end of their ministry. *Holiness* is the
great end. There must be a struggle and a toil here.' He was
aware, he told his mother, that his sermons contained
'truths which are unpalatable to the generality of mankind;
but the doctrine of Christ crucified is the only spring of real
virtue and piety, and the only foundation of peace and comfort. I know I must do good.' Certainly his sermons—even
the series of afternoon sermons in the summer, which he
instituted—were popular. He was confident; his voice grew
stronger; he knew his congregation. He thanked his mother
for suggesting texts for future sermons, but doubted whether
he would have occasion to use them for some little time. 'My

parish (I fear) wants to be taught the very principles of Christian doctrine. It has not got so far as to abuse them.'

Yet, under cover of this external confidence, he was being racked by doubt. On August 24, barely two months after his ordination, he wrote in his diary: 'I have been thinking much on the subject of grace, regeneration, etc., and reading Sumner's *Apostolical Preaching*, which Hawkins has given me. Sumner's book threatens to drive me into either Calvinism or Baptismal Regeneration, and I wish to steer clear of both, at least in preaching. I am always slow in deciding a question; and last night I was so distressed and low about it that the thought even struck me I must leave the Church. I have been praying about it before I rose this morning, and I do not know what the end will be of it. I think I really desire the truth, and would embrace it wherever I found it.'

If only Pusey were there! But Pusey, after winning the Latin Essay, was away in Berkshire, through the Long Vacation. Perhaps next year he would take orders and join his friend as second curate of St. Clement's. Meanwhile Newman took his parish problems of an evening to Hawkins, and Hawkins's self-assurance deepened his own self-distrust.

As the summer waned, Mr. Newman fell ill. At the end of September John was sent for. Three days later his father died. It was his first meeting with death. The differences of opinion he had had with his father; their difference of temperament and of outlook; these were all forgotten, swept away by a rush of filial emotions. 'The father and son' Miss Mozley pronounced 'were very dear to each other.' But was his father really very dear to Newman? It was not possible for his religious egotism to sink itself in family life. In so far as his relations loved him, he was touched by their love; in so far as they admired him, he would admit them to his intimacy. More he could not do. He is scarcely to be blamed for this. Genius is selfish; not less so in religion than in art. Nor can love be manufactured to the order of any conventions. Newman, so far as conscious control of affection is a possible thing, was an affectionate son and brother. There were no limits—at least in the earlier part of his life—to the trouble he would take, or to the time and the money he would spend for his family. But there was a limit, beyond or beneath his control, to his emotional responsiveness. Its existence was concealed by his habit of carrying in his mind an ideal picture of himself in relation to others—an artificial composition, which compelled the surface elements of his nature to arrange themselves in a similar pattern. His social personality was the gradual product of this process of imaginative character-building. He had an acute aesthetic appreciation of conduct; and he used this faculty, like the artist he was, to remedy his own defects. Again and again, in those private memoranda which he was constantly constructing for his own eye, sometimes even in his letters, he stands back and watches his behaviour almost as though it were the behaviour of another man, yet never with detachment, always with a passionate interest. These vivid and often dramatic impressions of himself he arranges upon his paper with instinctive and inevitable art. He saw himself in this way, upon Mr. Newman's death, the loved son of a loved father, experiencing all the emotions which such a son must feel on such an occasion. Then his thoughts leaped forward to his own future. Returning from the funeral, he wrote in his diary: 'Performed the last sad duties to my dear Father. When I die, shall I be followed to the grave by my children? My Mother said the other day, she hoped to live to see me married; but I think I shall either die within college walls, or as a missionary in a foreign land. No matter where, so that I die in Christ.'

Later, he saw himself, and told his mother that he saw himself, in relation to her and his sisters, as the prophet, not without honour, save among his own people and in his father's house. 'John' said his eldest sister Harriett 'can be most amiable, most generous. He can win warm love from all his friends; but to become his friend, the essential condition is, that you see everything along his lines, and accept him as your leader.' 'Harriett' said John to Frank, in the last stages of Tractarianism, 'has that in her which I cannot permit.' 'I would have no dealings with my brother' he wrote in the *Apologia* 'and I put my conduct upon a syllogism. I said, "St. Paul bids us avoid those who cause divisions; you cause divisions: therefore I must avoid you."' The ideal picture of the son and the brother was replaced, as time went on, by that of the zealot.

After Mr. Newman's death his family for some time had no fixed home. They lived for short periods at Brighton, Strand-on-the-Green (with Mrs. Elizabeth Newman, John's aunt), and elsewhere. Eventually they moved, at John's urgent request, to the neighbourhood of Oxford. But this was not till five years later.

Back at Oxford John renewed his arduous life. His name was beginning to become known as that of a promising young clergyman. In November he was invited to become a member of the newly formed Athenæum Club, but declined. He was immersed in his parish and his pupils. He was starting a Sunday School, and was dubbed a Methodist in consequence. Subscriptions for the new church were coming in fast. By January of the new year (1825) he had collected over £2,600, 'and the Colleges are yet to come.' Pusey was back in Oxford too. But the two friends were less together than they had been. Newman had his parish and his pupils, and had been obliged to give up going to Lloyd's lectures. Pusey was reading for the English Essay, and wrestling with the problem of 'Z's' infidelity.

Newman spent the Christmas vacation, or part of it, with his family. Was this at Brighton? And was this the occasion on which, as Frank maliciously relates, 'he kept us all agog by a tale of ghosts which seemed inexplicable except by believing in the spirits: then, after two or three weeks, he suddenly told

us he had found it all to be false'? Ghosts or no ghosts, the
question filling his secret mind was still this difficult question
of regeneration. By the middle of January he had reached the
point of deciding that 'the great stand is to be made, *not*
against those who connect a spiritual change with baptism,
but those who deny a spiritual change altogether.' Regeneration, whether it came by baptism or by conversion or by whatever means, must mean what it said and not be explained
into 'a mere opening of new prospects, when the old score of
offences is wiped away, and a person is for the second time
put, as it were, on his good behaviour.' Heartened by this
provisional conclusion he took coach to Oxford on the coldest
day of the winter, and began his Sunday duties next morning
by bathing in the cold bath at Holywell.

The pressure of work continued and increased. There was
the management of the subscription fund for the 'Boiled
Rabbit'. (Newman disclaimed all responsibility for its architectural character.) There was his new Sunday School—held
in St. Clement's since he could not find a large enough room
anywhere. The church being blocked with pews, Newman
built a gallery for his school, big enough to hold ninety-four
children, and found the money by private subscription,
Pusey presenting a stove. Besides his pupils, and his private
reading, and his ordinary parish duties, and his sermon-
writing, he had engaged to contribute to the *Theological
Review*. On the top of all this he accepted a commission to
write for the *Encyclopaedia Metropolitana* 'the memoir of Apollonius Tyanaeus, and the argument on Miracles, as connected
with it.' A very difficult subject, as he said, involving not only
a great deal of research into an obscure period but a great
deal of hard thought on miracles generally. He divided
miracles sharply—as indeed he was expected to divide them
by his editor—into the scriptural miracles, which were of
course to be received, and the so-called ecclesiastical miracles,
which were to be rejected. Later on he 'saw that they were to

be regarded according to their greater or less probability', and developed this more subtle view in the *Essay on Ecclesiastical Miracles* which he published in 1842. As for Apollonius of Tyana, how many modern readers, asked to say who and what he was, would answer, an early Christian Father? He was, in fact, a neo-Pythagorean philosopher from Asia Minor, who claimed miraculous powers and founded a school at Ephesus, about the time when St. Paul was preaching the gospel in the same city. 'Apollonius of Tyana' says Gibbon in one of his most slyly malicious notes 'was born about the same time as Jesus Christ. His life (that of the former) is related in so fabulous a manner by his disciples, that we are at a loss to discover whether he was a sage, an impostor, or a fanatic.' The summer, a very hot one, saw Newman grappling heroically with this essay. 'I hope' Hawkins wrote to him in August 'by this time your essay on Miracles *à priori* and *à posteriori* parts, and all the contents of all the books in the window-seat, are in a beautiful state of efflorescence.' Pusey, from Göttingen, reported that Less was not much use in the matter of miracles. Hawkins, in September, replaced forty books for him in the College library, but perceived that he had taken several more away with him to the Isle of Wight. The article was finished by the end of the year, but it took Newman ten days in January to verify his quotations. 'Apollonius' he complained to Harriett 'is a crafty old knave.'

There remains, from that hot summer, a note from the casebook of the young physician of souls, which shows how little he allowed his other labours to interfere with his parish work; and shows, too, how suspicious he had become of canting repentances.

'John C., perhaps thirty-five: had been a coachman, and all his life in the society of coachmen. . . . I have called from time to time, and particularly left Doddridge's "Rise and Progress". At length, the day before yesterday, I was sent for. He seemed very near his end, and was very desirous

of seeing me. He talked of sin being a heavy burden, of which
he wished to be released. . . . To-day I found that he had suddenly declared the weight of sin was taken off him, and tears
burst from him, and he said he was *so* rejoiced. He seems very
humble and earnest, and willingly listened to what I said
about the danger of deception. I was indeed much perplexed,
fearing to speak against the mysterious working of God (if it
was His working), yet equally fearing to make him satisfied
with a partial repentance and with emotions, and should do
harm to his wife, etc. [*sic*]. I spoke *very* strongly on our being
sinful and corrupt till death. . . . All this he seemed to admit,
and thanked me very fervently. I am thinking of the *cause* of
all this. His mother, I see, is a religious woman. She cannot
be indiscreet? Doddridge *could not* mislead him—or is it the
work of the Holy Spirit even in its suddenness?'

No easy dupe, this 'nice young gentleman' of twenty-four!

To all these demands on his time and energy yet another
was added, when in March 1825 Whately was appointed
Principal of St. Alban Hall and asked Newman to be his
Vice-Principal. St. Alban Hall dated from the early fifteenth
century; in 1882 it was merged into Merton College. At the
time of Whately's appointment it had a poor reputation. It
had become, says Whately's biographer, 'a kind of "Botany
Bay" to the University—a place where students were sent
who were considered too idle and dissipated to be received
elsewhere.' Whately was not the man to tolerate this state of
affairs. He and Newman between them soon changed the
character of the Hall. There remained, after the purgation, a
number of men 'well-conducted and respectable, but beyond
the usual age of undergraduates'. Whately called them the
Albani Patres. There is a glimpse in Mozley's reminiscences of
the Principal lying on his sofa, with one leg thrown over its
back, while he lectured to his awkward squad of elderly undergraduates.

The addition to Newman's income was small—about £50

a year; and the addition to his burden of work was large. The finances of the Hall had been left by the late Principal in a tangle which it took him months to straighten out. He was 'Dean, Tutor, Bursar, and all—in Whately's absence, indeed, Principal'. In Whately's presence he was also a hard-working anvil again. For Whately was composing his *Elements of Logic*, and Newman—as the preface generously acknowledged—'actually composed a considerable portion of the work as it now stands, from manuscript not designed for publication, and is the original author of several pages.'

Mrs. Newman was delighted. 'Next, my dear,' she wrote with mock seriousness to Harriett, urging her to return home to meet her brother on a flying visit. 'I must beg you to be prepared to treat John with the proper respect due to a real "Don".' And then, having imparted the wonderful news: 'Were it anyone but John I should fear it would be too much for his *head* or his *heart* at so early an age; but in him I have the comforting anticipation that he . . . will be sedulous to avail himself of his talents and authority, to correct and improve a Hall.'

Others besides Mrs. Newman were beginning to think that there was a future before this latest of Oriel's dark horses. The Vice-Chancellor invited him 'to favour the University with a sermon at St. Mary's' on Whitsunday. He declined, on the ground of inexperience, being still only a deacon. At the end of May he was ordained priest. His mother and sisters spent the Long Vacation in Whately's lodgings at St. Alban Hall, and were in the congregation when he administered Communion for the first time on August 7 at St. Clement's. In September he paid a short visit to his Trinity friend, Bowden, in the Isle of Wight. It was supposed to be a holiday for the sake of his health, but it was impossible for him to be idle. In between drives, and sailings, and musical evenings, he read Davison on *Primitive Sacrifice*, meditated sermons, and worked at his Essay on Miracles. But he enjoyed himself, in spite of the chronic indigestion which overwork had begun to induce and from which he suffered for the whole of his long life. 'The beauty of water and land', he wrote to Harriett 'only makes me regret that our language has not more adjectives of admiration.'

The winter term put Newman under very heavy pressure. The essay on Apollonius and Miracles was taking shape. 'I have taken bark according to Dr. Bailey's prescription for three weeks;' he told his mother in November 'and this, added to my excursion, has made me so strong that parish, hall, college and "Encyclopaedia", go on together in perfect harmony. . . . It is a great thing to have pulled out my mind. I am sure I shall derive great benefit from it in after life.' No doubt this was true. But all was not going quite so smoothly as he pretended to his mother. 'I have been involved in work against my will', he confessed to himself. 'The Hall accounts have haunted me incessantly. Hence my parish has suffered. I have had a continual wear on my mind, mislaying memoranda, forgetting names, etc.' Looking back on this period of his life, many years later, he admitted that he had overworked himself.

CHAPTER V

THE TUTOR OF ORIEL AND THE VICAR OF ST. MARY'S

I. THE NEW BROOM

Soon after the new year opened, a gap occurred unexpectedly in the ranks of the Oriel Tutors. Jelf became private tutor to Prince George of Cumberland, and Newman was made a college tutor in his place, along with Tyler, Hawkins and Dornford. He was to start work at Easter. Another curate was found for St. Clement's, and another Vice-Principal for St. Alban Hall.

The new tutor was in no doubt how to regard his responsibilities. 'May I engage in them' he wrote in his diary 'remembering that I am a minister of Christ, and have a commission to preach the Gospel, remembering the worth of souls, and that I shall have to answer for the opportunities given me of benefiting those under my care.' There were, he said, two incompatible views of a college tutor's office: the view which he held, and for which he found authority in Archbishop Laud's Oxford statutes, that the tutor should be 'a moral and religious guardian of the youths committed to him'; and the view which was held by Hawkins, that the tutor's concern with his pupils did not extend to their religious views. Of these two opposing views, that of Hawkins has triumphed so completely that Newman's seems to belong to the scrap-heap. But in the Oxford of 1826 Newman's conception of his duties corresponded more to outward circumstances than Hawkins's.

It was one of those periods which precede reform—a period

in which those who look back can find more ostensible authority for their opinions than those who look forward. Hawkins, though a formalist and a conservative, had been trained in a school of reformers. He had an intuitive sense of what was practical and what was not. A degree of conformity with the uses of the Church of England was, he knew, all that could be tolerably required of undergraduates. Any direct attempt by the tutors to force the religious convictions of their pupils would be deeply resented, not so much perhaps by the young men themselves as by their parents. Nor had he spent so much of his life in the society of Copleston and Whately without acquiring an instinctive, if unformulated, conviction that the young men had a right to call their minds as well as their souls their own, and to arrive at truth by their own efforts. The tutor's task was to teach them how to use their minds, not to make up their minds for them. The pressure of a mature mind upon a young one could very easily be a form of coercion. He may also have reflected that even college tutors sometimes changed their opinions, and that different tutors had different opinions. While Mr. X was teaching his young men that their hope of being saved depended on conversion, Mr. Y might be assuring his pupils that grace was only to be had through the sacraments, and Mr. Z might adopt both positions in successive years.

Newman had no such scruples. What he believed, he would teach. Did he not believe it to be true? Was he not sure that the attainment of religious truth was the most important object in human life? What did it matter whether young men arrived at the truth by their own or somebody else's route, so long as they arrived at it? Undue influence? How could the *right* influence be too strongly exerted? Confident of his mission, as he told himself, he felt that 'the tutorial office was but another way, though not so heroic a way as a mission to idolaters, of carrying out his vow.' The thought that his own views might change even further than they had changed already was not allowed to enter his mind—in this connection. Yet, just as he was about to take up his new duties, he wrote to his mother in reply to her enthusiastic letters about his sermons:[1] 'Do not be run away with by any opinion of mine. I have seen cause to change my mind in some respects, and I may change again. I see I know very little about anything, though I often think I know a great deal. I have a great undertaking before me in the tutorship here. I trust God may give me grace to undertake it in a proper spirit, and to keep steadily in view that I have set myself apart for His service for ever.' Would he, then, warn his pupils that his opinions were liable to change? Of course he would not.

The idea of directly influencing young minds was altogether too attractive to Newman to be put in any danger by such considerations as these. And there were plenty of reasons to justify him. After all, Oxford still was, as it always had been, a place where men were supposed to be made 'fit to serve God in Church and State'; the Reformation made little difference to the monopoly of the Church in the ancient seats of learning. The Universities remained barred against Dissenters and Roman Catholics until Gladstone's Universities Tests Act of 1871. At Cambridge the barrier was sometimes lifted for Dissenters, though they were not allowed to take degrees. At Oxford all undergraduates were required to subscribe to the Thirty-nine Articles before they were matriculated, and to attend Holy Communion once a term. Not that Newman approved of this latter compulsion. On the contrary, it was horrible to him that young men should be compelled 'or even suffered as a matter of course' to receive the symbols of Christ's body and blood in the spirit of a schoolboy attending a roll-call. In this matter he was in direct opposition to Hawkins. There is a story told of F. W. H. Myers at the table of a successful man of business, asking his host after dinner if he believed in personal immortality and

[1] Mrs. Newman's letters have been quoted already. See page 8.

receiving the answer: 'Of course I believe in heaven and eternal bliss; but I do wish you wouldn't start such an unpleasant topic.' This is a nice inversion of the answer Newman received, when he told a colleague that it was the practice of certain undergraduates to celebrate their return from the Communion Table with a champagne breakfast. 'I don't believe it;' said the indignant don 'and, if it is true, I don't want to believe it.' One of the differences between Newman and most other Oxford men of his time was that once a fact had forced itself on his attention he could not rid his mind of it, however disagreeable it might be.

The overwhelming pressure of public opinion was gradually to break down these ecclesiastical barriers. The nation willed that the Universities should be, in fact, Universities— places of education for *all* men, of whatever creed or origin. The Church has been slow to relinquish her hold over forms, the trivial appearance of an authority long in fact extinct; Royal Commissions and University reformers have been tender to long-lived anachronisms. Every College still possesses its Church of England Chaplain and maintains its Church of England services. The rule that undergraduates must go to morning chapel on a certain number of weekdays, unless they were given special leave to attend a roll-call instead, has only been relaxed in recent years and still (I believe) obtains in some colleges. Until 1931 every undergraduate must pass an examination in Holy Scripture, unless he obtained exemption on grounds of conscience. Masters of Arts, of whatever race or creed, are still admitted to their degrees 'to the honour of our Lord Jesus Christ and the increase of most holy mother church' 'in the name of the Lord the Father the Son and the Holy Ghost.'[1] The great (and now for all practical purposes secular) educational foundation of Christ Church is still ruled by the Dean of the

[1] 'Ad honorem Domini nostri Jesu Christi et ad profectum sacrosanctae matris ecclesiae . . . . in nomine Domini Patris Filii et Spiritus Sancti.'

Cathedral Chapter. The visitors of more than half the Colleges are Bishops or Archbishops. The Faculty of Theology still takes pride of place; of its eight Professors, five are Canons of Christ Church and all except one are in the Orders of the Church of England. The appointment of the Select Preachers before the University is still a matter of high formal importance. The Vice-Chancellor and the Proctors, whether they be Jews or infidels, still attend, either in person or by proxy, the University Sermon on Sunday mornings in St. Mary's and the Latin Communion celebrated at the beginning of each term. Everywhere the usages of the Church are imposingly dominant. Oxford likes the taste of old wine too well; is too afraid of losing some subtle unanalysed residual value, to throw it away.   But the wine has lost its potency.

These observations are not so remote from Newman and his tutorship and the Tractarian Movement as they may have seemed. It was always obvious to Newman that once the gates of Oxford were opened to non-Churchmen, the close connection between the University and the Church would be destroyed. 'The admission of Dissenters' he wrote to Bowden in 1834, when the Dissenters University Admission Bill was before Parliament, 'would be a repeal, not of one, but of all our statutes.' It was the clear right and duty of the Church to fight for her monopoly over education. Then, as now, most Oxford men wanted things to remain as they were, but hesitated to draw unambiguous conclusions. 'Newman, on the contrary,' (to quote his own description of himself) 'when he had a clear view of a matter, was accustomed to formulate it, and was apt to be what Isaac Williams considered irreverent and rude in the nakedness of his analysis, and unmeasured and even impatient in enforcing it.' No two things could be more odious, in his eyes, than an insincere worship and a pasteboard church. The whole of the Oxford Movement was, in effect, a passionate assertion that the Church must rule or society cease to be Christian.

The opposition between the views of Newman and Hawkins existed from the beginning, but it was not obvious to either of them in 1826. It was, however, implicit in their attitudes to the vexed question, 'whether a college tutorship was or was not an engagement compatible with the ordination vow.' They both considered that it was compatible. Hawkins thought that it was no breach, but also no fulfilment, of his vow. Newman that it was one way, amongst others, of fulfilling his vow. But neither realized at first how deep the cleavage was; and it was not until the strength of Newman's religious influence began to show itself that Hawkins understood the danger which threatened Oriel.

A few days before Newman took up his new office, the annual Fellowship examination took place. Two candidates were elected—Robert Wilberforce and Richard Hurrell Froude. They were both undergraduates of Oriel. Both were to be amongst the new tutor's closest friends. Wilberforce was the second of the four sons of William Wilberforce, the great Evangelical philanthropist, whose bill for the abolition of slavery had become law twenty years earlier. He and his youngest brother Henry, also of Oriel, were to be swept, after Newman, into the Roman Church; leaving Samuel the third son ('Soapy Sam') to become Bishop of Oxford and of Winchester and *persona ingrata* to the Anglo-Catholics. Of Froude Newman as yet knew little, but had heard a good deal. Writing to his mother on the morrow of the election, Newman called him 'one of the acutest and clearest and deepest men in the memory of man'. But their intimacy was not to ripen for another couple of years.

It was very soon understood in Oriel that the new tutor meant business. He was out of his shell and not afraid of speaking his mind to anybody. He spoke it most clearly to the gentlemen commoners, whom he considered to be the scandal and ruin of the place, as well as to those of his colleagues who treated these idle and dissolute youngsters with special indulgence. Perhaps he remembered their arrogant ill manners towards him when he sat next them at table, as a tongue-tied probationer. If so, he had his revenge now. He treated them 'with a haughtiness which incurred their bitter resentment.' Of the relationship which he found to exist between tutors and undergraduates he wrote in his diary, at the end of the first month: 'There is much in the system which I think wrong; I think the tutors see too little of the men, and there is not enough of direct religious instruction. It is my wish to consider myself as the minister of Christ. Unless I find that opportunities occur of doing spiritual good to those over whom I am placed, it will become a grave question whether I ought to continue in the tuition.'

Characteristically he set about creating his own opportunities. His first step was to go outside the round of routine lectures to classes of undergraduates, which most College tutors in those days took to be the beginning and end of their duty. Men reading for honours used to hire private tutors for themselves. When Mark Pattison came up to Oriel in 1832 the great days of Newman's tutorship were over, and the bad old methods had re-established themselves. 'A college lecture in those days' Pattison complained 'meant the class construing, in turns, some twenty lines of a classical text to the tutor, who corrected you when you were wrong. Of the value as intellectual gymnastic of this exercise there can be no question; the failure as education lay in the circumstance, that this one exercise was about the whole of what our teachers ever attempted to do for us.' Pattison was obliged to hire his own tutors, chose them badly, and failed to get a first class in the Schools.

Such a state of affairs was intolerable to Newman. No other man should come between himself and his own pupils, doing the work that he was there to do and robbing him of his influence. He was not strong enough yet to reform the whole College. But the pupils allotted to him were his own property. If they showed any reasonable promise, no trouble was too great for him to take over them. He was not content to help them in their reading. 'With such youths' he wrote of himself 'he cultivated relations, not only of intimacy but of friendship, and almost of equality, putting off as much as might be the martinet manner then in fashion with college tutors, and seeking their society in outdoor exercise on evenings and in Vacation.' Like Pattison in his best period, he discovered in himself a peculiar genius for charming young men. Very soon he had a devoted following, with the result that 'when he became vicar of St. Mary's in 1828, the hold he had acquired over them led to their following him on to sacred ground, and receiving directly religious instruction from his sermons; but, from the first, independently of St. Mary's, he had set himself in his tutorial work the aim of gaining souls to God.' One of his first pupils was Tom Mozley, who was to marry his sister Harriett and write his chaotic and inaccurate *Reminiscences* of Oriel and the Oxford Movement. Mozley found his new tutor 'very attentive and obliging' and abounding in good advice.

After the overwork of the previous year, 'the delight of having but one business' was very great. 'No one can tell' he confessed to Harriett 'the unpleasantness of having matters of different kinds to get through at once. We talk of its *distracting* the mind; and its effect upon me is, indeed, a *tearing* or *ripping open* of the coats of the brain and the vessels of the heart.' No literary millstone hung round his neck. He had an absorbingly interesting job, and he was doing it extraordinarily well. His *Life of Apollonius* and *Essay on Scripture Miracles* had given him the beginnings of a public reputation. He preached, in July, his first University Sermon. 'It was to me' he said in the *Apologia*, writing of this time, 'like the feeling of spring weather after winter.' His religious opinions had ceased for the moment to trouble him. He was in a state of temporary equilibrium. True, there was something a little disconcerting about Froude. He took the brilliant youth for a walk, and was told to read a book which had just appeared, called *Letters on the Church by an Episcopalian*. Froude said that it would make his blood boil. Newman read it, and found that his blood boiled very pleasingly. The anonymous author argued, firstly, that the Church ought to be completely independent of the State, neither interfering with the proper domain of the other; secondly, that the Church was entitled to retain her revenues, even if she became independent. Opinion said that the author was Whately. 'It was certainly' thought Newman 'a most powerful composition. One of our common friends [common, that is, to himself and Froude] told me, that, after reading it, he could not keep still, but went on walking up and down the room.' It was indeed an exciting idea, that the Church might have all the benefits of the Establishment and none of the disadvantages.

Altogether 1826 was a happy year, perhaps the happiest in his whole life. He made up his mind to read the Fathers right through, and commissioned Pusey in Berlin to buy them for him, nothing daunted by Jemima's comment that it had taken Archbishop Ussher eighteen years to carry out the same programme. Perhaps the resolution was a protest of conscience against a certain slackening of his ideals. He was 'beginning to prefer intellectual excellence to moral'. So at least he believed when he wrote his *Apologia*. But the preference was not unduly marked. He was on his guard against 'the danger of the love of literary pursuits assuming too prominent a place' in his thoughts. Life, he told his mother, in an apology for seeing so little of her, 'is no time for enjoyment, but for labour, and I have especially deferred ease and quiet for a future life in devoting myself to the service of God.' Nor did his advice to Harriett, in search of something to do, suggest that secular interests were occupying too much of his mind. She was to compare St. Paul's speeches in the Acts with his Epistles; and to make a tabular comparison of the

doctrines conveyed in the teaching of Christ, St. Peter, St.
John and St. Paul.

With his fifteen-year-old sister Mary his correspondence
was in a lighter vein. 'Dear John,' she wrote breathlessly, 'how
extremely kind you are. Oh, I wish I could write as fast as I
think. . . . I wish I *could* see your rooms. Are they called generally by the titles you give them? I hope the "brown room" is
not quite so grave as the name would lead one to suppose. . . .
I did not imagine, John, that with all your tutoric gravity,
and your brown room, you could be so absurd as your letter
(I beg your pardon) seems to betray.'

The cup of family satisfaction was filled to overflowing by
Frank's brilliant double first in June. John addressed his
brother in a set of verses upon his birthday, June 27:

> Dear Frank, we both are summon'd now
>   As champions of the Lord;—
> Enroll'd am I, and shortly thou
>   Must buckle on thy sword;
> A high employ, nor lightly given
> To serve as messengers of heaven!

2. THE BEGINNINGS OF LEADERSHIP

Newman was unwell during the summer term. An invitation from Rickards to act as his *locum tenens* at Ulcombe
offered exactly the kind of rest that he could enjoy with a clear
conscience. He took Harriett with him, to keep house in the
Rectory, and there for two months or so lived like any
bachelor country clergyman, 'commencing Hebrew' in the
fashion set by Pusey, pottering about the garden, and giving
Harriett his attention when she came into his study with her
domestic problems—as she very frequently did. With a good
deal of satisfaction he wrote and told Keble and Jemima all
about the Hebrew. His method was characteristic. He made
no attempt to get any preliminary idea of the language, but
plunged straight into the task of reading Genesis in Hebrew
with the use of a crib—the Greek version in the Septuagint.

At Ulcombe in August he preached the sermon which stands first in the first volume of his *Parochial Sermons*. It was on the same text as Pusey's first sermon at Badger Hall: 'Holiness, without which no man shall see the Lord.' Written for delivery to a country congregation, a little retouched later, it is a simple, on the whole unrhetorical, composition. Its theme is the necessity of holiness, if a man is to go to heaven. Holiness cannot be acquired in a day, or by any sudden change of mind and heart. Good actions are nothing, except that they are the only means of inducing holiness. Holiness is 'a frame and temper of mind'. Just as no one who has not got this temper can be happy in a church, so he cannot hope to be happy in heaven. For heaven is like a church; and, as he rightly says, would be hell to an irreligious man. And he draws a vivid imaginative picture of 'a man of earthly dispositions and tastes, thrust into the society of saints and angels', wandering forlornly through the courts of heaven and shuddering under 'that Eye of holiness, which is joy and life to holy creatures', but seems to him 'an Eye of wrath and punishment'.

Readers of Swedenborg's *Heaven and Hell* will see a startling resemblance between this imagination of Newman's and the pictorial visions of Swedenborg. But the Swedish seer's conception of the future life had a breadth and humanity wholly absent from Newman's. The latter never grew beyond a savage demarcation of heaven and hell—the one all bliss, the other all misery; never saw any prospect, for the great bulk of mankind, but of eternal punishment, however he might try 'in various ways to make that truth less terrible to the reason'. He dared not 'set bounds to God's mercy and power in cases of repentance late in life'; but 'God cannot change His nature', and no man could be saved who had not achieved holiness in his earthly life. To Swedenborg, on the other hand, holiness was rather a latent than an actual condition of the soul during life. An ordinary human being underwent, at death, a process of transmutation; all that was of value was taken into full account; a kind of balance was struck, and the transfigured soul thenceforward inhabited that state, in heaven or in hell, for which it was eternally fitted and where it could find most happiness or least misery. Even in hell, as Swedenborg saw it, there might be pleasurable occupation, if not happiness; and even in the highest spheres of heaven the happiness of the saints could not be perfect, but was subject to a periodical dimming. Swedenborg's system, in spite of its strange apocalyptic form, is as strictly logical as Newman's. If Newman had been brought into contact with it, at this period of his life when his opinions were in flux, it must have fascinated and might have deeply influenced him.

There are several points of special interest about this sermon at Ulcombe. First, it shows how definitely Newman had now abandoned the Evangelical doctrine of sudden conversion. Secondly, it shows to perfection (what so brief a summary can only suggest) the close, relentless, transparently clear logic, never slurring a point, never giving the hearer time to formulate objections, which, combined with his mastery of rhetoric and his magical delivery, gave him a more complete command over his congregations than any other English preacher has ever possessed. Other men have known better how to stir up a sudden tempest of emotions; others have argued as skilfully; but few, if any, have equalled him in the art of using reason as a lever for the prising of hearts. He was too consummate a master of a too subtle art, for his practice to be capable of easy reduction to a formula. But there was one specially favoured and specially effective device, of which the Ulcombe sermon is a good example—the device of fear. Fear is the driving-force of his arguments. Looking at the technical structure of the sermon, I call it—I think rightly—a device. But in using it, he was using upon others what had most influenced himself. This was the inheritance from Evangelicalism which he was never able to discard, by which he was always to be distinguished from those happier spirits to whom the tidings of the Gospel were kindly tidings. Again and again in his sermons it seems as if he had to force himself to speak of God's love and mercy. The assurance of these is less real to him than the fear of condemnation and wrath. The fact of sin, its heinousness, its inconceivably ghastly consequences in the world to come—it is when he speaks of such topics as these that he speaks most obviously from the heart and with most effect. Love and mercy come in, most often, as half-reluctant afterthoughts. And so, after telling the rustics of Ulcombe how far distant was the multitude of men from that holiness, which he had painted in sublimely impossible colours and held out to them as the absolute prerequisite of salvation (and assuredly his congregation, except for the Rectory party, to a man belonged to that multitude), he begins reluctantly to hedge: 'I wish to speak to you, my brethren, not as if aliens from God's mercies, but as partakers of His gracious covenant in Christ.' This would do for Ulcombe. For his Oxford readers something a little stronger was needed. So he adds, in the second edition: 'and for this reason in especial peril, since those only can incur the sin of making void His covenant, who have the privilege of it. Yet neither do I speak to you' (he is addressing Ulcombe again) 'as wilful and obstinate sinners, exposed to the imminent risk of forfeiting, or the chance of having forfeited, your hope of heaven. But I fear . . .' Poor farmers and labourers, where were they? 'Be you content' he comforted them 'with nothing short of perfection; exert yourselves day by day to grow in knowledge and grace; that, if so be, you may at length attain to the presence of Almighty God.' Or did he, perhaps, add part of his final exhortation for the benefit of the University public, for which the sermon was printed?

The thickest root of Newman's religious life lay in an unanalysed, he would have said unanalysable, sentiment—a deep and terrifying sense of sin. In his first University sermon, preached a month earlier, he put his finger on the distinction,

as he saw it, between philosophy and religion. 'The philosopher confesses himself to be imperfect, the Christian feels
himself to be sinful and corrupt.' This sense of sin he shared,
of course, with religious men of all ages, and particularly with
his own contemporaries. But with him it came first and overshadowed everything else. It drove him, like a child running
from the terror of the dark to be comforted by its mother, into
the consolations of religion—into, finally, the arms of his
adopted Mother, the Church of Rome, and his Father, St.
Philip Neri. It is the dominant theme of sermon after sermon,
from the earliest to the latest. 'This secret dominion of sin'
was the subject of a parish sermon he preached while he was
still curate of St. Clement's. 'Who is there' he asked his congregation in 1832 'but would be sobered by an actual sight
of the flames of hell-fire and the souls therein hopelessly enclosed?' 'It is' he wrote in the *Apologia* 'because of the intensity of the evil which has possession of mankind, that a
suitable antagonist [i.e. the Church of Rome] has been provided against it.'

The Rickards's came back to Ulcombe before the Newmans left, and all four became instantly fast friends. Harriett
wrote and told her mother and Mary all the details of the
meeting, and how Mr. Rickards (who had a terrifying reputation as a judge of character) had put John through his
paces, and how she herself had a headache. Here is the delightful beginning of Mary's answer: 'I sit down, dear Harriett, in a frenzy of delight, sorrow, impatience, affection and
admiration; delight at your happiness, sorrow at your letter,
disappointment, impatience to see you, admiration at you all!
How much I should like to know Mr. and Mrs. Rickards!
And yet, I don't know, perhaps I should be afraid; but no, I
should not be afraid. O Harriett! I want to say such an
immense number of things, and I cannot say one. I will try to
be a little quiet; but how is it possible while Mamma is reading to Aunt your charming description of John's "ordeal"?

Poor girl with a headache, poor girl—"outrageous"; sweet girl! nice girl! dear girl! Oh, what shall I begin with?'

From Ulcombe Newman, leaving Harriett behind him, went to the Bowdens and then to Mudiford. 'A very bracing place,' he wrote to his mother 'and the air and bathing did me more good than the air and sea of Worthing or the Island. The sands are beautiful. The truth must be spoken. The air of Oxford does not suit me. I feel it directly I return to it.' News of his fellow-tutor, Tyler's, coming departure from Oxford had reached him. Copleston had already been appointed to the Bishopric of Llandaff. Clearly great changes were impending at Oriel. But, after Ulcombe and Mudiford and a Long Vacation for once spent away from business, he felt his spirits rise, as they always, 'most happily, rise at the prospect of danger, trial, or any call upon me for unusual exertion; and as I came outside the Southampton coach to Oxford, I felt as if I could have rooted up St. Mary's spire, and kicked down the Radcliffe.' An ominous jest. But no particular danger awaited him in Oxford. He went back happily to his pupils, and played the fiddle with Blanco White. 'He has an exquisite ear. I wish I could tempt him to Brighton.'

The first part of the next year (1827) passed very uneventfully. Toothache took him to London in February, where he looked up Bowden in Somerset House and found him 'prepared for my arrival by a notice in the *Morning Post* among the "fashionable arrivals" . . . Fine subject for quizzing for my pupils!' He gossiped easily to his mother. 'The new Bishop [Lloyd] presented himself in his wig in church last Sunday. He is much disfigured by it, and not known. People say he had it on hind part before.' In June a slight shadow falls across him—he finds that he cannot escape being an examiner in the Schools in the near future. And all is not going quite smoothly at Oriel. 'We are having rows as thick as blackberries.' He had 'hunted' two men out of the College in the previous month. But the tone of his letters home is light-hearted. 'What a thing it is to be vigorous, J. [Jemima], and to be dignified, H. [Harriett]. I am so dignified it is quite over-powering.' His party was beginning to grow round him. 'I cannot but feel most grateful to you for your kindness to me, which has indeed, I can say without affectation, been to me that of an elder brother' wrote Henry Wilberforce to his tutor, confessing his jealousy of another young man of whom Newman was making a good deal, 'while I am deprived of the advantage which, however, I prize, I believe, as much as he can.' This was Golightly, of whom the reader will hear again, at a later date.

In September Newman and Richard Wilberforce stayed at Ulcombe with the Rickards's, and Mrs. Rickards wrote admiringly to Harriett: 'I trust we shall keep John till he must go to Oxford. . . . His looks bespeak that he has been reading too hard. He was very tired all the evening, but we managed to talk a good deal, and R. Wilberforce was as merry as he generally is. This morning I was treated by all three gentlemen coming into the drawing-room after break-fast, when a long discussion began which lasted near two hours. . . . And now here is John come to keep me company, or rather to be plagued by the children. I wish you only could see him with both on his lap in the great armchair, pulling off and putting on his glasses.' On the following day, a Thursday, rainy and cold: 'We have actually fires in each sitting-room. The gentlemen are all together in the larger room employed upon the Epistle to the Romans. . . . I cannot describe to you the enjoyment I have in listening. There is no intellectual pleasure so great or any from which one ought to profit so much as such conversation. . . . We have read one of Keble's hymns all together and shall have more of them I hope.'

The hymns were *The Christian Year*, which had just been published.

From Ulcombe Newman went for a few days to stay with the Wilberforces at Highgate, and was 'much taken with Mr.

Wilberforce. It is seldom indeed we may hope to see such simplicity and unaffected humility, in one who has been so long moving in the intrigues of public life and the circles of private flattery.' In spite of his gradual drift away from Evangelicalism—the firmament in which William Wilberforce was the brightest star—he was still in sympathy with Evangelicals. In the strong religious atmosphere of Highwood he felt perfectly at home, with its daily morning and evening prayers fully as long as Matins and Evensong, and its homemade Sunday services attended by neighbours. The complete unworldliness of the old philanthropist was in accord with his own scale of values. The Wilberforce fortune was running out; the sons 'found themselves' as Mozley said 'moving adrift from the world they had belonged to.' But they were too devoted to their father and too unworldly themselves to feel the least resentment at the comparative poverty to which his generosity had reduced them.

They must have been a very attractive group of young men, honest and humorous and high-spirited. Robert was the quietest and most studious of the three brothers at Oriel, the most wrapped up in his friends; an intimate and colleague of Newman's, and a figure in the Movement, but never so close to the great man as his younger brother Henry. Whether, as he afterwards told a friend, it was true or not that he had suspicions, about this time, of Newman's sanity, it would seem that there was something in Newman's mind which he disliked and distrusted. And although, in the end, he too joined the Roman Church, his conversion was due to Manning's rather than to Newman's influence. But Henry, charming and impressionable and talkative, and equally unambitious, was from the first Newman's devoted and impudent pupil, follower and friend. 'That plague', 'that wretch', he is called affectionately in Newman's letters. The story of Newman's attitude over his marriage has been told already.[1] He

---

[1] See pages 28-9.

was slow to follow Newman to Rome—perhaps his marriage
held him back, for he was in orders and of course knew that
he must resign his ministry—but he and his wife went at
length. 'My dearest Henry', Newman called him, sparing as
he was of Christian names even to his closest friends. With
Samuel, the future Bishop, Newman was never on intimate or
familiar terms; and Tract 90 'gave the *coup de grâce*' to their
acquaintance. Samuel had a robust determination to make
his way in public life. He was cast in the mould of the leader,
not of the disciple. As Henry said, he was the kind of man
who was always on the platform at a public meeting and
always spoke.

Newman had no lectures in the autumn. He was set free
for his duties as an examiner in the Schools. The two recently
elected Fellows—Robert Wilberforce and Hurrell Froude—
were added to the tutorial staff, Pusey having refused to become a tutor. Wilberforce, Froude and Pusey were all dab-
bling at this time in liturgical studies—they went round to
Blanco White's lodgings to learn from the ex-priest the order
of the Roman Service of the Breviary. Newman was not yet
quite at this point. But he found his rooms full of the ancient
Fathers. 'Huge fellows they are, but very cheap—one folio
costs a shilling!' What with dipping into these irresistible
folios, and attending to his mother's troubles—we are not
told what these were; they may have been financial, or connected with the tiresome Charles; but, whatever they were,
'dear John Henry is, as usual, my guardian angel'—what with
these distractions, preparation for his examinership in the
Schools was being scamped. Oriel was humming, too, with
discussion about its new Provost. Copleston had been consecrated to his Bishopric and resigned the custody of Oriel.
Who was to succeed? In these discussions Newman took, of
course, a leading part.

3. SHOCK

On November 26 Newman, while examining in the schools, was suddenly taken ill. His collapse was apparently complete. He was at once 'leeched on the temples'. Robert Wilberforce took charge of him—perhaps it was then that he began to have doubts of Newman's sanity—and carried him off to Highwood to consult a Dr. Babington, who became his 'valued medical adviser' for many years. He stayed at first with the Wilberforces. By December 11 he thought himself well enough to return to Oxford, and wrote a very disingenuous account of his illness to his mother. 'I have been at Wilberforce's several days; finding myself tired with my Oxford work, he kindly proposed it and I accepted it.' But Mr. Babington put his foot down. His patient travelled to Brighton on December 14 and remained there until the end of January.

Very little indeed is known about this mysterious illness of Newman's. It made a profound impression upon his mind—'I was beginning to prefer intellectual excellence to moral: I was drifting in the direction of liberalism. I was rudely awakened from my dream at the end of 1827 by two great blows—illness and bereavement.' Does not the language of this passage in the *Apologia* suggest that the illness was not a mere physical illness? Is not this suggestion powerfully reinforced by the otherwise incomprehensible suspicions of Robert Wilberforce about his sanity? The illness was, almost beyond doubt, a hysterical breakdown, than which nothing can be more terrifying to a man of active mind or, to a man of Newman's type, seem more evidently a visitation of divine wrath. 'Where have I erred?' would be his private interrogatory, as he climbed back shudderingly from the abyss, so suddenly opened beneath his confident feet.

There were two conceivable answers. The first, hardly within the compass then of either Newman or Dr. Babington,

M   F.O.A.

was that he had betrayed his human inheritance, branded as sinful what had been given him in the course of nature, surrendered himself to a creed of fear, and had yet behaved as though there were no impediments to the free expenditure of every ounce of nervous energy. I do not say this was the right answer. I have already tried to suggest that the psychological laws which we have so far formulated do not adequately explain the behaviour of a Newman. The weakness of the answer is obvious at once. After his breakdown Newman went on as before, only more so, and with increased and increasing demands upon his nervous energy. Yet there was no further actual breakdown, in spite of the fact that the circumstances attending his secession to Rome were infinitely more painful and trying than the trivial immediate cause of his breakdown in November 1827, which was, certainly, his inability to play the part of an examiner as he felt it ought to be played. There may, evidently, have been secret factors at work in 1827 of which we know nothing at all. There must, if our psychologists are right, have been some powerful and deep-seated conflict, which necessitated collapse as the only way out of an intolerable situation. It is, at least, very curious that the second, and worse, collapse took place in the actual scene of his first collapse. *Then* he was an examinee, unable to do himself justice; *now* he was himself an examiner. Is there not, in that simple fact, given the morbid war between his members, enough to satisfy modern psychological theory?

Psychopathological breakdowns are never the result of a single cause; the apparent cause is 'the last straw that breaks the camel's back'. All his life Newman had lived under a continual strain; he was two men at once, the master and the servant, the one ambitiously determined to leave his mark upon the world, the other going in perpetual fear of consequences, the one always successful, the other always turning success into failure. These are crude verbal representations of a conflict, too subtle to be exactly described, in which each

half of his personality changed, like Proteus, in the very grasp
of the other. An observant friend told him once that he had
had a near escape of being a stutterer. Stuttering is a well-
known symptom of nervous strain. The 'near escape' is significant of Newman's peculiar power of preventing his repressions from wrecking his conscious life. For the most part the
conflict remained out of sight. Sometimes it emerged into
consciousness, in the form of a struggle between self-will and
obedience to the will of God. It was generally possible, then,
to effect a reconciliation; it was the will of God that he should
be an active minister of the Gospel. But these periods of, so
to speak, sanctified success always came to a more or less
catastrophic end; the servant found some new way of betraying the master. The first period of his tutorship ended in a
nervous breakdown; the second period in a losing battle with
the Provost; the leadership of the 'Movement' in the abandonment of his whole position; his whole history in the Roman
Church was one long series of enthusiastic advances and painful failures. The blame for these failures is put by his biographer on outside causes, such as the counter-scheming of
Cardinal Manning; but part of it at least rested with Newman himself, in that the whole man was never engaged in the
advance. He went forward with an absurd disregard of facts;
caution stayed behind, with his other self. Only at the very
end of his life, sitting enthroned at Trinity in his Cardinal's
robes and receiving the ladies of Oxford 'in semi-royal state',
enjoying the pomp without the reality of power, was he suffered to remain in the eyes of the world at the height of his
achievement.

In the Schools in 1827 the conflict between success and
failure took a ludicrously trivial and yet temporarily disastrous form. For two years his masterful self had had a clear
run. He had been building up a position of authority and
dignity and influence over others. 'I am so dignified it is quite
overpowering.' The idea of examining in the Schools was

distasteful to him; he did not want to do it, but he had to give
way. Why was he so reluctant? He could not have explained.
The *work* was nothing. Any reasonably well-equipped college
tutor could take it in his stride. Beyond doubt the reason for
his reluctance was that the Schools were associated with his
extraordinary collapse in 1820. He must revisit that scene,
and strut on its stage in false colours, and he must go through
the whole business without any religious sanction. As a tutor,
he could always tell himself that he was carrying out his
ordination vow. As examiner he was a purely secular official.
How could he sit in judgment upon others, when he had been
found wanting himself? The conflict, so nakedly present, was
irresolvable, except by flight. Flight was out of the question.
A breakdown, complete enough to make return impossible,
was the inevitable result.

Such, at any rate in general outline, would be a modern
psychologist's answer to the self-questioning of the convales-
cent. There is no hint that any idea of the kind suggested
itself to Newman. This ghastly glimpse of the abyss was a
direct warning from God that he had been travelling upon
the wrong road. This was the kind of thing that happened to
a man when he began to think for himself, 'to prefer intellectual excellence to moral'. He had been wanting in obedience to God's will. That will must have been clearly expressed, or how could he be punished for not following it?
The dangerous path of independent thought must be re-
traced. Fortunately he had not travelled very far along it.
To what point must he go back? Not, certainly, to Evangelicalism. The logic of Hawkins, the saintliness of Pusey, had
made that refuge impossible. To what, then, but God's
visible Church, overlaid by human error, but still surely to be
discovered by one now so desperately in need of authoritative
guidance? And his pupils? Had he been honestly discharging
his sacred mission towards them? Was it not his duty to re-
double his spiritual efforts on their behalf? On some such

lines as these his thoughts must have been moving as he
journeyed down to Brighton on December 14. But his diary
and his letters tell us nothing. We have only the course of
events to use in our reconstruction, and that strange sentence in the *Apologia*: 'I was rudely awakened from my dream
at the end of 1827 by two great blows—illness and bereavement.'

At Brighton he found his mother and his three sisters—
Jemima and Mary returned from a visit to Ulcombe. 'It is
enough' Mary had written to him on the day after he was
taken ill 'to make one feel glad only to look at Mr. Rickards
and Mrs. Rickards makes me laugh so. . . . O John! how
absurd of me to tell you all this, which you know. How I long
to see you! . . . I can fancy your face—there, it is looking at
me.' And a week later, having got back to Brighton, she
wrote to her brother again (not, of course, knowing that he
was ill) telling him how Mr. Rickards had advised her to read
a number of earnest books and to turn "Telemachus" into
verse. Poor Mary! How determined they all were to make an
earnest young lady of her! 'I am so impatient to see you. How
long is it before you come? Can it be three, nearly four weeks?
I think it seems longer since I saw you than ever before. . . .
Dearest John, your most affectionate sister, M. S. N.'

Mary was the best medicine for John in this strange mental
agony of his, about which he dared not speak to anyone. But
Brighton held another distraction—Pusey, recovering like
Newman from a breakdown of health. And there was this
important topic of the Provostship to discuss. Who should
succeed Copleston? It must be either Keble or Hawkins.
There was no one else in the running, except Tyler. But
Tyler, to his own bitter chagrin, was held to have lost his
chance by his recent acceptance of the London rectory of
St. Giles-in-the-Fields. The two friends consulted earnestly
together and decided that they must vote for Hawkins. Pusey
had, in fact, already written to Keble and told him so. New-

man followed suit, with a longer and considerably more tact-ful letter, to which Pusey added a postscript. This done, New-man settled down to spend a quiet Christmas with his family, and to formulate his New Year resolutions in the light of the lesson which he supposed himself to have learned.

Early in the New Year, on January 3, two visitors came to stay with the Newmans, Maria and Fanny Giberne. Maria Giberne was a sister-in-law of the Rev. Walter Mayers, New-man's old schoolmaster and friend—a tall dark handsome girl, an artist, a good talker and letter-writer, and a warm admirer of Newman. She followed him into the Roman Church, became a nun, 'Sister Maria Pia', and died in a con-vent at Autun in 1885.

The following account of the tragedy of January 5 is taken from a letter written by Sister Maria Pia to Cardinal Newman more than fifty years later.

'I forget about the dinner and evening on that day for I was doubtless under considerable awe of you in those first days; but the next day Mr. Woodgate and Mr. Williams dined there, and dear Mary sat next you, and I was on the other side; and while eating a bit of turkey she turned her face to-wards me, her hand on her heart, so pale, and a dark ring round her eyes, and she said she felt ill, and should she go away? I asked you and she went: I longed to accompany her, but dared not for fear of making a stir. It was the last time I saw her alive. Soon after Jemima went after her; and then your Mother, looking so distressed, and she said, "John, I never saw Mary so ill before; I think we must send for a doctor." You answered as if to cheer her, "Ah, yes, Mother, and don't forget the fee.". . . Next morning Harriett came to walk with us about one o'clock—after the doctor had been, I think—but though she said Mary had had a very bad night, she did not seem to apprehend danger. We went to dine with a friend, and only returned to your house about nine. I felt a shock in entering the house, seeing no one but you—so pale

and so calm, and yet so inwardly moved; and how, when I
asked you to pray with us for her, you made a great effort to
quiet your voice, sitting against the table, your eyes on the
fire, and you answered, "I must tell you the truth; she is dead
already.". . . You told us a little about her, with gasping
sobs in your voice, and then you left us.'

In this way fell the hammer of God for the second time.

4. ST. MARY'S PULPIT

Newman made a fatiguing journey back to Oxford, and
arrived at Oriel a day or two before the election of Provost
Hawkins.

The election was merely formal. There was no other candidate. Keble had withdrawn. Newman's influence was
evidently decisive. If he had supported Keble, such was his
ascendancy now in the College that Keble would probably
have been elected. He preferred Hawkins because he knew
Hawkins well, and had an affectionate respect for him, while
Keble was hardly more than an acquaintance; Hawkins was
a disciplinarian and a man of method and business, Keble
was not; he supposed Hawkins to think much as he did on
religious and College and University matters, and Keble to
think very differently. When Froude urged 'that Keble, if
Provost, would bring in with him quite a new world, that
donnishness and humbug would be no more in the College,
nor the pride of talent, nor an ignoble secular ambition', he
merely laughed and said they were only electing a Provost,
not an angel. And when a former Fellow, described by
Mozley as 'a quaint patriarchal man, with a century of
wisdom on his still young shoulders', wrote 'You don't know
Hawkins as well as I do. He will be sure to disappoint you', he
paid no attention to the warning. Nor did he ever regret his
action; for it made him Vicar of St. Mary's and gave him a
new power of influencing Oxford; it led to the loss of his tutor-

ship, and therefore left him free to devote his time to the Church; and so it led to the Tracts and the Movement, and in the end to Rome. Pusey, on the contrary, mourned over it to the end of his life.

At first all seemed to be going excellently. At the end of the new Provost's first year Newman wrote to Rickards defending Hawkins against ill-natured criticism. 'If X. has railed to you, don't believe him. We have gone through the year famously.' The number of the hated gentlemen commoners had been reduced by more than half. The 'incurables' were sent down for good. Discipline was tightened up all round. 'Unprepared candidates' were refused admission. The Chapel sermon at the Sacrament was revived. The lecture system was entirely reorganized. First classes were once more looming in the offing. It was true that the Provost did not seem to be in very good spirits. 'He has not (nor should a Head) taken the initiative in these innovations, but has always approved— sometimes kept abreast with us—and at Collections has slain the bad men manfully.'

Hawkins, it is clear, had begun to feel that he was being driven by his team of tutors a good deal faster and farther than he wanted to go. No doubt first classes were excellent things. But after all Oriel did not exist to gain a brace or so of first classes every year. Hawkins recalled that Copleston was apt to be sarcastic about 'the quackery of the Schools'. Copleston had had no qualms about the state of Oriel, whether the Fellows or the undergraduates. Were things really so bad as Newman made out? Was it really a sound move to frighten all the men of good family away? Hawkins's sensitive nostrils sniffed the reforming breeze. There was surely a strange heretical smell in it, faint but extremely disagreeable.

It was in March, 1828, that the new Provost resigned the living of St. Mary's, and Newman was appointed Vicar in his place.

EDWARD HAWKINS
PROVOST OF ORIEL 1828-1882
*From the painting by Sir Francis Grant
in the possession of Oriel College*

The Church of St. Mary the Virgin stands, as all the world that has visited Oxford knows, in the very centre of the town in the High Street, between All Souls and Brasenose. It is commonly called the University Church, because it is used for the University sermons, which are preached every Sunday morning in full term and on certain other occasions by the Divinity Professors or the so-called Select Preachers in rotation 'before the University'. It is also the scene of the biennial Bampton Lectures and of a Latin Communion when term is about to open. But in fact St. Mary's is not a University Church at all. It is an ordinary church, with a parish in the middle of Oxford; and the advowson belongs to Oriel, whose founder Adam de Brome was Rector of St. Mary's in the early fourteenth century.

Up to the time of Newman's appointment the Vicar of St. Mary's had been content with 'the High Street shopkeepers and their housemaids' who formed the staple of his congregations. But Newman, whether by accident or design, changed all this. His pupils at Oriel naturally, as he put it, followed him on to sacred ground. He could not help writing his sermons with them in his mind. His reputation as a preacher grew with astonishing swiftness. Other undergraduates from other Colleges caught the contagion from Oriel. Young dons followed suit. In a short space of time the Sunday afternoon service and sermon at St. Mary's became a *de facto* University institution far better attended and more influential than the University sermon of the morning. There were those at Oxford who resented this bitterly—among them possibly the previous Vicar, certainly the new Vicar's own brother. The English public, at large, even many of the country clergy, got it into their heads that Newman preached in the University Church by University appointment. 'This natural mistake' Frank complained indignantly 'immensely enhanced his importance.' Frank Newman, now a Fellow of Balliol, went regularly to hear his brother in the pulpit, but never gained from his sermons 'the instruction or the pleasure that others did. *Distrust had sunk roots too deep.*' The old apostate viciously underlined the last six words.

These sermons at St. Mary's continued over a period of fifteen years, from Newman's induction in 1828 to his resignation in 1843, with only an occasional break. Many of them were collected in the seven volumes of his *Plain and Parochial Sermons.* Some of Newman's characteristics as a preacher have been noticed already. But no reader can form an accurate impression, whether of his art or of his message, if he leaves the sermons themselves unread. I have said that the message was, in the main, a message of fear; and that the use of fear to carry the pauseless argument home was his most favourite device. It is but fair to quote a contrary opinion. 'A tone, not of fear, but of infinite pity,' declared J. A. Froude 'runs through them all, and along with it a resolution to look facts in the face; not to fly to evasive generalities about infinite mercy and benevolence, but to examine what revelation really has added to our knowledge, either of what we are or what lies before us.'[1] The contradiction is perhaps not so flat as it may seem. In Newman's subtle technique pity was only a variant of fear. The facts which the preacher looked in the face were facts, as he believed, of terrible urgency. The consequence of disobedience was dreadful and certain. His humanity pitied those who refused to live as he bade them; his theology allowed them no hope. He might, in his softer moments, lead his congregation to 'imagining by a stretch of fancy the feelings of those who, having died in faith, wake up to enjoyment.' But the enjoyment of heaven was not to be purchased by the enjoyment of earth. And the unspeakable excellence of the lot which awaited the few bore, on its re-

---

[1] *Short Studies*, iv. 200. Since the above was written I have noticed a passage in a letter of F. W. Faber's, written in 1836, explaining his reconstruction of his religious beliefs under Newman's influence. 'Under God's grace, I will raise my superstructure of love upon a solid groundwork of holy *fear*—the *beginning* of wisdom, the persuader of men.'

verse side, the unspeakable misery of the lot which awaited
the many.

I have suggested, also, that the sermons are rich not only in
logic but in rhetoric—meaning by the word not a florid use of
language for its own sake, but the exquisitely simple literary
art which gives body to abstract argument without seeming
to do so, and concentrates itself every now and then into
some specially moving illustration. It is fair, again, to quote
the contrary opinion of Professor Stewart, who thinks the
style of Newman's preaching in his Anglican days deliberately 'austere, unadorned, even bald'. At first sight the sermons may have this look. But the art—the rhetorical art—is
there, in the very baldness of the carefully phrased and
grouped sentences, in the sudden illumination which one
sentence will give to all the rest, one paragraph to the argument which has gone before; and it is the more effective because it is unobtrusive. I open a volume at random, and find
such a sentence as this: 'We are two or three selves at once,
in the wonderful structure of our minds, and can weep while
we smile, and labour while we meditate.' Or this: 'Had we
no bodies, and were a revelation made to us that there was a
race who had bodies as well as souls, what a number of powerful objections should we seem to possess against that revelation!' Or this: 'Still there is joy in heaven, though no echo of
it reaches the earth.' Or I find such a passage as the following,
with its evident memory of a horror which had hung over his
own mind in November 1827, and must have been familiar to
many of his overstrained hearers:

'For one instant a horrible dread overwhelmed Him, when
He seemed to ask why God had forsaken him. Doubtless
"that voice was for our sakes". . . . Perhaps it was intended to
set before us an example of a special trial to which human
nature is subject, whatever was the real and inscrutable manner of it in Him, who was all along supported by an inherent
Divinity; I mean that of sharp agony, hurrying the mind on

to vague terrors and strange, inexplicable thoughts; and is, therefore, graciously recorded, for our benefit, in the history of His death, "who was tempted, in all points, like as we are, yet without sin."'

Or, to take one further illustration (worth quoting not only as a piece of almost perfect figurative prose, but for its bearing on the preacher's own thought):

'Such is the City of God, the Holy Church Catholic throughout the world, manifested in and acting through what is called in each country the Church visible; which visible Church really depends solely on it, on the invisible,—not on civil power, not on princes or any child of man, not on endowments, not on its numbers, not on anything that is seen, unless indeed heaven can depend on earth, eternity on time, Angels on men, the dead on the living. The unseen world through God's secret power and mercy encroaches upon this; and the Church that is seen is just that portion of it by which it encroaches; and thus though the visible Churches of the Saints in this world seem rare, and scattered to and fro, like islands in the sea, they are in truth but the tops of the everlasting hills, high and vast and deeply rooted, which a deluge covers.'

Of the manner of the preacher, and of the extraordinary effect which his sermons had upon the young men who flocked to hear him, there is no lack of evidence. The best account, perhaps, is Principal Shairp's.[1] Shairp's description refers to the late 'thirties, but it is equally applicable to the whole period of Newman's vicarship.

'The service was very simple,—no pomp, no ritualism . . . the most remarkable thing was the beauty, the silver intonation, of Mr. Newman's voice, as he read the Lessons. It seemed to bring new meaning out of the familiar words. . . . When he began to preach, a stranger was not likely to be

---

[1] *Studies in Poetry and Philosophy*. But I have taken the quotation from Ward's *Life of Newman*.

much struck, especially if he had been accustomed to pulpit oratory of the Boanerges sort. Here was no vehemence, no declamation, no show of elaborated argument, so that one who came prepared to hear "a great intellectual effort" was almost sure to go away disappointed. . . . The delivery had a peculiarity which it took a new hearer some time to get over. Each separate sentence, or at least each short paragraph, was spoken rapidly, but with great clearness of intonation; and then at its close there was a pause lasting for nearly half a minute; and then another rapidly but clearly spoken sentence, followed by another pause. It took some time to get over this, but, that once done, the wonderful charm began to dawn on you. . . . He laid his finger—how gently, yet how powerfully!—on some inner place in the hearer's heart, and told him things about himself he had never known till then. Subtlest truths, which it would have taken philosophers pages of circumlocution and big words to state, were dropt out by the way in a sentence or two of the most transparent Saxon. . . . And the tone of voice in which they were spoken, once you grew accustomed to it, sounded like a fine strain of unearthly music. Through the silence of that high Gothic building the words fell on the ear like the measured drippings of water in some vast dim cave.'

This general description fails only to do justice to the occasions when the preacher exercised his full power of moving his hearers. This was all the more tremendous for being commonly held in reserve. Such an occasion is vividly described by J. A. Froude. Newman had been picturing the incidents of Christ's passion. 'Then he paused. For a few moments there was a breathless silence. Then, in a low clear voice, of which the faintest vibration was audible in the farthest corner of St. Mary's, he said, "Now I bid you recollect that He to Whom these things were done was Almighty God." It was as if an electric shock had gone through the church, as if every person present understood for the first time the meaning of what he had all his life been saying.'

At this date the Vicar of St. Mary's was also responsible for the cure of Littlemore, a village lying on the high ground above Iffley, three miles to the east of Oxford. There was no church or chapel at Littlemore, and no means of serving the parishioners except by house-to-house visiting. The new Vicar took this part of his work no less seriously than the rest. Almost every day he rode or walked to Littlemore; 'almost always' says Mozley 'with some young friend, who greatly valued the privilege.' Frank, in spite of his growing distrust of his brother's opinions and his own movement to the left, used to help him at first by going out to Littlemore himself. The sight of Newman striding rapidly in his black tail-coat along the road towards Iffley was one which became very familiar to Oxford men during these fifteen years. Other men might have found the walk becoming monotonous, even though the Iffley road a hundred years ago was a winding country lane, instead of the dull suburban thoroughfare it is to-day. But Newman loved it. Every yard of it became a part of himself. He trod it in every variety of mood, from confidence to despair, down to the day when he turned his back upon Oxford and stumbled blindly along it, wetting his companion's hand with his tears.

So Newman was again living two lives at once. The occupation of his mind with the double work of the tutorship and St. Mary's prevented him from dwelling too much on the loss of his youngest sister. But whenever the pressure slackened the sense of desolating grief took its place. The tears welled up, whenever he thought of her. It agonized him that he and his sisters could only talk of Mary in the third person as if she were no more than a stick or a stone. He urged Jemima (who, like himself, had a passion for dates and anniversaries and past things) to write down all the trivial things she could remember of her sister, so that they might keep the

memory, at least, of her personality alive. To his mother, however, the young Vicar wrote with his usual careful avoidance
of depressing topics. 'I take most vigorous exercise, which
does me much good. I have learned to leap (to a certain
point) which is a larking thing for a don. The exhilaration
of going quickly through the air is for my spirits very good.'
He meant, of course, jumping on horseback, not with his own
long legs, though imagination abandons the latter vision with
extreme unwillingness. Out riding every day, by his doctor's
orders, in the lovely month of May, he felt the beauty of the
countryside with an almost painful intensity. 'I wish it were
possible for words to put down those indefinite, vague and
withal subtle feelings which quite pierce the soul and make it
sick. Dear Mary seems embodied in every tree and hid behind
every hill.' Still, in June, 'not one half-hour passes but dear
Mary's face is before my eyes'; and when, in November, he is
taking his solitary morning ride, 'I have learned to like dying
trees and black meadows—swamps have their grace and fogs
their sweetness. A solemn voice seems to chant from everything. I know whose voice it is—her dear voice.' How much
of Newman is in that 'solemn voice'! Because Mary was dead,
she must be thought of no more as the gay spontaneous child,
whose breathless letters to her adored brother touch the
stranger's heart to read after a hundred years. All that made
her humanly lovable must be discarded now. She is holy.

CHAPTER VI
SECRET FORCES

I. FROUDE AND ISAAC WILLIAMS

How real was Newman's love for Mary? The answer, if one goes by the book, would have to be that he loved her because she so ardently loved him. On her birthday, in 1826, he never troubled to write to her. He put his birthday wishes into a letter to Harriett. 'Pray wish Mary, from me, many happy returns of this day, and tell her I hope she will grow a better girl every year, and I think her a good one. I love her very much; but I will not say (as she once said to me) I love her better than she loves me.' He took her, poor Mary, while she lived, as so much impressible human material. In the stilted poem *Consolations in Bereavement* which he sent to Harriett in the April after her death, the thought is more for the living than the dead. Perhaps that is as it should be, given the title of the poem. But it is hard not to feel a little impatience with the egotism of the postscript: 'It goes to my heart to think that dear Mary herself, in her enthusiastic love of me, would so like them [the lines of the poem] could she see them, because they are mine. May I be patient! It is so difficult to realize what one believes, and to make these trials, as they are intended, real blessings.'

Now, however, for the first and only time in his life Newman was to be tied in earnest to someone else's chariot wheels.

'Hurrell Froude' Lytton Strachey pronounced 'was a clever young man, to whom had fallen a rather larger share of self-assurance and intolerance than even clever young men usually possess. What was singular about him, however, was not so much his temper as his tastes. The sort of ardour which impels more normal youths to haunt Music Halls and fall in love with actresses took the form, in Froude's case, of a romantic devotion to the Deity and an intense interest in the state of his own soul.'

There is just enough truth in this thumbnail sketch to make it pass as a caricature. But in the art of biography caricatures, even good ones—and this is not a very good one—are bad substitutes for portraits. 'Human beings' Strachey prefaced his *Eminent Victorians* 'have a value which is eternal and must be felt for its own sake.' All the more reason, surely, for resisting the temptation to knock them down with a few clever phrases. The 'bright and beautiful Froude' whom his friends cherished in their memory is unrecognizable in the self-centred and disagreeable youth invented by the essayist's selective cunning. Froude's own friends tell a very different story.

'Froude was a man' said his younger contemporary Tom Mozley, speaking for all that wide circle, 'such as there are now and then, of whom it is impossible for those that have known him to speak without exceeding the bounds of common affection and admiration.' Lord Blachford's description[1] speaks of the 'delicate features and penetrating grey eyes, not exactly piercing, but bright with internal conception, and ready to assume an expression of amusement, careful attention, inquiry, or stern disgust, but with a basis of softness'; of the 'bright low laugh when gravity had been played out'; of his entire freedom from any false sentiment or odour of sanctity. Newman's account of his friend in the *Apologia* needs to be quoted at greater length.

'He was a man of the highest gifts—so truly many-sided, that it would be presumptuous in me to attempt to describe him, except under those aspects, in which he came before

[1] Church, *Oxford Movement*, pp. 50-56.

me. Nor have I here to speak of the gentleness and tenderness of nature, the playfulness, the free elastic force and graceful versatility of mind, and the patient winning considerateness in discussion, which endeared him to those to whom he opened his heart. . . . [It is in his intellectual aspect that] I speak of Hurrell Froude, as a man of high genius, brimful and overflowing with ideas and views, in him original, which were too many and strong even for his bodily strength, and which crowded and jostled against each other in their effort after distinct shape and expression. And he had an intellect as critical and logical as it was speculative and bold. Dying prematurely, as he did, and in the conflict and transition-state of opinion, his religious views never reached their ultimate conclusion, by the very reason of their multitude and depth.'

He goes on to enumerate some of these views: Froude's admiration of Rome, and hatred of the Reformers; his delight in the notion of a powerful independent hierarchical church; his contempt for purely Biblical religion; his reverence for Tradition; his 'high severe idea of the intrinsic excellence of Virginity' (the phrase which specially exasperated Strachey); his devotion to the Virgin and the Saints; his 'keen appreciation of the idea of sanctity'; his disposition to believe in 'a large amount of miraculous interference' in the early and middle ages; his faith in the Real Presence; his preference for the mediaeval church; his 'insight into abstract truth' coupled with a love of concrete facts; his interest in the classics, in philosophy and art and history and ecclesiastical politics; his 'eager courageous view of things' in general.

Newman indicates the gaps in this unusual range of interests. Froude, he says, had no turn for pure theology, no appreciation of the ancient Fathers or of doctrinal controversies and pronouncements. 'His power of entering into the minds of others did not equal his other gifts.' Mozley and Blachford add to the catalogue of omissions. He had no ear

for music, and no eye for colour; and though he was interested in architecture, and had 'a soul for beauty', he liked
architecture to be 'scientific'. The dome of the Pantheon at
Rome distressed him, because he thought it ought to have been
built to a catenary instead of a simple semicircular curve.
But Mozley adds, also, to the catalogue of his positive qualities. Above all things Froude was a hater of shams.

This hatred of shams was, indeed, the dominant feature of
his character. It was the determining cause of his passionate
High Churchmanship. As Newman put it, he was impatient
of 'the contrariety between theory and fact', between the
theory of the indivisible Church and her miserable subordination to a host of compromises. It was the cause, also, of the
painful efforts in self-discipline, recorded in his published
Remains. Lytton Strachey made the inevitable hilarious use of
the opportunity which the *Remains* gave him, but his hilarity
was nothing new. The enemies of the Tractarians rejoiced
with equal and not less effective malice. But Froude's *Remains*
(as we shall see) are not, to any reasonably humane reader, a
subject for easy sarcasms. If they are comedy at all, they are
tragi-comedy and make more for tears than for laughter.
Only a very shallow scepticism can extract mere amusement
from the spectacle of a mind endeavouring to be ruler in its
own house, in agony because it cannot control thought and
desire in little things as well as in great, just as impatient of
'the contrariety between theory and fact' within itself as in
the world at large. The effort at self-discipline was impossible,
and even a little absurd, but it was heroic. The results aimed
at may have been wrongly conceived; but they were honestly
conceived. If religion was real, was it altogether ridiculous
to try to be religious in fact as well as in theory? The contemporary critics who laughed at the *Remains* could do so
because they believed in the necessity for compromise between
their ideals and their instincts. The sneers of Lytton Strachey
are without that excuse. It is legitimate to mock at the ideal;

but to mock at the effort to realize the ideal is to beg the entire question.

The study of religion in action is a ludicrous beating of the wind, if the critic fails to understand that belief, whether it is right or wrong, whether it has been reached consciously or unconsciously, is in itself a rational state. No man of any worth can lock it up in a cupboard of his mind and go his own way. He must try to act upon it, or cease to be a coherent personality. Experience and reason may convince him that his belief is wrong; it may be forced into a new pattern or disintegrated altogether by the upward thrust of hidden forces whose right to existence it has refused to recognize. But so long as he has it, it must be dominant. I may criticize his intelligence for continuing to accept it, though my criticism will not be much to the point if it ignores or misstates the circumstances in which his belief was formed. But by treating belief as a pathological curiosity, unworthy of influencing his conscious actions, I defeat my own object of making the dead bones live. If I reduce the belief of a Newman or a Froude to a mere morbid symptom, I reduce them to puppets. And what are the *Eminent Victorians* but a diverting puppet-show, designed to tickle the self-conceit of a cynical and beliefless generation?

Richard Hurrell Froude was the son of the Venerable Robert Froude, Archdeacon of Totnes and Rector of Dartington in Devonshire. He was the eldest of a family of eight. Two of his younger brothers reached distinction; William, seven years his junior, who became a railway engineer and naval architect, and James, ten years younger than William, who achieved fame as a historian and essayist. Richard himself was born in 1803, and was two years younger than Newman.

The Archdeacon was a fine specimen of a Tory High Churchman of the old school. He was a landowner, a justice of the peace, a keen rider to hounds. But he was also an artist, an antiquary, a man of wide knowledge—'very amiable,' said

RICHARD HURRELL FROUDE
From the engraving by Edward Robinson
after the drawing by George Richmond

Keble, 'but provokingly intelligent, one quite uncomfortable to think of, making one ashamed of going gawking about the world as one is wont to do, without understanding anything one sees.' He ran his parish and the bench of magistrates and the whole countryside. Subtleties of doctrine left him uninterested. 'The Church itself he regarded as part of the constitution; and the Prayer Book as an Act of Parliament which only folly or disloyalty could quarrel with.' But, solid man as he was, he had no objection to exorcising a ghost; and it was not the act of a conventionalist to allow the publication of his son's *Remains*.

Richard's mother died some time between his seventeenth and twenty-second year. She was, according to Sir John Coleridge, 'very beautiful in person, and delicate in constitution, with a highly expressive countenance, and gifted in intellect with the genius and imagination which his father failed in.' Richard combined the qualities and perhaps the defects of both parents. He had his father's quick practical intelligence and retentive memory and impatience with fools; his mother's charm and sensibility, delicate physique, idealistic temperament and introspective habit.

He grew up tall, straight, very thin, restlessly active; dark haired, grey-eyed; handy with a tool or a pencil; passionately fond of sailing; 'absolutely unlike Newman in being always ready to skate, sail, or ride with his friends—and, if in a scrape, not pharisaical as to his means of getting out of it.' 'I remember,' wrote Lord Blachford 'e.g., climbing Merton gate with him in my undergraduate days, when we had been out too late boating or skating.' (This, by the way, was not in Froude's undergraduate days; he was then a tutor of Oriel.) In everything that he did he gave an impression of intense, enjoyed energy. He loved paradox, slang, exaggeration. Solemnity was a bubble to be pricked whenever opportunity offered. The hearty 'muscular Christianity' of a later day would have been a perfect target for his disrespectful irony.

He revelled in argument, which he practised without unnecessary regard for his opponent's feelings. If he had a
perverse pleasure, it was in shocking, not only his enemies,
but also his friends. But there was always a practical point in
his most violent *étourderies*. He told a pious Protestant friend,
who wanted to build a large church in a populous centre, that
for most of his parishioners a pudding was worth twenty
prayers. He scandalized the solemn and pedantic Palmer,
who was anxious to decorate some manifesto with a number
of dignified signatures, by declaring that he meant to dictate
to the clergy and had no intention of allowing anyone else to
get on the box. If only people would avoid humbug and say
what they meant! There was much in this to remind Newman of Whately, but Froude's personal habits were more to
his taste than Whately's. Newman's senses were acute; he was
thought to be the best judge of wine in Oriel. But he detested indulgence. Whately's monstrous appetite must have
been a perpetual distress to him. Froude was the most
abstemious of men. He and Newman shared the same
ultimate contempt for the things of the body. They both
hated luxury, and despised (or feared) comfort. Both gave
the smallest possible space in their lives to the beautification
of their own immediate surroundings. But there was a difference between them in this respect. Newman had it in him
to care for these things; Froude had not.

The boy went to school first at Ottery St. Mary, and in 1816
he was sent to Eton. When he was about sixteen years old he
had a dangerous illness. He was obliged to leave Eton and
for a time he lived the life of an invalid. He passed several
months in the care of an aunt (or some other near relation),
and it was not until his health had improved that he was able
to go home to Devonshire. He had not been very long at
home before Mrs. Froude addressed to him one of the most
curious letters that a mother can ever have written to a son,
under the same roof as herself.

This letter, which Richard carefully kept, explains so much in his character that it must be quoted and summarized at some length. It takes the pretended form of a letter to a stranger, and begins as follows:

'Sir, I have a son who is giving me a good deal of uneasiness at this time, from causes which I persuade myself are not altogether common; and having used my best judgment about him for seventeen years, I at last begin to think it incompetent to the case, and apply to you for advice.

'From his very birth his temper has been peculiar; pleasing, intelligent, and attaching, when his mind was undisturbed, and he was in the company of people who treated him reasonably and kindly; but exceedingly impatient under vexatious circumstances; very much disposed to find his own amusement in teazing and vexing others; and almost entirely incorrigible when it was necessary to reprove him. I never could find a successful mode of treating him. Harshness made him obstinate and gloomy; calm and long displeasure made him stupid and sullen; and kind patience had not sufficient power over his feelings to force him to govern himself. His disposition to worry made his appearance the perpetual signal for noise and disturbance among his brothers and sisters; and this it was impossible to stop, though a taste for quiet, and constant weak health, made it to me almost insupportable.'

No parent of experience can help sympathizing with Mrs. Froude. But it is evident that she was not free from the special vice of parents, the vice, namely, of trying to regulate their children's behaviour by their own low standards of vitality. Small wonder that to Hurrell, as he grew up, his vigorous instincts became objects of moral suspicion.

The letter goes on to point out her son's good qualities—his naturally noble temper, his relish and his good taste 'for all the pleasures of the imagination', his dislike (when untempted) for his own faults. As he grew older 'his mind expanded and sweetened', 'his promising virtues became my most delightful hopes, and his company my greatest pleasure.' Then came his illness, which he bore with the most excellent patience and cheerfulness. When he came home, 'his manners were tender and kind, his conversation highly pleasing, and his occupations manly and rational.'

But alas! 'the ease and indulgence of home is bringing on a relapse into his former habits.' The other day, in an argument, he told the near relation who 'has attended him through his illness with extraordinary tenderness . . . that "she lied, and knew she did", without (I am ashamed to say) the smallest apology. I am in a wretched state of health' poor Mrs. Froude continued 'and quiet is important to my recovery, and *quite essential* to my comfort; yet he disturbs it, for what he calls funny tormenting, without the slightest kind of feeling, twenty times a day. At one time he kept one of his brothers screaming, from a sort of teazing play, for near an hour under my window. At another, he acted as a wolf to his baby brother, whom he had promised never to frighten again.' And with an appeal to her correspondent for his advice, she signs herself 'a very anxious parent, M. F.', adding the following postscript: 'P.S. I have complained to him seriously of this day, and I thought he must have been hurt; but I am sorry to say that he has whistled almost ever since.'

A year or so later, Hurrell—he was always called by his second name—went up to Oriel. There he came at once under the influence of Keble, who was his tutor, and from that time onward there was small risk of his speculations taking the dangerous turn which his father seems to have feared. 'He continued', so the Archdeacon told Isaac Williams, 'to throw out strong paradoxes, but always for good.' Tutor and pupil were formed for each other. Nothing, in the life of either, is so delightfully easy and unaffected as their correspondence. Keble's High Churchmanship, a good deal more self-conscious and idealistic than Archdeacon Froude's, stimulated

Hurrell into bolder flights than those of his elders. Keble's winning simplicity and consideration for others took him captive and riveted finally upon him the moral fetters which his mother had already persuaded him into wearing. Keble's scholarship dazzled him; he relished his humorous turn of phrase, his love of plain rustic speech just touched by some hint of classical elegance, his freedom from any sort of pose or pomposity. And behind, beyond, all this, the unabashed emotionalism of Keble's temperament, which might perhaps have seemed a little sloppy, if it had not been boxed in by scholarship and blessed by religion, called to the simple sentimentalist, whom Froude's wit and irony concealed from the world but not from his intimate friends. And Keble, on his part, surrendered to the wilful charm, the impetuous energy, the respectful impertinences of his brilliant and affectionate pupil.

In 1823, when Hurrell had been up at Oriel for nearly two years, Keble resigned his tutorship. He was tired of life in Oxford, 'criticizing sermons, eating dinners, and laughing at Buckland and Shuttleworth', and longing to 'get away to some country curacy'. Soon after the Long Vacation had begun he settled down at Southrop, near Fairford, with three young men reading for their schools. Hurrell was one, Robert Wilberforce another, and Isaac Williams of Trinity was the third. The reading party was almost an accidental affair. It came about, Williams was convinced, 'by the gracious ordering of Him, who disposeth all things.' The Provost had asked Keble to take Wilberforce with him. Keble was not very keen to do so; evidently he had planned to have Hurrell all to himself. Two's company, and three's none. And, besides, Wilberforce was a sad Evangelical. But happening to see Williams still in Oxford he suggested that he should join the party with Wilberforce.

Isaac Williams was the son of a well-to-do Welsh barrister practising in London. But he was born in Wales, and the mountains and the poetry and the passionate romanticism of his native land were in his blood. He had the long dark sensitive Welsh face, thin pointed nose and chiselled lips, high forehead, black hair and sparkling black eyes. The sensitive Welsh conscience was his too. When he first went to school he was shocked by the wickedness of other boys, and given to reflecting on the shortness of life and the transitory nature of all human things. 'I was greatly taken' he said 'with Sherlock on death, sentences of which haunted me like some musical strain.' He took to Latin as a duck to water; so that at Harrow, if he was told to write an English essay, he had to translate his ideas out of Latin into English as he wrote. He took equally readily to cricket. But, full and happy as his life at Harrow was, he looked back upon it in after life with horror. He remembered, with painful incredulity, 'the very warm and strong attachments I formed with boys not in every case of the best principles.' He shuddered at the subtle poison which he imbibed from the poems of Lord Byron, left loose, so to speak, in the school library. He mourned the total absence of religious instruction of any kind. In this unspiritual state, devoted to cricket and Latin, dances and country visits, and quite indifferent to religion, he came up to Trinity, 'in good estimation outwardly among men, yet with ruin within me, almost irretrievably fixed'. Somebody suggested that he should compete for one of the new open scholarships; he entered and was elected. Then Keble paid a visit to a Mr. Richards, 'an excellent old clergyman living at Aberystwyth' who had once been curate of Fairford. The Williams's had come into possession of a large estate near by, on which they spent some months in the year; and Isaac was introduced to Keble and 'rode with him on his returning home the chief part of the way to the Devil's Bridge.' Nothing particular came of this. But next year, on his winning the Latin Verse prize, Keble looked him up, and a few days later asked him to join the Southrop reading party.

On all three undergraduates these summer months made their impression. For Hurrell Froude they served to deepen his devotion to Keble, and gave him the friendship of Isaac Williams. Robert Wilberforce was a little out of the picture, beside the old disciple and the new. Neither Froude nor Williams approved of his Low Church principles. But the reading party marked the beginning of the long slow revolution which was to carry him into the Roman Church thirty years later. On him too Keble's curious spell was working. 'What a strange person Keble is!' he confided one day to Williams; 'there is Law's *Serious Call*. Instead of leaving it about to do people good, I see he reads it and puts it out of the way, hiding it in a drawer.' But Keble's reverence for the *Serious Call to a Devout and Holy Life* was not far removed from his reverence for the Bible. He said to Froude one day, while they were waiting for the younger man to take a coach, bringing the words out with difficulty almost at the moment of saying good-bye: 'Froude, the other day you called Law's *Serious Call* a pretty book. Isn't that like saying that the Day of Judgment would be a pretty sight?'

The deepest impression of all was that made on Isaac Williams. He came down to Southrop a happy heathen; he left it a miserable sinner. So great can be the force of example on an impressionable mind. Everything about Keble struck him like a revelation. Here was 'the first man in Oxford' burying himself in a tiny Gloucestershire parish, simply because he loved the work of ministering to the souls of a handful of rustics; taking three young men into his house and teaching them 'with much pains and care', without any thought of payment; treating them on terms of absolute equality, himself (as his factotum used to say) 'the greatest boy of the lot'; and (what was strangest of all to the Harrovian cricketer) preferring the society of the poor to the rich and even referring to them as his instructors in the wisdom of God. 'Religion a reality, and a man wholly made up of love, with charms of conversation, thought, and kindness, beyond what one had experienced among boyish companions—this broke in upon me all at once. . . . Each of us was always delighted to walk with him, Wilberforce to gather instruction for the Schools, and the rest of us for love's sake.'

Thereafter Williams was Keble's man. All that he could take over from Keble he took—renunciation of the world, High Church theology, simplicity of language, avoidance of display, distrust of 'mere intellect'. The result was not, perhaps, entirely happy. Even Dean Church found 'something forced and morbid in it'. But there was 'something forced and morbid' in all the Tractarians, even in Keble himself, though some concealed it from view more effectually than others. Human nature cannot be made to fit a superhuman standard without showing the signs of distortion. The Tractarians perceived as much for themselves, though they phrased it in different language.

Other undergraduates came to Southrop in the vacations which followed, and fell under the same spell. They were all, or nearly all, Oriel men; and so the soil was turned over by Keble for Newman's later tillage. Williams, spending much of his time in the vacations with Keble, came to know them well and to be as much at home in Oriel as in Trinity. But it was not until much later that he and his greatest friend at Trinity, W. S. Copeland, became intimate with Newman. As an undergraduate he only met Newman once, at breakfast with Churton, one of the Oriel Fellows. 'He did not notice me, and was talking all the while with Churton, on the subject of serving churches, and how much they would allow him for a Sunday. He had then a less refined look about him, than when I knew him afterwards.'

When Williams went back to Oxford, after this first visit to Southrop, 'preyed upon by secret shame and sorrow', Froude took the place of his former companions. There is little with which to fill up a picture of the next two years in the lives of both young men. They read hard for their Schools, and each in his different way developed what he most admired in Keble. Froude's letters to Keble during this period are full of half-digested learning, pictures of the scenery at Dartington, and accounts of adventures and mis-adventures on the water. He tells Keble how he hates Milton and 'his, not in my sense of the word, poetry'; how he adores King Charles and Bishop Laud; how he is reading, or not reading when he ought to be reading; how a French fishing-boat had been held up for ten days within ear-shot of the people on the coast and its crew was to be heard on Sunday 'singing the Roman Catholic service so beautifully', and what jolly grateful fellows they were. There is nothing morbid in these earlier letters. He is afraid that it is not in his stars to be ever contented; nothing worse than that.

In August 1825 Isaac Williams stayed with the Froudes in Devonshire. He and Hurrell went by steamer from Cowes (where 'the tantalizing sight of the beautiful yachts, with their glittering sails, skimming along in the breeze which had just started up after the violent rain which had fallen', moved Hurrell's soul to most unchristian covetousness) to Plymouth; and Isaac was sick all the way, while Hurrell watched the sun rise and concluded that 'there is nothing in the least sublime in the mere fact of being out of sight of land.' Isaac, a little surprisingly, fell for the Archdeacon at once, and be-came popular with the whole family. Hurrell's little brother James remembered 'his genial laugh, the skill and heartiness with which he threw himself into our childish amusements, the inexhaustible stock of stories with which he held us spell-bound for hours.' There were merry evenings on the Dart; picnics on the Island; and Mrs. Williams felt with relief, as she read Isaac's letters home, that he was in a happier mood than he had been for the last two years.

About this time Keble sent Froude his 'verses' to read. They must have been the poems of *The Christian Year*—or some of them. He had already shown them to Williams 'carefully written out in small red books'. Williams 'did not much enter into it.' No more did Froude. But it was not in Froude, young as he was and revering Keble as he did, to say otherwise than he felt. 'You seem to me' he wrote, after apologizing for his presumption, 'to have addressed yourself too exclusively to plain matter-of-fact good sort of people . . . and not to have taken much pains to interest and guide the feelings of people who feel acutely.' Things like Gray's *Elegy*, he thinks, 'which turn melancholy to its proper account, by pointing out the vanity of the world without telling us so, seem to me more to answer the purpose.' Sound criticism; that 'without telling us so' goes very near the essential weakness of Keble's poetry. And did it not need real courage, as well as independent judgment, to say that 'there is some-thing which I should call Sternhold-and-Hopkinsy in the diction'? Keble's answer does him no less credit. 'My dear Fellow,' he writes. 'As Tyler begins when he is in a jolly mood, these are to thank you very much for the trouble you have taken about them there things of mine, and still more for your telling me exactly what you think about them; for wch I shall hold you in greater honour as long as I live.' And he goes on to say that he has no illusions about his own 'crockery'. He will be quite content if it is of any use to the plain sort of good people. At any rate it is the best he can do; and 'there is no making a silk purse out of a sow's ear.'

2. FROUDE'S JOURNAL

The extracts from Hurrell Froude's Private Journal begin soon after this with the New Year (1826). For the first six months of the year they consist of a few scattered entries, expressing irritation with his own idleness; but in July they take a serious turn. From this point onwards until the ex-tracts end—that is to say, from the summer of 1826 to the summer of 1828 during his twenty-fourth and twenty-fifth years—they are an arsenal of ammunition for his enemies.

He was elected to his Oriel Fellowship at Easter 1826—not altogether to his own surprise. But his delight in his success knocked him off his feet. 'My dreamy sensations' he wrote to Keble a few weeks later 'have at length subsided, and I cannot think how I was such a fool as to be so upset.' He determined to set to steadily at divinity and other sobering studies. A Fellow of Oriel must make a serious job of his life. A little later he gave Keble his impressions of the personalities of the common room. The *Remains* do not print the names; but to whom else can the following description apply but Newman? '— is to my mind the greatest genius of the party, and I cannot help thinking that, some time or other, I may get to be well acquainted with him; but he is very shy, and dining with a person does not break the ice so quickly as might be wished.'

The first remarkable entry in the Journal is dated July 1. He has decided that the Journal must be used to keep him in order about more things than reading. 'I am in a most conceited way, besides being very ill-tempered and irritable. My thoughts wander very much at my prayers, and I feel hungry for some ideal thing, of which I have no definite idea. I sometimes fancy that the odd bothering feeling which gets possession of me is affectation, and that I appropriate it because I think it a sign of genius; but it lasts too long, and is too disagreeable, to be unreal. There is another thing which I must put down, if I don't get rid of it before long: it is a thing which proves to me the imbecility of my own mind more than anything; and I can hardly confess it to myself; but it is too true.' The published extracts do not explain what the 'thing' was.

The cause of this sudden resolution was the reading of his mother's papers, which included a private journal and some prayers. He found in these evidence that she had suffered from just the same inner restlessness and unhappiness as himself. She wrote it all down, as he was doing now. And amongst other things she had written down in her journal during the last year of her life what she, poor lady, in her hypersensitive condition, considered her son's unkindnesses, with prayers for his improvement. 'I did not recollect' wrote the tortured Hurrell 'that I had been so unfeeling to her during her last year. I thank God some of her writings have been kept; that may be my salvation; but I have spent the evening just as idly as if I had not seen it. I don't know how it is, but it seems to me, that the consciousness of having capacities for happiness, with no objects to gratify them, seems to grow upon me, and puts me in a dreary way. Lord, have mercy upon me.'

Fits of depression followed, punctuated by fits of reaction, when the entries of the preceding days seemed like sheer nonsense. But his mother's journal had got such hold of him that he could hardly think about anything else. He resolved to copy her method of recording the shortcomings of each day in detail, instead of writing a general account. His only hope, he felt, was to watch his mind at every turning.

In September his distress reached an acute stage. He went to stay with Isaac Williams at Cwmcynfelin near Aberystwyth. George Prevost was there, another of Keble's Oriel young men, in the process of becoming engaged to Isaac's sister, and Hurrell struck up a friendship with him. They walked up the Rheidol valley to the Devil's Bridge; 'the walk was an attempt at romance, and it answered to a certain extent.' But all through this visit Hurrell's nerves were on edge. He blamed himself for eating and drinking too much, for looking with greediness to see if there was a goose on the table, for being jealous of the intimacy between Isaac and Prevost, for not being sociable, for failing to read the psalms and the second lesson before breakfast, for wanting to show off his abstinence at table, for pretending to be a better shot than he was, for throwing Isaac his greatcoat when he was on horseback, for a score of such trivialities. It is on these that Froude's critics have fastened. But beneath them there lay a surging discontent with himself—the product of a number of complex causes, his mother's cruel legacy, his own ruthless candour, and no doubt also those sexual repressions, which Lytton Strachey considered to be the whole of the story. Perhaps there was a physical cause too, in the feverish energy, which so often marks the victim of consumption and sinks every now and then into an equally abnormal lassitude.

While he was at Cwmcynfelin he wrote three, four times to Keble. The first three letters were never sent; one was (apparently) torn up, the other two were kept and are printed in his *Remains*. They are revealing documents—more revealing even than the obviously expurgated diary, for they show the deeper discontent of which the diary only records symptoms. The diary, it is true, shows a divided personality—the normal healthy self-satisfied youngster in conflict with his mother's son. But the letters show more clearly the united personality, struggling to reconcile the division. 'With me this last summer' he says in the first letter 'seems to have gone very strangely; and I do not see any ground why my reason should contradict my feelings because the things which affect me are either in their nature confined to the person who feels them, or are thought trifles by people in general.' He was on the point of telling Keble what his trouble really was, or seemed to him to be. But the letter slides off. 'I have been trying almost all the Long to discover a sort of common-sense romance.' . . . Who can now say what Hurrell Froude meant by this curious phrase? Some means of satisfying his aching need of deep emotional pleasure, without stepping outside the tidy *parterres* of the Christian gentleman's garden? He does not explain what he means. He is sure that 'there is such a thing, and that nature did not give us a high capacity for pleasure without'—without what? His pen or his courage fails him, and he completes the sentence: 'without making

o   F.O.A.

some other qualification for it besides delusion.' And then he
makes an academic problem of it, and thinks it may be
solved by learning Hebrew and reading the early Fathers.
Clearly such a letter wouldn't do. Keble would smell some
very horrid rat.

So a fortnight later he tries again. 'I have been in a very
odd way . . . a letter that I tried to write to you seemed so
strange when I read it afterwards that I resolved not to send
it. . . . All this summer I have been trying a sort of experiment
with myself, which, as I have had no one to talk to about it,
has brought on great fits of enthusiasm and despondency.'
He goes on to describe his journal, and how foolish it all is.
And then, with a sudden confused insight into his own
nature: 'It made me seem to myself as if I was two people,
and that the fellow who would act and feel as I have let myself do, could never be the same person who has the high
notions of happiness and the capacities of man which I am
making in theory.' How right he was! But having perceived
this he falls back into the character of the diarist. He confesses to Keble 'that I am disingenuous, sneaking to those I
am afraid of, bullying to those who are afraid of me'; and
implores his old tutor to assist him with advice as to the best
way of disciplining himself.

This letter, too, was not sent. Two days later, in despera-
tion he tried again. 'I have made three attempts to write . . .
but all of them ran off into something wild.' In this final
letter his confession boils down to 'fits of enthusiasm or
despondency', and to a less desperate-sounding appeal for
help. 'I wish you would say anything to me that you think
would do me good, however severe it may be. You must have
observed many things contemptible in me, but I know worse
of myself, and shall be prepared for anything.' Such an
avowal seems pretty safe. It was almost common form.

But Keble, if he was not a profound thinker, was shrewd
enough to read between lines like these. We do not know what

he said to his hard-driven correspondent. But Hurrell got from his letter 'something more like happiness than I have known since my Mother died.' He knew now that he could open his heart to Keble and not be rebuffed. And if the advice he got was not what a modern psychoanalyst would have given him, at least it was consistent and sensible and without destroying the ideal he had set up brought it nearer within his reach. 'It is much better' writes Hurrell gratefully 'to give up all notion of guiding myself and "seek first the kingdom of God and his righteousness, and all these things shall be added.". . . It is very frightful to see people like Mr. Bonnell' (whose life Keble, with a true physicianly instinct, had advised him to read) 'so alarmed about themselves, and expressing so strongly the wretchedness of their moral condition.' The correspondence continued in this vein for only a little while longer. There was another letter from Keble of 'the greatest comfort' to Hurrell, warning him 'not to reckon tranquillity and cheerfulness a bad sign', but to allow his mind 'to rest on other subjects than the presence of that High Being, in the light of whose countenance are set my secret sins.' And there was another letter from Hurrell to Keble, from which these phrases are quoted, resolving 'for the future to conduct myself in the presence of men with such humility, that to the Angels I may be an object rather of pity than of scorn', and admitting that self-imposed penance 'though it has in it the colour of humility, is in reality the food of pride. . . . Even fasting itself, to weak minds, is not free from evil, when, however secretly it is done, one cannot avoid the consciousness of being singular.' This letter was dated January 8 1827. Thereafter Froude's letters to Keble are in his old impetuous natural vein.

He came back to Oxford in October (1826) determined to begin a sort of monastic austere life, and to do his best to chastise himself before the Lord. Keble's answer to his first letter came a day or two later. It is remarkable that, in spite

of Keble's advice, he still continued to fill his diary with his
backslidings and fastings and attempts at self-discipline.
'Read steadily to-day; had no dinner, but a bit of bread.'
'Felt an impulse of pleasure, on finding that Wilberforce was
not at chapel this morning.' 'Slept on the floor, and a nice
uncomfortable time I had of it.' 'It crossed me that I should
like Newman to observe, that I had studied the service before
I came to chapel, by my finding the lesson before it was given
out.' And so on. But on the whole the tone of the Journal,
after Keble's letter, is steadier than it had been, and there are
passages of refreshing good sense and candour. Why, he asks
himself, very puzzled, is he 'so very indulgent to the lax
actions and notions of those who go on in the way of the world
and yet so excessively bitter against those who set up to be
good and wise?' This reflection makes him wonder if 'his own
peculiar feelings may not be as erroneous' as he sees those of
the self-righteous to be.

None of Hurrell's friends ever had the least suspicion of
these painful efforts to subdue his body to his soul, and his
soul to the pattern required of him by his religion. Indeed
many of the traits he noted in his own character as detestable
affectations were those which made him so attractive to
others. Somebody asked to borrow his umbrella; he replied
with 'a grotesque desire to affect a gentlemanlike carelessness'
that they could go by Loder's and he would get one there.
And instantly he was filled with shame, while his friend no
doubt told himself in a pleased way: 'How like Hurrell!' It is
very difficult, in reading the Journal not to fall into the error
of imagining that he must have been living a double life
every minute of the day—one half talking and behaving in
the well-known character of Hurrell Froude, the other whispering 'What a fraud this fellow is!' It is necessary to remember that the Journal was a deliberate attempt at the end of
each day to analyse the motives of his trivial daily actions.
But it is not to be supposed that the Froude, who seemed so

bright and real and spontaneous to his friends, seemed otherwise, in his intercourse with them, to himself. At the beginning of the Journal it is true that the effort of daily analysis
does seem to be reacting upon the spontaneity of his behaviour. He was, in fact, trying very hard to substitute an
ideal character for his real one—though any sensible Deity
(one cannot help thinking) would greatly prefer him as he
was to the colourless nincompoop he was trying to become.
But after his exchange of letters with Keble, and Keble's
sound advice to 'burn confessions', he gradually relaxed the
analysis. He closed the Journal altogether 'on principle' between December 9 1826 and February 8 1827; and when
he reopened it it was only to make an occasional entry until
it ceased altogether in May 1828. At least the published
Remains do not print any entry of a later date.

   The real Hurrell, then, maintained himself against his own
efforts at self-reform. But the fastings and abstinences were
not dropped. It is pathetic to watch their effect upon his
physical strength, and sometimes even upon his mind. In an
hour of clear self-judgment he owned that he used self-denial
'because I believe it the way to make the most out of our
pleasures; and, besides, it has a tendency to give me what is
essential to taking my place in society, self-command.' If this
was not altogether true, it was certainly true that his motives
were mixed. It pleased his vanity to be able to control his
appetites. It was a time-honoured way of pleasing God, or at
any rate of fitting the soul to please God better. It was also,
perhaps, a pleasure in itself. His natural vigorous self, the self
which his mother had pursued every means of suppressing,
was often triumphant over his resolutions. But the idea of
fasting had a curious attraction, all its own. 'I used to specu-
late' he writes 'on the delight of keeping fasts upon the river
in fine weather, among beautiful scenery.' And the thought of
a young girl who killed herself by fasting gave him a peculiar
satisfaction. 'She died a few months back,' he wrote to New-

man in the year before his own death 'and, from what W. tells me, must have been a little saint; all last Lent she fasted so strictly as to hurt her health, in spite of being constantly ridiculed; and where she got her notions from I cannot guess.'

Froude's fasts were not of the nicely fried fish type. 'Fell quite short of my wishes with respect to the rigour of to-day's fast. . . . I tasted nothing till after half past eight in the evening.' This is a common type of entry. Small wonder that he suffered from bad dreams (and dreams of giving 'flash' dinners), and fits of terrible lassitude, and absurd fancies (such as that Keble thought him a bore), and was always falling asleep in his chair instead of reading religious books. His doctor told him that he must indulge in a more generous diet. 'I was glad of the excuse,' he notes 'but I must take care to prevent a relapse. The vacancy left in my mind by abstinence, fits it for spiritual ideas.'

There are two peculiarities about Froude's Journal and Occasional Thoughts. The first is the very curious fact, to which the editor of the *Remains* (i.e. Newman) calls special attention, that nowhere does he use the name of Christ—not even in the prayers in which he confesses his sins and implores pardon and help. Newman's explanation carries very little conviction. He assures the reader that Froude's faith in the Saviour's 'grace and merits was most implicit and most practical', and that of course 'where he speaks of "God" and "Lord" he includes an allusion to Christ under those titles.' Yet Newman admits the strangeness of the omission. He explains it by saying that 'a mind alive to its own real state, often shrinks to utter what it most dwells upon, and is too full of awe and fear to do more than silently hope what it most wishes.' Most readers, I think, will agree that this only makes matters worse. Is not the whole point and message of Christianity, as the Church has formulated it, in Christ's mediation between man and God? Is it not, then, an act of presumption for the sinner to make no acknowledgment and no use of this

(*ex hypothesi*) all-important fact? Is it not absurd to shrink
from speaking the name of Christ, but not to shrink from
speaking direct to God? Absurd, that is, upon the hypothesis.
But not at all absurd if the religion of the supplicant is not
specifically Christian; if what moves his imagination is God's
majesty and holiness on the one hand, the visible and traditional splendours of the Church on the other; if Christ is little
more than the obvious corollary of Christianity, and the
supplicant's 'implicit and practical' faith in Him little more
than the necessary consequence of his acceptance of the
teachings of the Church. If a man's written thoughts ever
reveal his mind, it is when he writes for his own eye, without
any thought that others will ever see them. In his sermons
Froude, of course, uses the name of Jesus Christ. No preacher
could do otherwise. But even in the sermons his language
about Christ is of the ordinary conventional kind. It is charged
with no particular emotion. And in his private mind Christ
seems to have had no place at all. It is not to be supposed that
he, unlike Newman, was conscious of the omission. But the
omission tells its own plain tale.

3. VIRGINITY AND FRIENDSHIP

The other singular omission is that Froude betrays no
consciousness of that 'high severe idea of virginity' which
Newman ascribed so definitely to him. The Journal is not
printed in its entirety. Passages too delicate for publication
may very likely have been omitted. But it would certainly
seem that in the years 1826 to 1828 the idea of virginity, as
such, did not hold a very definite place in his mind.

This is awkward ground to tread upon. Nevertheless it is
too important a matter to be passed over in silence. We are
bound to come to some conclusion about this 'idea of virginity'. Whether it is in itself a noble or a worthless idea is a
question that we are fortunately not obliged to discuss. But

that it was an idea which played a prominent part in the minds of some of the Tractarians we have already seen.[1] We are entitled to ask whether it came into their minds of its own right, so to say, or whether it was not, primarily, there as a working solution of their own psychological problems.

There have been two attempts, in the west, to study the nature of homosexuality—in Athens of the fifth and fourth centuries before Christ by Socrates and his followers, and in twentieth-century Europe by psychologists of various schools. The methods of approach in the two cases differ *toto coelo*. In Athens, and in other Greek cities, homosexuality was not regarded with public horror. On the contrary the tendency was to regard physical connection between men and women as no more than an animal act, pleasing in itself and involving a momentary emotion, or as a social duty, necessary for the continuance of the race. Love between persons of the same sex was thought by most Greeks to be of a higher, more ideal, character. The typical Greek romance was not a story like that of Tristan and Iseult, but a story of passionate friends like Achilles and Patroclus, Orestes and Pylades, Harmodius and Aristogeiton. There were exceptions, of course. But in many parts of Greece the natural occurrence of such friendships was deliberately used by the state as a means of welding the male community together. Particularly was this so in the hardy Dorian states; most of all in Sparta.[2] And it was thought no shame if the friendship was accompanied by physical intimacy. It was as much 'the thing' for a man to be in love with a youth, as it is for a young Englishman or American to be in love with a girl. It is hardly necessary to say that ideal love between persons of the same sex was no more the universal rule than ideal love between persons of opposite sexes is the universal rule in the modern world. Prostitution—that is,

[1] See pages 25 *et seqq.*

[2] Mrs. Mitchison's novels, e.g. *Black Sparta*, give a faithful and sympathetic picture of this remote society.

physical intimacy without love—and indiscriminate amusement on every kind of level were as common in Athens as in London or Paris. But it was the spiritual, ideal love which interested Socrates. The physical act, if it did not in itself disgust him, was at best a concession to animalism, impeding love's gift of wings to the soul.[1]

Very different is the modern psychological approach. Regarding love as no more than an emotional accompaniment or refinement of the sexual instinct, and the sexual instinct as obviously existing for the sole purpose of procreation; acting, also, under the powerful pressure of social opinion; psychology has tended to treat homosexuality as a disease, out of which nothing good can come, or at best only an inferior kind of good. It is true that this is not quite the whole story. Most psychologists will agree that no man is perfectly 'normal'. Most, if not all, psychologists will agree that every human being, in his progress towards 'normality', passes through a definitely homosexual stage. Many will go so far as to admit, with McDougall, 'that, in some small proportion of human beings, the sex instinct is innately inverted, is innately homosexual.'[2] And some may even be bold enough to suggest that emotional attachments between persons of the same sex have as much intrinsic right to existence and recognition as emotional attachments between persons of opposite sexes.

In the main, however, psychology sees in what it calls inversion a falling short of the proper human standard, treating it as a diseased condition, which it seeks to cure or to palliate. And neither psychology nor philosophy, with rare exceptions, attempts (at least, in England) to consider what of value this condition—so common as it is—may have in it for humanity.

No one familiar with Greek literature can feel entirely comfortable over the modern view. It is difficult to think that

[1] Plato, *Phaedrus*, chapter 37.
[2] W. McDougall, *Outline of Abnormal Psychology*, p. 223.

the Greeks built so much of their society and their art on a
specifically diseased basis. Through the study of Greek literature, and especially of the Platonic dialogues, the sense of a
godlike excellence in the Greek ideal of love between friends
has entered into the minds of generation after generation of
young Englishmen. In no generation has this been more
clearly marked than in that of the Tractarians. In them it
entered into close union with another ideal, the ideal of the
sanctification of earthly loves by the love of God. Their
strenuous efforts to tame the body—'the unruly horse' of
Socrates—gave to the combination of these two ideals an
almost desperate intensity. Psychology had not yet taught
men to look for the roots of spiritual ideals in their animal
nature. Love, therefore, was not an object of suspicion. But
psychology lies between us and them. We cannot help looking
for those animal roots. And though we may declare to ourselves that the origin of a sentiment has nothing to do with its
value, the very terminology in which we are obliged to speak
of it seems often to imply a sneer at its pretensions. Let us try
to keep our language clear of these question-begging implica-
tions. Both Froude and Newman may have derived the ideal
of virginity from a homosexual root; but this does not of itself
justify us in sneering either at the ideal or at the condition
which gave rise to it. On the other hand, we cannot possibly
begin to understand their emotional life if we shut our eyes
to everything except its surface appearance.

What, then, is the evidence for the existence of such a temperamental bias in Hurrell Froude? Mostly it is indirect. The
bias is to be inferred from the tone and temper of his Private
Journal, and the fervour of his masculine friendships. But
there is some direct evidence. 'O Lord,' he wrote in one of his
agonies 'the thoughts which sometimes come into my head
are too shocking even to name.' This is the unmistakable
language of conflict with sexual temptation. What was the
nature of the desire which laid him open to temptation? For

the most part it escaped his censure by sublimating itself into an idealized and sanctified love. But there is a period during which it is impossible not to suspect that it took a form which he could not idealize or sanctify.

On December 9 1826 he closed his journal 'on principle', after five months of exhausting effort to remodel his character. He had decided to take private pupils. After detailing his reasons for this decision the entry continues: '—— has applied to Tyler to ask him if I will take him as a pupil, just as I have come to the determination of employing myself in this way. If the thought was sudden on his part, the coincidence is still more curious; at any rate it seems the fates have thrown us together. I must repress all enthusiastic notions about the event . . . must keep down anxiety about his class . . . and above all watch and pray against being led out of the way by the fascination of his society; but rather by steady persever-ance in the right course, do what I can with God's assistance, to be of some little service in guiding his ways.'

There can have been no immediate companionship with the unnamed undergraduate, since the vacation had already begun. But the prospect of it was enough to produce a terrible tumult in Froude's mind.

'O God,' he writes on January 10 'I stand in my naked filthiness before Thee, whose eyes are purer than to behold ini-quity. . . . O my God, I dare no longer offer to Thee my dis-eased petitions in the words by which wise and holy men have shaped their intercourse between earth and heaven. Suffer me, with whose vileness they can have had no fellowship, to frame for myself my isolated supplication. . . . Thou hast cast me away from Thy presence, and taken Thy Holy Spirit from me, giving me over to vile affections and a reprobate mind. Yet praised be Thy Holy Name, Thou hast not even thus utterly left me destitute; but with hideous dreams Thou hast affrighted me; and with perpetual mortifications Thou hast disquieted me; and with the recollections of bright things fascinated me; and with a holy friend Thou hast visited me.'

On January 12 he writes again: 'O may the recollection of these dreadful things so fill my soul with deep humility. . . . O Lord my God, I, who am even as a beast before Thee . . . do yet . . . venture to intercede with Thee for others. Bless, O Lord . . . that high spirit, whom, as Thy type upon this earth, Thou hast interposed between me and the evils I have merited.' On January 15 again: 'Strengthen me, O Lord my God, that I may dare to look in the face the hideous filthiness of those ways, in which, for the sins that with open eyes I have acted, Thou hast permitted me blindly to stray.' And on January 21: 'My soul is a troubled and restless thing, haunted by the recollection of past wickedness.' But term has now begun. And whether it is that his pupil has reasserted his fascinations, or for whatever reason, he continues: 'But though I feel how bad I am . . . yet my miseries pass away like a cloud, and my soul refuseth to conceive its wretchedness.' The next passage shows him even prepared to entertain the notion that a man might cease to believe the Bible, as he ceases to believe fairy stories.

All these prayers are among the Occasional Thoughts printed apart from the Journal. But on February 8 he re-opens the Journal with an entry which shows that the storms of the last two months cannot have been unconnected with the entry made on December 9.

'Since I left off,' he writes 'I have been punished for the feeling that dictated the last line [about guiding his pupil's ways]. I hope God may not permit me to relapse; but experience has taught me that I cannot by myself prevent it, and I am now frightened at seeing in myself many symptoms of returning pride.' Two days later he prays to be saved from the snares of a double mind. But the struggle is over. Keble, the holy friend, has vanquished the dark angel in his heart. And on the 22nd he can say thankfully: 'I am no longer in the

company of those who scorn the appearance of piety, nor
dazzled with examples of fascinating vice. I live among those
who profess Thy fear, and I lean on one to whose friendship
I have no access but through Thee.'

The Journal ceases in 1828, and the Letters after 1827,
lively and plain-spoken as they are, make no further exposure
of the writer's inmost mind. But the victory was perhaps not
so complete as Keble and Newman supposed. Among the
verses which he left behind him is a stanza (dated 1833)
which strongly suggests that his mind was not (as the editors
of his *Remains* asserted) 'freed from the solicitudes which at
one time troubled it.' The stanza is the first of an unfinished
poem:

> Lord; I have fasted, I have prayed,
> And sackcloth has my girdle been,
> To purge my soul I have essayed
> With hunger blank and vigil keen.
> O Father of mercies! Why am I
> Still haunted by the self I fly?

In the *Lyra Apostolica* (where this poem may be found)
there is another set of verses from Froude's pen, which con-
tains a curiously recondite hint that the old 'vile affections'
still had their way with him. It is number 79 in that miscel-
lany of 'faded devotion'. His New Self is colloguing with his
Old Self.

> I mourn for the delicious days,
> When those calm sounds fell on my childish ear,
> A stranger yet to the wild ways
> Of triumph and remorse, of hope and fear.

So speaks the Old Self. And the New Self replies:

> Mournest thou, poor soul! and wouldst thou yet
> Call back the things which shall not, cannot be?
> Heaven must be won, not dreamed; thy task is set,
> Peace was not made for earth, nor rest for thee.

And in a footnote to the last line Froude quotes a couplet
from the seventh of Virgil's Eclogues:

> Haec memini, et victum frustra contendere Thyrsim.
> Ex illo Corydon, Corydon est tempore nobis.

'These things I remember,' says the shepherd Meliboeus at
the end of the Eclogue, after narrating a contest in song between two other shepherds, Thyrsis and Corydon; 'and how
Thyrsis, though defeated, went on vainly contending. Ever
since that time Corydon, none but Corydon, is our poet.'

By this quotation Froude clearly means to compare the
Old Self and the New Self of his own poem with the Corydon
and Thyrsis of the Eclogue. Which corresponds to which?
Which is defeated, which triumphant? The obvious answer
is, of course, that the Old Self is defeated, and the New Self is
the triumphant Corydon. But in the Eclogue it is Thyrsis who
has the last turn, just as in Froude's poem it is the New Self
who has the last word. It is Thyrsis who still goes on trying,
although he is defeated; just so it is the New Self who goes on
trying, although defeated. Corydon is the Old Self. But Corydon is a name with an unforgettable association attached to it
in the Eclogues. *Formosum pastor Corydon ardebat Alexim*—'The
shepherd Corydon was in love with the beautiful Alexis.' It is
quite impossible to suppose that for a mind so steeped in Virgil
as Froude's the name did not bear the associations for which
the second Eclogue has made it notorious, and which were
such a shocking stumbling-block to poor Professor Conington
in his commentary upon the poet.

Does it not appear, then, that the Corydon who stood for
the unregenerate Froude was the Corydon of the second as
well as the seventh Eclogue? The only transformation he was
able to effect in this temperamental bias was to give it a religious instead of a pagan colouring. Alexis gave way to
Keble and Isaac Williams and Newman. This religious sub-
limation of love was accompanied by the growth of a conscious 'idea of virginity'. His sexual appetites must be somehow appeased. A negative abstinence was not enough. Only a
positive ideal could subdue the beast within him. The idea of
virginity fulfilled this function as nothing else could. Unlike
Keble, and Williams, and Pusey, and Henry Wilberforce, he

could find no solution in marriage, whereby 'such persons as
have not the gift of continency' may ordinarily 'keep themselves undefiled members of Christ's body.'

To what extent was this true of other participators in the
movement? That Newman himself was in very much the
same case as Froude can scarcely be doubted. It was probably never such a problem to him, as it was to Froude; but
upon this we have no evidence. Newman's peculiar power of
representing himself to himself as a complete person, of tying
up or tucking away unpleasing loose ends, enabled him to
avoid, or to appear to avoid, the cruder moral conflicts. If
he was not able to silence them completely, he was at any rate
careful that no sound from them should reach the world.
Moreover, his friendships were never of the kind that Froude
found it so difficult to escape from. He had no worldly con-
nections clinging round him; he never found himself on intimate terms with 'flash' companions, or allured by visions of
'fascinating vice'. All his friends were high-minded and
deeply religious. There was no conflict between the dark
angel and the white.

Of all his friends Froude filled the deepest place in his
heart, and I am not the first to point out that his occasional
notions of marrying definitely ceased with the beginning of
his real intimacy with Froude.[1] It is most curious and interesting to notice how different his relations with Froude were
from his relations with his other friends. With them he was
the beloved, rather than the lover. Between him and Froude
the relation was reversed. He loved Froude more than Froude
loved him—at least that is the impression continually conveyed by their correspondence. The younger man's death
from consumption in 1836, long expected as it was, dealt him
a deadly blow. In a strange letter to Bowden, written the day
after the news of Froude's death reached him, he said that he
had often found himself confusing Bowden and Froude to-

[1] Edwin Abbott, *Anglican Career of Cardinal Newman*, i. 187.

gether and only calling Froude by his right name by an act of
memory. The reason for this is not far to seek. They were the
only two friends who had ever stood at the very centre of his
life, and of these two Bowden was the one of whose love he had
always been perfectly certain. Bowden had married and, to
that extent, deserted him. There was no danger of Froude
deserting him for a wife; but he was never really certain that
Froude's love was equal to his own. Bowden was colourless,
Froude was all colour and life; Bowden's mind lay completely open and subservient to his own, Froude's remained secret
and independent. The confusion of names was an unconscious
effort to make as sure of his present friend as of his earlier.

There were many dearly loved friends in Newman's life.
Whately, Keble, Pusey, Isaac Williams, William Copeland,
Henry Wilberforce, John Christie, Frederic Rogers (Lord
Blachford)—the list descends from his elders to his juniors.
Buried in the Oratory at Birmingham his heart yearned painfully for his old intimates. When Copeland at last came to see
him at Birmingham in 1862, Newman's affection almost unlocked the restraints of speech. 'I want you to live many years,
and never, never again to be so cruel to me as you were for
near 17 long years.' But there were only three who occupied
a central position in his heart. The needed succession was
continued, with an interval after Froude's death, by a friend
of very inferior mental calibre, Ambrose St. John, who accompanied Newman to Rome and served him with dog-like devotion until he, too, died in 1878. St. John gave him something that neither Bowden nor Froude ever came near to
giving him—something for which, one cannot but think, he
was unconsciously craving all through his Oxford career.
The Romans called him, 'because he was fair and Saxon-
looking', Newman's Angel Guardian. 'From the first' said
Newman 'he loved me with an intensity of love, which was
unaccountable.' In the second volume of Wilfrid Ward's *Life*
there is a half-comic half-pathetic photograph of the two men,

taken when Newman was between sixty and seventy; Father St. John, stout and middle-aged, is standing, with his hand on Newman's shoulder, looking down benevolently at Newman, who is seated on a chair. Newman is awkwardly fingering his tie, and responding to St. John's look with a kind of anguished scowl. But there is nothing comic about Newman's account of St. John's death. As the latter lay dying, or rather sitting on the edge of his bed a few hours before his death, unable to speak or to express his emotions except by the oldest of all methods, 'he got hold of me' (Newman wrote to Lord Blachford) 'and threw his arm over my shoulder and brought me to him so closely, that I said in joke, "He will give me a stiff neck." So he held me for some minutes, I at length releasing myself from not understanding, as *he* did, why he so clung to me. Then he got hold of my hand and clasped it so tightly as really to frighten me, for he had done so once before when he was not himself. I had to get one of the others present to unlock his fingers, ah! little thinking what he meant. At 7 p.m. when I rose to go, and said "Good-bye, I shall find you much better to-morrow," he smiled on me with an expression which I could not and cannot understand. It was sweet and sad and perhaps perplexed, but I cannot interpret it.' Never afterwards could he speak of St. John without weeping and becoming speechless; by his own wish his body was buried in the same grave.

Keble and Pusey were differently constituted from Newman and Froude. But both of them maintained their masculine friendships on a peculiarly high emotional level. And indeed this was true, with few if any exceptions, of all the Tractarians. There were Isaac Williams and William Copeland of Trinity, 'close friends' as Dean Church says, 'with the affection which was characteristic of those days', for both of whom Newman 'had the love which passes that of common relation.' There were all the younger disciples of Newman, united in adoration of their master and devotion to each other.

There was the *gauche* unworldly Charles Marriott who loved Newman beyond anyone else on earth.

'And why' (some will exclaim indignantly) 'should it not be so? Is not love the very life-blood of Christianity? Is there anything surprising, anything that needs roundabout quasi-psychological explanations, to account for the fact that men who engage in a Christian revival are held together by a love greater than that of common friendship?' Perhaps not—if an emotional disposition is a special gift from heaven to earnest Christians. If such an explanation seems a little too extravagant, why then the cart must stay in its usual place behind the horse, and we must suppose that the emotional disposition came first, the religious use of it later. Love certainly is not under men's conscious control. If I am a Christian and believe that it is my duty to love my neighbour I am no better able to *love* him than I was before. I can tell myself that he is a better man than I am; I can choose to be friendly with him, I can turn the other cheek to his buffetings, I can pray for him, I can give him my old clothes or my last penny. But I cannot persuade myself that I love him, unless I love him with or without Christian motives, or unless I rob the word of all proper meaning. And if all this is true, then it becomes an obvious as well as a very interesting and significant question to ask:—What part did this unusual capacity for emotional friendships play in the genesis of the Oxford Movement?

'Unusual', because to most modern readers the capacity will probably seem unusual, and even indecent, except in the very young. Perhaps a conventionalized and devitalized conception of friendship provides us with a poor standard of comparison. It might be no less foolish to write the Tractarians down as fundamentally unbalanced, than to think they were specially equipped for their providential purpose by a peculiar emotional sensibility. It might be better simply to observe that they were not ashamed of being emotional, and that in consequence, few as they were, and contrary as their aim was to the intellectual tendencies of the time, they were able to produce a lasting impression upon their own century and possibly even upon ours.

So much cannot be denied by any sensible reader of the letters and memoirs of the day. The momentum of the Tractarian revival was powerfully increased by these emotional friendships. But was there in fact any causal connection between this particular emotional tendency and the ideas of virginity and celibacy, which were for a time so marked a character of the movement? Did not these ideas exist in their own right? If they did exist in their own right, it is more than strange that so little is said about them. They were accepted, by those who accepted them, as self-evident. We have noticed how guarded and reluctant Newman's own language about them was.[1] In his novel *Loss and Gain*, a picture of the Oxford Movement with the principal character left out, written two years after his own conversion, he devotes two short chapters to a discussion about the celibate ideal between Charles Reding (the undergraduate convert-to-be who is a projection of Newman's own ideas) and his friend Carlton. The discussion is very convincing, in the sense that it is true to life; very unconvincing, in that Charles, like Newman himself, has really very little to say about the ideal which (to his friend's distress) has taken possession of him, and (again like Newman) is extremely reluctant to talk about it at all.

Carlton is shocked to discover that Reding has a sneaking kindness for celibacy. He tries to laugh him out of it. Then he urges that the genius of the English Church goes against celibacy. Not until near the end does the conversation show signs of going below the surface.

' "Tell me, Reding," said Carlton, "for really I don't understand, what are your reasons for admiring what, in truth, is simply an unnatural state."

' "Don't let us talk more, my dear Carlton," answered Red-

[1] See page 30.

ing; "I shall go on making a fool of myself. Let well alone, or bad alone, pray do."

'It was evident that there was some strong feeling irritating him inwardly; the manner and the words were too serious for the occasion.'

But Carlton presses his question, only to be answered that celibacy is 'supernatural', and the talk rides off on a discussion upon the meaning of this word. Then Charles gets nearer to saying what he thinks. 'Surely the idea of an Apostle, unmarried, pure, in fast and nakedness, and at length a martyr, is a higher idea than that of one of the old Israelites sitting under his vine and fig-tree, full of temporal goods, and surrounded by sons and grandsons.' Carlton, unfortunately, fails to ask the much-needed question, *why* the one idea should be higher than the other. And Charles then produces the text *In sin hath my mother conceived me*. In marriage, he thinks, over and above the doctrine of original sin, there is great danger of sin—by which he presumably means copulation for its own sake or for the sake of the accompanying emotion. But though he has evidently not said all that is in his mind, he refuses to go further, and the talk ends with a debate upon the nature and value of penance.

Now all that really emerges in this curious passage is the idea that copulation is sinful, and hence that abstinence from the sexual act is praiseworthy. Yet Reding's embarrassment, which is also Newman's, is as clear an indication as could be given that this was only a superficial account of the matter. For Reding, as for Newman, the idea of sexual union had evidently *no* fascination. It was a 'sin', but not a temptation; and the idea of celibacy seemed to have a positive value, which he failed altogether to put into words. It may have been that he could not possibly put it into words, for the reason that it did not really exist. The physical side of marriage was deeply repugnant to him; love must be ideal, but in marriage it was bound to be carnal; he translated his repugnance, in itself a weakness, into a virtue. And Newman, for all his powers of introspection and logical analysis, was defeated here by something obscure in his own nature; and showed his defeat by his reluctance and his inability to explain in what the value of the celibate ideal really consisted.

In one of the younger members of his party the interdependence between virginity or celibacy and a disposition formed for romantic friendship was more obviously marked than in Newman's subtler temperament. Frederic Faber came up to Balliol from Harrow in 1833. He migrated from Balliol to University College, where he won a scholarship and was elected to a Fellowship, defeating Mark Pattison, the future Rector of Lincoln. 'Faber' wrote Pattison in his memoirs 'belonged to the college, in which he was a great favourite, was a dashing talker, though like myself only a second class.' A very intimate friend wrote of him more than fifty years later: 'In person he was extremely prepossessing—of good height, slender figure, fair complexion, bright blue eyes, well-formed features, almost feminine grace. The attraction of his looks and manners, and our agreement in poetical tastes, soon made us friends; and our affection for each other became not only strong, but passionate. There is a place for passion, even in friendship. . . . His opinions, originally Calvinistic, then, as the phrase was, "Tractarian", and finally Roman Catholic, underwent great changes; but his religion under each phase of opinion was intensely earnest and sincere, and his life and conversation pure and without reproach.' He was known in Oxford by the nickname 'Water-lily Faber', from his poem called *The Cherwell Water-lily*, in which he apostrophized that flower as a type 'of virgin love and purity', emblem 'of all a woman ought to be.' He won the Newdigate in 1836 with a poem on 'The Knights of St. John', and the Johnson Divinity scholarship next year; published several volumes of romantic poetry and was made much of by Wordsworth. But the church bells were always ringing in his heart. He took orders and settled down as a country clergyman, only two years before the landslide of 1845, which swept him into the Roman Church.

As a Roman priest Father Faber satisfied his poetical instincts by writing hymns, and his romantic instincts by an extravagant and credulous Italianate piety which Newman came to distrust and dislike. But as Rector of the Brompton Oratory he played a part not less influential than Newman's in the Romanist Revival which followed Tractarianism. Though disease attacked him in his early thirties, and converted the graceful and beautiful youth into a distressingly corpulent, prematurely aged man, he never lost his peculiar fascination over others. 'Nothing' said his brother 'could mar the beauty of his countenance.' He showed no trace of regretting his physical degeneration. It was a trifling cross to bear. The inner life of devotion—a devotion which seemed at times to dwell almost more upon the Virgin and the Saints than upon the Persons of the Trinity—made the accidents of the flesh seem of no account. He died at the age of forty-nine. On the title page of the brief memoir, with which his Protestant brother supplemented the official Catholic *Life*, stands a quotation from *Cymbeline*:

> Such a holy witch
> That he enchants societies unto him:
> Half all men's hearts are his.

And the quotation was not inept. 'I cannot tell why it is, but that Faber fascinates everybody' said a friend of his at Harrow. The remark was carried to him. He recognized its truth and resolved to 'lay this talent at the feet of my Redeemer'. At Oxford he was the centre of an admiring circle of earnest youths. 'He was a great priest' said Monsignor Manning to his own congregation; 'he was the means of bringing multitudes into the One Fold.'

There was a moment—it was hardly more—when Frederic Faber pleased himself and half scandalized his friends with

FREDERIC WILLIAM FABER
From a water colour drawing

the notion of marriage. But how little he can have been in love with the lady is evident from a letter which he wrote only three or four weeks later. His first collected volume of poetry had been published, and some critics had objected to the extravagant tone of his language about his friends. He answers: 'Strong expressions towards male friends are matters of taste. I feel what they express to *men*: I never did to a born woman. Brodie thinks a revival of chivalry in male friendships a characteristic of the rising generation, and a hopeful one.'

His earlier letters to his friends are full of such 'strong expressions'. He tells his 'dearest A' that he is 'one whom I love above all created beings, one whom alas! I often fear I love too much.' The fear grew in him. He palliated it by adoring 'the love of our heavenly Father, who by His grace is leading us in beautiful brotherhood on our Christian path.' But— was there not something a little dishonest (he began to ask himself) in this rendering of a pagan sentiment?

> Alas! it was a most unworthy dream
>   That with my youth had grown,—
> An earthly lure with a false winning gleam
>   Of Heaven about it thrown. . . .
> It may not be: I and my dreams must part,—
>   Part in the blood that flowed,
> Where the stern Cross ran deepest in my heart,
>   Tearing its cruel road.

And so the romantic paganism was by degrees transmuted into 'a romantic devotion to the Deity', the Wordsworthian love of nature into a craving for the courts of heaven.

> O Paradise! O Paradise!
>   'Tis weary waiting here,
> I long to be where Jesus is,
>   To feel, to see Him near.

But until Rome provided him with the means of carrying the process of transmutation to the necessary extreme, he remained, just as Froude did, susceptible to the 'earthly lure'. Travelling in Greece in 1841 he was attended for five weeks

by a young servant named Demetri; the boy kissed his hand
at their parting, 'and rubbed it with his forehead for the last
time', and went away weeping. The master was no less distressed. He had been deeply attracted to Demetri, and had
found an outlet for his affections in trying to combat the lad's
'loose Greek notions'. Such partings, he wrote in his journal,
'would be intolerably heavy-hearted events, if it were not for
the Christian hope which shines with such an awful sweetness
on the places beyond the grave.'

Reading between the lines of their correspondence, one per-
ceives that there was something in Frederic Faber from which
Newman shrank. Was it the younger man's fashionable success? Or was it that in him Newman felt his own romantic
sensibilities exposed, as it were, for all to see, without any of
the careful screens which he set about them? Did he see, in
this transition from extravagant friendship to extravagant
piety, a too naked and obvious rendering of his own emotional progress?

CHAPTER VII

BECOMING A CHURCHMAN

The growth of the intimacy between Froude and Newman was a rather slow process. It was in 1826, Newman
says, that he 'began to know Mr. Hurrell Froude.' That, of
course, was when Froude was elected a Fellow. At the end of
1827 Froude joined the teaching staff as an additional tutor.
During 1828 the two men saw a good deal of each other; but
it was not until 1829, and well on in that year, that they drew
really close together. The steps are, some of them, recorded
by Froude.

In October, 1826, he took a walk with Newman. They
talked about ghosts—a favourite topic of Newman's. The
conversation left an unpleasing taste in Froude's mouth. He
felt, for a moment, that it had shaken the steadiness of his
faith. Next month there was another walk. 'Insensibly got
talking in a way to let him infer I was trying to alter myself.
Also allowed myself to argue. Was puzzled as usual, and have
been uncomfortable and abstracted ever since. Once doubted
whether I had not been wrong, which made me ridiculously
uneasy.' In December he was annoyed with himself for
allowing Newman 'to ask me, without resenting it, whether
I and S. were not "red-hot High Churchmen".' A sense of
irreconcilable opposition between Newman's religious views
and his own kept them apart until the tutorship brought
them together. In the summer of 1828 there are signs of increasing intimacy. In May Newman rides over to Cuddesdon

with Wilberforce and Froude. Correspondence starts in the Long Vacation. Newman writes to ask: 'Did you read Pusey's book on the coach-top as you intended?' Froude sends a long letter about his own idleness ('though I ought to work hard to prepare for Orders'), about his 'dreams of faëry land', about telescopes and astronomy, about religious affectation in a friend's parish at Torquay. And he confesses to Wilberforce that Newman 'is a fellow that I like more, the more I think of him; only I would give a few odd pence if he were not a heretic.'

That summer was memorable to Newman for many reasons, and not least because, through Froude's good offices, he was asked to stay with Keble and his father at Fairford. 'Yours ever affectionately' he signs his answer, but hints that he is still what Froude called a 'heretic' by referring to John Sumner's appointment to be Bishop of Chester—Sumner being an Evangelical—and saying that it has given him sincere pleasure. The few days that he spent at Fairford in August were wet and dull, and Newman felt that he had not done himself justice. But he found himself in 'quite an affecting and most happy world. . . . Keble's verses are written (as it were) on all their faces. My head ran so upon them that I was every minute in danger of quoting them. Mr. Keble as well as John shows much playfulness and even humour in his conversation.'

Newman's mother and sisters spent the last weeks of the vacation in a cottage at Nuneham Courtenay lent to them by Dornford, Newman's senior colleague in the tutorship; and Newman stayed there with them. According to Mozley it was the very cottage in which Jean-Jacques Rousseau had lived for a time. An ironical kind of coincidence! There, no doubt, he persevered with his reading of the Fathers; it was, the *Apologia* says, in the Long Vacation of this year that he set about the task. And a cloud no bigger than a man's hand rose upon his tutorial horizon. He and Wilberforce were elaborating a scheme for the reorganization of the tutorship system, subject to the Provost's approval.

The tutors seemed at first to be getting their way. At any rate Newman, writing to Rickards [1] early in 1829, explained their plans, as though they had been finally agreed upon. 'The most important and far-reaching improvement has been commenced this term—a radical alteration (not apparent on the published list) of the lecture system. The bad men are thrown into large classes, and thus time saved for the better sort, who are put into very small lectures, and principally with their own tutors quite familiarly and chattingly. And besides, a regular system for *the year* has been devised. But we do not wish this to be talked about.'

But this confidence was premature. It must have been very soon afterwards that a definite difference of opinion showed itself between the Provost on the one hand, the four tutors on the other. Hawkins 'maintained that Newman was sacrificing the many to the few, and governing . . . by a system . . . of mere personal influence and favouritism.' Newman felt that the Provost preferred 'a heartless system of law and form in which the good and promising were sacrificed to the worthless and uninteresting.' But this statement of the quarrel is too guarded. The real difference lay much deeper. It was not merely that Hawkins objected to the tutors giving too little time to the inferior men—though the objection was a perfectly reasonable one; nor was it that he objected to each tutor having his own special batch of pupils; he felt deeply suspicious of the influence which the tutors were beginning to exercise on the best men. Newman was getting such a hold over their minds as might well startle and alarm any prudent Head of a College. His three colleagues—the swashbuckling Dornford, the painstaking Wilberforce, the eccentric Froude—they were all succumbing, or had succumbed, to his masterful influence. The

---

[1] The letter already quoted on p. 184.

Provost reflected with amazement on the rapid advance of
this young man, who had sat so humbly at his own feet only
four years earlier, to the dominant position in the College.
Looking across to St. Mary's he saw the pulpit which he had
occupied with so much force and learning becoming, now
that Newman stood in it, a sudden power in the University.
He saw Newman hobnobbing with 'red-hot High Churchmen'; he detected a change of opinion, leading God knew
where, but passing certainly beyond the sensible point at
which he, Hawkins, had hoped to stay it. Something odd was
afoot. Was the Provost to be a mere cypher in his own
College? Was he to look on and see Oriel become an object
of suspicion to the country at large? Newman 'held almost
fiercely that secular education could be so conducted as to
become a pastoral cure. He recollected that Origen had so
treated it, and had by means of the classics effected the conversion of Gregory the Apostle of Pontus, and of Athenodorus
his brother.' Whether he quoted these instances to Hawkins
or not, the Provost knew well enough the kind of ideas that
now filled his mind, and resolved at least to limit the opportunities which the four tutors sought for proselytizing their
pupils.

It is impossible not to feel the strongest sympathy with
Hawkins in the position in which he found himself. He was
new to his office; he felt the great responsibility which was
his as a successor to two Provosts of genius—Eveleigh and
Copleston—who had succeeded in placing Oriel *hors concours*
in the University; there was no question of the exceptional
ability and energy of the tutors; he owed his own election
to the support of Newman; he was one with them in his
conviction that the tutorial system needed reform. Yet the
particular reform for which they asked had these two great
defects—that it tended to leave the ordinary or stupid or
indolent undergraduate to work out his own salvation or
damnation, and that it sought to put the clever promising

young men completely into the hands of their tutors. Even on secular grounds there was a case to be made against this— and a strong case. But the Provost's difficulty lay in the fact that the secular objection was as nothing to the religious one. Gentlemen did not send their sons to Oriel in order that they might be turned into religious prigs or fanatics. And yet the Provost could not be sure what the tutors really proposed to do. The Oxford Movement was not yet begun. He was compelled to rely on his instincts; and, in his arguments, to fall back upon the least important of the two grounds for his opposition. And in the end, after a largely meaningless battle of words, he was obliged to enforce his view by a mere exercise of his authority, which eviscerated Oriel and reacted unhappily upon his own prestige and character. The tragedy of Hawkins was the tragedy of many a ruler and statesman, repeated *in petto*.

But while there still seemed some possibility of compromise, he did his best. This is how Newman himself concluded his account of the quarrel, and with it the reader can be left to judge where his own sympathies lie.

'The main practical argument which the Provost urged upon him, on behalf of his continuing tutor on the old system of lecturing was, "You may not be doing so much good as you may wish or think you would do, but the question is, whether you will not do some good, some real substantial good." Mr. Newman used to laugh and say to his friends, "You see the good Provost actually takes for granted that there is no possible way for me to do good in my generation, except by being one of his lecturers; with him it is that or nothing."'

Agreement between the tutors and the Provost becoming thus, at length, evidently impossible, Hawkins put an end to the dispute by the use of the authority, which he had hitherto kept scrupulously in the background. In June, 1830, he wrote to Newman—and in similar terms to Wilberforce and Froude—a letter which concluded: 'And I am most reluctant to do so still, but I yield to what you seem to desire, and feel bound, therefore, to say that, if you cannot comply with my earnest desire, I shall not feel justified in committing any other pupils to your care.'

The result was, in Mark Pattison's words, that 'from this date the college began to go downhill, both in the calibre of the men who obtained fellowships and in the style and tone of the undergraduates.' Oriel had become a house divided against itself.

2. FIRST BLOWS FOR THE CHURCH

The end of 1828, then, found Newman entering upon his battle with Hawkins, beginning his intensive study of the Fathers, preaching to crowded congregations at St. Mary's, and moving into a close intimacy with Froude and Keble. It found Pusey married, Professor of Hebrew and Canon of Christ Church, and engaged in a somewhat violent controversy with Mr. Hugh Rose of Cambridge over the state of Protestantism in Germany. Keble was still at Southrop and Fairford.

Pusey's appointment was a pleasant excitement to his friends. Keble was 'a little apprehensive of his reading himself to death. For I suppose, by the Rule of Three, Fellowship : Canonry :: Headache : Apoplexy.' But though Pusey was never at any time of his life a man of the world, there were other things besides scholarship to claim his attention just now. He had a young wife 'of striking appearance, handsome and handsomely dressed'; there were calls and dinnerparties; 'their domestic establishment was well-appointed'; they kept a carriage and pair, and Pusey—except when he forgot where he was and what he was doing—enjoyed exhibiting his skill as a whip to young Mrs. Pusey. Children were on their way. And Newman felt a twinge of envy. For a moment his 'deep imagination' was shaken. Had Pusey chosen the better way? 'Seek we lady-lighted home,' he concluded a poem on *My Lady Nature and her Daughters*,

> Nature 'mid the spheres bears sway,
> Ladies rule where hearts obey.

And, with Pusey's dedication of himself to sacred learning in his mind, he uttered a sigh to Harriett: 'How desirable it seems to be to get out of the stir and bustle of the world, and not to have the responsibility and weariness of success!'

An unreal wish, and he knew it. He was incapable of idleness. At this time he was Treasurer of Oriel, and exhibiting a practical skill in the management of the College finances which actually drew a compliment from the late Provost. And a storm blew up early in the new year which made him discover in himself a further range of unsuspected enthusiasms and capacities.

It was one of the many dramatic ironies in Newman's career that he should have learned his powers as a leader of difficult causes by successfully opposing the political emancipation of the Church which he afterwards joined. If it had not been for the Peel by-election in Oxford and the extraordinary stimulus which it gave to the aggressive elements in Newman's character, it is conceivable that he would never have pressed the Tractarian movement so hard and fast and far, and that he might have died an Anglican Bishop or Archbishop instead of a Cardinal.

Robert Peel was the senior Burgess of the University of Oxford. He had hitherto opposed Roman Catholic Emancipation. But in 1828 O'Connell, though a Catholic, was elected to Parliament as member for County Clare. The law prevented him from taking his seat. Peel and Wellington perceived that unless the law was altered there would be civil war in Ireland. They resolved, in face of their political past, to force Emancipation through Parliament.

On February 5, 1829, Convocation at Oxford adopted a

petition against this surrender to the Irish agitation, and
Peel felt it his duty to resign his seat as a representative of
the University. On February 8 Newman, writing to his
sister, said that he had no opinion on the Catholic question.
But within the week he had become the head and forefront
of the opposition to Peel's re-election. A series of breathless,
excited letters to Harriett and his mother revealed to them a
novel fierce exultant John. 'Our meddling Provost'—'disgust
of Mr. Peel'—the 'intolerable insolence' of the Peelites—these
were unpleasant-sounding phrases. And why this inexplicable
passion over a question to which he had proclaimed himself
indifferent? 'We have achieved a glorious victory. It is the
first public event I have been concerned in, and I thank
God from my heart both for my cause and its success. We
have proved the independence of the Church and of Oxford.'
'My mind is so full of ideas in consequence of this important
event, and my views have so much enlarged and expanded,
that in justice to myself I ought to write a volume.' And what
strange paradoxical ideas they seemed to Mrs. Newman to
be! The Church likely to be separated from the State—all
the talent of the day concentrated against it—its principles
only to be maintained by 'prejudice and bigotry', qualities
not to be despised, since they transmit the truth. As for
Catholic Emancipation, that had not been the *crux* of the
election. He was 'clearly *in principle* an anti-Catholic'; but
'the intelligence of the country will have' Emancipation; to
oppose it was inexpedient, perhaps impossible. Why, then,
had John been so bitter against poor Mr. Peel? Mrs. Newman
wondered. Ought not a statesman to take inexpediency and
impossibilities into account as much as a young clergyman
at Oriel? Ah! but that was not the point. The point was to
strike a blow for the Church. John began to feel that he must
have tired his mother about the Catholic question. Had he
said 'bewildered and alarmed' instead of 'tired', he would
have chosen his words more accurately.

The short sharp battle which resulted in Sir Robert Inglis representing the University instead of Mr. Robert Peel, and so committed the foremost intellectual centre of England to opposing, not only Catholic Emancipation, but parliamentary reform, Jewish relief, and the repeal of the Corn Laws, brought Newman and Keble still closer together. Pusey ranged himself on the other side. But the two chief intractables were indulgent to him. 'I do not reckon Pusey or Denison among our opponents,' Newman reassured Harriett 'because they were strong for concession beforehand.' But all Oriel, all the resident Fellows, were solidly behind Newman and Keble.

The Peel election was followed by the election of two new Fellows of Oriel, both of whom belonged whole-heartedly to Newman's camp. One of these was John Christie, 'a sound and elegant scholar' who 'read all the novels and all the poetry of the day, and took to Tennyson, it may be said, at first sight.' The other was Thomas Mozley. Newman was delighted. Mozley, he told Rickards enthusiastically, 'will be one of the most surprising men we shall have numbered in our lists. . . . He is not quick or brilliant, but deep, meditative, clear in thought, and imaginative. His ἦθος is admirable . . . he is amiable and, withal, entertaining in parlance, and to sum up all somewhat eccentric at present in some of his notions.' Mozley had many excellent qualities; but depth and clearness of thought were conspicuously not among them. He was a shrewd observer, an admirable *raconteur*, but his mind moved on the surface of things. As he said of himself, he could never concentrate his attention on a serious matter for even ten minutes; in his capacity as one of Newman's disciples he was like the 'poor weakling, who insists on joining an Alpine adventure when he cannot but break down at the first pinch.' He panted cheerfully behind Newman, and even dreamed of following him to Rome. But by that time he had begun to build a church; and the idea of aban-

Q

doning an unfinished building was really much more objectionable than a mere change of creed. So he stayed where he was, anchored by Harriett and his architectural enthusiasms.

In the summer the Newmans left Brighton and settled for the Long Vacation in the little village of Horspath near Oxford. John rode into Oxford in the mornings. A piano was borrowed. Blanco White came out and played the fiddle. The devoted Henry Wilberforce took lodgings nearby. Mozley came to stay for a few weeks. Altogether 'an harmonious period, that might well live in the memory of all concerned in it, and perhaps raise gloomy contrasts as time went on.' John had intended to sink back into Irenaeus and Cyprian. But the riding in and out of Oxford, and the musical evenings, and the cares of St. Mary's, and routine college duties, and his favourite occupation of sorting and arranging and burning his papers, left no time for the Fathers. There was some correspondence between himself and Froude and Pusey. He wanted Froude to become his curate and take Littlemore off his hands. But Froude refused: 'You see I am a double-minded man, unstable in all my ways.'

As for Pusey, he was at work on his answer to Mr. Rose and wrestling with the problem of Inspiration. What, please, did Newman think of his observations upon this matter? Newman thought very well of the observations. 'His view of inspiration,' he reported to Froude 'I think you will be much pleased with. It is one which has by fits and starts occurred to me. He has put it into system, and I do believe it is the old Orthodox doctrine. He holds the inspiration of the Church and of all good men, for example Socrates.' Froude was also pleased. 'I hope Pusey may turn out High Church after all', he replied. The topic was a delicate one. In his first book Pusey had contended that historical passages in the Bible, on which no question of doctrine turned, were not necessarily inspired. Study had revealed to him the existence of 'historical contradictions' in the sacred text—minute and unimportant certainly, but uncomfortably difficult to reconcile with the doctrine of plenary inspiration. But Pusey's reservation had much upset Keble; and it had been distorted by Rose into a denial of the inspiration of the Gospels. It looked to many as if Pusey, writing about German rationalism, had himself been infected by that dreadful disease of the sceptical intellect. It was important to get the matter straight. But by Hawkins's advice the discussion upon inspiration was abbreviated in the second book. And for the rest of his life poor Pusey never heard the last of it. It is to be doubted if he ever did get the matter straight even in his own mind. In 1841 he floundered painfully in the effort to explain to a correspondent that he had never doubted the plenary inspiration of Holy Scripture; he had only ventured to think that the Holy Ghost did not extend His guidance 'into such minute details and circumstances as in no way affected the truth.' And in his will he directed that neither of the offending books should be republished.

'I hope Pusey may turn out High Church after all', Froude could now say to Newman. Certainly Pusey would turn out High Church. Newman himself was already at that point, and already moving past it into some as yet unformulated position. Since the Peel affair he had definitely broken with Whately. 'Still in my rooms at Oriel College,' he wrote as he sat there alone one day in this September, remote from the family circle at Horspath, 'slowly advancing and led by God's hand blindly.' The tone of his sermons changed. 'We are the English Catholics' he told his congregation this autumn. 'There is not a dissenter living but, inasmuch, and so far as he dissents, is in a sin.' And as he penned these words he thought of his brother Frank standing on the brink of separation from the Church. He must have known well what pain this opinion would give his mother. Yet, since it was now his opinion, he had no option but to express it; no

option but to send her the sermon, as he always sent his
sermons, for her to read. Mrs. Newman read it and said
nothing. But Harriett—writing now from Dornford's cottage
at Nuneham, to which the three women had moved from
Horspath at the end of October, with thick snow outside and
a chill sense of desolation within—asked him to 'give us a
decent lengthened call. I should like a quarter of an hour's
quiet talk with you. . . . We have long since read your two
sermons; they are very High Church. I do not think I am
near so High, and do not quite understand them yet.'

Since March Newman had been one of the secretaries of
the Oxford Branch of the Church Missionary Society. This
was, of course, an Evangelical body. But since March he had
moved very rapidly from his old Evangelical associations.
Some kind of step had to be taken; and the step which Newman actually took was a highly characteristic one. He began
by protesting to his fellow-secretary on the score of certain
offensive doctrines put forward by two preachers in aid of
the Society's funds. Dissatisfied with the reply which he
received, he attacked the senior secretary in committee by
moving an enormous number of amendments to his report.
Such was his persuasiveness that these amendments were
only negatived by the chairman's casting-vote. Defeated at
the centre, he changed his tactics, and circulated an anonymous pamphlet (February 1830) in which he urged Churchmen of his own way of thinking to swamp the Society by
becoming members. It was well known that Newman was
the author. And though some of his immediate friends
thought his action, if impracticable, yet bold and praiseworthy, others took a different view. Rickards warmly
denied that Newman could possibly have written anything
so mean, and was mortified to discover that he was wrong.
The Society took instant revenge, and turned him out of the
secretaryship in March. A few months later the last strand
of the rope was cut; and he removed his name from the Bible

Society. Almost simultaneously—this was in June—the Provost terminated the argument about the tutorship by stopping the flow of further pupils to Newman, Wilberforce and Froude.

'We die gradually with our existing pupils', he wrote to his mother, who had returned to Brighton. 'This to me personally is a delightful arrangement. . . . But for the College I think it a miserable determination. . . . I am full of projects what I shall do. The Fathers arise again full before me. This vacation I should not wonder if I took up the study of the Modern French Mathematics.'

3. THE CHURCH IN DANGER

It is not easy to trace the course of Newman's deepening intimacy with Froude during these years. The correspondence of each is only represented by scraps. The little which survives is of no great interest in itself, except that it shows Froude leading, Newman following, with a show of independence and an occasional attempt to dig himself in, before he is finally pulled across the boundary between tradition and private judgment. On January 9, 1830, (while he was meditating his attack on the Church Missionary Society) he wrote to Froude a rambling letter on various topics. Blomfield, Bishop of London, he is glad to note, 'maintains the propriety and expedience of the Athanasian Creed', and he hopes that this will recommend the Bishop (an Evangelical) to 'worthier thoughts' in Froude's mind. At this stage it would seem that Newman was meditating a kind of amalgam between the High Church and Low Church parties. There are parts of the Creed, he goes on, which he 'would willingly see omitted, if it could be done silently, and could not defend if attacked'; but, on the other hand, 'to cut it out would be to lose the damnatory clauses, and to curtail it even would be to flatter the vain conceit of the age.' His objections to

the Creed lay, in fact, not at all where the ordinary man
feels them to lie, but in such theologically inexact expressions
(so he considered them) as 'the Son is equal to the Father.'
From theology the letter passes to politics. 'I have doubt' he
writes, 'whether we *can* consider our King as a proprietor
of land on the old Tory theory. The rightful heir was lost in
the Revolution; then the nation took the property of the
island and gave it to William, and then to George, on *certain
conditions*—that of being chief *magistrate*. Has not the Constitution since that time been essentially a republic?' From
politics to Arnold's newly published Sermons, which he had
lent to a friend and dipped into himself. Really, they were
not at all bad. From the sermons to University politics. And
here, again, he is for a sensible compromise. There was a
movement on foot to 'exclude Aristotle and bring in modern
subjects'. This should be forestalled by reasonable concessions.
'I should like to make Modern History, or Hebrew etc. etc.,
necessary for the M.A. degree.' At the end of the letter come
two references to something which Froude must have said.
'I have thought vows are evidences of *want of faith*.' Editing
the letter in old age Newman added some explanatory
words to this sentence. After 'vows' he wrote 'e.g. of Celibacy'; and after 'faith' he wrote 'N.B. trust'. Now why
should he have altered 'faith' to 'trust'? Was it that Froude
had suggested that they should exchange vows of celibacy,
and that he felt that such an exchange would imply a want
of trust in each other? The other reference is an obscure
defence of private judgment. 'Qy. What is meant by the
right of private judgment? The *duty* I understand; but no one
can *help* another's thinking in private.' Later, he was to go
the whole way with Froude in condemning private judgment
as the fount of all evil.

In the summer Newman found time for a fortnight's visit
to his mother at Brighton. He rode by stages all the way there
and back. As he passed over the downs and through fields

and woods and villages, 'the fascination of a country life nearly overset' him. He began to think, in the very manner of Hurrell, that a lonely romantic curacy would have inexpressible charms. And as for a country living! Well, it was the only great temptation he had to fear, 'for as to other fascinations which might be more dangerous still, I am pretty well out of the way of them' (all this in a letter to Rickards) 'and at present I feel as if I would rather tear out my heart than lose it.' At least he earnestly desires that he may never be rich; and (though he is less sure of his sincerity over this) that he may never rise in the Church. This was the vein for Rickards, whose good opinion of him, since the Church Missionary Society pamphlet, needed a little fostering. But to Hurrell he wrote in a somewhat different strain, describing a misadventure on the road. His mare 'came down the last morning, her knees quite uninjured, but my nose cut pretty deep with the silver of my glass. It seemed to promise a scar, but will be nothing. I shall leave off glasses in riding. So I finished by walking twenty-one miles in a broiling sun on a dusty road.' Then at the end of his letter: 'I think of setting up for a great man; it is the only way to be thought so.'

Outside Oxford events of every kind were working towards the overthrow of the system of ideas to which Newman was binding himself. The repeal of the Test Act and Catholic Emancipation were already accomplished facts—accomplished, too, by a Tory government. The end of that period of grudging reform was very near. In the country at large the tide of dissatisfaction was rising—dissatisfaction with the whole *régime* of Tory squire and Tory parson; with the tyrannies of tradition, clericalism, religious dogma, hereditary power; with social and economic misery and injustice; with the fossilized institutions of Church and State. Authority, in the person of the great Duke, clung to the past because it was the past. But there was a new and vigorous challenge to authority growing up, in the persons of the industrialists great and small, for whom there was no place in the antiquated structure of English government and English society. These men were not to be subordinated to the squirearchy for ever. Later on, their highest ambition would be to become squires themselves. But first they had to fight their own battle. The mass of the common people in the industrial and rural areas alike was equally discontented. Consequently, the movement for reform had an irresistible weight as well as an irresistible impetus. Parliamentary reform was the immediate objective. But the reform of everything was in the air. The slow working in the heavy English intellectual soil of the principles which inspired the first French Revolution was beginning to be evident. Authoritarianism was being breached. In 1827 Brougham founded that 'godless institution', University College in London, where dissenters and rationalists might receive the education denied to them at Oxford and Cambridge. Newman's own brother was to become one of its Professors. Now in July, 1830, came the news of the second French Revolution. Charles X had tried to restore the Church in France to its ancient supremacy; he had even attempted to make sacrilege punishable with death. The mob overthrew him. Early in August he was obliged to abdicate, and Louis Philippe replaced him, in a constitutional monarchy upon English lines.

The effect of this revolution upon English opinion was enormous. 'It gave Englishmen' says Professor Trevelyan 'the sense of living in a new era, when great changes could safely be made.' To Froude and Newman it gave, on the contrary, the sense of living in an era when every institution of value was in danger, only to be saved by heroic exertions. 'What a horrid affair this is in France', wrote Froude to his friend. 'I admire the spirit of the King and Polignac . . . and, if I were king, would rather lose my head than retract one step. As to English affairs, the Whigs seem to be successful everywhere. . . . Such thoughts are too gloomy to pursue.' And to Keble he wrote a month later: 'The fate of the poor King of France, whose only fault seems to have been his ignorance how far his people were demoralised, will give spirits to the rascals in all directions.'

Newman shared these opinions. 'The French' he wrote to Froude 'are an awful people. How the world is set upon calling evil good, good evil! This Revolution seems to me the triumph of irreligion. . . . The effect of this miserable French affair will be great in England.' Froude's letters continued to reflect his discomfort. 'Things' he told Keble next January 'are still in a bad way down here [i.e. in Devonshire]. The labouring population, as well as the farmers, seem thoroughly indifferent to the welfare of the parsons and squires. . . . Two very great fires have taken place in our neighbourhood. . . . I have now made up my sage mind that the country is too bad to deserve an Established Church.' And in the following June: 'You see they almost persecute the Roman Catholics at Paris.'

Indeed the situation in England was alarming. 'All autumn', to quote Professor Trevelyan again, 'the agitation in the country was deeper than political. Economic misery, pauperism, starvation and class injustice had brought society to the verge of dissolution. Rick burning . . . kept the rural south in terror. In the industrial north the workmen were drilling and preparing for social war. The middle classes clamoured for Reform.' Even at Windrush, where Isaac Williams was now a curate, 'there occurred some agrarian riots, and every one was much alarmed and panic struck; John Keble rode with the mob fearlessly and good-naturedly, entreating them not to demolish the farmer's machines; they put forth a Methodist preacher to answer him, as he stood on a machine begging them to desist.'

The political events of these years led so directly to the

birth of the Oxford Movement, that the reader may like to refresh his memory of them by a very brief summary. The new Parliament, elected on the death of George IV, met in November 1830. The Duke, challenged by the Whig leader Lord Grey upon the question of Reform, replied that the existing system of Parliamentary representation possessed the full and entire confidence of the country. This was too palpably not the truth. The Government was defeated in the House of Commons, the Duke resigned, and the new King sent for the veteran champion of reform, Earl Grey. Grey's administration was predominantly aristocratic. This was as it should be, since the House of Lords was at once the principal stumbling-block to reform and contained the ablest champions of reform. The Reform Bill was produced in March. It was a bold measure, extinguishing the rotten boroughs without compensation to their owners. As such it was too strong for the stomachs of some of Grey's supporters. Unable to carry his Bill without emasculating it, he persuaded the King to agree to a dissolution. At the General Election of May the Bill swept the country; Grey returned to power with a large majority. The Bill passed the Commons; but in October it was thrown out by the Lords. Feeling in the country was bitter in the extreme. But in the event, after a prolonged struggle, the Lords capitulated under the threat of a wholesale creation of peers, and the Reform Bill became law in May 1832.

That the opinions of Keble, Froude and Newman were antipathetic to Reform is almost self-evident. It was a Whig measure, inspired by utilitarians and 'useful knowledge people', as Newman contemptuously called men earnestly concerned in such matters. It was shocking to see so much waste of passion upon a purely secular question. There could be no question that Reform would not stop at Parliament. The Church would inevitably be attacked; at worst 're-formed' from above by Bishops who were not believers in

Christianity in any true sense of the word, but Liberals in matter of religion. 'And in saying this,' said Newman to Bowden 'I conceive I am saying almost as bad of them as can be said of anyone.' At best the Church would be disestablished; and Newman, at any rate, felt that he would 'rather have the Church severed from its temporalities, and scattered to the four winds', than have 'such a desecration of holy things' as the elevation to the episcopal bench of men like Samuel Parr, the clerical 'Whig Johnson', who had died before the Whigs could make a bishop of him.

But Newman was more of a realist than his friends. Not that he, any more than they, had the smallest understanding of social problems. His interest in the lower orders was confined to their souls. Poverty and subjection are, it is well known, good for the soul. He was, as Mozley observed, 'no morbid philanthropist or indiscriminate almsgiver'. The task of the servant—the slave even—is to be a good servant, or a good slave. Tom Mozley tells an anecdote of him which illustrates his natural attitude towards his inferiors. Newman had been staying with his brother-in-law at Cholderton. Mozley's gardener drove him into Salisbury and chattered amiably to him all the way—eleven miles. 'Pony went well,' Newman wrote in his next letter 'and so did Meacher's tongue. Shoot them both. They will never be better than they are now.' But if he expected the lower orders to accept their lot in life with Christian fortitude, he had a natural sense of their power, when they moved together in a mass. 'The nation (i.e. numerically the $\pi\lambda\hat{\eta}\theta o\varsigma$) is for revolution. ... They certainly have the physical power.' This of the Reform Bill. The thing must come. There is no more to be said about it. Let the Church look to her defences. 'It is the sophism of the day to put religious considerations out of sight.'

After the Reform Bill had been passed, the Whigs set to work to reform all round—and very necessary the effort was. And naturally one of their first moves was against the

anomaly of the Established Church in Ireland. 'Twenty-two
Protestant bishops' as Trevelyan concisely puts it, 'drew
£150,000 a year, and the rest of the Church £600,000 more,
very largely from the Catholic peasants.' These revenues
were mainly derived from the tithes payable to an alien
Church, which was there against the wishes of the great
majority of Irishmen, who had a perfectly good Church of
of their own. The position was one plainly impossible to
maintain, in face of the growing resentment of the Irish. It
could only be, and was being, maintained by armed force.
Yet the feeble attempt of the Whig government in 1833 to
ease the Irish ecclesiastical problem by suppressing ten out
of the twenty-two Irish bishoprics roused a storm of indignant protest in England and resulted in its own immediate
downfall. Not until 1869, when Gladstone disestablished and
partly disendowed the Protestant Episcopal Church in Ireland, did Englishmen come to their senses—as always, in
Irish matters, a generation too late.

It was the abortive attempt to suppress the ten Irish
bishoprics which gave the initial impetus to the Oxford
Movement. We are still not arrived, in our narrative, at that
point. But all the factors are now assembled. And we may
now ask ourselves the question, how it could possibly have
seemed to Newman that this was a platform on which he
could confidently take his stand. That men like Keble, all
passionate loyalty to the English Church and ingeniously
stupid resistance to every kind of reform, or like the pedantic
Palmer of Worcester, or even like the extravagantly thorough-
going Froude, should dig themselves in over the Irish Bishoprics—that need not astonish us at all. But Newman! With his
sense of the inevitable; and, still more remarkable, with his
sense of 'that vast Catholic body broken into many fragments by the power of the Devil'—the Catholics in England,
the Roman Catholics, the Greek Catholics, and so on [1]—how

---

[1] *Parochial Sermons*, iii. 208. This sermon was preached in 1830.

could he, with any respect for his own logic, fail to see that the real Church of Ireland was one of these fragments, and a quite different fragment from the Established Church of England?

The Whig attack failed. But the succeeding Whigs, while they left Ireland alone, fulfilled the expectations of Newman and his friends; though not quite in the way expected. They laid impious hands on the finances of the Church. In 1836 they set up the body known as the Ecclesiastical Commissioners. No one nowadays would dream of regarding this as anything but an obviously beneficial reform. Wakeman, the High Church ecclesiastical historian, writes of it: 'The State itself passed somewhat under the influence of the new spirit [i.e. the Church revival] and ceased to present an unsurmountable obstacle to Church development . . . the incomes of bishops and capitular bodies were fixed, and as far as possible equalized, and funds thus set free for the endowment of new parishes and the assistance of poor benefices.' Not so was the Act regarded by the parents of Anglo-Catholicism. 'Pusey' wrote Newman to Bowden in 1838 'is writing a most elaborate article on the Church Commission, which (so far as I have seen it) is a most overpowering and melancholy exposure of it by a mere statement of facts.'

These events lie a little ahead of the point we have now reached. But the common apprehension of them drew the friends together, and tightened Froude's hold over Newman. Little by little—so Newman summarized Froude's influence upon him—'he made me look with admiration towards the Church of Rome, and in the same degree to dislike the Reformation. He fixed deep in me the idea of devotion to the Blessed Virgin, and he led me gradually to believe in the Real Presence.'

4. 'A VOW HAD BOUND HIM'

Family matters were filling up Newman's time at the end of the summer of 1830. His mother and sisters had decided to leave Brighton for good. They moved to Iffley, close to Oxford and to Littlemore, to a small house made out of two old cottages knocked into one, which they called Rose Hill. A little later they exchanged Rose Hill for a pretty modern house called Rose Bank. From this new point of vantage they were able to mix in Oxford society, to take in hand the school and the poor parishioners of Littlemore, and to watch John's alarming progress at close quarters. Frank went, as it was thought, for good to Persia as a Nonconformist missionary. 'God guide us' (not Frank) 'in His way!' noted his brother in his diary. Charles was preparing to make his life a curse to himself and a burden to his relations. He went to Bonn at the expense of his two brothers to take a literary degree, and came away without seeking the degree. John got him a clerkship in the Bank of England; but he could not be restrained from writing letters of advice to the Directors, and soon lost his post. After that he was a charge upon John and Frank and Tom Mozley until his death. This August, while John was preparing Rose Hill for his mother, he received a letter from Charles attacking the Christian faith. He answered it in twenty-four closely written foolscap pages 'all about nothing', and wrote in great despondency to Froude. 'All my plans fail. When did I ever succeed in any exertion for others?' It was a mood which recurred more and more frequently as life went on.

At the end of the year Newman was 'weak and deaf' from overwork, and sleeping very badly. What the cause of the overwork was, it is not easy to see. He still had his pupils to finish off, and his sermons to write, and the petty business of the Bursarship. But these had been with him for some time, and he had no big task on his hands. Presumably he was reading in his Fathers. A proposal had been made to him to take part in a projected Ecclesiastical History. But this did not take definite shape till the early spring. In March he was in correspondence with Hugh Rose—Pusey's adversary—who was editing for Rivington, the publisher, a series of books forming a Theological Library. Two proposals were made to him. First a book on the Thirty-nine Articles; second a history of the Councils of the Church. The first was dropped, the second accepted; and in the summer of 1831 he began his reading. He set to work at once on the Council of Nicaea—the great assembly of ecclesiastical dignitaries summoned by the Emperor Constantine in the year A.D. 325 to settle the dispute upon the nature of Christ which had arisen between the Bishop of Alexandria and the deacon Arius. Arius taught that the Son was a different person from the Father, by whom he had been created. He was not truly God, nor was he truly Man, though he had worn the appearance of a man. It was an early version of the heresy which Pusey had noted in Germany—Christ was no more than a superior embodiment of the divine manifestation. It was a heresy which barely escaped becoming orthodoxy. Although the Nicene Council condemned it by a large majority, Arianism became for a great part of the fourth century the dominant religion in the Eastern empire.

In tackling the Nicene Council, therefore, Newman found himself in contact with something very much more complicated than a mere assertion of the right over the wrong doctrine. It became necessary to trace the ancestry and to follow the fortunes of the wrong doctrine, which had so nearly usurped the place of the right one; to understand, or to seek to understand, the significance of the theological quarrel which seems to a modern rationalist, as it seemed to the Emperor Constantine, the most insane which had ever convulsed society.[1] But rationalists ought to keep their heads,

---

[1] J. M. Robertson, *Short History of Christianity*, chapter ii. § 2.

where emperors may be excused for losing their patience. The dispute went very deep. Arianism, had it been allowed to develop unchecked, must have resulted in the dilution of Christianity into a philosophical Pantheism. We may regret that this was not permitted; but it is mere prejudice to suggest that the quarrel was one of no importance.

Certainly it did not seem so to Newman. The task of un-ravelling its complexity fascinated him. 'It was launching myself on an ocean with currents innumerable; and I was drifted back to the ante-Nicene history; and then to the Church of Alexandria. The work at last appeared under the title of *The Arians of the Fourth Century*.' It was, in fact, refused by the editors of the Theological Library. Rivington himself thought it dull. It was published in 1833 by Lumley; the actual writing of it occupied Newman from the summer of 1831, when he began his reading, to the summer of 1832—a short enough time, if his distractions are taken into account. But, if the book was imperfect, its results upon his own mind were far-reaching. He was in the grip now of a master current, which drifted him in the end from Alexandria to Rome.

July was spent in a visit to Dartington. The two friends travelled down together. They went by sea from Torquay, sleeping on deck, and Froude caught a cold which turned to the epidemic influenza, and was the beginning of his long fatal illness. The holiday was rather spoiled by the influenza, which was everywhere. The whole Rectory was down with it—Newman alone escaped. He wandered idly about, en-joying the rich colouring of the midsummer Devonshire scenery. 'The rocks blush into every variety of colour, the trees and fields are emeralds, and the cottages are rubies. . . . My very hands and fingers look rosy, like Homer's Aurora, and I have been gazing on them with astonishment.' The delicious, fragrant, air made him 'languid, indisposed to speak or write, and pensive', the lusciousness of the grass

and the foliage, and the steepness of the hillsides enclosing
the deep valleys, gave him a certain sense of oppression.
These beauties, exquisitely as he was able to appreciate
them, were not for him. He jotted down some lines for
Harriett:

> There stray'd amid the woods of Dart
>   One who could love them, but who durst not love;
> A vow had bound him, ne'er to give his heart
>   To streamlet bright, or soft secluded grove.

And in something of this spirit he preached in his gloomiest
vein to Archdeacon Froude's parishioners on 'Scripture a
Record of Human Sorrow', bidding them beware of taking
a pleasant sunshine view of the world; for God's dark view
'is the ultimate *true* view of human life.'

Froude stayed in Devonshire reading Plato and writing
letters to his friends and trying to shake off his cough. Plato's
metaphysics passed over his head. But 'as to Socrates, I can
scarcely believe that he was not inspired.' He was playing
with the idea of becoming a historian of the Church in the
Middle Ages. Newman went back to Rose Hill and Oriel and
the Arians. Frederic Rogers (afterwards Lord Blachford),
now his favourite pupil, was reading for his schools at Iffley
and the two spent much time together. They were walking
over Magdalen Bridge into Oxford on September 18 when
someone told them that Whately had been appointed Archbishop of Dublin.

The news produced a strange commotion in Newman's
mind. In spite of the formal break between his old master
and himself which his part in the Peel by-election had
brought about, and in spite of the fact that his path was to
Whately's what a tangent is to a circle, he jumped at once to
the conclusion that Whately would want him to go to Dublin.
A month passed, and no word came. Still Newman believed
that it would come, and vexed himself and Harriett with the
answer that he would make. How could he leave the Arians?
Would his health stand the Irish climate? Moreover, 'if times

R   F.O.A.

are troublous, Oxford will want hot-headed men, and such I
mean to be, and am in my place.' On the other hand, might
it not be his duty to go? For some time he had thought that
a post in Ireland was the one thing that could draw him from
Oxford. Had not Harriett heard him say so? The question
seemed to convey a doubt. But the balancing of *pros* and *cons*
was needless. No word ever came from Whately. When next
they met in Oxford, in 1834, Newman cut him in the street.
Whately had 'made himself dead to me.' True, the younger
man put his conduct on Whately's supposed betrayal of his
frontier post. But how much injured vanity lurked under
that stern judgment?

A few days with Keble at Fairford, this time with a much
more comfortable sense of intimacy. 'I want some of your
criticism,' Keble had said, inviting him, 'for somehow I can't
get it out of my head that you are a real honest man.' And
after the visit: 'I don't care how soon I have an opportunity
of the same kind again.' Then back to Oxford again for the
winter term. Froude was still away trying to get the better of
his cough. Newman suppressed his uneasiness, and threw himself into his History of the Arians. Coming back from a walk
he found thirty-six splendid folios of the Fathers in his room
—a farewell present from his pupils. A few days later a scare
of the cholera reached Oxford. Mrs. Newman instantly
evolved a plan of campaign. She would be head nurse at
Littlemore. 'I have the whole in my head, should it be
ordained that our vicinity is to suffer under the visitation.'
But the cholera did not reach Oxford that winter, and Newman ploughed onwards through 'the twenty-six tomes of
the Concilia'.

One thing happened in the winter to please him—Keble's
election to the Professorship of Poetry. It was not then, and
it is not now, a full Professorship. The Professor gives a
lecture once a term, and he is elected by the members of the
University, not by a small board of electors. A century ago

JOHN KEBLE
*From the drawing by George Richmond
in the National Portrait Gallery*

the election was often governed by religious and political
rather than by literary considerations. The lectures were
delivered in Latin. Matthew Arnold was the first to break
with tradition and lecture in English. Keble's lectures have
not, therefore, received very much attention. Mr. Lock in
his study of Keble deals with them at length. I must confess
that his chapter has not sent me to the original text. He took,
says Mr. Lock, 'as his final guide the poems of the Old
Testament. . . . The canon for which he contends is this, that
the best poets are those who have felt throughout their life
the deepest feelings about Nature, about man, and about
God which were possible at their time.' As a canon of
criticism this may be thought, in our more exacting time,
more than a little inadequate. But it pleased his contemporaries very well. It was, Dean Church claimed, 'the most
original and memorable course ever delivered from the
Chair of Poetry in Oxford'. And indeed, since the poets
directly dealt with were all heathens, it must certainly have
required a good deal of ingenuity to classify them according
to the degree in which they anticipated the Christian
verities.

Soon after this the nature of Froude's disease began to
declare itself. He wrote to Newman a letter 'most welcome,
sad as it was; I call it' said Newman answering it 'certainly
from beginning to end a sad letter, and yet somehow sad
letters, in their place and in God's order, are as acceptable
as merry ones.' He passed the news to Keble, who commented that Froude didn't take proper care of himself. This
was early in January, 1832. A fortnight later Froude was a
little happier about himself; but on February 17 he wrote
to Newman: 'I am afraid I cannot disguise from myself that
within these ten days I have had an attack on my lungs.'
And this was followed by a letter from the Archdeacon to
the effect that he had offered 'to be Hurrell's companion to
the Mediterranean or any other part of the world', though

he doubted whether it would do him any good. But Froude's next letter was more encouraging. He had been thoroughly examined. Whatever had been wrong, he was now thoroughly well and was allowed to return to Oxford. So at least the doctor told him. 'At the same time, he says I must be very cautious, as the thing which formed in my windpipe proves me to be very liable to attack, and he looks upon it as an extraordinary piece of luck that I got rid of it as I did. I am to wear more clothing than I have hitherto done, and to renounce wine for ever: the prohibition extends to beer: *quò confugiam?*' He went from the doctor to Fairford to stay with the Kebles. At least he was there at the beginning of April, still vexed by his inflamed throat, when Newman consulted him about a sermon he was due to preach before the University.

This, his fifth University Sermon, deserves more than a bare mention, for it displays, with peculiar force and clarity, Newman's governing conception of religion. It is a conception so severely limited, and yet so powerful by the very fact of its limitation; so absolute in its assumptions; so fundamentally opposed to the humanistic temper of our own times, as well as to the utilitarian temper of Newman's; that it needs a certain effort to understand it. Yet to understand it is necessary, if we are to understand Newman and Newman's progress through Oxford. It is his *governing* conception. That is not to say that it is the whole of Newman. It is the form in which his philosophy reconciles three different things—his own fear of himself, his inherited or acquired religious principles, his interpretation of history. It leaves out a great deal—his delight in the world of the senses, his enjoyment of a shaped and finished society, all his tenderest and happiest feelings.

The sermon is called 'On Justice as a Principle of Divine Governance'. It was preached on the text from Jeremiah viii. 11: 'They have healed the hurt of the daughter of my

people slightly, saying, Peace, peace; when there is no
peace.' It was directed (Newman told Froude) 'against Sir
James Mackintosh, Knight'. Mackintosh was a leader in the
reform of the savage criminal laws; he was a Benthamite; he
argued that it was impossible to revere a God who was not
completely benevolent.

Newman had no difficulty in refuting that simple proposition, to his own satisfaction. Benevolence is all very well.
But 'if it be natural to pity and wish well to men in general
. . . it is also natural to feel indignation when vice triumphs.'
Moreover, though the instinct of justice implanted in us
tends to *general* good, 'it evidently does not tend to *universal*
good, the good of each individual, and nothing short of this
can be the scope of absolute and simple benevolence. Our
indignation at vice tends to the actual misery of the vicious
—nay to their *final* misery.' Benevolence is certainly admirable. But what about Justice? It is only man's guilty conscience
which prevents him from delighting in 'the traces of God's
justice, which are around us.' Benevolence wins our love.
But Justice commands us. It is a primary notion in our
minds, not to be resolved into other elements. What presumption to suggest, out of our own reason, that the happiness of His creatures is the sole end of God's government!
What does Reason know about it? It cannot even say that
man's creation may not be altogether subservient to some
further divine purpose.

Turn then from these idle hypotheses to the facts. How
does God regard sin? 'A solitary act of intemperance,
sensuality, or anger, a single rash word, a single dishonest
deed, is often the cause of incalculable misery in the sequel
to the person who has been betrayed into it.' A single
example is enough to destroy the idea that God is mere
benevolence. The fact that the punishment is not always
visible on earth can only mean that a worse punishment still
is reserved for the hereafter. As for repentance—how can

repentance wipe out the everlasting consequences of a man's single sin upon the lives of others? 'A man publishes an irreligious or immoral book; afterwards he repents and dies. . . . Shall *he* be now dwelling in Abraham's bosom, who hears on the other side of the gulf the voices of those who curse his memory as being the victims of his guilt?'

'Against these fearful traces or omens of God's visitation upon sin' (the preacher continued) 'we are, of course, at liberty to set all the gracious intimations given us in nature of His placability.' Effort and repentance have some palliative effect. God's rule is not one of absolute unmixed justice, 'which, of course, would reduce every one of us to a state of despair.' But nature tells us nothing of how love and justice can be reconciled. And a religious man 'would hardly wish the rule of justice obliterated. It is something which he can depend upon and recur to. . . . Different, indeed, is his view of God and of man . . . from the flimsy self-invented notions of the mere man of letters, or the prosperous and self-indulgent philosopher!' Let the seeker after truth quit the public haunts of business and pleasure, and consider the tears shed in secret, 'the wearing, never-ceasing struggle between conscience and sin . . . the harassing, haunting fears of death, and a judgment to come,—and the superstitions which these engender. Who can name the overwhelming total of the world's guilt and suffering,—suffering crying for vengeance on the authors of it, and guilt foreboding it!'

Tantum relligio potuit suadere malorum, the philosopher might have retorted to the preacher. But the possibility of such an answer is not in Newman's mind. Even the outward face of the world—the world to which the 'theophilanthropist' appeals for the approval of his flimsy hypothesis—proves 'the extreme awfulness of our condition, as sinners against the law of our being'. Whenever the world thinks of its Maker 'it has ever professed a gloomy religion, in spite of

itself.' Human sacrifice, self-torture—these are man's
natural means of propitiating the unseen powers of Heaven.
Superstition? Yes, relatively to true religion; but 'man's
truest and best religion, *before* the Gospel shines on him. . . .
They who are not superstitious without the Gospel, will not
be religious with it: and I would that even in us, who have
the Gospel, there were more of superstition than there is.'

Our guilt is a growing and an overwhelming misery, as
our eyes open on our real state. God's terrible justice needed
the strong act of Christ's death, 'to counterbalance the
tokens of His wrath which are around us, to calm and
reassure us, and to be the ground and the medium of our
faith.' Precisely *how* Christ's death has secured man's
salvation 'will ever be a mystery in this life.' Yet we have not
merely God's word for it, but the deed itself. 'His reconciliation with our race' is 'no contingency, but an event of past
history'. Our part in the bargain is to believe; if we believe,
though we must still be tried by the rule of God's justice, we
are assured of pardon and justification.

In something of this stern mood he wrote a sharp rebuke
to young Mozley, who was seeking a curacy. 'You have lost
much time in the last four or five years. . . . I have expected
a good deal from you, and have said I expected it. Hitherto
I have been disappointed.'

5. THE STREAMS CONVERGING

The streams, this summer, were beginning to converge.

Froude was in Oxford again, almost his old self. So was
Isaac Williams. So, on occasion, was Keble. Mr. Palmer of
Worcester, the learned authority on the Anglican liturgy,
was become one of Newman's chief admirers. In his rooms
early in June Newman met Pusey's Cambridge adversary—
Hugh Rose. But Pusey and Rose were, in fact, both of the
same mind. Both were alarmed at the inroads of scepticism—

only Rose was more alarmed than Pusey. He and Newman
took to each other instantly. Newman made Pusey call with
him upon Rose; and the call was, he noted in his diary, 'the
termination of their quarrel about German writers'. Froude
also was introduced to the Cambridge visitor, who left
Oxford delighted with his new friends. 'I derived' he told
Palmer 'the very highest gratification which such times as
these admit, from seeing such a body of learned, powerful
and high-minded men.'

Newman was able to hand to Rose the MS. of his *History
of the Arians*, which he had just completed, 'tired wonderfully, continually on the point of fainting away, quite worn
out'.

The British Association met in Oxford this June. The
University, clerical and ignorant as it was, had the courtesy
to confer the honorary degree of D.C.L. upon Brewster,
Faraday, Brown and Dalton. This action was not universally
approved. The new Professor of Poetry was furious. That
this 'hodge-podge of philosophers' should be so honoured!
Oxford had 'truckled sadly to the spirit of the times.' The
Provost of Oriel, on the other hand, thought that the University had done very sensibly in conciliating the scientists.
Dr. Carpenter, the Unitarian amateur scientist, and parent
of scientists and reformers, was tactless enough to say that
Oxford had 'prolonged her existence for a hundred years by
the kind reception he and his fellows had received.'

Newman was a whole world away. He was walking and
talking with Hurrell Froude and Isaac Williams. 'Our principles then' Williams recalled 'were those of the Caroline
Divines, thinking much of the Divine right of kings, and the
like; but we approached perhaps more to those of the non-
jurors. Newman was now becoming a Churchman.'

Becoming! But Williams was a little behind the times. He
had only just come back to Oxford, to be a tutor at Trinity,
from his two years' isolation in a curacy at Windrush. He

was something over full of the Kebles. John Keble had
opened the Christian life to him, while he was still an undergraduate. Thomas, John Keble's brother, the Rector of
Bisley in the Cotswolds, described by Dean Church as 'a man
of sterner type than his brother, with strong and definite
opinions on all subjects' and a severely simple and practical
style of preaching, had completed his religious education.
To Williams the 'Bisley-Fairford' school was the alpha
and omega of Christianity. Everything was judged by
reference to that double standard; everything of merit, in
Froude or in Newman, was derived from it. His mind, too,
had not rid itself of the suspicions about Newman's heterodoxy which Thomas Keble had implanted in him. When
Newman paid his first visit to Fairford, Thomas had been
most uncomfortable at the idea of introducing such a
'liberal' into his father's sacred circle.

Nevertheless Williams was 'greatly charmed and delighted
with Newman', when he was thrown now for the first time
into his society. At first, indeed, he felt uncomfortable.
Was it the mark of a true Christian to be always 'looking
for effect, for what was sensibly effective', as Newman
seemed to be doing? Bisley and Fairford both said that one
ought to leave the effect to God. And Newman seemed
still to have strong traces about him of that dreadful Oriel
set of Noetics—people who thought that it was necessary
and even desirable to use their intelligence in matters of
religion. Later on, Williams felt sure that he had 'always
looked upon the combination of these two schools'—i.e. the
Noetic and the Bisley-Fairford school—'in Newman, who
was first a disciple of Whately's and then of Keble's, as the
cause of such disastrous effects, which have now, in him,
united German rationalism with the Church of Rome, in
their full developments.' Poor Williams! he was, indeed, out
of his depth. But Newman's fascination prevailed over these
doubts; and when the Vicar of St. Mary's astonished him

by asking him to become his curate and look after the
poor of Littlemore, and Thomas Keble told him (with an
abrupt change of mind) that he could not have too much
of the society of such a man, he accepted the offer with
alacrity.

Very soon after that the cholera came to Oxford, this time
in earnest. The vanguard of it reached Oxford in June, in
the last week of the term. Newman had been seriously
alarmed about his own health. One night, after finishing the
Arians, he fell into a panic and 'played the fool' by sending
for the doctor. It was arranged that he should go away for
a month or so, leaving his new curate to look after his parish.
'It was an awful time' wrote Williams in his autobiography
'from the uncertainty which then overhung the nature of
the disease. Froude continued great part of the time with
me in Oxford.' A Fellow of St. John's died, and Williams
buried three persons at St. Clement's. But St. Mary's and
Littlemore remained unaffected. Still, it was a great relief
when Newman came back, and the nervous Williams, after
preaching a sermon on the text 'Let them that suffer according to the will of God commit the keeping of their souls
to him', escaped safely to Aberystwyth.

Newman meanwhile had been to Cambridge, where he
failed to see Rose (who was ill) but was captivated by the
beauty of the sister University, in spite of his 'regret at her
present defects and past history'. In fact, he thought the
place finer than Oxford. From Cambridge he went on to
Ulcombe, and was back in Oxford before the end of July,
to find a note from Palmer: 'Let me hear, my dear friend,
of your health, and may God have you under His protection.' The alarm about the cholera in Oxford and London
was nearing a panic. This ill-bred disease, in spite of Palmer's
comforting reflection that 'few persons in the better classes
of society have taken it yet', was not confining itself to the
poor. Henry Wilberforce could not persuade his mother to

let him visit Newman at Oriel. 'The deaths in the upper classes this week in London have too much alarmed her.' A cousin of the Wilberforces, a lady, had been attacked by the cholera on her way to church at midday on Sunday, and was dead at midnight. The London gentry were flying in every direction. There had been a fatal case at Littlemore, though not in Newman's own parish. The danger was very near.

'The obstinate blockheads' he wrote to Rogers 'have actually first, not burnt, but buried, and now again actually dug up, the bed furniture of the poor patient which they were ordered to destroy. Is not this the very spirit of Whiggery: opposition for its own sake, striving against the truth, because it happens to be commanded us?' As for himself, he is in God's hands; and he cannot rid himself of the strong impression, unreasonable as it may be, 'that one is destined for some work, which is yet undone in my case. Surely my time is not yet come. So much for the cholera.'

Evidently he was not quite comfortable about his absence from his cure in the early stages of the epidemic. 'It is not yet formidable here,' he told Rogers 'or I should not have gone away.' And he wrote to Williams thanking him for taking his place, and received a slightly ambiguous reply: 'my dear Newman, you have yet to learn how to be a vicar, or you would see the impropriety of saying to a curate "I am obliged to you for staying"; for it is my business to be here [? there] always.'

At the end of July Froude went home. The double shadow of the cholera and of consumption lay over their parting. Newman held his friend's hand and 'looked into his face with great affection.' A deep presentiment sent a pang of anguish through his heart. And though it was not to be immediately fulfilled, and nearly four years of earthly companionship lay before them, this remained in his memory as their real parting. He had it (as he tells us) in his mind, though he was actually with his friend at the time, when he wrote next year in Sicily:

> And when thine eye surveys,
> With fond adoring gaze
> And yearning heart, thy friend,—
> Love to its grave doth tend.
> All gifts below, save Truth, but grow
> Towards an end.

The cholera died away, and the autumn was beginning, when Froude wrote to make a startling proposition. He and his Father were to spend the winter in the Mediterranean. They would see Sicily and the south of Italy. Why should his friend not come too? The idea made a sudden inroad on Newman's imagination. He lay awake with excitement. Why should he not go? His book was off his hands. Williams, with his excellent notions of a curate's obedience to his vicar, could be persuaded to look after St. Mary's. He would never have such an opportunity again. The Mediterranean! and in company with Hurrell! Was he not in danger of becoming a little narrow-minded? Travel would enlarge his views. A voyage would be good for his health—not that he expected to be ever regularly well. He must be back by the beginning of April. How much would the tour cost? All this he poured out to Froude. The only thing which really stood in his way was the idea that he might be 'intruding' upon the Archdeacon. But how childish to be so excited! 'Indeed, it makes me quite sad to think what an evidence it has given me of the little real stability of mind I have yet attained. I cannot make out why I was so little, or rather not at all, excited by the coming of the cholera, and so much by this silly prospect you have put before me.'

Three weeks later he is able to reassume his dignity. 'Did I consult my wishes, I should stop at home. I grudge the time, the expense, the trouble, the being put out of one's way, etc. But it may be a duty to consult for one's health, to enlarge one's ideas, to break one's studies, and to have the name of a travelled man.' For all this pretence of indifference, his spirits remained in a state of pleased excitement. The Fathers stayed unopened. He spent much of his time playing the fiddle. With *regular* attention to that instrument, he decided that he might do what he pleased with it. He even toyed with the idea of preaching an extempore sermon—a terribly low-church thing to do—but was 'afraid'.

The arrangements for the journey were soon settled. He was to join the Froudes at Falmouth on December 5. The interval was filled with the necessary preparations and one or two visits. He met Rogers in London and went down with him to his home at Blackheath for a few days. Some good advice followed. Rogers was suffering from eye-trouble, but he must not let himself be idle. 'You may hunt in Hampshire three days in the week, and I shall never call it muddling; that is, *it will not incapacitate you from working in due season.* But to be doing absolutely nothing *is* injurious.'

He preached on Sunday December 2 a University Sermon on 'Wilfulness the sin of Saul'. At the afternoon service the second Psalm, chosen by the organist, was Psalm 121, 'I will lift up mine eyes unto the hills. . . . The Lord shall preserve thy going out, and thy coming in.' It was 'an omen or a promise'. Early next morning, satisfied that he was not being wilful, but only performing a moral duty, he took the coach for Whitchurch.

CHAPTER VIII

MEDITERRANEAN INTERLUDE

I. FIRST IMPRESSIONS OF TRAVEL

Monday, at one o'clock, saw him in Whitchurch, confronted by a wait of ten hours for the night coach. He sat down in the inn to write verses. A semi-secret plan had been concocted between Rose, who ran the *British Magazine*, Newman and Froude. They were to write, and get their friends to write, a number of short religious poems—'a mixture', as Froude put it '—some fierce and some meek—the plan is to have none above twenty lines.' They were to appear in the magazine, under the title of *Lyra Apostolica*. Ten hours at Whitchurch, and nothing else to do. It was an excellent opportunity to make a start. The sense of being guided on this extravagant adventure of foreign travel possessed him. It had seemed as if his guardian angel rode with him on the coach from Oxford. A sonnet formed itself.

> Are these the tracks of some unearthly Friend,
> His foot-prints, and his vesture-skirts of light . . .

A lovely opening. But the inspiration faded out in uneasy moralizing. He was interrupted by a loquacious fellow-traveller and forced to be 'talkative and agreeable without end'. At last he was free to write to his mother. It seemed miserable to be going away for such a long time. 'Yet I doubt not, in after life, I shall look back on this day . . . as the commencement of one of the few recreations which I can hope, nay, or desire to have in this world, for the only cessation from labour to which I may look without blame. I really do *not* wish (I think) that it should be anything else than a preparation and strengthening time for future toil.'

By one o'clock on Tuesday he was at Exeter. At seven in the evening he left by the Falmouth mail. It was 'a beautiful night, clear, frosty, and bright with a full moon'. Riding outside, as he always did, the Vicar of St. Mary's forgot for a while the stern purposes of religion and let his senses be taken captive by the dark mysterious loveliness of the countryside. His mind translated each image into words. But next day it was all gone 'like a dream'. A slightly Pickwickian incident marked the journey. Riding with Newman on the top of the coach were 'a man, called by courtesy a gentleman, on the box', and 'a silly goose of a maid-servant'. Newman was offended by their conversation and roundly told the gentleman that he was talking great nonsense. To which the gentleman replied that Newman was a damned fool; but, upon recollecting that he was talking to a parson, insisted on shaking him warmly by the hand. After which, it is to be supposed, the night unrolled itself in peace.

Newman was not a very peaceable traveller. He travelled with the same concentrated energy that he gave to every other pursuit. Journeying one day from Derby to London he was obliged to change coaches at Leicester. He found the London coach waiting, and made for the seat corresponding to the one he had occupied on the other coach. Another passenger soon turned up to claim it; it was his seat, he had occupied it all the way from Nottingham to Leicester. Newman refused to budge. The coach was no longer the Nottingham and Leicester coach; it was now the Leicester and London coach. The seat was his as its first occupier. And he remained successfully in possession all the way from Leicester to London.

The mail reached Falmouth between seven and eight on Wednesday morning. Newman enquired for his friends at the inn. They had not yet arrived. So he went straight to bed and

stayed there till one o'clock, when he got up and had 'breakfast'. Their vessel was to be the *Hermes*, the largest in the
Malta service, a steam packet of 700 tons, with engines of 140
horse-power and a crew of fifty, 'fitted up in the most comfortable way imaginable'. 'A lubberly craft,' Hurrell called
her 'with a bottom as flat as a dish.' She had been sighted
'miserably perplexed with the gales off the Downs' and was
now expected hourly. As he finished the letter to his mother
recording the incidents of his journey the Froudes arrived.

The *Hermes* put out again about midday on Saturday. As
night fell on the afternoon of their first day at sea they passed
the Lizard and stood out into the Atlantic. Newman's fancy
leapt ahead. What would this adventure do to him? Would it
perhaps not enlarge his mind so much as to unfit it for the
less romantic virtues? Watching the Lizard, he began to
compose a poem called 'Wanderings'.

> I went afar; the world unroll'd
>   Her many-pictured page;
> I stored the marvels which she told,
>   And trusted to her gaze.
>
> Her pleasures quaff'd, I sought awhile
>   The scenes I priz'd before;
> But parent's praise and sister's smile
>   Stirr'd my cold heart no more.

It is a little strange that he should have sent the verses home
to Harriett, even though he did describe them to her as one
of his follies.

The Atlantic roll began to affect the three passengers—
there were no others on board. As Newman went down to
dinner a strange sensation visited him. 'The heaving to and
fro of everything seemed to puzzle me from head to foot, but
in such a vague, mysterious way, that I could not get hold
of it, or say what was the matter with me, or where. On I ate:
I was determined, for it is one of the best alleviations. On I
drank, but in so absurdly solemn a way, with such perplexity
of mind, not to say of body, that I laughed at myself.' After

another twenty-four hours he had become used to the motion of the boat. The Archdeacon succumbed completely and stayed in bed. But Hurrell, like Newman, put up a stout resistance to this meaningless 'trouble without a crisis'. Together they succeeded, though not without moments of danger, in getting through the service on Sunday morning, Hurrell reading, Newman responding, and listened to the captain's address to the crew, which amused them both by being 'so much to the point'.

Sunday and Monday were spent crossing the Bay of Biscay, under an overcast sky, but in a reasonably calm sea. Newman was soon well enough to take stock of his surroundings, and to master the technique of making himself comfortable. He was struck by the practical good sense and good humour of the ship's young officers. 'It amuses one to scrutinize them. One so clever, the others hardly so. They have (most of them) made very few inductions, and are not in the habit of investigating causes—the very reverse of philosophers.' He was pleased with himself for getting his sea-legs so quickly, for writing evenly while the sea was rocking up and down, for so easily doing many things which seemed difficult. Indeed, he told his mother with a rush of self-confidence, 'I am disposed to think that hitherto I have been working under a great pressure, and, should it please God ever to reverse it, I shall be like steam expanding itself.'

As there were only the three passengers, they each had a double-berthed cabin to himself. 'Cabin' is not quite the right word. There was a central cabin, lit at night with an oil lamp, out of which the passengers' sleeping berths opened, mere cubby-holes containing two berths, one above the other. The berths had no ventilation except through the central cabin, and were stuffy and damp and musty. He turned the bedding out of the lower berth, and unpacked and arranged his belongings in it, and slept in the top berth. All this he explained in his letters at great length, and with a

wealth of descriptive detail which could not be bettered by
any modern novelist. The creaking of the vessel, for example:
'it is like half a hundred watchmen's rattles mixed with the
squeaking of Brobdingnag pigs, while the water dashes, dash,
dash against the side. Then overhead the loud foot of the
watch, who goes on tramping up and down for more or less
the whole night. Then in the morning the washing of the
deck; rush comes an engine pipe on the floor—ceases, is renewed, flourishes about, rushes again: then suddenly half a
dozen brooms, wish-wash, wish-wash, scrib-scrub, scratching
and roaring alternately. Then the heavy flump, flump of
the huge cloth which is meant to dry the deck as a towel or
duster.'

When the passengers came on deck on Tuesday morning
they caught their breath at the glorious beauty of the sea
and sky and coast. The sky was clearing, the wind blowing
fresh but warmly from the east. On the horizon stood up
Cape Ortegal and the Cantabrian Mountains beyond to the
east—'the first foreign land I ever saw.' As the *Hermes* stood
in nearer to the Spanish coast, three lines of mountains became clearly marked, 'magnificent in outline', in places very
precipitous. The sun was shining; the rocky coast glittered;
the wind sang; the sea was wild and grand and full of colour.
'A deep black blue' said Hurrell, or 'a black purple'. Newman could not describe it, and sought almost clumsily for
words: 'so subdued, so destitute of all display, so sober—I
should call it, so gentlemanlike in colour; and then so deep
and solemn, and, if a colour can be so called, so strong; and
then the contrast between the white and the indigo, and the
change in the wake of the vessel into all colours—transparent
green, white, white-green, etc. As evening came on, we had
every appearance of being in a warmer latitude. The sea
brightened to a glowing purple, inclined to lilac; the sun set
in a car of gold, and was succeeded by a sky, first pale orange,
then gradually heightening to a dusky red; while Venus

came out as the evening star with its peculiar intense bright-
ness. Now it is bright starlight.' A lost painter speaks in the
exactness of this description. The senses—the deceitful,
usurping senses—had given him 'the most pleasurable day—
as far as externals go—I have ever had that I can recollect; and
now in the evening I am sleepy and tired with the excitement.'

Thursday was another such day. The *Hermes* steamed close
in along the coast of Portugal about a mile from the shore,
and Newman was in raptures about 'all that indescribable
peculiarity of foreign scenery which paintings attempt. . . .
The cliffs are high, composed of sandstone. They form a
natural architecture—pyramids, and these in groups. The
water, which is beautifully calm, breaks in high foam; the
sun is bright and casts large shadows on the rocks and downs.
Above, all is exposed, barren, or poorly cultivated; an immense plain, irregularly surfaced, slopes down to the brink
of the cliffs, a beautiful pale reddish-brown. Through the
glasses we see houses, flocks of sheep, windmills with sails like
a spider's web, martello towers with men lounging about the
walls, woods of cork trees with very long stems, all as clear
and as unnaturally bright as you can fancy.' Then 'the lines
of Torres Vedras and the rocks underneath passed before us
like a pageant', in which he noted with his careful exactness
of description every hue and gradation of colour. Pagan
similitudes rose instinctively in the minds of the two friends.
'At the base of the cliffs the waves are dashed, the foam
rising like Venus from the sea.' Hurrell, who thought in
Greek rather than in Latin terms, was put in mind of Aphro-
dite. Then came the rock of Lisbon and the mouth of the
Tagus. Could he be only five days from England? Newman
asked himself. 'How is the North cut off from the South!
What colouring! A pale greenish red which no words can
describe, but such as I have seen in pictures of Indian landscape—an extremely clean and clear colour. We shall make
Cadiz by to-morrow evening, while Williams is lecturing at

Littlemore. The sunset has been fine—the sky bright saffron,
the sea purple. The night is strangely warm. Latitude 39° or
38°. The Great Bear almost in the water. The glass 66° in my
berth, which is cooler than the cabin, which opens upon the
external air.'

Some sound of music must have travelled poignantly across
the water, as they passed Lisbon and he wrote his tale of verses
for the day:

> Cease, Stranger, cease those piercing notes,
>   The craft of Siren choirs;
> Hush the seductive voice that floats
>   Upon the languid wires.
>
> Music's ethereal fire was given
>   Not to dissolve our clay,
> But draw Promethean beams from Heaven,
>   And purge the dross away.
>
> Weak self! with thee the mischief lies,
>   Those throbs a tale disclose;
> Nor age nor trial has made wise
>   The Man of many woes.

They reached Gibraltar after dark on Saturday. Sunday
was spent in coaling—a most uncomfortable day. 'A Sunday
without the signs of a Sunday I can hardly understand.'
Next day the party landed and explored the Rock. Newman's faculty of delighted observation was fully employed
all day—on the geological formation of the rock, the con-
struction of the old Moorish fortifications, the presence of
Hugh Rose's *British Magazine of Ecclesiastical Information*
among the periodicals at Government House, the 'superb
Cyprus wine' on their host's table. As they rowed back to
their ship in the evening he observed a beautiful electric
phenomenon. 'The edge of the water, where it broke against
the pier, was all on fire. Wherever the oar went it was a
sheet of liquid flame, sparkling besides, wherever the
splashes fell. It was as if the under surface of the water was
fire and the oar turned it up.'

> As if such shapes and sounds which come and go
> Had aught of Truth or Life in their poor show!

So ended a sonnet which he had written at Falmouth
before the *Hermes* started, as if to guard himself in advance
against the witchery of the senses. The sad thing was that his
senses were so keenly alive to this poor show of the outward
world. They delighted in it all—colour, line, taste of food
and drink, natural scenery, sounds, smells, the look of human
beings, buildings, cities, the complex appearances of
societies and nations and institutions—from the simplest
impressions to the most intricate. But the delight, if not
actually wrong, was very dangerous. Pantheism was the
child of it. What place would there be for it in a soul devoted
to God? A reaction against the extreme enjoyment of this
first fortnight set in. It is shown very clearly in a letter which
he wrote to his mother soon after leaving Gibraltar. He
wishes that he were back 'in the midst of those employments
and pleasures that come to me at home in the course of
ordinary duty.' There is something too dangerously strong
and enchanting in these strange sights. For what are they all
'but vanities, attended too, as they ever must be, with
anxious watchfulness lest the heart be corrupted by them,
and by the unpalatable necessity of working up oneself to
little acts of testifying and teaching, which mere indolence,
not to say more, leads one to shrink from!'

But the historical associations of the Mediterranean soon
return to overbear this reactionary mood (which nevertheless
recurs constantly throughout his travels). And if the thoughts
of Greece and Carthage and Rome, which come first to his
mind, are a little unworthy of a Christian clergyman, the
comfortable facts remain that 'here Jonah was in the storm;
here St. Paul was shipwrecked; here the great Athanasius
voyaged to Rome.'

2. THE ISLES OF GREECE

And now the *Hermes* entered the Mediterranean. She was to touch at Algiers, and at Malta, cross the Ionian sea to Patras, thence to Corfu and back to Malta. The travellers had decided to stay with the ship until her return to Malta. By doing so they would have a glimpse of Greece and the Ionian islands. On their return to Malta they would be obliged to spend fifteen days or even longer in quarantine, after leaving the ship, before they would be free to move about Sicily and Italy. Malta was then, as Newman put it, the gate for the whole continent; and the British Government was 'forced to be strict in its rules by the jealousy of other Powers.' Quarantine over, they planned an expedition into Sicily. From Sicily they would go to Naples; from Naples to Rome.

Even to-day, when the Mediterranean is full of pleasure cruisers, a Northerner's first visit to Greece, to Sicily, to Italy is an almost overpowering experience. How much more so a hundred years ago, when it was a rare and difficult adventure, long and costly and even sometimes dangerous, at the best excessively uncomfortable, even for wealthy young noblemen making the grand tour in their own carriages; and when the travellers had been soaked from childhood in the literature and history of Greece and Rome. Add to this the devouring interest of these travellers in the great Church which had swallowed up the relics of that magnificent pagan civilization; add, too, their consciousness of separation from that so visibly triumphant Church, their anxiety to discover evidences of her present degeneration, hard to reconcile with their glory in her ancient triumph; add, at least in Newman's case, an extreme sensibility of the past, an extreme delight in the colours and shapes of foreign scenes; and imagine all this bought at the expense of time dedicated to a stern moral and religious aim. Is it any wonder that for Newman, if not for

Froude (who was ill all the time), his Mediterranean adventure was a supremely important event in his life? He needed the stimulus of the *Lyra Apostolica* to remind him from time to time where his heart was moored.

'Tyre of the West' he apostrophized England as the Rock of Gibraltar changed outline and dwindled behind him,

> Tyre of the West, and glorying in the name
>   More than in Faith's pure fame!
> O trust not crafty fort nor rock renown'd
>   Earn'd upon hostile ground.

And, as Algiers grew distinct, his thoughts turned from England to the Church of England.

> E'en now the shadows break, and gleams divine
>   Edge the dim distant line.
> When thrones are trembling, and earth's fat ones quail,
>   True Seed! thou shalt prevail!

This was Newman, the professional clergyman and prophet. A different Newman spoke in a shrewd comment upon the Gibraltar fortifications. 'When Marshal Gourmont was here two years ago, his criticism on Gibraltar was that its fortifications were overdone. This may be true, but such a judgment will vary with possession and non-possession.' This was the Newman who might easily, if the shift of circumstance had been a little different, have been a Nelson or a Gordon; the Newman whose first observation on the Devonshire scenery was that the Duke of Wellington would be in an itch to find some height from which he could survey the whole country; the amateur of war who said of Gurwood's *Despatches of the Duke of Wellington* that it made him burn to have been a soldier; who wrote a series of letters to the Press on the causes of the Crimean *débâcle* and followed every detail of the campaigns in Egypt and the Soudan with three large maps hung upon the walls of his room; the man of whom Father Ryder said that he might have been great in any department of life—a great general, a great lawyer, a great parliamentary debater.

After leaving Gibraltar engine-trouble delayed the *Hermes*, and it was not until Thursday afternoon that she reached Algiers. Up till then the weather had been perfect, and the travellers sat on deck reading the *Odyssey* and watching the superb panorama of the Atlas mountains. Newman thought the town looked as interesting as any place they had seen. Hurrell thought it detestable—a wasps' nest. A storm was blowing up. The 'infamous tri-coloured flag' on the French ships was a red rag to his irritated nerves. A boat came out for their letters, 'with such fellows in it!' he complained 'red, tough, and apathetic, to a fearful degree'. Newman said that they could not be descendants of Adam. The friends were very indignant at not being allowed to land. 'This nest of insects' Newman told his mother, echoing Hurrell's phrase, 'affected to put us in quarantine on account of the cholera . . . and would not receive our letters till they were cut through (to let out the cholera, I suppose), and then only at the end of a pair of tongs. How odd it is I should have lived to see Algiers!'

The storm came up in the early evening, and the wind blew a gale all night and was followed by an uneasy swell next day. All the passengers and half the crew were sea-sick.

'I care little for sea-sickness,' Newman wrote graphically to his mother 'but the attendances on it are miserable. . . . The worst of sea-sickness is the sympathy which all things on board have with it, as if they were all sick too. First, all the chairs, tables, and the things on them much more, are moving, moving, up and down, up and down, swing, swing. A tumbler turns over, knife and fork go, wine is spilt, as if encouraging like tendencies within you. In this condition you go on talking and eating as fast as you can, concealing your misery, which you are reminded of by every motion of the furniture around you. At last the moment comes; you are seized; up you get, swing, swing, you cannot move a step forward; you knock your hips against the table, run smack at the side of the cabin, try to make for the door in vain, which is your only aim.' The smell of the bilge-water, stirred up by the gale, was 'like nothing I ever smelt, suffocating'.

However, the weather improved rapidly, and Sunday was a lovely day. Newman was shown the track to Carthage between two islands. Nothing he had yet seen touched him so nearly. He thought of the Phoenicians, Tyre, the Punic Wars, 'of Cyprian, and the glorious Churches now annihilated', and almost forgot the physical exhaustion, which had followed the bout of sea-sickness. But he was sure that he had not had a night's sleep since he left England, except the night when they were anchored off Gibraltar. This was an unconscious exaggeration—he slept like a log the night after Gibraltar. He told Hurrell that he did not think his health had perceptibly improved, and Hurrell reported this without comment to Isaac Williams. 'I am sore all over with the tossing and very stiff,' he wrote to his mother from Malta 'and so weak that at times I can hardly put out a hand. But my spirits have never given way for an instant, and I laughed when I was most indisposed.' Newman had the makings of a first-class valetudinarian.

They were at Malta on Christmas Eve, Monday, and left again on Wednesday for Patras, of course without landing. Christmas Day was spent on board—a 'most wretched Christmas Day, a sad return to that good Providence who has conducted us here so safely and so pleasantly. By bad fortune we are again taking in coals on a holy day.' He was exasperated by the fact that when the coal had been got in the ship's company was to have, not a service, but a Christmas dinner. All the morning the air was full of the sound of bells, and there he was, unable to go to church. He could not even imitate the behaviour of a 'poor fellow' in the quarantine building on shore, whom he could see 'cut off from the ordinances of his Church, saying his prayers with his face to the house of God in his sight over the water'. What

an example! 'It is a confusion of face to me that the humblest
Romanist testifies to his Saviour as I, a minister, do not. Yet
I do what I can, and shall try to do more, for I am very
spiteful.'

The trip to Patras and Corfu lasted for fifteen days. The
Hermes touched at Zante after dark on the 28th, for a few
hours, and the travellers landed and walked about the town,
listening to men singing in parts as they worked in the shops
open to the street, and drinking the red and white wine of
the island, which Newman pronounced to be very good.
This brief glimpse of night life in a Greek island had a queer
unreality which made him think of the theatre. His Evangelical prejudices still hung about him. But is there (he asked
Jemima) any real objection to going to a playhouse for the
sake of seeing what it is like, any more than to visiting a
heathen country? If, indeed, one goes for the sake of the
amusement, that is wrong. But just to go and see, as one goes
and sees a coffee-house, a billiard-room, or a mosque—there
can surely be no harm in that?

Next day, after being thrilled by the sight of Ithaca and
the mountains about the Gulf of Corinth, they came to
Patras. They walked about the town for an hour or two,
drank coffee, 'almost the best' Newman had ever tasted, and
returned to their ship as night fell. He added a postscript to
his letter to Jemima: 'I have landed on the Peloponnese.
High snowy mountains, black rocks, brownish cliffs—all
capped with mist, shroud us. The sunset, most wild, har-
monises with the scene.'

The *Hermes* carried despatches for the Greek Government
recently established at Nauplia, ninety miles away in Argolis.
Greek independence was very newly born. Prince Otho of
Bavaria had been proclaimed King; he was on his way from
Germany now to take possession of his kingdom, accompanied by a suite of high officers, thirty ladies, a hundred
horses and a throne finer than anything in Europe. He and

his *entourage* were expected at Corfu in a few days' time. Meanwhile a local brigand had seized Patras, and the whole of Greece was overrun with bandits. It was not safe for Newman and his friends to attempt a cross-country journey to Athens, and there was no boat to take them round the Peloponnese. They thought of striking inland from Corfu and making their way to Athens through Turkish territory; but this formidable adventure was abandoned.

So Newman never got nearer to Athens than Patras. Had the *Hermes* reached Malta a day or two earlier the party might have been taken to Nauplia by Sir Henry Hotham, the admiral commanding the Mediterranean fleet, to whom Archdeacon Froude had introductions. But the chance was missed. It was symbolic. Not Athens, but Rome, was Newman's lifelong destination.

> Let heathen sing thy heathen praise,
> Fall'n Greece! the thought of holier days
> In my sad heart abides.

North from Patras to Corfu steamed the *Hermes*, passing close to Ithaca. Newman stayed on deck watching it for hours, labouring under an emotion he could not analyse. It was not, he thought, the Homeric associations of the island of Odysseus which stirred him so deeply. No. Ithaca revived some poignant recollection of childhood, when he had known the story of Ulysses and his dog Argus by heart. 'I thought of Ham, and of all the various glimpses which memory barely retains, and which fly from me when I pursue them, of that earliest time of life when one seems almost to realise the remnants of a pre-existing state. Oh, how I longed to touch the land, and to satisfy myself that it was not a mere vision that I saw before me.'

The travellers spent the first week of the new year in the lovely island of Corfu, mostly in fine weather, riding all about it, dining out almost every night, and attending a ball at the Palace. One of Newman's most entertaining letters was

written from Corfu to Harriett. It is full of detailed observation. A week or two of study on the spot, and Newman (one
feels) could have made an ideal administrator of Corfu or
any other island or province. He had the knack of piecing
together what he saw, and making sense out of disconnected
facts. But the chief interest in this letter is the account he
gives of his own state of mind—his double consciousness, as
actor and spectator of his own acts—which throws a flood
of light upon his whole career.

'No description can give you any idea of what I have seen,
but I will not weary you with my delight; yet does it not
seem a strange paradox to say that, though I am so much
pleased, I am not interested? That is, I don't think I should
care—rather I should be very glad—to find myself suddenly
transported to my rooms at Oriel, with my oak sported, and
I lying at full length on my sofa. After all, every kind of
exertion is to me an effort: whether or not my mind has been
strained and wearied with the necessity of constant activity,
I know not; or whether, having had many disappointments,
and suffered much from the rudeness and slights of persons
I have been cast with, I shrink involuntarily from the contact of the world, and, whether or not natural disposition
assists this feeling, and a perception almost morbid of my
deficiencies and absurdities—anyhow, neither the kindest
attentions nor the most sublime sights have over me influence
enough to draw me out of the way, and, deliberately as I
have set about my present wanderings, yet I heartily wish
they were over, and I only endure the sights, and had much
rather *have* seen them than *see* them, though the while I am
extremely astonished and almost enchanted at them.'

On January 10 the *Hermes* was back at Malta, and Newman, weary of sight-seeing, was longing for the fifteen days
of peaceful quarantine, which he had been dreading a fortnight before as a waste of time. He was longing also for news
from home; dreaming that letters were brought him, but were

illegible 'or I wake up, as if there were men trying to tell me and others preventing it. And the ship bells are so provokingly like the Oriel clock, that I fancy myself there.' But he saw the *Hermes* go with a pang of regret. 'It was a kind of home.' Her departure seemed somehow to cut him off from England.

Life in the Lazaretto, where the period of quarantine had to be passed, was comfortable enough. Huge stone rooms, twenty feet high; mild sunny weather; windows wide open; olive-wood fires on which they boiled their eggs and heated their milk. The Froudes drew and painted. Newman hired a violin—'bad as it is, it sounds grand in such spacious halls'— and wrote verses, and learned Italian, and walked up and down the rooms for exercise, and rowed about the harbour with Hurrell.

Two or three days before their incarceration ended Newman caught a bad cold. He heard a loud noise in the Archdeacon's room—certainly not made by the Archdeacon, who was 'audibly fast asleep'. The noise was so loud that he smiled to himself in the dark, and said 'Clearly this is too earthly to be anything out of the way.' But when it had been repeated three times he shouted out 'Who's there?' and sat up in bed. Nothing happened. He waited a long time, and so caught his cold. Next day he compared notes with the Froudes. They, too, had heard peculiar noises—footsteps in the middle of the night—not however on that particular night. Newman recalled that a few nights previously he had dreamed, very vividly, that somebody had come to wake him up. 'Evil spirits' he concluded 'are always about us; and I had comfort in the feeling that, whatever was the need, ordinary or extraordinary, I should have protection equal to it.'

If the evidence for supernatural visitation was somewhat slight, there was no doubt about the cold. The party moved out of the Lazaretto into rooms in Valletta. Newman, after

one effort at sight-seeing, was obliged to go to bed. He wrote
home in a despondent and irritable mood. He was all alone.
The Froudes were out all the morning, and dining out every
night, and now they had gone off on a two days' visit accompanied by the servant whom they shared with Newman.
'Well, I am set upon a solitary life, and therefore ought to
have experience what it is; nor do I repent. But even St. Paul
had his ministers. . . . I wonder how long I shall last without
any friend about me. . . . I am glad Frank has the comfort of
friends about him.' A few days later the cough was cured; and
the three travellers made a brief expedition into Sicily before
going north to Naples.

John's irritable references to the callous absence of the
Froudes, and his despondent account of himself, not unnaturally disturbed his mother and sisters. Jemima wrote
blaming Hurrell for deserting his friend. Mrs. Newman wrote
anxiously enquiring about his health. Some explanation was
necessary. 'As to Froude,' he wrote 'whom Jemima blames,
I cannot fully have stated how it was I was left alone at
Malta. I had suffered much from being so much with
strangers for five or six weeks, and I wished to be left alone,
as the only remedy of my indisposition. In answer to Froude's
many solicitations, and his offer to sit with me or read to me,
I had assured him, all I wanted in order to recruit myself was
perfect solitude. . . . You know I can be very earnest in entreating to be left alone. If I said anything else in my letter,
it was the inconsistency of the moment.'

But the inconsistency of the moment is often an index to a
man's real feelings. No explanation could gloss over the fact
that Newman had felt sore about Hurrell. 'Suffered much
from being alone with strangers.' Strangers! A curious word
to use of his dearest friend. Yet not a word used at random.
He loved Hurrell; but it was hard to be with him and yet not
to have him to himself. There was the Archdeacon, with the
first claim. And Hurrell was perhaps not an easy person to

live with at close quarters. His was a dominating personality
—more so even than Newman's. Also he was in consumption.
Both the younger members of the party were accustomed to a
great deal of complete privacy in their daily lives. It is easy
to understand how weeks of perpetual companionship in
confined quarters, with Hurrell sometimes in a fretful and
critical mood, made Newman genuinely long to be by himself. But it was a queer sort of revenge for wounded sentiment
to speak of Hurrell as a 'stranger'. The cold exaggeration
shows how painfully tender his feelings were. It was not
without cause that in the Lazaretto his thoughts ran on
David; or that he took for the text of his poem in the *Lyra
Apostolica* (written on January 16, a few days before the
quarantine came to an end) 'Thy love for me was wonderful,
passing the love of women.' Had Jonathan lived (he thought)
to stand before David's throne, would their love have lasted
so intensely? David's

> spirit keen and high,
> Sure it had snapp'd in twain love's slender band,
>   So dear in memory;
> Paul, of his comrade reft, the warning gives,—
> He lives to us who dies, he is but lost who lives.

Nor was it without cause that ten days later, ill of his cold, he
wrote those lines, already quoted, about the fond adoring
gaze and yearning heart that cannot prevent love tending to
its grave.

In the solitude of his friendless bedroom his thoughts
turned yearningly to St. Mary's and Littlemore. 'All the
quiet and calm connected with our services is so beautiful in
memory, and so soothing, after the sight of that most exciting
religion which is around me—statues of the Madonna and
of the Saints in the streets etc. etc.—a more poetical but not
less jading stimulus than a pouring forth in a Baptist chapel.'
Thirty years later the boot was on the other leg. 'I do hereby
profess *ex animo*,' he said in a letter to the *Globe* in 1862 'with
an absolute internal assent and consent, that Protestantism

is the dreariest of possible religions; that the thought of the Anglican service makes me shiver.'

He shivered, in his Valletta bedroom, as he lay with a mustard-plaster on his chest, at the dangers menacing the Church which then seemed to him sole true inheritor of the Christian tradition. 'How awful' his letter continued 'seems (to me here) the crime of demolition in England! All one can say of Whigs, Radicals, and the rest is, that they know not what they do.'

Newman's cough prevented him from seeing much of Malta. Just as he was recovering and able to go about, a steamer arrived from Naples, Glasgow-built, 'beautifully appointed', with seventy or eighty passengers, including 'counts and princes numberless who spat about decks and cabin without any concern.' The Froudes and Newman joined this early model of a pleasure cruiser as far as Messina, whence they embarked again for Palermo, which they reached on Sunday morning (February 10), the sea calm, the sun hot, and everything beautiful to a degree. 'We had' said Newman 'a difficulty in getting lodged.' Froude's account is more detailed and amusing. He and Newman, foreseeing trouble, made a rush for the ladder and were first into the boat. But the boat made for the wrong landing place. They had to run for it, on landing. Froude soon dropped out. But Newman and the boatman succeeded in outstripping 'the wife of the Governor of Moldavia and Wallachia', who was their most formidable competitor. However, she had the better of them, for she hired a coach and had made assurance doubly sure by sending two servants ahead, who 'when Newman came up with them raced him and, being fresh, contrived to keep ahead by a foot or so, so as just to bespeak Jacqueri's whole house before he could speak to the land-lord.' They were lucky, in the end, to discover an apartment without fleas. Such were the indignities of travel in 1833, for even a Vicar of St. Mary's, and on a hot Sunday morning.

They were up early the next morning for the main object
of their brief visit to Sicily—the expedition to Egesta.

3. EGESTA

Why, wedded to the Lord, still yearns my heart
　　Towards these scenes of ancient heathen fame?
　　Yet legend hoar, and voice of bard that came
Fixing my restless youth with its sweet art,
And shades of power, and those who bore a part
　　In the mad deeds that set the world on flame,
　　So fret my memory here,—ah! is it blame?—
That from my eyes the tear is fain to start.

So Newman had written, as they waited at Messina for the
crossing to Sicily, and answered his question with the lines:

　　'Tis but that sympathy with Adam's race
　　Which in each brother's history reads its own.

The answer was untrue. Round the remnants of pagan
civilization in the Mediterranean there hung, for Newman
as for such apparently different men as Shelley or F. W. H.
Myers or Matthew Arnold, a wholly peculiar enchantment,
at war—as he well knew—with his other allegiance. His
childhood and youth and early manhood had been largely
spent in learning the languages and studying, however un-
systematically, the poets and historians and philosophers of
Greece and Rome. So the enchantment came no doubt very
largely from their association with the romantic dreams of
adolescence. But was there not a deeper, subtler attraction?
Did not the old pagan culture, at its best, accept and glorify
the life of the senses, and show how beautiful and splendid
such a life could be? These were thoughts not easy to reconcile with perfect loyalty to the Christian dispensation as it
was interpreted by Keble. Newman suppressed them; and
made believe that his yearning toward heathen scenes was
nothing but an intelligent interest in human history.

He had seen practically nothing of Greece—only the

T   F.O.A.

shapes of mountains in the distance. But the Greek cities of
Sicily were quite as exciting to his imagination. He knew his
Thucydides. 'The mad deeds that set the world on flame' were
the deeds of the Peloponnesian War. The policy of Nicias,
commander-in-chief of the Athenian expedition to Sicily,
was a topic of light conversation among the characters of
his novel *Loss and Gain*. And it was Egesta, the city whose
ruins they had come to Sicily to visit, who persuaded the
Athenians to undertake that ill-fated adventure. The great
temple was then just built, or building—for it was never
quite finished. After the collapse of the Athenian expedition,
she saved herself from revenge at the hands of her neighbours
by becoming a subject of Carthage. A hundred years later
she was destroyed by Agathocles the tyrant of Syracuse, and
her whole population was massacred with horrible ferocity.

It was four in the morning and still dark when the carriage,
drawn by three mules with bells, carrying the Archdeacon,
Hurrell and Newman, as well as the driver and his boy and a
hired servant named Francesco, set off for the forty-three-
mile drive to Calatafimi. As they stopped for hot coffee and
a morsel of bread at a café in Palermo there was a sudden
quickening of life in the empty street, revellers returning
from a masquerade. Then up the long ascent to Monreale,
and over the mountain pass, where the dawn revealed a
wonderful prospect of 'wild, grey, barren eminences tossed
about, many with their heads cut off by clouds, others
lighted up by the sun'. Soon there burst upon the travellers
the vision which astonishes all who go that way—the bay of
Castellammare, 'an enormous garden, spread out at the foot
of the mountains', with the blue sea curving beyond and the
bold hills embracing it. After that, as the sun grew higher
and warmer, the descent into 'a richly fertile plain, large
every way, full of olives, corn, vines, with towns inter-
spersed', while Newman reflected how Sicily, for all its rocky
barrenness, had been the granary of the Roman empire. At

Partinico they changed mules. They drove, as tourists drive
to-day, through the main street of Alcamo lined with 'large
and sometimes very ornamented houses, extremely dilapi-
dated'. But the impression of these things was blotted out for
them by the liquid filth through which their carriage rolled,
and then by the far distant sight of a tiny box-like structure
—the temple of Egesta. The road dipped, and the little box
vanished. At half past one they came to Calatafimi. Even
Newman's stomach demanded some attention. They had 'an
egg or two' apiece, examined their sleeping quarters with an
apprehensive eye, instructed Francesco to make them ready,
collected mules and boys, and started off for their afternoon
among the ruins.

Even to-day the first sight of the great temple is an experience not easily forgotten, though one drives up in a
motor-car, crossing the river Gaggera by a brand-new bridge
at the point where Agathocles slit the throats of his more
fortunate captives, and coming to a stop where the new road
ends in a wide staring circular sweep just below the temple
beside an enterprising American bar.

But Newman and his friends approached Egesta by
another route. Their mules carried them through groves of
olive and prickly pear and orange orchards to a steep hill
covered with ruins, where a savage-looking bull was feeding
between the stones. 'Oh that I could tell you one quarter
what I have to say about it!' wrote Newman to Jemima, forgetting his rôle of the wearied sightseer. They were standing
on Monte Varvaro, the site of the ancient town, on the top
of a rocky hill, some 1400 feet above the level of the Bay of
Castellammare, which lay in full view seven miles away,
overlooked by high mountains. Between the sea and the hill
the great plain of Alcamo. All about them the austere
Sicilian heights, climbing slowly at first from the plains
and valleys and then abruptly lifting up their limestone
escarpments. This was the kind of scenery which stirred him

most—the 'extensive view with tracts bold and barren in it', reminding him of the music of Beethoven. Set in the crown of the hill, so as to command from its seats the view towards the sea, curves the ancient Greek theatre, as the Romans remodelled it. The back wall of the stage, which the Romans rebuilt so high that the view of the surrounding country must have been shut out from all but the topmost seats, is in ruins. The whole theatre lies naked and open to the plain and the sea, almost a part of the desolation which surrounds it.

From the back of the theatre, as Newman looked away from the sea, he saw the hillside falling steeply away to an upland valley, on the other side of which rose a majestic and precipitous line of hills, higher by far than the hill on which he was standing. Down in the valley on a lower rounded hill, a thousand feet above sea-level, four hundred feet below him and three-quarters of a mile away, with these stern hills behind it, stood the great temple. Here was the art which moved him most deeply. These pagans had done their best. Even Christianity had something to learn from them. 'Such was the genius of ancient Greek worship—grand in the midst of error, simple and unadorned in its architecture: it chose some elevated spot, and fixed there its solitary witness, where it could not be hid.'

The party made their way down the steep track (paved now by the Fascists with a profusion of marble chips) which connected the town with the temple. There was an encampment of shepherds in front of it, with wolf-dogs and wild Salvator-like dresses. Newman, somehow separated from his friends, found the wild men swarming round him with threatening cries of *Date moneta!* He was sure they would have taken it by force, if the custodian of the temple had not appeared with his gun and overawed them. This was perhaps the only occasion in his life when he was threatened by anything like physical violence.

The temple, when they got to it, was overwhelming. There it stood, all its pediments and columns perfect, and only differing—as they thought—from what it was at first in the deep rich colouring of the weather stains, and (of course) in the absence of its roof and furniture. They may have been right. For the temple at Egesta was never finished. It may never have looked, as its builders intended it should look— smooth, trim, painted with blue and red, a bright and coloured work of art in triumphant contrast to the wild and barren hills behind it. But of that Newman and Froude could not have dreamed. In a way they misinterpreted all they saw; missed the chief secret of the civilization whose poets they had got by heart; reading into its ruins the fugitivism of Wordsworth and Coleridge and Southey. 'It is the most strangely romantic place I ever saw or conceived', exclaimed Hurrell. What arch-romantics these old Greeks must have been! How sensitive to the parable of the hills! How reverent towards the solemn mystery bounding human life, though the true God had not yet been revealed to them! This simple, noble building of roughly dressed natural stone—by what a perfect instinct it seems to have been summoned out of the landscape, to which it stands indeed in the contrast inevitably existing between the works of man and the works of nature, but also in the intimate relationship of a Cotswold cottage to its own countryside. Just that might be the instinctive excellence of unrevealed religion. All the more so, because this landscape is not mild, but stern and gloomy and magni- ficent. Paganism could have made no more tactful appeal to the Vicar of St. Mary's.

But the tact was the tact of time, or of accident. If, by a miracle such as Newman would have been delighted to experience, he and Hurrell could have been allowed for a moment to see the temple with the eyes of its chief architect, what would they have felt? After the first shock to their preconceptions, would they have admired or detested? Per-

haps it is a little foolish to ask the question. Yet I fancy that
they would both have found something exciting in the super-
lative insolence of the Greek's challenge to his native
scenery. Just at the back of the temple, a stream, the Torrente
Pispisa, flows through a precipitous ravine two or three
hundred feet deep and only a few yards wide. An ancient
path, cut and worn in the rock, winds round the hill on
which the temple stands down to the bottom of the gorge.
From this point half the temple is visible, rearing itself above
the edge of the rocky wall. This ravine, Hurrell rightly observed, gives a grandeur to the whole scene even beyond
what it gets from the mountains and the solitude. It would
have given—must have been intended to give—the crowning
touch of pride to the superb self-sufficiency of the temple.
The Oxford visitors, if they had seen it in its intended perfection, would have marvelled that an idolatrous religion
could dare to be so bold. They would have envied, while they
reprobated. And Newman would have written a poem for
the *Lyra Apostolica*, mournfully comparing the timidity of his
own Church with the self-confidence of the heathen.

But no such thoughts came into his mind, and he was able
to let his imagination indulge its romantic bent. 'Mountains
around and Eryx in the distance. The past and the present!
Once these hills were full of life! I began to understand what
Scripture means when speaking of lofty cities vaunting in the
security of their strongholds. What a great but ungodly sight
was this place in its glory! and then its history; to say nothing
of Virgil's fictions. Here it was that Nicias came; this was the
ally of Athens; what a strange place! How did people take it
into their heads to plant themselves here?'

Darkness fell, as they returned to Calatafimi. Francesco
had a good dinner ready for them, and three beds in the
dining-room. The fleas made them pay heavily for their
adventure. Hurrell slept till midnight, and then devoted
himself to the task of retaliation. The Archdeacon slept till

ten; Newman not at all. They were up at four, and after a
scratch breakfast took the road for Palermo.

4. NAPLES

A day of sightseeing at Palermo and Monreale, and then
the travellers left in the Glasgow-built pleasure-steamer for
Naples. Newman's mind was filled with two topics—Sicily
and the Roman Church. The attraction of Sicily for him was
overpowering. To have seen Egesta was 'a day in his life'.
That had been a wonderful sight, 'full of the most strange
pleasure'. But the whole island drew him like a loadstone.
And this in spite of the horror and disgust which he felt for
the filth and poverty of the population. 'Oh, the miserable
creatures we saw in Sicily! I never knew what human suffering was before. Children and youths who look as if they did
not know what fresh air was, though they must have had it
in plenty—well, what water was—with features sunk, contracted with perpetual dirt, as if dirt was their food. The
towns of Partinico and Alcamo are masses of filth; the
street is a pool; but Calatafimi, where we slept!—I dare not
mention facts. Suffice it to say, we found the poor children
of the house slept in holes dug into the wall, which smelt not
like a dog-kennel, but like a wild beast's cage, almost overpowering us in the room upstairs.' But his sense of human
dignity was comforted by the sight of many handsome
Sicilians and Calabrians—'a striking and bright-looking
race—regular features and very intelligent. Sparkling eyes,
brownish skins, and red healthy-looking cheeks. At Amalfi
yesterday we were quite delighted with them.' And there
brooded over Sicily, over the wide fertile plains and hillsides
and desolate heights, the spirit which never failed to put its
unanalysable spell upon his mind—the spirit of an irretrievably vanished past.

In Palermo the past was also the present—the Cappella
Palatina, the churches of San Giovanni and La Marterana,
the Duomo, the splendid cathedral of Monreale. All these
were 'superb'. But upon what evil days they had fallen! The
Oxonians shook their heads together over the Roman priesthood, and collected scandalous stories of its degraded state.
Hurrell lent perhaps the readiest ear to these. There was
Mr. X. 'who went into a Benedictine convent at Monreale,
is now in Naples without permission, leading a gay life, and
the Church has not proceeded to any severe measures
against him.' With his own eyes he saw priests laughing as
they heard confessions. Newman agreed that the priesthood
was in a bad way, but reflected that he had really very little
experience to go by. Still, the state of the Church was evidently appalling. Satan had been let out of prison to roam
the earth once more. The Church was being stripped of her
temporalities. The Bishop of Monreale received only a
beggarly £2000 a year out of the £10,000 (Hurrell said
£20,000) which belonged to him by right. As the steamer
journeyed towards Naples Newman and Froude talked with
an American Episcopalian—'a pompous man, and yet we
contracted a kind of affection for him.' He had 'better principles far than one commonly meets with in England, and a
docile mind'. The fantastic imagination came to Newman
that the Book of Revelation might only be concerned with
the Roman Empire; just as the first verses of Genesis summed
up ages of geological time, so the future of Christianity in
America and China might be 'summed up obscurely in a
few concluding sentences; if so, one would almost expect
some fresh prophecy to be given when the end of the European period comes.' Could the future of the Church lie in
the far East or the far West? Alas! he discovered that the
American was a Wesleyan Episcopalian—in fact a Dissenter.
How could anything good come out of Dissent? Perhaps, after
all, England was destined to be the 'Land of Saints' in the

dark hour of the vague but dreadful crisis, towards which the whole western world was visibly tending.

Such was the confused state of his reflections at Naples, where the first shocking news of Lord Grey's Irish Church Reform Bill appears to have reached him.

Naples seemed a very dreadful place. The poverty of the Church was deplorable. All its property had been confiscated —so they were told. The people were infidel and profane. The life of the town was nothing but frivolity and dissipation. It was carnival time—'real practical idolatry', Hurrell called it. 'Religion' lamented Newman 'is turned into a mere occasion of worldly gaiety.' The sooner they were out of so bad a place the better. The weather was abominable, the beds damp. Even the famous bay disappointed them. Watering-place scenery, they decided contemptuously, for watering-place people—a place for animal gratification in fine weather.

There were memories, however, to be treasured. They visited Pompeii, which Newman found wonderfully interesting, but somehow he was not much moved. More thrilling was the expedition to Paestum—a long drive of some sixty miles along the shore of the bay of Naples, and across the mountains by Nocera and Cava to Salerno. They spent the night at Salerno, in a comfortable inn, and set off at five next morning (February 26) for the temples at Paestum. 'The large temple far exceeded my expectations; it is as far superior to the temple at Egesta as its situation and the scenery round are inferior. It is, indeed, magnificent.' That night they spent again at Salerno, and next morning they drove along the coast-road to Amalfi. 'Such cliffs, ravines, caves, towns perched aloft, etc., that I am full of silent, not talkative delight.' At Amalfi they climbed the hillside, all 'beautifully cool and sweet', with some vague idea of striking across the heights to Castellammare on the other side of the peninsula of Sorrento; but at the sight of the

difficulties they thought better of this wild plan, and returned
to the town, passing a bevy of boys in training for the
priesthood, 'so bright and smiling and intelligent looking'.
They got back to Naples by sea, in the evening, very tired
and hungry, rested and packed next day, and on Friday,
March 1, shook off the dust (or mud) of the heathen city
and started for Rome, which they reached, after a tedious
journey, on Saturday evening.

5. ROME

Writing to Harriett on the Monday after his arrival in
Rome Newman graphically described the last stages of the
journey.

'The approach to Rome from Naples is very striking. It is
through ancient towns, full of ruin, along the Via Appia;
then you come to the Pontine Marshes; then, about fourteen
miles from Rome, to a wild, woody, rocky region; then
through the Campagna—a desolate flat, the home of
malaria. It is a fit approach to a city which has been the
scene of Divine judgments. After a time isolated ruins come
to view, of monuments, arches, aqueducts. The flat waste
goes on; you think it will never have done; miles on miles the
ruins continue. At length the walls of Rome appear; you
pass through them; you find the city shrunk up into a third
of the space enclosed. In the twilight you pass buildings
about which you cannot guess wrongly. This must be the
Coliseum; there is the Arch of Constantine. You are landed
at your inn; night falls, and you know nothing more till next
morning.'

In point of actual fact the travellers sallied forth on the very
evening of their arrival and made for St. Peter's. They found
it of a prodigious size. As he stood in St. Peter's, and again
next day in the basilica of St. John Lateran, *omnium urbis et
orbis ecclesiarum mater et caput*, where five of the great Councils

of the Church were held, Newman experienced an unfamiliar but not unpleasant sensation. How vast and, at the same time, how exact in their proportions were these marvellous edifices! How small and mean the wavering outline of his own personality!

By Monday many things had happened. They had visited the Coliseum, and the Forum, and the Capitol. They had attended divine service in the English chapel and listened contemptuously to a semi-evangelical 'watering-place' sermon. They had found themselves comfortable quarters in the Via del Babuino, a few doors from the Wilberforces and Edward Neate, whose brother Charles was one of the younger Fellows of Oriel. And Newman had proposed to Neate that they should visit Sicily together.

The plan of going back to Sicily and postponing his return to England until the end of May had evidently been forming itself for some time in Newman's mind. It was a natural enough plan for any ordinary traveller to make. But for Newman it was exceedingly strange. It meant parting with Hurrell, as well as being absent from the Oriel Fellowship election on April 11. It meant doubling on his tracks, spending more money, travelling alone—for in the end Neate did not go. It meant staying longer out of England, while the Whigs were already at their wicked work. It meant leaving Isaac all alone at St. Mary's, through the Trinity term. Excellent as these reasons for not going back to Sicily were, there was a much stronger reason for going—he wanted to. It was one of the few occasions in his life when he was obliged to indulge his self-will without demonstrating to himself and to others that to do so was an incontestable duty. Still, he did his best. 'Impatient as I am to return on every account, I feel it would be foolish, now that I am out, not to do as much as ever I can.' He thinks that at any moment he may receive a summons from his Bishop to return; but 'to return without summons seems absurd; so I must be content.' To Frederic

Rogers, his favourite now of the young men, who was to
stand for an Oriel Fellowship at Easter, he explains his
absence from the election at length. Two votes might
perhaps make a difference; one could not. He and Froude
had worked it all out. And as the Archdeacon wouldn't hear
of Hurrell's going back, what would be the good of Newman's doing so? If he went back, really he would 'have seen
nothing, hardly, and scarcely done more than wander about
the wide sea.' The note of anxious self-justification is very
audible. And trying so to justify himself to his young admirer
he forgot the astonishing impropriety of assuming—and
letting Rogers share the assumption—that his vote was pre-
determined. He remembered the necessity of keeping up
appearances when he wrote a few days later to Tom Mozley:
'being at a distance, I may say without breach of decorum,
that I am earnestly desirous that Rogers should succeed;
were I on the spot, to say this would be inconsistent with
the impartiality of a judge.'

And Hurrell? Was it possible that one could have too much
of the company even of his dearest friend? Hurrell was
restless and discontented. 'Being abroad is a most unsatis-
factory thing,' he wrote to Keble from Rome 'and the idleness of it deteriorating. I shall connect very few pleasing
associations with this winter.' And he complained to another
correspondent that it was really melancholy to think how
little one had got for one's time and money. Hurrell's mood
may well have spoiled much of Newman's enjoyment.
Hurrell's persistent cough (no better than when they left
England) must have got on his nerves. It must have been
irksome to be always deferring to a robust and masterful
Archdeacon. There seems to have been some slight disagreement over the first visit to Sicily. The original project of a
longer expedition was given up for unexplained reasons.
Why should he not leave the Froudes and go again to Sicily
by himself? The island drew him back with an irresistible

attraction. He had the money—a hundred pounds had lasted him all the way to Rome. Whatever protestations Hurrell and his father may have made, he resolved to carry out this plan.

A batch of long letters put his friends *au fait* with his journeyings. In these and in Hurrell's letters the chief topic is naturally—Rome. Their attitude to the Holy City was compounded of thrilling admiration and defensive horror. Newman poured it all out, as it came to him, appropriately dressed for his correspondent of the moment. Hurrell was less copious and enthusiastic. But to him, no less than to Newman, 'Rome is the place after all where there is most to astonish one, and of all ages, even the present.' What laid hold of Hurrell's imagination most deeply was 'the entire absorption of the old Roman splendour in an unthought-of system'—pagan marbles built into Christian churches, St. Peter buried in Nero's circus. It was he who took Newman to interview an English Monsignor, in order to discover if 'they would take us in upon any terms to which we could twist our consciences.' The two friends found to their 'dismay' and 'horror' that the way was irretrievably barred by the 'atrocious' Council of Trent, 'for which Christendom has to thank Luther and the Reformers.' They retired from their interview more than ever convinced that their only hope lay in a return to the doctrines and practices of the ancient Church of England—which, for Hurrell at least, meant 'Charles the First and the Nonjurors'. The authority who administered this cold douche was Dr. Wiseman, whose article in the *Dublin Review* in 1839 was to give Newman his 'first real hit', now in 1833 Rector of the English College in Rome, the future patron of Newman and his fellow-converts, and the first Cardinal-archbishop of the new Roman hierarchy in England.

The account which Hurrell gave of this curious interview to Keble was marked by his characteristic exaggeration of phrase. It was not, said the editor of his *Remains* (who was, of course, Newman) to be taken literally. The visit was for the purpose of ascertaining 'the ultimate points at issue between the Churches'. But Hurrell's language is too definite to be disposed of quite so easily. It is impossible not to think that the two friends went to the interview, unofficial as it was, in something of the spirit in which Lord Halifax met Cardinal Mercier, nearly a hundred years later, at Malines.

For Newman the fascination of Rome was instant and complete. 'This is a wonderful place' he told his mother, the day after his arrival '—the first city, mind, which I have ever much praised. . . . Everything is so bright and clean, and the Sunday kept so decorously.' The next day to Harriett: 'And now what can I say of Rome, but that it is the first of cities, and that all I ever saw are but as dust (even dear Oxford inclusive) compared with its majesty and glory? Is it possible that so serene and lofty a place is the cage of unclean creatures? I will not believe it till I have evidence of it.' And a few days later: 'Rome grows more wonderful every day. The first thought one has of the place is awful—that you see the great enemy of God—the Fourth Monarchy, the Beast dreadful and terrible.' The ruins, and all their associations, 'brand the place as the vile tool of God's wrath and Satan's malice.' So much must have been necessary to soothe the quick apprehensiveness of the three women at Iffley. Skilfully he corrects his denunciation with the Apollo Belvedere and the celebrated pictures of Raffaelle; and ends up with a good word for the Roman clergy, 'a decorous, orderly body', though there are signs of timidity and indolence and a dislike of fasting, and the choristers at St. Peter's 'are as irreverent as at St. Paul's'. An appendix of verses seems to redress this mild commendation, but leaves the question of Rome's wickedness open:

> How shall I name thee, Light of the wide West,
>   Or heinous error-seat?

> O Mother, erst close tracing Jesus' feet,
>   Do not thy titles glow
> In those stern judgment-fires which shall complete
>   Earth's strife with Heaven, and ope the eternal woe?

A week later he confesses to a friend that he could not
'conceive a more desirable refuge, did evil days drive me
from England.' But that is absurd. He has his duties 'even
were we cast out as evil'; and, besides, he cannot rid himself
of the idea that 'Rome Christian is somehow under a
special shade, as Rome Pagan certainly was,' though he has
seen nothing to confirm it. 'Not that one can tolerate for an
instant the wretched perversion of the truth which is
sanctioned here'; but there is nothing obviously reprehen-
sible, and in spite of the fact that the canons laugh and talk
at service the clergy 'though sleepy, are said to be a decorous
set of men.'

To Jemima, two days later, mindful perhaps of what the
family expected, he is less indulgent to Roman backslidings.
The religion of Italy is 'very corrupt', for all the superficial
appearances of piety. It must receive severe inflictions. 'I
fear I must look upon Rome as a city still under a curse,
which will one day break out in more dreadful judgments
than heretofore.'

By Good Friday (April 5) he cannot refrain from telling
his mother that, profoundly as he still detests the *Roman*
Catholic system, 'to the Catholic system I am more attracted
than ever, and quite love the little monks [seminarists] of
Rome; they look so innocent and bright, poor boys!' No
doubt there are grave scandals in the Italian priesthood and
'mummery in abundance'; but 'there is a deep substratum
of true Christianity', infinitely to be preferred to that of
'Mr. B., whom I like less and less every day.' (Mr. B. was
the semi-evangelical chaplain at Rome with the watering-
place manner.) On April 11, writing to Jemima from
Naples, he betrays how nearly his heart had been taken. 'Oh
that Rome were not Rome! but I seem to see as clear as day

that a union with her is *impossible*. She is the cruel Church, asking of us impossibilities, excommunicating us for disobedience, and now watching and exulting over our approaching overthrow.'

In a letter to Rickards, as if to excuse himself for finding so much to admire under the shadow of the Pope, he develops one of his most fantastic speculations. There is, he thinks, a curse upon Rome—upon the place itself—quite apart from its pagan or Christian associations. The argument is a little mixed, for he goes on to speak of Rome as 'the first cruel persecutor of the Church and as such condemned to suffer God's judgments, which had [? have] not yet been fully poured out upon it, from the plain fact *that it still exists*.' So there is more and worse to come. The truth is that the city of Rome possesses an evil *genius loci* 'which enthralls the Church which happens to be there.' He is not so clear about this as he could wish. Indeed, he is really in a worse muddle than he realizes. For he is, as he says, a great believer in *genii locorum*. When he went to Cambridge he instantly felt the power of a genius *loci*, like the genius of his own dear Oxford. And the genius of the place was not, for Newman, as it is for us, a metaphorical figure. It was a real being—as real as himself, or his guardian angel, or the Persons of the Trinity. If, then, the genius of Rome was as he described it to Rickards, how was it that he had found the place so delightful? Well, it was 'a very difficult place to speak of, from the mixture of good and evil in it.' Against the *genius loci* could be set impalpable influences emanating from the dust of the Apostles. The religion of Rome 'is still polytheistic, degrading, idolatrous.' It derives its power from the locality—as Napoleon found when he tried to uproot the Papacy and re-establish it in Paris. Inextricably intertwined with this devilish power is another, spiritual, power—the true Church. The latter is the slave and captive of the former. One day the captive will be set free. Meanwhile,

helpless as it is, it is strong enough to furnish Newman with
an inexplicably soothing memory.

Could a strong intelligence be more uncomfortably bogged
by its own wilful credulity?

The five weeks in Rome were passed in the usual strenuous
round of sightseeing. As Hurrell put it, he and Newman
'tried hard to get up the march-of-mind phraseology about
pictures and statues.' Unfortunately they met one of those
tiresomely knowledgeable Cambridge men, 'who, though he
had not been in Italy much longer than ourselves, had
attained an eminence so far beyond what we could even in
thought aspire to, that we gave the thing up in despair, and
retired upon the τόπος, that "we don't enter into the techni-
calities."' So they cultivated the rather dangerous company
of Dr. Wiseman, whom Hurrell thought 'really too nice a
person to talk nonsense about', and took the march of mind
for granted.

The news from England was disquieting. Arnold's plan of
Church Reform had just been published. Newman treated
it with heavy ridicule. If the parish churches were to be
thrown open to all the various sects—Quakers and Roman
Catholics excluded—would there not be too many sects in
some places for one day? Why not pass an Act to oblige some
persuasions to change their Sunday? The Evangelicals would
naturally keep Sunday on Saturday and could then call it
the Sabbath without fear of criticism. 'This would not interfere with the Jews (who would of course worship in the parish
church) for they are too few to take up a whole day. Luckily
the Mahommedan holiday is already on a Friday, so there
will be no difficulty in that quarter.'

But the 'wicked spoliation Bill' of the Whigs was too serious
a matter for ridicule. The feelings of the travellers fluctuated
between optimism and despair and an uncomfortable indifference. Newman, on March 20, is in the first of these
moods. Keble is at last roused; once up, he will prove a

U　　　　　　　　　　　　　　　　　　　　　F.O.A.

second St. Ambrose. Others are moving, too. He has strong
grounds for believing that before long the Prussian Communion will be applying to the English Church for ordination. M. Bunsen, the Prussian Minister, has received them
very kindly. Great things may be hoped for from Germany.
Even the German painters in Rome are animated by a
high reverential spirit, and (as Hurrell puts it) 'think grace
and beauty bought too dear, if they tend to disturb the mind
by pagan associations.'

Alas, M. Bunsen's efforts, in 1841, to ally the Prussian and
the Anglican Churches, were to prove (as we shall see)
one of the blows which finally broke Newman's allegiance
to the Church of England.[1] Had they succeeded—had
Pusey followed his own first instincts in favour of Bunsen's
scheme and not surrendered his judgment to Newman—had
Tractarianism not thrown up an impassable barrier to
Protestant unity—had the Anglo-Prussian Bishopric in
Jerusalem not been a mere flash in the pan—the whole
course of the relations between England and Prussia might
have been changed, and the European War of 1914 might
never have occurred. To the Newman of 1840, fighting (in
Dean Church's phrase) 'for the historical and constitutional
catholicity of the English Church', or to the Newman of his
Roman Catholic period, holding the extremest agonies of
millions as nothing in comparison with the toleration of
even one venial sin, such a prospect would have made no
appeal. But in 1833 he was, it seems, still able to take a
statesmanlike, if excitable, view of ecclesiastical politics.

Meanwhile, it was incredible to hear that there were
actually people in Oxford who had got up a petition in
support of the Irish Spoliation Bill. Who were they? Let
them, said Newman to Hurrell, be sent to Coventry. Let
them not be spoken to by serious people. Hurrell, for once
following a little behind, was disposed to make exceptions,

[1] See p. 428.

which Newman thought capricious. But, on the whole, he agreed with his friend.

A little before their time at Rome was up, the travellers visited Frascati. There Newman wrote some strangely confessional lines on Temptation for the *Lyra Apostolica*.

> O holy Lord, who with the Children three
>   Didst walk the piercing flame,
> Help, in those trial-hours, which, save to Thee,
>   I dare not name;
> Nor let these quivering eyes and sickening heart
> Crumble to dust beneath the Tempter's dart.
>
> Thou, who didst once Thy life from Mary's breast
>   Renew from day to day,
> Oh might her smile, serenely sweet, but rest
>   On this frail clay!
> Till I am Thine with my whole soul; and fear,
> Not feel a secret joy, that Hell is near.

What secret communication had passed between himself and Hurrell, that he should so closely echo the very language of his friend's private journal?

6. ISOLATION

Easter in 1833 fell on April 17. On Easter Monday the Froudes started for England, going by Genoa and thence by sea to Marseilles, and drifting slowly northwards through France, where Hurrell, in spite of his hatred of the Revolution and the tricolor, fell in love with the people themselves.

Newman stayed a day longer in Rome. He wandered about 'with a blank face' and desolation in his heart. He was left to himself in a foreign land for the first time in his life. Even the tombs of the Apostles could not comfort him. Rome, in five weeks, had become as much a part of himself as Hurrell. He revisited its holy places, a hurried forlorn pilgrim, as he supposed for the last time. To leave Rome was like tearing a piece out of his heart. What had he been about to separate himself not only from Rome (which was inevit-

able) but from his friend? Why had he not gone with him to
the South of France, 'where there was so much both interesting and new'? Simply, he told himself bitterly, 'for the
gratification of an imagination, for the idea of a warm fancy
which might be a deceit, drawn by a strange love of Sicily
to gaze upon its cities and mountains'.

Such were his feelings on Tuesday afternoon as he prepared for his own departure. But next day he recovered his
equanimity. He gave Jemima one of his pen-pictures. 'On
Wednesday morning, when I found myself travelling, as the
light broke, through a beautiful country, which I had in
March passed in the dark, I began to gain spirits. We had
passed Terracina (Anxur) with its white rocks by moonlight; at dawn we had before us a circle of beautiful blue
hills, inclosing a rich plain, covered with bright green corn,
olives, and figs just bursting into leaf, in which Fondi lies.
Then came Mola, where Cicero was murdered, and the
country I saw was still more beautiful; so at length we got to
Naples in twenty-nine hours from Rome, including two
hours' stopping, the distance being about 148 miles.'

Meanwhile the election to two Oriel Fellowships was
taking place. As Newman sat writing to Jemima he was
interrupted by the thought that at that very moment the
Provost and the Fellows were sitting round the common
room considering their votes. Seldom were his affections
more passionately engaged in the contest. It must, it should,
be Rogers; and after Rogers, Charles Marriott. And so it
was. An hour or two later Keble was writing the news of
their election 'without a dissentient voice' into what used
to be called, in the eighteenth century, a 'Cheddar' letter—
that is, a letter written by several people. Mrs. Newman,
Harriett and Jemima, John Christie, Isaac Williams, Tom
Mozley, and Keble were the joint authors; and the postage
paid at Oxford was 2s. 5d. But when Newman got the letter,
he was too ill to decipher the close writing. He first saw the

news of Rogers's election in a newspaper at Palermo, and
'kissed the paper rapturously.'

On Friday morning, just as the names of the new Fellows
were being given out, Newman started on an expedition to
Vesuvius, with his friend Mr. Bennett, the English chaplain,
and another Englishman. They drove to Resina, where they
took mules and asses to the foot of the principal cone, eight
hundred feet high. This had to be negotiated on foot. It
consists of loose ash; and Newman, wearing a pair of Italian
shoes rather too large for him, which were continually filling up with the ash, found the struggle to the top exhausting. Arrived at the first crater, they sat down to cook
some beef and drink some wine, 'most delicious wine, though
it is the common wine of the place—so common as hardly
to be drinkable anywhere else.' Then they explored the
volcano, climbing the secondary cone of loose ash, which
at that date rose 150 feet or more in the centre of the old
crater. From the top they gazed down into the true crater,
'an awful sight . . . resplendent with all manner of the most
various colours from the sulphur', emitting clouds of white
unbreathable fumes. 'The utter silence increased the im-
posing effect, which became fearful when, on putting the
ear to a small crevice, one heard a rushing sound, deep and
hollow, partly of wind, partly of the internal trouble of the
mountain.' The party descended into the crater. Newman's
loose shoes filled with the hot ash, so that he could not put
his feet to the ground and had to cling by his hands. Feet
and hands were blistered by the heat. 'I assure you I quite
cried out with the pain.' And so back to Naples, no more
than four shillings out of pocket, from 'the most wonderful
sight I have seen abroad'.

Then followed several days of enforced idleness and solitude in the Italian Brighton, while he waited for a passage
to Sicily. The weather was bad—continual heavy rain and
stormy winds. Yet, oddly enough, he began to repent his

harsh judgment of Naples. On his first arrival from Rome he
liked it no better than before. The sun was shining then; the
glare and the bustle displeased him, by the contrast with
'the majestic pensiveness' of Rome, 'where the Church sits in
sackcloth calling on those who pass by to say if anyone's
sorrow is like her sorrow.' Now with the rainy weather he
began to see a beauty he had been blind to at first. There
was colour everywhere. And though the people were heathen,
they were civil and good-natured and clever and humorous.
'They are quite Punches. Just now a ragged boy persecuted
me with a miserable whining for coppers, following me for a
minute or so. When he found that would not do, he suddenly
began to play a tune upon his chin, with great dash and
effect. All the boys are full of tricks more harmless than that
of filching pocket-handkerchiefs, in which they certainly
excel.' His attitude to his surroundings became, in fact, one
of leisurely amused observation. There was no Hurrell at
his elbow, perpetually jolting him into violent thought. He
resigned himself to the unavoidable waste of time; even to
abandoning a half-formed plan of catching up with the
Froudes at Sens or Chartres. It was pleasant to potter round
the library, the pictures, the museum, all by himself; to go
up the Castello Sant' Elmo, and drive out to Virgil's tomb.
It was pleasant to enjoy the excellent fare in his hotel.
Italian cooking gained on his fancy. He liked their fondness
for oil; their onions 'like full-flavoured apples'. Over-in-
dulging in a 'tempting cheese' he opened the doors of his
mind to a remarkable nightmare, which he set down on
paper for his mother's amusement.

'First a weight and horror fell on me, after which I found
myself in the tower at Oriel. It was an audit, and the
Fellows sat round. Jenkyns and the Provost had been
quarrelling, and the latter had left the room, and Jenkyns
to expedite matters had skipt on in the accounts and entered
some items without the Provost's sanction (the extreme

vividness of all this was its merit; after waking I could hardly believe it was not true). I shook hands first with one Fellow then with another. At last I got a moment to shake hands with the gallant Dornford, who was on my right, with Denison, who stood next, and then Copleston, who said: "Newman, let me introduce you to our two new Fellows", pointing to two men who stood on his right hand round the table. I saw two of the most clumsy, awkward-looking chaps I ever set eyes on, and they had awkward unintelligible names. With great grief of heart, but a most unembarrassed smiling manner, I shook hands with them and wished them joy, and then talked and chatted with the rest as if nothing had happened, yet longing to get away, and with a sickness of heart. When I got away at length, I could find no means of relief. I could not find Froude nor Christie. I wished to retire to the shrubberies, which were those of Ham. "There," thought I to myself, "on this seat or that arbour, which I recollect from a boy, I shall recover myself"; but it was not allowed me. I was in my rooms, or some rooms, and had continual interruptions. A father and son, the latter coming into residence, and intending to stand for some Sicilian scholarship. Then came in a brace of gentlemen commoners with hideous faces, though I was not a tutor, and, lastly, my companion with whom I travelled down here from Rome, with a lady under his arm (do what I will I cannot recollect who I thought it was—I saw him with a lady at St. Peter's on Good Friday). This was part of the dream, but only part, and all, I say, so vivid. What shall we say to a bit of cheese awaking the poetical faculty?'

This dream is worth examining in some detail. It is centred upon Newman's struggle with Hawkins for the mastery of Oriel. He could not bear to think of this as a personal quarrel; nor could he bear to think that any blame lay with him for his own defeat. So the dream opens—or the recorded fragment opens—with a transference of his part in the

quarrel to Jenkyns. To Jenkyns, because only a few months
before Newman had been in correspondence with Jenkyns
on the possibility of his (Newman's) becoming Dean of
Oriel. The Dean of Oriel was more than the ordinary Dean
of an Oxford College. He was, in effect, the ruler of the
College, subject only to the veto of the Provost. In his dream,
then, the Jenkyns who quarrels with the Provost (as the real
Jenkyns never did, Newman noted with surprise in a subsequent comment) is a symbol for that masterful part of
Newman's own self, which was bent on dictating the policy
of Oriel. This Jenkyns is victorious. The Provost retires; and
Jenkyns—symbolizing Newman's genius for affairs as well
as his desire to rule the roost—manipulates the accounts as
he chooses. So far the dream is specially vivid; it is all balm
to wounded vanity. But now comes a change. Dornford,
Denison, young Copleston start up. These are the new body
of tutors—the Provost's men. And here—oh, horror!—are
the dreadful consequences of the Provost's misguided policy.
Two awkward louts, with impossible names. Two new
Fellows of Oriel. Not the beloved Rogers—nor Marriott.
And yet . . . why these epithets of 'clumsy' and 'awkward-
looking'? Do they not belong, quite inevitably, to Charles
Marriott, whose ways and talk (even Dean Church admitted)
were 'such as to call forth not unfrequent mirth among
those who most revered him'? The uncouthness of the dream-
Fellows serves, as dream-images do, a double, even a triple,
purpose. It symbolizes at once the ultimate success of the
dreamer's own wish, the measureless folly of his opponent,
the triumph of the spirit over externalities. Every way Newman is justified; though the dream cannot exclude the bitter
brooding sense of failure, which is a *leit-motiv* of his career.
Even to that, in the dream, he is superior. The mask of
good breeding obscures his defeat. His enemies shall not
suspect his real feelings. The dream, with consummate skill,
shores him up on every side.

So far, it is a dream. Now it becomes a species of night-mare. Perhaps a dream turns into a nightmare when the machinery of symbolism becomes unable to cope with the load placed upon it. Perhaps the symbolism becomes— to speak in the loosest of metaphors—too confident, too adventurous. If the more superficial difficulties are so easily resolved, why not those which lie at the very root of the waking personality? The buried trouble in the soul is stimulated too far. The dream-surface grows disturbed and threatening. Something which terribly menaces the dreamer's settled character is approaching. He seeks to cover it with some deceitful symbol. He cannot bear to look upon this thing, this part of himself which he has thrust out of his life for ever. The shadow of the monstrous crow darkens the dream-world. One of two things may happen now in his dream. The attempt of the monster to manifest itself may have gone too far to be stopped. There is an age-long moment of shattering fear. Some commonplace object or sensation is charged with a ghastly significance. Tweedledum is transfixed; struggles to escape and cannot; screams, awakes. This is the true nightmare. Or Tweedledum may, in the dream, succeed in making a partial escape. The mani-festation may be prevented. But the dreamer's vanity is shaken. He is no longer master of the situation. His escape is foiled; he is at the mercy of a series of uneasy events. Running the course of these he may in the end succeed in out-distancing the nameless pursuer. The dream may tail off into less disturbing images.

Newman's dream takes the second road—with a differ-ence. The shadow of the monstrous crow scarcely begins to darken the sky, for Tweedledum is already running away. He is in search of comfort and consolation. But he cannot find them. His own friends are invisible. He is driven back into childhood, into the time when defeat was synonymous with safety and the settled heavenly order of his father's garden. But he is denied that means of escape. He has set himself up to be a responsible person, to create a new order of his own, to impose his own will upon the world. He has failed, and the dream, having got him on the run, will not let him go so easily. Barred from the shrubberies of Eden, he doubles back into manhood. He would be alone in his rooms at Oriel, enjoying the student's escape from reality. But this too is denied him. The dream mocks him with uncomfortable images. First the father and son. Who can they be but the Archdeacon and Hurrell? It is as if the Archdeacon were resigning his place to Newman, and Hurrell—standing for a Sicilian scholarship—were submitting himself to Newman's will. The dream is tempting the dreamer back into the dangerous zone of human relationships. It is a trap. He is not a tutor. Hurrell is not his pupil. The father and son vanish; the two hideous gentlemen commoners take their place. Why two? The dualism runs insistently through the whole dream. No doubt it was suggested by the topic uppermost in Newman's mind—the election to the two vacant Fellowships. But it had, evidently, a deeper significance. It is the sign of incompleteness in isolation, of man's need to be mated. And the dream shows Newman troubled by this need and by his inability to satisfy it in the ordinary way of the world. His spiritual affections are useless to him. His friends have failed him. The brace of gentlemen commoners symbolize a tougher combination than his refined intimacies with Bowden or Froude or Rogers. They swagger into his rooms, and he is powerless to forbid them. They are real, active, triumphant—and hideous. Why? Because they represent the natural man, the sinful concupiscent man, the old Adam, to whom he has denied the right of existence. They are, in fact, his 'baser' self; and they are in his rooms, because they are a part of himself; but they are external and hostile to his dreaming consciousness, because he has disdained their help in building his personality. The dream cannot alter this personality; but it can, and does, exhibit the division between it and them as the cause of his ineffectualness. And then they vanish, and a man comes in with a lady under his arm. The dream grows polite. 'Desire' it seems to say 'may be satisfied in a civilized aesthetic manner. But even this is not for you. Look at this gentleman, and consider if he is not to be envied.' Waking, Newman struggled to recall the lady. She had been somebody in particular. But who? His mind refused to surrender that perplexing, significant secret. And that was not surprising, if (as we guess) the lady was none other than Newman himself.

7. JUDGMENT

'Spring in Sicily! It is the nearest approach to Paradise of which sinful man is capable.' So he had written to Jemima from Rome. And now he stood on the edge of this wilful, delicious experience. It would, he told Jemima, be far more pleasurable in retrospect than in actual performance. The prophecy was truer than he knew.

The sirocco came to a sudden end in the night of Thursday, April 18; and his ship sailed early on Friday morning. He left Naples with positive regret. Sunday saw him at Messina, failing to 'achieve a service', and preparing for his expedition. On Monday he set off for Taormina, along the coast-road. He had hired a servant named Gennaro in Naples; and his train consisted of himself, Gennaro, two mules and several muleteers. It was all rather fantastic and unreal. He felt unlike himself, in a light-coloured hat and coat, 'my neckcloth the only black thing about me, yet black without being clerical'. He was tired, irritated by a delay over his passport, rather depressed. The weather threatened. The baggage kept coming off the mules. There was nobody to talk to. 'A tour is the best time for turning

acquaintances into friends, and I was losing a great opportunity.'

A day's journey of twenty miles brought them to a flea-
ridden inn at San Paolo, and next day they came to Taormina by breakfast-time. 'The last two miles we diverged
from the road up a steep path, and soon came to the ancient
stone ascent leading to Taurominium. I never saw anything
more enchanting than this spot. It realised all one had read
of in books about scenery—a deep valley, brawling streams,
beautiful trees, the sea (heard) in the distance. But when,
after breakfast, on a bright day, we mounted to the theatre,
and saw the famous view, what shall I say? I never knew
that nature could be so beautiful; and to see that view was
the nearest approach to seeing Eden. O happy I! It was
worth coming all the way, to endure sadness, loneliness,
weariness, to see it. I felt, for the first time in my life, that I
should be a better, more religious man if I lived there.' The
poor show had some truth and life in it, then, after all?

In the afternoon Newman continued his journey along
the coast to Giarre. All the way he listened with pleasure to
the croaking of the frogs ('the most musical animals I have
hitherto met with—they have a trill like a nightingale').
The way lay across some of the wide stony river-courses
(*fiumari*) characteristic of Sicily. 'The hills receded—Etna
was magnificent. The scene was sombre with clouds, when
suddenly, as the sun descended upon the cone, its rays shot
out between the clouds and the snow, turning the clouds
into royal curtains, while on one side there was a sort of
Jacob's ladder. I understood why the poets made the abode
of the gods on Mount Olympus.'

The night-quarters at Giarre were even worse than those
at San Paolo. The fleas were innumerable; they bit with a
sting. All through the night he lay sleepless, listening to a
clock striking quarter after quarter. Next day he resolved,
instead of going on to Catania by the coast-road, to strike

inland to Nicolosi and make the ascent of Mount Etna.
There were said to be some marvellous chestnut trees on the
way, six miles out from Giarre. But they proved to be
'nothing but roots cut level with the ground'. Disappointments were beginning. He ate some breakfast in a house
where there was a sick man, and then set out for the five
hours' journey to Nicolosi, over fields of lava, under a very
hot sun. When they reached the inn, Gennaro was tired and
Newman had strained his leg walking. The ascent of Etna
seemed unattractive. The snow was lying later than usual
on the mountainside. The visitors' book was discouraging.
'If you have been a fool in coming,' one entry ran 'do not
be twice a fool in going up.' Newman decided to follow this
advice. His spirits were at a low ebb, and they sank further
still when he looked at his bedroom—the worst he had
hitherto encountered. Gennaro, on whom he was already
beginning to depend, had gone out. The spirits of wine,
which he used as a dressing for his dinner, had failed. He
had eaten almost nothing for two days, and was feeling
'altogether out of sorts'. He lay down miserably on the
plank bed, which looked as if it would come to pieces in the
night; and at once the fleas renewed their merciless attacks.
Well! He had come on this expedition to Sicily (so he now
persuaded himself) not merely for pleasure's sake, but
because he 'wished to see what it was to be a solitary and a
wanderer.' His imagination went back, as it always did when
he felt defeated by circumstances, to his childhood. He
thought of the school sick-room at Ealing. There, at least,
he had been looked after by others. Here, at Nicolosi, even
his servant had deserted him. 'My mind felt very dry, and
I thought, "What if I should lose my reason?"' And then
Gennaro reappeared, and all was changed. The excellent
fellow poached his master some eggs, and sprinkled the floor
with water (to discourage the fleas). Soon Newman was
asleep. He slept soundly for eight hours. Early next morning

he walked down to Catania for his breakfast—a pleasant descent of twelve miles, with a comfortable town to receive him at the end of it. The morbid anxieties of the previous evening melted away.

Common sense would have suggested a rest of two or three days at Catania; but, in spite of his strained knee and the blisters on his feet and his 'considerable languor', he was off next morning to Syracuse. He went by sea, in a large open boat called a *speronaro*, with an awning at the stern, taking nothing with him but his cloaks and a few bottles of wine. There was nothing to eat, except a little bread provided by the sailors. They got to Syracuse in the early hours of the following morning, after an excessively uncomfortable night on board, during which Newman composed perhaps the worst of his contributions to the *Lyra Apostolica*, the lines called *Taurominium*.

Into the twenty-four hours which he spent at Syracuse Newman crammed an incredible amount of exertion. He read Thucydides; interviewed the consul; got a new passport; saw the fountain of Arethusa; rowed up the Anapus; went out to Epipolae; visited the amphitheatre; wrote at great length to Harriett and Jemima; dined with a party of Anglo-Indians at his hotel; attended a reception after the marriage of a local dignitary. The sirocco had returned. The rain came down in torrents. On the next morning, which was Sunday, he left again by boat for Catania. This irked his conscience; but the wind was fair, and he was impatient against the risk of further delay. As if to punish him for his godlessness, everything went wrong. The wind changed again; another wretched night was spent on the boat. On Monday morning they were obliged to put in at Agosta, near the ancient Megara. There, after hours of delay with the authorities, he obtained mules and a guide, and set out in the afternoon under a broiling sun for Catania. The track lay across wild heathlands, then through cornfields and woods, down into a sandy plain intersected by rivers. Darkness came on, and the guide lost his way. It was nearly midnight when he reached Catania, more dead than alive.

Next day Newman felt feverish. He could not eat; and, though the fever seemed to abate, he suffered from choking sensations in the evening. The day was close. There was a slight earthquake. He had the feeling that he had gone through more fatigue and vexation than ever in his life before. Nevertheless he wrote another long letter home, and prepared to leave Catania next morning (Wednesday, May 1) on the long trek to Girgenti, which he expected to reach by Saturday. Then he would enjoy a quiet Sunday, reading aloud to Gennaro, his servant, who could neither read nor write. He would explore the ruins of Girgenti, and go on to Selinunte, and then strike north to Palermo. There he would take boat for Marseilles. Only another three or four weeks, and this arduous pilgrimage would be over. Oh! to see Oxford and be among friends again!

Wednesday's trek was uneventful. They spent the night at Adernò, at the foot of Etna. For the first time, as if his blood had become noxious to them, the fleas left him alone. On Thursday, ill though he felt, he continued his journey. At first he went on foot, and in spite of his sickness he was able to look about him with delight. 'The scene was most beautiful—hills thrown about on all sides, and covered with green corn, in all variety of shades, relieved by the light (raw sienna) stone of the hills. The whole day the scene was like the Garden of Eden, most exquisitely beautiful, though varying, sometimes with deep valleys on the side and many trees, high hills with towns on the top as at S. Filippo d' Argirò, Etna behind us, and Castro Juan before in the distance.' As he looked at the view, he thought of his sister Mary and his eyes filled with tears. At Regalbuto, a dozen miles out, he was too ill to go on; but after lying down for an hour or so he climbed on to his mule. The journey was continued, with

frequent halts while he lay down and rested, as far as Leonforte, a little town two thousand feet up in the hills in the
heart of Sicily, some forty miles from Adernò. There he
spent a miserable night, obsessed with the idea that he must
at all costs *get on*.

Next morning he was too ill to get out of his bed. For three
days he lay in the peculiar misery of mind and body, which
belongs to the early stage of severe illness. At first he supposed that the trouble was gastric. He made Gennaro get
some camomile flowers and brew him some tea. He thought
the tea 'beautiful'. It had the effect (delicately hinted by
dots in his detailed account of his illness) of loosening his
bowels. 'I recollect thinking at last I had found out what was
the matter with me, and the whole night I passed in that
distressing way . . . which I used often to do at home before
I went abroad.' He said so to Gennaro; but Gennaro, feeling
his pulse, thought he had a fever. 'Oh no!' he said confidently 'I know myself better.'

Any kind of interference with the normal course of events
was significant to Newman; and a severe illness was inevitably, in his mind, a punishment or an education. His
Sicilian fever was, for many years afterwards, the most
important episode in his experience. In the shortened per-
spective of the *Apologia*, written thirty years later, it shrinks
into a sentence, and his torment of mind into the prophetic
assertion to Gennaro: 'I shall not die, for I have not sinned
against light.' But in the last years of his Anglican career his
mind was constantly preoccupied with the detailed recollection of his illness. It was a topic to which he fell back in his
conversations with his young disciples at Littlemore. And
at intervals between 1834 and 1840 he wrote the remarkable
memorandum, called *My Illness in Sicily*, which is printed
with his *Letters and Correspondence*, prefacing it with the observation that 'the remembrance is pleasant and profitable.'

There was more than one reason for this fascinated pre-occupation, though Newman himself was unable to understand all of them. 'What am I writing it for?' he asks at the end of the memorandum, in his library at Littlemore. 'For myself I may look at it once or twice in my life, and what sympathy is there in *my* looking at it? . . . Who will care to be told such details as I have put down above? Shall I ever have, in my old age, spiritual children who will take an interest?' That craving to be appreciated as uniquely important, in his own personal right, was a perpetual note sounding in Newman's consciousness. It was, possibly, the determining factor in his religious life. What religion gave him, ultimately, was the assurance that if men did not value him rightly God did. Up to the very end of his long life, for all the patient humility in which he schooled himself, the sharp sense of his own individuality never left him. 'I, alas, alas, am 86.' The repetition of the word 'alas' was full of meaning. He watched himself, as a very old man, wasting under the dramatic passage of time, with the same absorbed surprise as he watched himself struggling in the grip of his Sicilian fever. Sight, hearing, feeling, movement—all might fail him, but the essential John Henry Newman remained, the most interesting, important, indubitable of all existences.

More upon the surface was the relation which the fever bore to his life before and after. Like the illness which (as he believed) had been sent to shock him out of an inclination to Liberal opinions, this illness was sent to remind him that his time was not his own. It marked a division in his life. He prefaced his memorandum by noting 'its remarkable bearing on my history'. It was, first, 'a punishment for my wilfulness in going to Sicily by myself'. And, secondly, it in some way prepared him for the coming call to action. He seemed to be dying; but he was sure that he would not die, *because* there was work for him to do in England. He recovered, and came

back to England, and instantly he was plunged into the
Movement.

About this reason for his excessive interest in the details
of his illness—the only reason he was able to assign—it can
only be said that, so stated, it is no reason at all. Any biographer would be delighted if he could make three weeks
between life and death into the turning-point of his hero's
career. But, though Newman himself always thought of it in
that light, the connection cannot be sustained. Already in
Rome, to Monsignor Wiseman, he had impressively declared that he had a work to do in England. His temper of
mind, about the Whigs and the crisis descending upon the
Church, was already fully developed. Keble's Assize Sermon,
which set the Movement on foot, would have been preached
whether Newman had been ill or well in Sicily; and the
content of Newman's response would have been just what
it was. The contrast between the illness and the sudden
fierce outburst of energy on his return to Oxford was exciting,
in his own mind; but there was no causal relation. Or, it
would perhaps be truer to say, his own account of the matter
entirely fails to disclose the causal relation which he felt to
exist.

What, then, was this deeper relation, which he obscurely
perceived? It was an example—the chief example—of that
oscillatory rhythm which was the pattern of his whole career.
He never failed but he followed up failure with success; never
succeeded but he fell from success into failure. Every
collapse was followed by a recovery, which went just as far
above normality as the collapse had fallen below it. The
pendulum swung to and fro with the most astonishing
exactness. The measure of his weakness at the one stage was
always the measure of his strength in the next. It is not a
difficult matter to plot the peaks and abysses in a graph of
his career. The attempt to do so discloses a pattern of such
extraordinary regularity, that its shape cannot have been

due to chance. At first sight it might seem that chance must, nevertheless, have determined it. It was chance (if it was not Providence) which provided the external facts—the pegs, so to speak, in the board round which the thread of his mental life is stretched, to exhibit these alternations of vitality and collapse. Chance (or Providence) gave him the Vicarage of St. Mary's and the anti-Peel campaign after his breakdown in the Schools and Mary's death; just as it gave him the opportunity of annihilating Kingsley after what his biographer called 'the low-water mark of his life-story'. Besides providing these and other opportunities of success, it sometimes—as now in Sicily—determined the points of collapse. But on a closer view the conclusion irresistibly emerges, that the regularity of these rhythmical alternations was due, not to accident or to Providence, but to Newman himself. The relation of peak to abyss was not a one-way relation. If he climbed out of the abyss, it was only to fall back into it. If he fell into the abyss, it was only to climb out of it again. When accident fixed the point of ascent or descent unusually high or low, Newman's unconscious management of his own history fixed the next turning-point at an equivalent distance below or above the normal level.

I have suggested that recovery was exactly equivalent to collapse. The dynamics of personality are not susceptible of measurement. One cannot, in fact, establish this supposed equivalence. One can do no more than form an intuitive judgment. Using such a judgment, I find myself obliged to qualify my hypothesis of exact equivalence. On the whole, and throughout his entire life, Newman's power of recovery appears to me rather greater than his liability to collapse. He climbs out always to a point higher than that to which he fell. Fanciful or not, this speculation helps to account for the significance of his illness in 1833, in its relation to the events which followed. The extremity of weakness was followed by the extremity of vigour—by a period of 'exuber-

ant and joyous energy' such as he 'never had before or
since', which lasted from 1833 to 1839.

There were two minor reasons for the intensity of his own
interest in the course of his illness. It gave him a perfect field
for the exercise of his genius for introspection. There lay
before him, almost as if its contents were spread out on the
table of some superhuman vivisectionist, a mind, undergoing
a peculiar experience—and a very interesting mind, since
it was his own. That was one reason. And the other reason
was that, side by side with this exercise of detached self-
observation, the remembrance of the illness allowed him to
indulge his self-pity. He dwells on his loneliness, his pain and
weakness, his dependence on Gennaro. In the confident six
years which followed his return to England there was little
room for self-pity except in such recollections. Perhaps this
was why they seemed so pleasant to him. When, in 1840, he
brought the memorandum to an end he recalled how he had
refused to let Gennaro have the blue cloak which had
'nursed me all through my illness.' It was still with him at
Littlemore. 'I have so few things to sympathize with me' he
wrote 'that I take to cloaks.' Self-pity was with him again;
for the six years of confidence were over, and the six years'
descent into the abyss had begun.

Lying, then, in bed at Leonforte too ill to move, all that
Friday, the third of May, he was tormented by the idea that
he was being punished by God for his self-will. The Froudes
and all his other friends had been against his going to Sicily.
Why had nobody pointed out that he was being self-willed?
'Then I tried to fancy where the Froudes were, and how
happy I should have been with them in France, or perhaps
in England. Yet I felt, and kept saying to myself, "I have
not sinned against light", and at one time I had a most
consoling, overpowering thought of God's electing love, and
seemed to feel I was His.'

Next day 'the self-reproaching feelings increased. I seemed to see more and more my utter hollowness. I began to think of all my professed principles, and felt they were mere intellectual deductions from one or two admitted truths. I compared myself with Keble, and felt that I was merely developing his, not my, convictions. I know I had *very* clear thoughts about this then, and I believe in the main true ones. Indeed [he was writing in December 1834], this is how I look on myself; very much (as the illustration goes) as a pane of glass, which transmits heat, being cold itself. I have a vivid perception of the consequences of certain admitted principles, have a considerable intellectual capacity of drawing them out, have the refinement to admire them, and a rhetorical or histrionic power to represent them; and having no great (i.e. no vivid) love of this world, whether riches, honours, or anything else, and some firmness and natural dignity of character, take the profession of them upon me, as I might sing a tune which I liked—loving the Truth, but not possessing it, for I believe myself at heart to be nearly hollow, i.e. with little love, little self-denial. I believe I have some faith, that is all. . . . Still more serious thoughts came over me. I thought I had been very self-willed about the tutorship affair, and now I viewed my whole course as one of presumption. . . . I recollected, too, that my last act on leaving Oxford was to preach a University sermon against self-will. . . . Yet still I said to myself, "I have not sinned against light."'

During these two days his throat was too painful to let him swallow. The door of his room had to be locked to keep it shut. Gennaro was a good deal away, and Newman lay in his room, a prisoner, counting the stars and flowers in the wallpaper 'to keep my mind from thinking of itself'. The whining of beggars in the street distressed him terribly, until Gennaro came back and drove them away. The sound of music—a harp, he thought, and a clarionet—made by some

travelling performers was a brief comfort. In the evening
Gennaro made him get up, and took him out for a walk—
perhaps in order to see if he was well enough to be moved to
Palermo. They sat under a fig tree and Newman wondered
how he came to be there. The continuity of experience was
beginning to disintegrate. There was something about a litter
for the journey to Palermo. Gennaro told him a story about
a sick officer whom he had attended in Spain, who left him
all his baggage and then got well. It was a hint to Newman
to do the same, but he 'did not see the drift of the story at the
time.' He gave Gennaro Hurrell's address, but said: 'I shall
not die. God still has work for me to do.'

That night Gennaro slept in his room, and Newman asked
him if he said his prayers. The man said, yes. While Gennaro
slept, Newman lay, like a child in a sick-bed, with that vivid
yet dreamlike consciousness of his surroundings, which belongs to fever. On the Sunday, he kept eating all day. Again,
in the evening, Gennaro took him out—this time riding on a
mule. Or was this on the Saturday? It was all mixed up in
his mind. Texts about the way, the paths of God, floated
through his head. He must go to meet God. He must go to
Palermo. They started at daybreak on Monday. After half
a mile he made Gennaro unpack the baggage and get out
the remains of a chicken, which he ate. Then he felt very
thirsty, and began sucking oranges, and eating the leaves of
the trees. The thirst increased. Only it was not thirst but 'a
convulsive feeling of suffocation almost about my throat—
very distressing'. He must have water. At last they came to
a hut, or shepherds' tent, where he was given water. He lay
there for some hours, only half conscious, an object of eager
commiseration to a crowd of 'different ages and sexes'. A
doctor came in and felt his pulse and recommended a drink
of camomile, lemon and sugar. A diligence passed, on its way
to Palermo. Newman insisted on speaking to one of the
travellers. A German came in, who could speak English; and

Newman gave him his letter of introduction to somebody at Palermo, and felt a sense of great relief. In the evening he was put, sideways, on to a mule and led up the steep four miles to Castro Giovanni, where a decent lodging was found for him. 'The parting with the poor people in the tent was very affectionate. . . . My servant burst into tears, though I should not have thought him specially tender.'

For nearly three weeks he lay at Castro Giovanni. He had been attacked by a virulent form of fever—according to one account a 'gastric' fever, according to another a variety of scarlet fever—which was raging in Sicily at the time. It was complicated in some way, which the dots in the printed version of the memorandum leave to the imagination—presumably by dysentery or diarrhoea. The complication was painful, but only lasted (as he seemed to remember) for five days. The fever came to its crisis (he believed) in eleven days. During much of this time he was delirious. It seemed as if he remembered 'sitting on a staircase, wanting something, or with some difficulty, very wretched, and something about my Mother and sisters.' He was bled—by an inferior doctor, with moustaches and a harsh voice, of whom he made much, corresponding with him, in his lucid intervals, in quite good Latin, since his Italian had perished of the fever. The heat was terrible. He had nurses, and Gennaro slept in his room, but for some reason it was the muleteer who sat up with him at first and relieved him, when he felt like fainting, by applying vinegar to his nose with 'great bullet-tips of fingers'. There were confused quarrels with the muleteer about his wages, and with the doctor about his remuneration. Gennaro conducted these disputes, before the magistrates, who made their appearance in a body in the sick-room.

All turned now on Gennaro. 'Gennaro ruled me most entirely. I was very submissive, and he authoritative.' There were quarrels with Gennaro. The doctor ordered cold lemonade. Gennaro was for warm tea. 'I insisted on the

lemonade, and made a formal complaint to the doctor that
he (Gennaro) changed the prescriptions (and I would not
see Gennaro for a while).' And when he wanted cold water
to his head, and the doctor and Gennaro would not let him,
'I managed to outwit Gennaro by pretending to dab my
temples with vinegar, and so held a wet cloth to them.' But
this was in his convalescence. While the fever was at its
height, Gennaro used to bathe with vinegar his master's
temples, ears, nose, face and neck. The daily Mass bell
tortured his nerves. 'I used quite to writhe about, and put
my head under the bed-clothes, and asked Gennaro if it
could be stopped. He answered with a laugh of surprise that
it should not annoy me, and of encouragement, as if making
light of it. I have since thought they might suppose it was
a heretic's misery under a holy bell.' All through his illness
he depended on Gennaro so much that he could not bear
him from the room five minutes. 'I used always to be
crying out, for I don't know how long together, "Gen-
na-ro-o-o-o-o-o!"'

Until the crisis was passed—about May 11—Newman
was very near death. The doctor gave him over. But Gennaro believed that he would recover, 'from the avidity with
which I always took my medicine.'

Gennaro was right. The avidity for his medicine was the
expression of a will to live—the same will which carried him
into his ninetieth year with all his faculties unimpaired in
spite of his frequent anticipations of death and apoplexy.
The crisis once passed, the blind will to live was transformed,
day by day, into the resurrection of his complete self-consciousness. At first he was like a child, coaxing Gennaro for
cakes; longing for the egg, baked by Gennaro in wood ashes
for his breakfast; crying out with delight over his tea. 'I
used to say, "It is life from the dead!" I never had such
feelings.' His senses, naturally so acute, were sharpened by
his illness. The master of the house had music played in the

next room. 'It was very beautiful, but too much for me. What strange, dreamy reminiscences of feeling does this attempt at relation raise! So the music was left off.' He watched eagerly for the coming of daylight, murmuring rapturously to himself as the dawn gleamed through the shutter of the window 'O sweet light! God's best gift.' When, at length, Gennaro carried him downstairs and put him in a chair outside the house, the sight of the sky moved him so that he sat helplessly crying, while the people stood round and stared at him.

Gradually his mind began to bury itself again, wandering amongst the events of his past life. He thought of his schooldays. Was Dr. Nicholas still alive or not? He could not remember, could not place himself accurately in time. Then his book on the Arians came vividly into his thoughts. He imagined how it might be improved. He planned ways of making money to pay for the expenses of his illness. He felt an inspiration for a poem, called for pencil and paper, and wrote the lines (No. cv in the *Lyra Apostolica*) beginning 'Mid Balak's magic fires'. Later, he found that he had composed them a month earlier at Messina. A letter came up from Palermo. It was the 'Cheddar' letter, containing the news of the Oriel election. He pored over the small writing, without his glasses, hoping to find Rogers's name. But it was not there—or, rather, he could not find it. The effort brought a rush of blood to his head. Panic seized him. The blood was mounting, mounting. It was up to his ears. If he fell asleep it would go higher, and all would be over. When he slept, it was to dream fantastically. He dreamed that he was at the Russian Court, talking to the Empress. He dreamed of armies and battles—a military expedition, in which he was taking part, from Reggio crossing to Messina and taking a town—an assault upon Castro Giovanni. The will to power was reinforcing the will to live.

At length, on May 25, still very weak, he set off for Palermo in a carriage sent for him from that town. Never had the world seemed so entrancingly fair. 'My joy was too great for me at first. I never saw such a country—the spring in its greatest luxuriance. All sorts of strange trees—very steep and high hills over which the road went; mountains in the distance—a profusion of aloes along the road. Such bright colouring—all in tune with my reviving life. I had a great appetite, and was always coaxing (as I may call it) Gennaro for cakes.' The next day was a Sunday—Whitsunday, though he did not realize this, having lost track of dates. They travelled through the Sunday, in spite of Newman's troubled conscience, and arrived at Palermo on Whit Monday. Either on the Sunday or the Monday morning he sat by the bedside, when he got up, crying bitterly. All he could say to Gennaro was to repeat that he was sure God had some work for him to do in England. He had said so to Dr. Wiseman at Rome, but 'not pointedly'. Now, however, the pulse of this conviction was 'intense and overpowering'. Gennaro, of course, could not understand him at all.

The journey to Palermo was an exhausting one for a healthy man. For anyone in Newman's condition it was foolhardy in the extreme. On one day they travelled sixty-two miles. When they reached Palermo he was almost prostrate. 'I could not read nor write, nor talk nor think. I had no memory, and very little of the reasoning faculty.' At the hotel where he lodged he was thought to be dying. He could not speak without drawling, nor move without assistance. His recovery was rapid; but it was fortunate for him that he was obliged to wait nearly three weeks for a passage to Marseilles. He spent the time sitting in gardens and churches, or being rowed about on the sea.

As life poured back into him, the thought of returning to England, which at Castro Giovanni 'seemed like a dream or an absurdity', became a painful longing. He wrote to Rogers to congratulate him on his election—having seen the news by chance in a paper—and added that he was '*very* home-

sick'. The churches of Palermo were his chief consolation.
'I began to visit the Churches,' he wrote in the *Apologia* 'and
they calmed my impatience, though I did not attend any
services. I knew nothing of the Presence of the Blessed Sacrament there.' On the day of his departure he put these
emotions into a poem for the *Lyra*:

> Oh that thy creed were sound!
> For thou dost soothe the heart, thou Church of Rome, . . .
> I cannot walk the city's sultry streets,
> But the wide porch invites to still retreats,
> Where passion's thirst is calm'd, and care's unthankful gloom.
>
> There, on a foreign shore,
> The home-sick solitary finds a friend . . .
> I almost fainted from the long delay
> That tangles me within this languid bay,
> When comes a foe, my wounds with oil and wine to tend.

In these quiet hours of his convalescence, in the hot still
Sicilian sunlight, and the cool shadows of the churches, a
tempting vision of a life spent in peaceful contemplation, in
'the green repose of the sweet garden-shade' or the seclusion
of church and cloister, came close to his heart. The poems
written at Palermo for the *Lyra* are its witnesses. He repudiated the vision, not with contempt, but with a bitter, fierce
exultation:

> Runs not the Word of Truth through every land,
> A sword to sever, and a fire to burn?

Like St. Gregory Nazianzen he longed secretly 'to muse
upon the past—to serve, yet be at rest.' Yet, surely, he had
not been saved from the jaws of death for this. 'Soft-clad
nobles' might count him and his fellows mad. But Liberalism,
bent on its presumptuous task of halving the Gospel of God's
grace, was now, in England, threatening all that lent
meaning to his profession.

> So will we toil in our old place to stand,
> Watching, not dreading, the despoiler's hand.

And not watching, only. Christ would avenge His Bride.
Even now the work was beginning. He, Newman, was

destined to spend his strength upon it. There would be rough deeds, trials and crimes. Not St. Gregory Nazianzen should be his guide, but St. Paul, who fought with beasts at Ephesus.

No. He had had his hour of musing, his hour of delight. He had lost himself in dreams of the remote, romantic past. He had seen nature at her most beautiful. And then God had stricken him. The purposes of God were fierce, not gentle. The Garden of Eden was not for him. Farewell to Sicily! Farewell to the honest, faithful, masculine Gennaro, to whose care he owed his life. What if he had once been deranged and was easily overset by liquor and had once or twice left his master alone for a whole day? He had stood to Newman in a relation which Newman had found, in his weakness, inexpressibly comforting—the servant turned master. Good-bye, now, to all that, except in the pleasure of recollecting it. The tide of life was rising again. Forward, then, to a place of command in the army of the Anglican Church Militant!

He left Palermo on June 13, in an orange boat bound for Marseilles. It was a wearisome journey. The boat was becalmed for a week in the Straits of Bonifacio. Chafing against the almost intolerable delay, with tears in his eyes when he thought of home, he sought to embrace the discipline of patience, of resignation to the will of God. In this mood, with the emotionalism of convalescence still upon him, he wrote the immortal prayer called *The Pillar of the Cloud*, known to millions as the hymn *Lead, kindly Light*. It needs an effort to dissociate the poem from the dreary drawling tune fitted to it by the Reverend John Bacchus Dykes. Amongst the laboured Biblical analogies and metrical sermonettes of the *Lyra Apostolica* it is, nevertheless, the one utterance of genius. It is the supreme expression, simple and beautiful and haunting, of spiritual surrender. To his friends it seemed to be the work of a Newman whom they did not know. He was

ill, when he wrote it; unlike himself. But whether it expresses
spiritual truth, or spiritual weakness, it came from Newman's
innermost self and was prophetic of his own future.

It was not, however, in this mood of passive submission
to God's will that he was to appear to his friends on his return
to England. Nor did he continue in it during his journey.
He dreamed one night, as the ship lay becalmed, that a
stranger joined him 'so meek in mien, It seem'd untrue or
told a purpose weak', yet on occasion speaking with a 'stern
force, or show of feelings keen', that must surely mask deep
craft or hidden pride. The stranger was St. Paul. Not in
passive submission, then, but in active controlled indignation
must his own duty lie. He put the angel faces behind him,
and planned a new rule of conduct:

> Prune thou thy words, the thoughts control
>   That o'er thee swell and throng;
> They will condense within thy soul,
>   And change to purpose strong.
> But he who lets his feelings run
>   In soft luxurious flow,
> Shrinks when hard service must be done
>   And faints at every woe.

At last, on June 26, his boat drew near the French coast.
Next day he landed at Marseilles. Thoughts of Hurrell
Froude, landing here just two months ago, rushed over him
—tender, passionate, anguished thoughts. Was Hurrell,
perhaps, already dead? That he was marked for death Newman, in his heart of hearts, well knew. He wrote a last lyric
for the *Lyra* on the Separation of Friends—twenty lines,
obscure to the point of meaninglessness. They had to be so,
since Hurrell (if he were still alive) would see them; and he
must not know for whom the speechless intercession of his
friends was mounting to Heaven. But after Hurrell's death
in 1836 Newman added a pathetic conclusion, which gave
the clue to the rest:

> Ah! dearest, with a word he could dispel
>   All questioning, and raise

Our hearts to rapture, whispering all was well
   And turning prayer to praise. . . .
Dearest! he longs to speak, as I to know
   And yet we both refrain.
It were not good: a little doubt below,
   And all will soon be plain.

Two days of travelling brought Newman to Lyons. There a last trial of patience awaited him. He was laid up for several days with inflammation of his ankles. On Tuesday, July 9, he reached England and his mother's house at Iffley, to find Frank there, arrived from Persia a few hours before him. 'The following Sunday, July 14,' he wrote in the *Apologia* 'Mr. Keble preached the Assize Sermon in the University Pulpit. It was published under the title of "National Apostasy". I have ever considered and kept the day, as the start of the religious movement of 1833.'

CHAPTER IX

THE WHIRLPOOL

I. GENERALITIES

I have tried to explain something of the antecedents, social and personal, out of which the Oxford Movement arose; and to explain some of the complicated elements in the character of the great man, whose personality was the dynamic centre of the whole disturbance. While Newman was its heart, it was (as Mark Pattison said) a whirlpool, sucking into it—or else violently repelling—all the talent of the day. Newman gone, it became a fixed system, a mere party in the Church, alive certainly, and even victorious, after a time, within the limited sphere of Anglican politics. But the sphere of possible victory contracted year by year, until Keble's assurance that victory would be 'complete, universal, eternal' (the words are from the famous Assize Sermon) may be said to have become a classical example of futile prophecy. In the two remaining chapters of the present volume I seek to depict only the first of these two stages. The other must be left to the ecclesiastical historians.

What, to begin with, was the Movement itself all about? It was, at its beginning, a vindication of the privileges of the Church of England, under the threat of spoliation by a Whig Government. 'The new governors of the country' in the words of Dean Church 'were preparing to invade the rights, and to alter the constitution, and even the public documents, of the Church. The suppression of ten Irish Bishoprics, in defiance of Church opinion, showed how ready the Government was to take liberties in a high-handed way with the old adjustments of the relations of Church and State.' This collision of politicians and ecclesiastics revealed profound contradictions of principle. To High Churchmen, as Keble expressed himself in the famous sermon, the nation was 'a part of Christ's Church, and bound, in all her legislation and policy, by the fundamental laws of the Church'. If public opinion denied this, then the nation was in a state of apostasy; and, whatever the consequence, such a 'direct disavowal of the sovereignty of God' must be implacably resisted. The Whigs might answer that a very large proportion of the people, especially in Ireland, were not members of the Church of England at all and cared not a fig for her articles of belief, her formularies, her ceremonies, her claims of divine authority. The Church answered—or, rather, the Tractarians answered—that this was irrelevant. The Church was a legal, constitutional, element in the government of the country. She was this, because she was more than this. By human law she was the Establishment. By divine law, and by the right of uninterrupted succession, she was the Apostolical Church of Christ in England—and in Ireland. To deprive her of her worldly goods was, as Pusey explained to his brother, an act of sacrilege, not to be justified by any argument of expediency.

This was the Tractarian view—the view of the Kebles, the Froudes, Newman, Pusey, Rose, Palmer and the rest. They spoke, in this matter, for Churchmen—clerical and lay—all over the country. The majority of those for whom they spoke had no considered theory of the Church, and no knowledge of the conditions which made the reform of the Church in Ireland so inevitable. They were merely afraid for the future, for their own pockets and prestige and the general order of things. The Tractarian leaders *had* a theory—or the beginnings of a theory—but they were either ignorant or reckless of Irish necessities. They, too, were afraid for the future—if candlesticks in Ireland could be so lightly put out, what might not happen in England? Their fears were intelligent fears.

The temper of the age was alarming to religious men. 'Allusions to God's being and providence'—so it seemed to Mr.
William Palmer looking back upon the year 1833 from the
year 1883—'became distasteful to the English parliament.
They were voted ill-bred and superstitious; they were the
subjects of ridicule as overmuch righteousness. Men were
ashamed any longer to say family prayers, or to invoke the
blessing of God upon their partaking of His gifts; the food
which He alone had provided. The mention of His name was
tabooed in polite circles.' There was a violent reaction against
the authoritarian mood, which had followed the victory of
Waterloo. Then, as now, disillusionment was general; and
the Church came in for more than her share of unpopularity.
One after another the iron bands were snapping—the archaic
franchise, the Test and Corporation Acts. Rationalism
seemed to be intoxicating the mob, as well as philosophers
and politicians. Prelates were being insulted in the streets;
the Bishop of Bristol's palace was burned. Here was a Government in power with its ear to the ground. The Irish Church
Temporalities Bill was a first, and a mild, instalment of a
programme which would reduce the Church of England to a
department of the Civil Service.

Was the fear—as a recent critic has suggested[1]—absurd?
Surely it was not. It is true that nothing worse succeeded the
enactment of the Irish Church Temporalities Bill. But was
this not, in part at least, the consequence of the great demon-
stration of feeling with which the Oxford Movement began?
Had certain men not exerted themselves in 1833 to prove to
the Government of the day that the Church of England was
still a power for politicians to reckon with, what further
measures might not have followed? Already, before Newman's return from Sicily, the acute and practical mind of
Rose (Pusey's old antagonist) had correctly appreciated the
situation. Something, he wrote in February to Palmer, must

[1] *A Century of Anglo-Catholicism*, Professor H. L. Stewart, p. 76.

be done. 'The only thing is, that whatever is done ought to be *quickly* done: for the danger is immediate, and I should have little fear if I thought that we could stand for ten or fifteen years as we are.'

In giving credit to the originators of the Movement for their tactical sense, the historian has to beware of adopting their judgments. If they were right about the risks into which their Church was passing, they were most certainly wrong about Ireland. What happened in Ireland was, no doubt, painful to Churchmen, but it was inevitable. Hence a division of opinion in the Church herself. The Primate, Archbishop Howley, though he had opposed the emancipation of the Roman Catholics and parliamentary reform, and was hostile to Jewish relief, was statesman enough to perceive that the position in Ireland was untenable. He consented at an early stage to the principle of the Irish Church Temporalities Bill, by which the Irish Church rates were withdrawn from the Church and the suppression of a number of sees followed as a matter of financial necessity. The Bishops in general acquiesced. The Archbishop of Dublin, Whately, voted for the measure in the House of Lords. For this honest and courageous action he incurred the lasting contempt of the Tractarians—of Newman, once his adoring disciple, in particular and of all Newman's circle.

But the Tractarians set no value on ecclesiastical statesmanship. There could be no compromise between temporal facts and eternal realities. If the whole world united with the flesh and the devil against the Church, the Church must abate no jot of her claim. Indeed she must restate it still more plainly and uncompromisingly, and leave the consequences to God. What if she were stripped of her possessions by wicked men and her ministers beggared and persecuted? 'Christ will avenge His bride.' And for her leaders, the Bishops, what more blessed termination of their course could there be (in the language of Tract No. 1) than the spoiling of their goods and martyrdom? Though this was not, perhaps, an accurate reflection of the minds of the Bishops themselves.

Such was the spirit by which the originators of the Movement were fired; and such was the spark which ignited it. But in a few months it had developed into something far more significant than a mere rally to the defence of an ancient and divine institution against political attack. What *was* the Church of England—the question was implicit from the beginning and soon became explicit—what *was* the Church of England, that she not only dared but must assert her rights against the State? The answer was simple. She was the Catholic and Apostolic Church, ordained by Christ Himself, tracing back her authority to the Apostles through the laying on of hands, and keeping in her sole gift the sacraments of baptism and the eucharist, by which God's saving grace was conveyed to sinful man. She bore on her shoulders the weight of accumulated error; she was shackled by her subordination to the civil power; the purity of her doctrine had been sullied by the self-confident imaginations of the Reformers. Nevertheless she was still the Catholic and Apostolic Church, no vain creation of human fancy, but the daughter of God, the bride of Christ, the mother of souls.

The answer opened up a vast range of dispute and research, at the same time as it tapped a new, or rather an almost forgotten, source of enthusiasm. It brought the Tractarians into collision on the one hand with the Evangelicals and the Latitudinarians, on the other with the Roman Catholics. To the Evangelicals this insistence upon the identity of the Church of England with the undivided pre-reformation Church was extremely unpalatable; equally unpalatable was the emphasis given to the sacraments. To the Latitudinarians the whole answer had the character of a mechanical superstition. To the Romans—soon to be brilliantly championed in England by Dr. Wiseman—the claim was an impertinent heresy, only not to be so described because, logically pursued, it must surely end in a recognition of Rome's claim to be still the Catholic Church in every corner of the world. But for those who could accept the Tractarian claim it is impossible to overstate the thrilling consequences of that acceptance. They found themselves divinely and directly commissioned, not for the thankless task of thinking out God's purposes for themselves, but for the restoration of His Church to her original purity and splendour. They addressed themselves to this exhilarating labour, under a leader of magnetic genius, in a spirit of high and confident excitement.

For, though the answer in broad outline was simple enough and derived its power from its very simplicity, it had to be worked out in detail under conditions of extreme present difficulty through a mass of complicated and often self-contradictory historical material. The present difficulties were given by the tangled constitution of the Church of England, the ambiguities of her Articles and formularies, the presence within the same body of powerful parties bitterly opposed to the new movement. The historical difficulties were given by the very causes which had produced the present difficulties—the war of influences from the Reformation onwards; and, to go farther back than this, by the long period during which the Church of England had been one with the Church of Rome. To what point, then, must the new Reformers go back? The obvious answer might seem to be: To Christ and the New Testament. That was, in effect, the Evangelical answer. But to the Tractarians it was the obviously wrong answer. Christ had commissioned the Apostles; but He had not provided them with a ready-made Church. The formation of the Church had been a gradual process—necessarily so, while the Faith gradually possessed the Roman Empire. But it had not been a haphazard, undirected process. The promise of the Father had been with the Apostles, and after them with the Saints and Fathers of the early Church. The Holy Ghost had dictated the pattern of the divine society. It was, then, to the earliest centuries of Christianity, while the Church was still one and undivided, before the first fatal schism of East and West had begun to develop, that Newman and his companions turned for the rediscovery of that divine pattern, still, as they held, preserved by God's providence, more truly than elsewhere, in the Church of England. In the clumsy language of her Articles of Religion, "Holy Scripture containeth all things necessary to salvation.' But this could not mean, as the Low Churchmen maintained, that the things necessary to salvation lay open on the face of scripture to man's unaided intelligence; still less could it mean that the services and sacraments of the Church were unnecessary to salvation. The Word of God needed authoritative interpretation. And this interpretation was to be found in the writings, not only of the Apostles, but of the early Christian Fathers, and in the decisions of the Oecumenical Councils of the Church, held at intervals from the fourth to the seventh centuries.

Here, then, was a field of study and thought, promising the richest rewards, suddenly opened in a desert. To the typical Oxford scholar of that day (as perhaps to his modern equivalent) the Fathers were like dead mutton. It is said that Dean Gaisford, as he showed Christ Church library one day to a visitor, walked rapidly past all the Fathers, with a 'Sad rubbish!' and a contemptuous wave of his hand.

The elaboration of the Tractarian answer issued in a special theory of the Church of England, to which Newman gave the name of the *Via Media*. This 'middle way', then a theoretical ideal, afterwards (or so the claim is made for it) a realized fact, was a highly subtle conception. On the face of it the phrase denotes a mean between two extremes—the errors of Rome on the one hand, of Protestantism on the other. But it meant a great deal more than that. It meant more, even, than a central position between all the many extremes—the

Greek as well as the Roman Church, Dissent as well as Protestantism. It meant a mean between the claim of infallibility
and the disclaimer of authority. Newman, in the words of
Dean Church, 'followed the great Anglican divines in asserting that there was a true authority, varying in degrees, in the
historic Church; that on the most fundamental points of religion this authority was trustworthy and supreme; that on
many other questions it was clear and weighty, though it
could not decide everything.' The middle way meant, again,
a reconciliation of virtues which had long kept different
company. In Wakeman's view it 'retains the essentials of
the Catholic Church in faith and organization, and yet con-
bines with it an appeal to Scripture, a rightful use of reason,
and an avoidance of superstitious exaggeration.' And, in the
words again of Dean Church, it insists 'on the reality and
importance of moral evidence as opposed to demonstrative
proof'. This last claim is of deep importance. The Tractarians
possessed all the moral earnestness and religious emotion of
the Evangelicals; but combined them with an intellectual
power of analysis and exposition, to a degree long unknown
in England.

It was this combination which gave the movement its
peculiar character and saved it from final collapse when Newman deserted it. It is surprising, in 1933, to find a modern
Evangelical, the Master of St. Peter's Hall, denying to the
Oxford Movement the character of a true religious revival.
It was, he is reported to have said, rather 'a needed rediscovery and development of the institutional aspect of religion
as expressed by the Church, than a proclaiming of that personal relationship between each individual soul and God which
has been the pulsing heart of every religious revival from
Elijah's day to our own.'[1] The criticism is no criticism at all;
it begs all the questions. The whole point of the Movement
lay in the assertion—no less passionately made than the Evan-

[1] *The Times*, April 7, 1933.

gelical's assertion of his private intimacy with God—that men deceive themselves if they seek God otherwise than through the Church. It should be needless to add that in the teaching of Keble, Pusey, Newman and the Tractarians generally the relationship of the individual soul to God was just as important as in the teaching of John Wesley. But the importance of that relationship was not to be thought of as transcending the importance of the Church. The Church was the divinely established means of grace. But she was something else and something greater. She was the continuing dwelling-place of God's spirit upon earth, and as such she was owed all the honour and glory within the power of men to pay to her.

This exalted conception of the Church made demands upon the intellect of a much more subtle and difficult kind than the demands made by the current Low Church philosophy of salvation. And the process of establishing the claim of the Church of England to be regarded as the true Church involved an extremely ambitious programme of learning and argument. The programme was undertaken by the leaders of the Movement. Palmer's *Origines Liturgicae*, Pusey's volume of tracts on *Baptism*, Newman's *Prophetical Office of the Church* were among the forerunners of a theological literature which certainly made full use of reason. Yet somehow the impression grew up and has never been dissipated, that the Movement was mystical, aesthetic, impulsive, irrational.

Every eager motion of man's mind towards a new way of life develops its own characteristic excesses. If the Evangelical revival shipwrecked many of its converts on desert islands of ugliness, stupidity and cant, the Apostolical bark grounded, not seldom, in the shallows of religious aestheticism or became entangled in a Sargasso-like sea of introspection. The latter danger was the correlative of the former. The truths of God were not to be apprehended by reason. The magnificent edifice of the Church rested, not on any metaphysic, but on the axioms of Christian morality. There were those—like

Isaac Williams—to whom the beauty of personal holiness was the first and the chief evidence of religion. They saw this beauty shining most brightly in the noble setting of the historic Church, a living part of the visible communion of saints. All the rest they took upon trust. They sought to refashion their own lives according to their vision. The attempt led many of them into a distressing wilderness, beyond the help of their inexpert spiritual guides. Others were caught by a different, an easier vision—the dreamlike spectacle of the Church herself, the remembered splendours of her past, the imagined splendours of her future. Amongst these were not a few who found in the revived exaltation of the sacraments and the priesthood a new enhancement of life, the more delicious because it was so mysterious. Discipleship became the vogue; ordination tickled the vanity of many a self-conscious youngster; coteries of undergraduates paraded their devotional extravagances before the eyes of irritated young Philistines; while the shallowest minds discovered a new form of pleasing excitement in the most trifling externals of religion—the interpretation of a rubric or the embroidery of a scarf.

The *Via Media*, ran a current sarcasm, was crowded with young enthusiasts who never presumed to argue, except against the propriety of arguing at all. There was, Dean Church himself admits, a good deal of foolish sneering at reason on the part of affected young disciples. The language of Pusey and Newman was often ill calculated to discourage this kind of inverted conceit. Obedience to the Church seemed to require the surrender of the right of private judgment—the right which had become anathema to Newman. His violent antipathy to the school which had nursed him as a young man—the school of Whately and the Oriel Noetics—led him to repudiate the 'pride of reason', in which he discerned the cause of Whately's fall from grace. Unquestionably Newman was afraid of his intellect. Only his moral sense had saved him, he believed, from shipwreck. 'I thank God,' he told Pusey on the eve of his secession 'that He has shielded me morally from what intellectually might easily come on me—general scepticism.' Nevertheless he used his intellect—if only within the framework of his moral certainties and religious intuitions—and used it with powerful effect.

Indeed the use of reason would have been forced upon the leaders of the Movement by controversy, if the nature of their conceptions had not already compelled them to take that road. Before long they were involved in a war of argument on two fronts. On the one hand they had to meet the accusation of Popery; on the other they had to maintain their middle position against the Papists. In this war Newman was, in the end, defeated. But the defeat was not a purely intellectual defeat. It was his imagination, not his reason, which was taken captive by Rome. Half-way between 1833 and 1845 his first doubt came to him. 'Who can account' he himself asked in his *Apologia* 'for the impressions which are made on him? For a mere sentence, the words of St. Augustine, struck me with a power which I never had felt from any words before. . . . "Securus judicat orbis terrarum!" By those great words of the ancient Father the theory of the *Via Media* was absolutely pulverized.'

It was only pulverized because its author desired that it should be. He had ridden too long on the crest of the wave; by the law of his nature he was already aching to sink into the trough, to submit himself to a superior authority. The descent took him six painful years. But they were not years of argument; they were years of imaginative adjustment to the complete reversal of his position. The adjustment was facilitated by the contempt into which the Movement had fallen in his own University, and in the ranks of his ecclesiastical superiors. Pusey's suspension; the condemnation of his own Tract No. 90; the succession of episcopal charges against the principles of the Tractarians—these events took the heart out of him. His own Church, it seemed, would have nothing to say to his efforts to re-establish her. His *Via Media* was but a dream of his own mind. He could have submitted to her, as he submitted to Rome; but only if she had the greatness of mind to be what Rome believed herself to be. 'O my mother,' he cried to her, in his last sermon at Littlemore, with a pathetic eloquence which moved his hearers to uncontrollable tears, 'whence is this unto thee, that thou hast good things poured upon thee and canst not keep them, and bearest children, yet darest not own them? . . . Thou makest them "stand all the day idle", as the very condition of thy bearing with them; or thou biddest them be gone, where they will be more welcome; or thou sellest them for nought to the stranger that passes by.' It was indeed a pathetic self-revelation of the inmost motives of the preacher. Two years later the stranger bought him, and eyed his bargain with suspicion.

But during these six years, while Newman remained the chief centre of dramatic interest, the real leadership of the Movement passed into the hands of Pusey. And Pusey, whatever his morbid peculiarities may have been, and for all his physical frailty, was of very different stuff from Newman. Where Newman was weak, Pusey was tough. His mind was not of the order which is shaken by sudden impressions. He had his teeth into the *Via Media*, and he was never going to let go his hold. Far more than Newman he knew what sorrow and responsibility could be. He had experienced the essential human passions. He was, in fact, what Newman never was—a man. Let Newman, with his escort of hermaphrodites, succumb to these alien, imperious fascinations. He would not believe it, until it had actually happened. He was broken-hearted when the incredible became accomplished fact. But it made no manner of difference to his own views. Everything became much more difficult than it had been. But all the feelings, all the arguments, which he and Newman had shared, were just as real, just as true, as they had ever been.

The *Via Media* was not shattered, though its inventor had lost faith in his own invention. Pusey took over the patent, and made it work. It must be admitted that, after a fashion, it is working still.

2. BEGINNING OF THE TRACTS

'On first confronting my brother on our joint return from abroad' wrote Francis Newman nearly sixty years later 'his dignity seemed as remarkable as his stiffness.' To John, overwhelmingly conscious of a mission, Frank was an unprincipled renegade. He did not put it to Frank quite so crudely; but he told him that his Evangelical formula was rank heresy, and he made it clear by his manner that intimacy between them was ended. For himself he was conscious less of dignity and stiffness (though he had always longed to acquire a 'stable' character) than of 'exuberant and joyous energy', such as he had never known before and was never to know again. Health and strength came back 'with such a rebound that some friends at Oxford, on seeing me, did not well know that it was I, and hesitated before they spoke to me.' Confidence in himself and in the cause he was to champion was so complete that he felt utterly contemptuous of disagreement. 'My behaviour had a mixture in it both of fierceness and sport; and on this account, I dare say, it gave offence to many; nor am I here [i.e. in the *Apologia*] defending it.' It pleased him to play cruelly with opponents of smaller calibre; to trick them with ironical phrases; to court misunderstanding. For all this he was to pay in bitter humiliation over a long stretch of years. But for the time being he was reckless of consequences. He did not, by his own account, set up for the leader of a party. He 'never had the staidness or the dignity necessary for a leader.' He declared, even, that to the last he never recognized the hold he had over young men. He had 'a lounging, free-and-easy way of carrying things on'. He would not allow that he and his friends constituted a party at all. That was how it all looked to him in retrospect in 1864. But he *was* leader, and he knew perfectly well that everyone so regarded him. It was not until things began to go badly, and the fountain of fierce energy began to dry up inside him, that he struggled to rid himself of the title. 'My good fellows,' he wrote to Pusey in August 1838 '*you* make me the head of a *party*—that is your *external* view; but I know what I am—I am a clergyman under the Bishop of Oxford, and anything more is accidental.'

An interesting picture of Newman in this first summer of the Movement is given in James Mozley's letters. James was the younger brother of Tom, and was at this date an undergraduate at Oriel and an ardent admirer of the great man. 'Newman has at last come,' he wrote to Tom on July 12 'and is looking very well, much better than when he went, and considerably tanned with his exposure to the southern sun.' After an excited description of Newman's adventures in Sicily he ended with an exhortation to Tom to come to Oxford. 'Newman, now that he is once back, does not intend to leave Oxford in a hurry, so all his friends who wish to see him must come to Oxford.' In September, after the earliest Tracts had appeared, he told his sister: 'Newman now is becoming perfectly ferocious in the cause, and proportionately sanguine of success. "We'll do them", he says, at least twenty times a day—meaning, by "them", the present race of aristocrats, and the Liberal oppressors of the Church in general.'

The first active step, after Keble's sermon, was not, however, taken on Newman's initiative. This was the conference of friends at Hugh Rose's rectory at Hadleigh, Suffolk, which lasted from July 25 to 29. Rose was the prime mover, the only Cambridge member of the party, a learned, sensible, practically-minded man. The others came from Oxford— Hurrell Froude from Oriel, Arthur Perceval from All Souls,

JOHN HENRY NEWMAN
*From the drawing by George Richmond
in the possession of Oriel College*

William Palmer from Worcester. Keble was to have been there, but for some reason decided at the last moment not to go. Newman preferred to remain outside, and receive a confidential report from Froude, who was somewhat critical of his company. Rose, though full of good notions, was 'not yet an Apostolical', and Perceval, though a very delightful fellow and a thorough-going Apostolical, was too excitable and extravagant. Palmer told Newman that both Perceval and Froude were 'very deficient in learning and therefore rash'. Nothing very definite emerged from this association of opposites, except that the two great objects must be to fight for the doctrine of the Apostolical Succession and to defend the integrity of the Prayer Book. Froude made up his mind that Rose was not the man to save the situation.

Soon after the Hadleigh conference action developed along two distinct lines. Rose and Palmer hankered for a Society and the drafting of Petitions and Declarations. The Society was to be called the Association of Friends of the Church. Palmer threw himself energetically into it, and travelled up and down the country. It was useful spade-work; the soil was turned over for the Tracts. But the Association came to little. 'Living movements' Newman thought 'do not come of committees, nor are great ideas worked out through the post, even though it had been the penny post'—which, of course, at that date it was not. But 6530 ministers of the Apostolical Church signed an Address to the Archbishop of Canterbury, drafted by Palmer, amended by Newman, and presented in February, 1834, to the Archbishop by twenty-four distinguished clergymen with the Archdeacon of Canterbury at their head. The Address was brief. It congratulated the Archbishop on his firmness and discretion (did its drafters know that he had approved the notorious Irish Church Temporalities Act?), assured him of the signatories' devoted adherence to the Apostolical doctrine and polity of the Church and their deep-rooted attachment to her venerable Liturgy, and promised him their support for any measures that might tend to revive the discipline of ancient times. Such amiable expressions of opinion were not likely to effect a great deal—and indeed it soon appeared that most of the signatories attached no special meaning to the one significant term in the Address—the word 'Apostolical'. Still, the Address showed that the Church was stirring; and it was followed by a much more remarkable manifesto—a Declaration of the Laity of the Church of England, presented to the Archbishop of Canterbury in May, with the signatures of no fewer than 230,000 heads of families. The Declaration, like the Address, extolled the Church's 'apostolic form of government', and indeed went even further than the Address by asserting that the consecration of the State by the public maintenance of the Christian Religion was the first and paramount duty of a Christian People, and by identifying that public maintenance with the Establishment of the National Church. And King William IV, on his birthday in the same month, took the opportunity of making a speech to the Bishops, not 'got by heart', in which he assured them of his firm attachment to the Church and resolution to maintain it, and made a pointed reference to recent unhappy circumstances and to 'the threats of those who are enemies of the Church'.

All this was good, so far as it went. The Whigs would see now that they were not to have it all their own way. But Newman and Froude meant that the Church should rise to the level of the great epithet used of her in these two documents. And while Palmer was indulging his own bent as a kind of general manager for the collection of signatures for the Address and the Declaration, Newman put his idea of the Tracts into execution. There was a good deal of preliminary scuffling with those who, like Palmer, were unsympathetic to the idea. But in the early autumn of 1833 the famous series began.

Every kind of difficulty had to be overcome. No competent

publisher would handle them. They had to be printed and circulated by private effort and at private expense, until they were subsequently taken over by Rivington. But there was no doubt, from the start, about the noise they were making. The earliest pamphlets were short, and (if allowance is made for the literary standards of the time) sharp. No. 1 was from Newman's own pen. It appeared on September 9, under the title *Thoughts on the Ministerial Commission respectfully addressed to the Clergy*. The very wordiness and flatness of the title emphasized the startling directness of its argument. The times are evil, yet no one speaks against them. The question must be asked, on *what* are the clergy to rest their authority, when the State deserts them? Upon nothing else than their Apostolical descent.

Amongst those upon whom this Tract, and those that followed it, made an immediate and powerful impression was Dr. Pusey. Keble had sent him a copy of his sermon on National Apostasy, but it survived in his library with its pages uncut. This perhaps meant no more than that Pusey was working too hard on his Catalogue of Arabic MSS. to pay attention to public events in which he was not immediately concerned. The stir made by the Tracts in Oxford was too considerable to pass over his head. The air hummed with violent censure and equally violent praise. Since his marriage and his appointment to the Chair of Hebrew in 1828 Pusey had been wrapped up in his work and his family, when he was not prostrated by illness. Four children had been born to him, one of whom (christened by Newman) had died. But the friendship begun by those earnest walks and talks in Christ Church Meadow ten years ago still united him to Newman. Newman was a frequent visitor at the Puseys' house. When Pusey fell dangerously ill Newman wrote him a 'very kind and loving letter'. Each thought of the other with affection and remembered him in his prayers. But perhaps the affection would have been in some danger of becoming little more than a conventional attitude, if it had not been for the renewal of intimacy brought about by the Tracts.

Pusey came into the circle at a time when Newman was beginning to need reinforcement. Palmer was constantly pressing him to discontinue the Tracts, and using all the influence he could muster to this end. Froude's health had broken down again. He spent three weeks in October with Newman at Oxford, and Newman learned then from the doctor (though the truth was kept from Froude) that he must abandon hope of his friend's recovery. He wrote to Keble, imploring him to persuade Froude to go to the West Indies. Their combined efforts were successful. Froude left England for Barbados in November, not to return for a year and a half. And Newman, who counted on his friend more than he dared confess to himself, was left to carry on the campaign alone. The correspondence between them took on a new and poignant urgency; there was a new tenderness in Froude's letters, as if he had come to realize how much he meant to Newman, an evident desire to use the language of affection; and on Newman's part an eagerness to be sure that he was doing what Froude thought it right for him to do. 'My dear Froude,' he wrote in November when Palmer was pressing him hardest to drop the Tracts 'I do so fear I may be self-willed in this matter of the tracts. Pray do advise me according to your light.'

So Pusey—though no longer the slight curly-headed youngster of Newman's first recollection—came to fill some part of the aching gap. It was an office that none of Newman's younger friends could fill. He needed someone whose mind he had not formed; someone external to himself and equal to himself. Isaac Williams, in his account of a conversation which must have taken place about this time, shows the way of Pusey's approach to the pedestal of leadership.

'Pusey's presence always checked Newman's lighter and unrestrained mood; and I was myself silenced by so awful a person. Yet I always found in him something most congenial to myself; a nameless something which was wanting even in Newman, and I might perhaps add even in Keble himself. But Pusey was at this time not one of us, and I have some recollection of a conversation which was the occasion of his joining us. He said, smiling, to Newman, wrapping his gown round him as he used to do, "I think you are too hard on the Peculiars, as you call them. You should conciliate them; I am thinking of writing a letter myself with that purpose." "Well!" said Newman, "suppose you let us have it for one of the Tracts!" "Oh, no," said Pusey, "I will not be one of you!" This was said in a playful manner; and before we parted Newman said, "Suppose you let us have that letter of yours which you intend writing, and attach your name or signature to it. You would not then be mixed up with us, nor in any way responsible for the Tracts!" "Well," Pusey said at last, "if you will let me do that, I will." It was this circumstance of Pusey attaching his initials to that Tract, which furnished the *Record* and the Low Church party with his name, which they at once attached to us all.'

The Tract which resulted from this conversation was No. 18 and was dated December 21, though apparently it was not in circulation until the new year. It was entitled *Thoughts on the Benefits of the System of Fasting, enjoined by our Church*, and was signed E.B.P. Longer than any of the preceding Tracts, it was temperately and persuasively argued. But fasting had fallen into desuetude. The Tract was received with a good deal of indignant or derisory criticism. 'I was not prepared' wrote Pusey to Newman, in pathetic astonishment, a few days after its appearance 'for people questioning, even in the abstract, the duty of fasting; I thought serious-minded persons at least supposed they practised fasting in some way or other. I assumed the duty to be acknowledged, and thought it only undervalued.' Dr. Arnold was much alarmed by the Tract. He thought that fasting belonged 'to the

antiquarianism of Christianity—not to its profitable history';
and he warned Pusey that he was associating himself with 'a
party second to none in the tendency of their principles to
overthrow the truth of the Gospel'. What would become of
his own plan for 'reunion all round' if they succeeded in re-
erecting the wicked 'idol of Tradition'? More insidious was
a comment of the Provost of Oriel. Pusey, who had been ill
all the winter, was due to preach on January 19 in the
Cathedral. He was unable to appear in the pulpit; his sermon
was read for him by the Archdeacon. He must, said Hawkins,
have been fasting too much.

The appearance of Newman's first volume of his Parochial
Sermons in March, with its dedication to Pusey 'in affectionate acknowledgment of the blessing of his long friendship
and example'—Pusey refused to pass a more eulogistic form of
words—was another indication to the public that Pusey was
drawing close to the Tractarians. Illness prevented him from
contributing another Tract 'on not keeping company with
notorious sinners'. But events were preparing this year (1834),
which were to give a further stimulus to the Movement and
to bring Pusey into still closer connection with its leaders.

The Professorship of Moral Philosophy had fallen vacant
in 1833, and up to the last moment it seemed that Newman
would be elected. What consequences might not have followed, if this expectation had been realized? The notion first
came into Newman's head in the August after his return from
Sicily. He mentioned it in a letter to Froude as 'a most
audacious scheme' which would not 'bear to be put on paper;
the ink would turn red.' But in January the scheme no longer
seemed audacious. He wrote of it to Bowden as a *chance*, for
which he had 'no especial wish'. In February it had become
'a fair chance'. But in the middle of March another candidate
presented himself—Dr. Hampden, the Principal of St. Mary
Hall—and was promptly elected.

3. HAMPDEN

Hampden was a former Fellow of Oriel, an intimate friend of Whately and Blanco White and Dr. Arnold, some eight years older than Newman. He was no longer a Fellow when Newman was elected, for he had married soon after being ordained. After a brief experience of various country curacies he settled down in London to a life of comfortable private study. He had ample private means, and his disposition was that of a retiring student. A shy, affectionate man, quietly following out his own original line of thought, able and learned but without any gift for controversy, he was completely unfitted to be the antagonist of a merciless fighter like Newman. Yet that was the part he was destined to play; and the Bishopric of Hereford was quite inadequate compensation for the troubles in which he was to be involved.

Every kind of imputation has been made by Newman's 'spiritual children' against the unfortunate Hampden, short of gross immorality. Dull, stupid, muddle-headed, rude, mean, ignoble, vindictive, cold, ostentatious, humourless—these are some of the epithets freely bestowed upon him. Even the fact that he spent £4,000 on the restoration of St. Mary Hall, and the rebuilding of the lodgings, was made a charge against him. The campaign of vilification did not spare his personal characteristics. He was 'the most unprepossessing of men . . . not so much repulsive as utterly unattractive . . . his face was inexpressive, his head was set deep in his broad shoulders, and his voice was harsh and unmodulated. Some one said of him that he stood before you like a milestone, and brayed at you like a jackass. It mattered not what he talked about, it was all the same, for he made one thing as dull as another.' Thus the ribald pen of Tom Mozley, retaining into extreme old age the prejudices of his hot youth. For the feud began when Newman was deprived of his pupils and Hampden came back to Oxford, at

Provost Hawkins's earnest request, to assist in the Oriel tutorship.

It was all shamelessly unfair, and most of it completely untrue. So far as personal appearance went, the lie is given to Mozley's malicious picture by the Christ Church portrait. He was a steady, sedate sort of a man, 'old Hampden' to his friends even when he was a boy; and something of his unresponsiveness to the lighter side of life shows in his expression. It is the face of a silent man, perhaps of an obstinate man; but it is certainly not the face of a stupid or disagreeable man. A lady, who knew him well, described him as having 'dark, bright eyes that kindled with animation; a clear, brown complexion; dark straight hair, the forehead peculiarly open; a well-proportioned figure, though not tall, and a finely-shaped leg and foot.' He was cursed with an intense shyness, which was very much to his disadvantage when the limelight fell upon him. But though he was stiff in company and a poor talker—or, rather, not a talker at all—in unsympathetic circles, he could be very easy and charming with his own friends.

The special line of thought which he took for his own was perhaps originally suggested to him by Blanco White. It was connected with the study of scholastic theology—a subject of which Oxford was completely ignorant. He conceived that the development of a complicated technical theology, resulting from the application of formal logic to the data of Christianity, had been of immense disservice to religion. This vast pretentious structure was, he held, a masterpiece of ingenious self-deception. The theologians of the schools thought they were establishing religious truth by elaborate argumentation, when they were only multiplying and arranging a theological language. There could be no compromise between such a view of dogma and that held by Newman, to whom dogma was the fundamental principle of religion. For Hampden the fundamental principle of religion was God's

RENN DICKSON HAMPDEN
From the painting by Sir Daniel Macree
in the possession of Christ Church

revelation of himself through Christ, with its attendant moral teaching and historical facts; and the subsequent revelation in the soul of each believing Christian. These were the facts; the rest was but a web of subtle theory.

How, then, (his enemies asked) could he profess his belief in the creeds which he recited in church as readily as everyone else? There were only two possible answers—in their opinion. Either he was a hypocrite and a humbug, or he was too stupid to understand that he had cut the ground from under his own feet. The latter was the most damaging account of the matter, and it was industriously spread abroad. His critics overlooked the fact that in the last of his Bampton Lectures he had anticipated the criticism and provided an explanation of his own. Suppose, he asks, that we suddenly became aware, for the first time, of the divine facts revealed in the Bible. Should we not shrink from reducing them 'to the precision and number of articles'? But, he continues, 'when theoretic views are known to have been held and propagated; when the world has been familiarized to the language of these speculations, and the truth of God is liable to corruption from them; then it is, that forms of exclusion become necessary, and theory must be retorted by theory.' The function of theory is only tolerable in religion when it denies wrong notions, not expressly sanctioned by revelation. 'This is the view which I take, not only of our Articles at large, but in particular, of the Nicene and Athanasian Creeds. . . . If it be admitted that the notions, on which their several expressions are founded, are both unphilosophical and unscriptural; it must be remembered, that they do not impress those notions on the Faith of the Christian, as matters of affirmative belief. They only use the terms of ancient theories of Philosophy—theories current in the Schools at the time when they were written—to exclude others *more obviously* injurious to the simplicity of the Faith.' Why, then, go on using them? Because (amongst other reasons) the tendency of the human

mind to identify words with things is not 'a transient phenomenon, peculiar to one age, or one species of philosophy', but
'an instinctive propensity of our intellectual nature'. What
has happened once will happen again; and imperfect and
obscure (to modern minds uninstructed in their real significance) as the safeguards of the Creeds may be, it would be
reckless to throw them away. The spirit of scholasticism still
lives.

Such, very much abridged, was Hampden's defence of his
own position, and it was not the defence of a fool or an
impostor.

The Bampton Lectures, in which his theory was fully
developed, were delivered in 1832. They were well attended,
and it was not until other circumstances brought the lecturer's
name into prominence that they began to undergo hostile
criticism. Effective as the criticism was upon University
opinion, in fact it left Hampden's position essentially un-
touched. Dean Church devotes several pages of his study of
the Oxford Movement to a destructive account of the
Lectures; but anyone who reads the Lectures with an open
mind will see at once that the Dean never allowed himself to
come to grips with their thesis, and confined himself to saying
that Hampden did not know what he was talking about. But
Hampden knew very well what he was talking about. Nor
had he (as malice asserted) got it all from Blanco White. The
charge, made three years after the Lectures were delivered,
had a special sting. For Blanco White, in the meantime, had
'turned Socinian' (which is, being interpreted, Unitarian),
and it was, as Dean Church puts it, 'fresh in men's minds
what language and speculation like that of the Bampton
Lectures had come to in the case of Whately's intimate
friend, Blanco White.' But the charge was demonstrably
false. The study of scholastic philosophy had been Hampden's special field for years. He had contributed the articles
on Aristotle and Aristotle's Philosophy to the seventh edi-

tion of the *Encyclopaedia Britannica*, and on Thomas Aquinas
and the Scholastic Philosophy to the *Encyclopaedia Metropolitana*. Five years earlier he had tried out his theory of the
limitations of technical theology in a published *Essay on the
Philosophical Evidence of Christianity*. It was far from being a
sudden and excitable speculation, as the egregious Tom
Mozley confidently asserted. Not content with describing the
Lectures as a self-contradictory plagiarism, the critics said
that they were unreadable, and even unintelligible. Only in
the Oxford of the early nineteenth century could such a
criticism have been made. The Lectures are not a literary
masterpiece. But they are written in an excellent clear
English; the argument is lucid and straightforward. What
made them unreadable and unintelligible was the *odium
theologicum* of their readers and the inelasticity of minds
wholly untrained in speculation. Not the least of Dr. Hampden's offences was that he had allowed himself to describe
the Fathers of the Church as if they were individuals, each
with his own marked character. He spoke of the 'shrewdness
and versatility' of Augustine, or credited Ambrose with 'the
practical dexterity of the man of the world'. Such language,
while it shocked Pusey unspeakably, certainly enlivened his
subject. The proof of the pudding was in the eating. Readable
or not, the Lectures went through three editions.

4. 'SUBSCRIPTION'

The year 1834, apart from the Addresses to the Archbishop of Canterbury, and the steadily swelling volume of the
Tracts, was devoid of remarkable incident in the history of the
Movement. It was a year of many vexations to Newman.
There were quarrels—quite serious quarrels—with Palmer
and Rose. The business side of the Tracts was a continual
worry, until Rivington consented to take them over from the
inefficient Howkins in April. The disappointment (real though

concealed) over the Professorship of Moral Philosophy was
followed in the summer by an incident of the sort which was
always happening to Newman. He refused to marry a
female parishioner, named Jubber, on the ground that she
(being a Dissenter) had not been baptized. A great deal of
publicity was given to the affair, and Newman fell back on
his customary cushion of self-pity. 'Till the last hour I have
felt to be one man against a multitude. No one, apparently,
to encourage me, and so many black, averted faces, that unless from my youth up I had been schooled to fall back upon
myself, I should have been quite out of heart. I went and sat
twenty minutes with Mrs. Small [the old dame schoolmistress
at Littlemore] by way of consolation.' He was in trouble, too,
with Rickards; and had come very near to quarrelling with
Henry Wilberforce for getting married. More and more he
missed the vital companionship of Hurrell Froude. 'I could
say much, were it of use,' he wrote 'of my own solitariness
now you are away. Not that I would undervalue that great
blessing, which is what I do not deserve, of so many friends
about me; dear Rogers, Williams, ὁ πάνυ Keble, and the
friend in whose house I am staying (whom I wish with all my
heart you knew, as *apostolicorum princeps*, Bowden), yet, after
all, as is obvious, no one can enter into one's mind except a
person who has lived with one. I seem to write things to no
purpose as wanting your imprimatur. Perhaps it is well to
cultivate the habit of writing as if for unseen companions, but
I have felt it much, so that I am getting quite dry and hard.
My dear Froude, come back to us as soon as you safely can,
and then next winter (please God) you shall go to Rome,
and tempt Isaac (who is very willing) to go with you. But
wherever you are (so be it) you cannot be divided from us.'

But the most shocking thing, which happened in the year,
was a painful exchange of letters with Whately. 'Of course no
one can know poor Whately now', he had said to his friends;
and in the spring, when the Archbishop of Dublin came to

Oxford and attended communion in Oriel Chapel, Newman was absent from the service. The gesture seemed unmistakable; and the supposed cause of Newman's absence was carried to Whately by current gossip. The Archbishop wrote, much distressed, to ask if he might deny the story. Newman answered, in flat and unconvincing terms, that it was untrue. But he went on to admit that his most intimate friends knew how deeply he deplored 'the line of ecclesiastical policy adopted under your archiepiscopal sanction'; and to charge the Archbishop with having been, by his sceptical principles, the true author of 'the perilous measures' in which he had acquiesced. This being so, he could not deny that it had been a relief to him 'to see so little of your Grace when you were in Oxford'. 'May I be suffered'—so the insufferable letter ended —'to add that your name is ever mentioned in my prayers, and to subscribe myself, Your Grace's very sincere friend and servant, John H. Newman?'

If this reply showed Newman at his worst, the response to it (not printed in Newman's correspondence) showed Whately at his best. He wrote simply as one who had once been Newman's friend, not as an older man in an office of high distinction who had been impertinently rebuked by a younger man for doing his best in a situation of extreme difficulty. Opinions, he knew, must necessarily differ, but 'God help us, what will become of men if they receive no more mercy than they show to each other!' Newman did scant justice to his (Whately's) principles. And why should *he* be so severely blamed for accepting what the Primate himself—whom nobody dreamed of blaming—had already accepted? But the burden of his letter was the complaint that Newman, who had once wished for nothing so sincerely as to be known as his friend, had never attempted to remonstrate with him for his supposed wrong-doing. For his own part he could not have brought himself to find relief in avoiding the society of an old friend, because of a difference on certain principles. 'But though your regard for me' he concluded 'falls so short of what mine would have been under similar circumstances, I will not, therefore, reject what remains of it.' To this letter Newman made no answer. No answer was possible.

There were consolations to be set against these troubles. It was something, after Henry Wilberforce's marriage, to extract from him such a *Liebeserklärung* as this: 'I have loved you like a brother' wrote the devoted young man; 'and my saddest feelings have been often in thinking that, when in the events of life I am separated far from you, you will, perhaps, disapprove or misunderstand my conduct, and will cease to feel towards me as you have done; or that our minds will grow asunder by the natural process of change which goes on in this changing world. . . . How wonderful will it be hereafter if we attain to a state where souls can hold intercourse immediately, and where space makes no division between them!' It was something to know, from Hurrell Froude's letters, that he was holding his own against his mortal enemy and feeling the pain of separation almost as deeply as Newman himself. There was pleasure to be had from the confession of an old Alban Hall pupil that he owed to Newman more than he could repay. There was a melancholy satisfaction in the decline of Oriel in the Schools, under the new tutors, in fulfilment of his own written prediction. And when the press of business became insupportable it was comforting to sit in the Bodleian, happily collating manuscripts for an edition of Dionysius Alexandrinus, which he had undertaken for the Clarendon Press. 'I reflect with some pleasure that some of our most learned men lived and acted in most troublous times.' Moreover, the political scene appeared (deceptively) brighter. The Whig coach was upset by a Cabinet quarrel over the sanctity of ecclesiastical property. In November Grey resigned, and the King sent for Wellington and Peel. The relief was short-lived, and served only to re-establish the

Whigs in power, after the April elections, under Lord Melbourne, more firmly than ever.

The leaven of the Tracts was beginning to work visibly. Agitated clergymen studied the reading-matter at the beginning of the Prayer Book and discovered for the first time that Morning and Evening Prayer were supposed to be read daily in every parish church or chapel, after the ringing of a bell to summon the faithful. An unheard-of practice! What was to be done about it? Newman himself started a daily morning service at St. Mary's in the Long Vacation. He had a desk put up near the altar. 'It seems to me that the absurdity, as it appears to many, of Tom Keble's daily plan is, his praying to *empty benches*. Put yourself near the altar and you may be solitary.' But even Newman lacked courage, as yet, to institute a weekly celebration of the Lord's Supper.

There were many other questions to challenge the energy of the newly fledged Apostolicals. The Dean of Westminster was allowing the Abbey to be desecrated by 'music-meetings'. There was to be a petition to the King against that. The Whigs contemplated a reform of the marriage laws; and another petition was organized. The Society for the Promotion of Christian Knowledge, which was showing dangerous symptoms of liberalism, became a battle-field. After the fall of the Whigs, Newman and Rose began to elaborate a plan for 'some really working Court of heresy and false doctrine'. If, then, a heretic were nominated by the Crown to a bishopric, 'his words would be censured by this Court, and the Archbishop strengthened to refuse to consecrate.' This would be much better than a frontal attack on the King's prerogative.

But the question of questions which filled this year and part of the next was 'Subscription'. At Oxford, though not at Cambridge, the Vice-Chancellor still required every undergraduate to subscribe to the Articles of the Church of England before matriculation. Dissenters, Jews, Roman Catholics, Unitarians, Freethinkers were, therefore, entirely excluded

from the University. At both Universities subscription was
necessary before taking any degree; and, of course, no one
could be a Fellow of a College or hold any University post
without a degree. It was not until Gladstone's Act of 1871
that the Church was finally forced to relinquish her practical
hold over the Universities. But an attempt was made in 1834—
and the impulse to it issued from Cambridge. Sixty-three
resident members of the Cambridge Senate petitioned the
House of Commons and the House of Lords in March for the
abolition of all religious tests. A Bill was accordingly introduced into the Commons, and passed by a large majority,
but rejected by the Lords.

The opposition to the Bill, strong even in the laxer air of
Cambridge, was fiercest in Oxford. Both Universities petitioned Parliament against it, but Oxford 'did a great deal
more than send petitions to Parliament.' Subsidiary petitions
were promoted in various parts of the country. And three
formidable Declarations were prepared. The first was signed
by members of the University 'immediately connected with
its instruction and discipline'; the second by members of
Convocation not so engaged; and the third by the parents
and guardians of undergraduates. Was there ever such a year
of petitions and declarations before or since?

Foremost in the ranks were Pusey and Newman, but the
opposition was not limited to the Tractarians. It was general.
Symons, the Warden of Wadham, afterwards a bitter enemy
of the Tractarians, was one of its warmest champions. The
Lords threw the Bill out in July, and a sigh of relief ran
through the University. But the snake was scotched, not
killed. Many of those who had opposed the Bill were uneasy
about the practice of making young men subscribe to Articles
of Religion, which most of them had never read and cared
nothing about. An alarming rumour greeted Newman and
Pusey on their return to Oxford for the Michaelmas Term
that the Heads of Houses were no longer to be relied upon.

The rumour was all too true. On November 10 the Heads decided by a majority of one to introduce a measure into Convocation for the abolition of subscription. Some mild formula would be proposed in its place.

The villain of the piece was Provost Hawkins. And it was his ally, Hampden, who rashly began the public battle with a pamphlet, entitled *Observations on Religious Dissent*. He argued against tests on a double ground: first, that the Articles were fallible human formularies and no one, least of all a young man, ought to be required to subscribe to them without a thorough knowledge of what he was doing; second, that as used in the University, they were a mere machinery of exclusion. The pamphlet had an immediate sale and went into a second edition. Hampden had such confidence in his arguments that he actually presented a copy to Newman. The letter in which Newman acknowledged the gift was (in his own phrase) 'the beginning of hostilities in the University'. He regretted that the pamphlet had been written; he felt an aversion to its principles; he lamented it as 'an interruption of that peace and mutual good understanding which has prevailed so long in this place.'

The fat was now in the fire. Between the dogmatists and the 'march-of-mind men' (to use one of Froude's and Newman's favourite phrases) there could be nothing but bitter war. What did it matter if the young men knew what they were subscribing to or not? 'Religion' said Newman 'is to be approached with a submission of the understanding.' And Pusey pointed with horror to Cambridge, where 'the tone of the clever Undergraduate Society, e.g. the Debating Society' showed the danger of letting young persons of unsound faith into the University, without any test at all. Pusey got quickly to work. He issued a fly-leaf containing twenty-three Questions. Shrinking from this bombardment, the Heads of Houses hastily rescinded their resolution. But the question was by no means disposed of. It came up again in the spring, with a proposal to substitute for subscription a form of declaration, assenting to the doctrines of the Church of England as set forth in the Articles, promising to conform to her liturgy and discipline, and undertaking to submit to instruction in the Articles. This might seem to tie the young men up even more tightly than before. But Pusey and his friends thought otherwise. A battle of pamphlets ensued. Pusey entered the lists with a fresh set of twenty-seven Questions. The Provost of Oriel replied with a set of Answers. Pusey retaliated with a set of Notes upon the Provost's Answers.

In May 1835 the parties gathered for the decisive vote in Convocation. 'If you like bitterness,' wrote Newman to Froude, who had just returned from the Barbados, 'we are on the high road towards it.' To Newman's surprise and delight, Froude, ill as he was, appeared in Oxford the day before the vote was taken. Anne Mozley, Tom's younger sister, the future editor of Newman's letters, happened to be passing the coach office with Mrs. Newman at the moment of his arrival. She saw him getting down from the coach and being greeted by his friends. 'He was terribly thin—his countenance dark and wasted, but with a brilliancy of expression and grace of outline which justified all that his friends had said of him. He was in the Theatre next day, entering into all the enthusiasm of the scenes, and shouting *Non placet* with all his friends about him.' The proposal was defeated by an overwhelming majority.

5. THE FIRST VICTORY

The Movement was hardly yet of a definite shape. It was a stir, rather than a systematic way of thinking. But it was beginning to be consolidated. Already Newman, in two tracts published in August 1834, had put forward in the form of a dialogue the first outline conception of the *Via Media*. Already, in these two tracts, he had declared his belief in the necessity of a second Reformation, defended himself against the accusation of Popery, and pointed the distinction of doctrine and manner between the Articles and the Liturgy. Pusey's accession—a definite and acknowledged fact before the end of 1835—was a powerful factor in the further growth of the party. 'He at once gave to us' said Newman 'a position and a name.' The fame of his great learning, his 'deep religious seriousness, the munificence of his charities, his Professorship, his family connexions, and his easy relations with University authorities'—it is easy to see what all this meant to the little group of Apostolicals. And his internal influence upon the Movement was equal to these external benefits. The first, almost careless, exuberance steadied into a plan. The short, plain-spoken tracts (which Newman in August 1835 was on the point of giving up)[1] lengthened into systematic studies, beginning with Pusey's three tracts on Baptism, a full-length treatise in themselves. The great Library of the Fathers was begun. And Newman himself, under Pusey's influence, took up the task of dealing at serious length with the relation in which he and his friends stood to the Church of Rome. The Romanist controversy, he said in Tract No. 71, published early in 1836, had overtaken them like a summer's cloud. Tract No. 71, and its successor No. 72, dealt somewhat tenderly with the errors of Rome, perhaps because Newman hardly recognized the magnitude of the problem with which he was dealing. In his book upon *The Prophetical Office of the Church*, published in 1837, he pressed the attack upon his chief antagonist with greater fierceness. Others besides Newman and Pusey were engaging in the hard labour of reviving a distinctive Anglo-Catholic theology. The time was ripe for the formation of a Theological Society. This

---

[1] 'The tracts are defunct, or *in extremis*. Rivington has written to say they do not answer. Pusey has written one on Baptism, very good, of ninety pages, which is to be printed at his risk. That, and one or two to finish the imperfect series (on particular subjects), will conclude the whole. I am not sorry, as I am tired of being editor.' (Newman to Froude, *Letters*, ii. 124).

was Pusey's special invention; and a very useful invention it was for the Tractarians. It was a regular breeding-ground for the Tracts and Rose's *British Magazine*.

The fuller development of the Tractarian notions frightened away some who began by being sympathetic. F. D. Maurice used to relate that he took Pusey's tract on Baptism with him on a walk 'and how, as he went along, it became more and more clear to him that the tract represented everything that he did not think and did not believe, till at last he sat down on a gate and made up his mind that it represented the parting point between him and the Oxford School. He always spoke of it with a kind of shudder, as it were of an escape from a charmed dungeon.'[1] And Golightly, once a favoured pupil of Newman's, was turned by degrees from a disciple into an enemy.

Nevertheless it was this solid weight of thinking which gave body and momentum to the 'paper religion' of the *Via Media*. External events played their part in converting the dream of Keble and Froude into a reality—defeats no less than victories. Indeed the spectacular nature of its reverses was one of the causes of its success. Without Newman's controversial genius the movement could never have reached the point when it began to be called more by Pusey's name than his. But, if Pusey had not identified himself with it, would Newman have ever been in a position to write, in such wondering language, of its miraculous growth? 'From beginnings so small, from elements of thought so fortuitous, with prospects so unpromising, the Anglo-Catholic party suddenly became a power in the National Church, and an object of alarm to her rulers and friends. . . . If we inquire what the world thought of it, we have still more to raise our wonder; for, not to mention the excitement which it caused in England, the Movement and its party-names were known to the police of Italy and to the backwoodsmen of America. And so it proceeded,

[1] *Life of F. D. Maurice*, i. 186, quoted in the *Life of Pusey*.

getting stronger and stronger every year, till it came into collision with the Nation, and that Church of the Nation, which it began by professing especially to serve.'

The first of the external events which gave a new stimulus to the party occurred at the beginning of 1836.

The Regius Professor of Divinity, Dr. Burton, died suddenly on January 19, and all Oxford was plunged into speculation about his successor. The Whigs were in power again, and anything might be expected from Lord Melbourne. The appointment of the Professor was a Crown—that is, a Government—appointment. Would Melbourne jest at Oxford, or would he act impartially, on the best advice? Melbourne, characteristically, jested—but with episcopal sanction. From Archbishop Howley he collected a list of eight names. Pusey came first on the list, Shuttleworth (the witty Warden of New College) second, Newman fourth, Keble fifth. The other names would be names, and no more, to a modern reader. He then sent the list to Whately. Whately consulted Copleston, the former Provost of Oriel and now Bishop of Llandaff. Together they advised Melbourne to ignore all the recommendations of the Archbishop of Canterbury, and to appoint Hampden. Melbourne cheerfully accepted their advice, and the Archbishop of Canterbury meekly endorsed the appointment.

And indeed it was an excellent appointment. That was the cream of the jest. Or, rather, it would have been an excellent appointment, if it had been made a generation later. At this particular moment it was like an insufficiently prepared raid upon a strongly entrenched position. And the unfortunate Dr. Hampden was not the man to execute such a forlorn adventure.

His appointment had been discussed in Oxford and dismissed as improbable. Something of Archbishop Howley's recommendations must have leaked out. Newman inclined to think Shuttleworth (a survivor of the Oriel Noetics) would be the new Professor. 'He would be nothing at all,' he said to Pusey 'and we might act as if *sede vacante*.' But he wrote very earnestly to Keble, now married and installed in his Hampshire vicarage, telling him that there was *some* chance of his (Keble's) being appointed and imploring him not to refuse it, even at the hand of a Whig prime minister.

But Hampden! What *could* be done to stop it? This was the burden of the agitated letters and notes which flew to and fro, and of an extempore dinner party given by Pusey, on the evening of the day when the dreadful news reached Oxford, to the leaders of orthodoxy in the University. Nothing, it seemed. There was, of course, a petition. But the petition was sent to the King, and the King (having exhausted his devotion to the Church by his famous address to the Bishops) did nothing. What, indeed, could he do? 'Another time' Lord Melbourne, with all the insolence of a Whig oligarch, observed to Pusey 'it would be wise, if you want anything done, to go to those who can *do* it.' Newman pursued a different method. He bought or borrowed a copy of Hampden's Bampton Lectures and sat up all night tearing them to pieces. His *Elucidations of Dr. Hampden's Theological Statements* was given to a hungry public five days after Pusey's dinner. The title was a stroke of controversial genius. It suggested, most unfairly, that the Lectures were obscure. The pamphlet strung a series of extracts from the book upon a string of acid comment. Of all methods of controversy this is at once the most unjust and the most effective.

Effective certainly in Oxford. But the *Elucidations* failed to shake Lord Melbourne. If the Lectures were beyond his power of understanding, so were the *Elucidations*. He dismissed them as 'abstruse', and two days later confirmed the appointment in the *Gazette*.

The usual events followed in Oxford. There were more petitions—addressed now to the Hebdomadal Board of the University—a committee, a report, a public declaration.

The report found Dr. Hampden guilty of rationalism, of 'the assumption that uncontrolled human reason in its present form is the primary interpreter of God's Word, without any regard to those rules and principles of interpretation which have guided the judgments of Christ's Holy Catholic Church in all ages of its history and under every variety of its warfare.' The phraseology was Tractarian, and the chief author of report and declaration very evidently Pusey. The Apostolicals were riding the crest of a wave. But, as they were to discover before many years had passed, the wave itself was not Apostolical. It was orthodoxy in a panic.

This volume of protest issued in a statute, by which the new Professor was deprived of his vote in the nomination of Select Preachers to the University. Since his vote was but one of five the practical effect of the statute was negligible. The statute also deprived him of his right to be consulted if a preacher was called in question before the Vice-Chancellor. This, too, did not seem at the time a very substantial matter. The sting of the statute did not lie, of course, in its practical effects. It was an insulting gesture, of the kind dear to the authorities of that day, which enabled them to censure a victim without specifying his offence. All that the statute committed itself to saying of Dr. Hampden's offence was that 'he hath in his published writings so treated matters theological that the University hath no confidence in him.'

The statute—according to an opinion signed by Campbell, afterwards Lord Chancellor, Lushington, afterwards Dean of the Arches, and Hull of the Chancery Bar—was certainly *ultra vires*. But it was supported by thirteen Heads of Houses against ten (counting the two Proctors) and submitted to a meeting of Convocation on March 22. In the meantime a rain of hostile pamphlets (including yet another from Pusey's unwearying pen) descended upon Hampden; the streets were placarded with anti-Hampden posters; and when the unhappy man walked down the High Street he saw an enemy in

every passer-by. His inaugural lecture was crowded by his
opponents. It was all sheer misery to him; he lost his appetite
and could not sleep. On the whole he bore himself, under
these extremely trying circumstances, with considerable
dignity. And when his natural indignation tempted him to
complain, a little stridently, to Melbourne, he took to heart
and gratefully remembered the advice given to him by that
insouciant man of the great world. 'Be easy' said Lord Melbourne, putting a kindly hand on his arm; 'I like an easy
man.'

One last pamphlet appeared on the eve of Convocation—
need it be said, by Pusey? The handful of Hampden's supporters hissed Pusey as he took his seat next day in the
Theatre. For two hours an excited and impatient crowd
waited for the proceedings to begin. There was a battle going
on behind the scenes. The Proctors were determined to veto
the statute, and to veto it before it was put to the vote. After
a prolonged wrangle they carried their point. The speeches
were made—all in Latin, except for one obscure orator's
attempt to express himself in his native language. But he got
no further than 'Mr. Vice-Chancellor, I trust that we shall
have no modern Liberalism or Whiggery here' before he was
silenced by a very proper rebuke. The proctors, amid a storm
of cries, were seen to open their mouths. Not a word could
be heard. But they had pronounced their veto, and the proceedings were over.

The respite was only temporary. The Proctors were near
the end of their term of office. The statute was introduced
again in May. This time there was no veto, and the statute
was passed by a majority of 474 to 94. Various attempts were
made in later years to restore to Hampden the powers of
which he had been deprived. None of these was successful.
For the rest of his Oxford career he remained under the ban,
and his nomination to be Bishop of Hereford in 1847 was
opposed with unrelenting bitterness. He wrote little more for

an uncomprehending generation, and in the House of Lords indulged his natural taciturnity by never once opening his mouth. But in his own diocese he made a popular and successful bishop.

Amongst those who supported the statute was Gladstone. He was not actually present in the Theatre, but that was due to an accident. Twenty years later the Bishop of Hereford was startled to receive a letter from Mr. Gladstone, expressing his deep regret for the attitude he had taken up in that far-off controversy. He was no longer, he confessed, 'able to master books of an abstract character', and could not pretend to pass any judgment upon the 'propositions then at issue'. But it had become clear to him that the charges brought against Dr. Hampden had not been made distinct, nor been properly investigated, and that no opportunity had been given to him to make his defence.

The violence which the Tractarians had shown in leading the attack upon Hampden, while it certainly helped to cement them into a definite party and to flatter their consciousness of their own powers, had its own evil consequences. Damaging attacks began to appear from various quarters. Specimens of their theological teaching were held up to scorn in a pamphlet which mimicked the manner of Newman's *Elucidations*. The witty chaplain of Archbishop Whately, Dickinson, published an anonymous *Pastoral Epistle from His Holiness the Pope to Some Members of the University of Oxford*. Pusey, to whom a joke of this order was like blasphemy, retaliated with an Earnest Remonstrance. But the most damaging attack of all was a savage article by Dr. Arnold, called *The Oxford Malignants*, in the April issue of the *Edinburgh Review*. Violent and unfair as the article certainly was, it was not more so than the attack on Hampden had been. If the Tractarians had honestly believed that Hampden's views were dangerous to dogmatic religion (as they certainly were), Dr. Arnold no less honestly believed that the Anglo-Catholic revival was dangerous to religious unity (as it certainly was). He had quite as much right to say that its promoters were conspirators, or fanatics, not over-scrupulous in their methods, as they had to say that Hampden was a blundering fool, wrecking the foundations of religion without knowing what he was doing. Honours were easy. But Arnold's attack (which nearly cost him the Headmastership of Rugby) did the greater damage. From that moment Dean Church dated the beginning of the unpopularity and suspicion which gathered round the Movement.

6. THE ZENITH

'March 1836' ran a note in Newman's hand on a packet of letters 'is a cardinal point of time.'

It was on March 1 that he received the news of Hurrell Froude's death two days earlier at Dartington. The news was not the less terrible to him because it was expected. Tom Mozley was in the room when he opened the Archdeacon's letter. 'He could only put it into my hand, with no remark.' Afterwards, in the company of Henry Wilberforce, he broke down and cried. Since Hurrell came back to England, he had only seen him twice—once at Oxford in the summer, and once at Dartington in the autumn. Newman remembered how, when he took leave of him in the evening, Hurrell's face lighted up and almost shone in the darkness, as if to say that in this world they were parting for ever. After that the disease gained rapid ground. The idea of wintering at Rome had to be abandoned. In February it became obvious that the end was very near. 'Who can refrain from tears' wrote Harriett in a postscript to one of her letters 'at the thought of that bright and beautiful Froude? He is not expected to last long.'

Froude's death eased Newman's passage to Rome in two ways. Keble, who knew Froude's inmost mind better even than Newman and had himself done much to form it, was always certain that, if he had lived, he would not have left the Church of England. It is hard to conceive that Newman would have broken away by himself, but with Froude dead he was at liberty to let his mind take its own course. And yet, by an odd accident, it was the dead hand of Froude which gave to his friend the first definite impulsion upon the path to Rome. As he looked over the shelves containing Hurrell's books, from which the Archdeacon had asked him to choose one for a keepsake, someone—it was, perhaps, Pusey— pointed to the Roman Breviary. 'It was the Breviary which Hurrell had had with him at Barbados. Accordingly I took it, studied it, wrote my Tract from it, and have it on my table in constant use till this day.' This Tract (No. 75) came out in the June after Froude's death. It is a treatise of over 200 pages, and must have involved a considerable amount of work. It was priced at 2s. 3d. and sold astonishingly. It also involved its author in serious difficulties with many of his friends.

The loss of Hurrell Froude was the beginning of a series of changes in his domestic life. In April his sister, Jemima, was married to John Mozley, and three weeks later his mother died. Her death was another emotional shock. 'Up to the time of the funeral' wrote James Mozley to his mother 'he was dreadfully dejected, his whole countenance perfectly clouded with grief, and only at intervals breaking out into anything like cheerful conversation.' But his spirits improved wonder- fully as soon as the funeral was over. He confessed to Jemima that for a long time he and his mother had been out of sym- pathy. She had 'much misunderstood my religious views, and considered she differed from me; and she thought I was sur- rounded by admirers, and had everything my own way; and in consequence I, who am conscious to myself I never thought anything more precious than her sympathy and praise, had none of it.' Then, in September, Harriett was married to Tom Mozley. It was the final break-up of the family. For Frank was now beyond the pale, and Charles had always been 'impossible'.

The record of these middle years, from the humiliation of Hampden in May 1836 to August 1838, is devoid of any important public events. The Tracts went on. Newman finished his long-projected church at Littlemore. The four-o'clock sermons at St. Mary's, and the informal lectures in Adam de Brome's chapel, continued to spread his influence among the young men. The older disciples went out into the world, into the law courts and the chancery chambers and the country parishes, carrying the new principles with them. New disciples presented themselves in their place—Frederic Faber of University, W. G. Ward the dialectical *enfant terrible* of Balliol, Mark Pattison and Richard Church of Oriel, and many another. Newman began his weekly tea parties for young men—it was at one of these that Pattison 'offered some flippant remark, such as young B.A.'s are apt even now to deal in. Newman turned round and deposited upon me one of those ponderous and icy "very likelies"; after which you were expected to sit down in a corner, and think over amending your conduct.' Pusey sold his carriage and horses, and Mrs. Pusey her jewels, in order to give £5,000 to a fund for building churches in East London and to finance the *Library of the Fathers*. Newman published *The Prophetical Office of the Church* and the *Lectures on Justification*, and much against his will, early in 1838, took over the editorship of the *British Critic*.

A 'tiny flame' was also rearing itself, in imitation of the Oxford blaze, at Cambridge, and Oxford became 'a place of pilgrimage' in the eyes of young Cambridge devotees. J. F. Russell, an undergraduate at Peterhouse, was receiving long letters from the great Dr. Pusey. He was able to tell his distinguished correspondent that a Mr. Carus 'has embraced the doctrine of baptismal regeneration, and inculcates it at his parties.' Accompanied by an older friend, the Rev. W. J.

Irons (who was, however, an Oxford man) young Russell paid
a thrilling visit to Oxford in the winter of 1837.[1] They made
at once for St. Mary's and were gratified by a sight of Newman's back as he knelt before the altar. In the afternoon they
had an audience of Dr. Pusey, 'a young-looking man, about
my height, very pale and careworn, with a slight impediment
in his speech'. The conversation ran on 'the Canons of Nice'
and the celibacy of the clergy. They dined at Queen's, and in
the common room after dinner listened to the one universal
topic of conversation. 'It was allowed that the Doctor and
Newman *governed the University*, and that nothing could withstand the influence of themselves and their friends. Every
man of talent who during the last six years has come to
Oxford has joined Newman, and when he preaches at St.
Mary's (on every Sunday afternoon) all the men of talent
in the University come to hear him, although at the loss of
their dinner. His triumph over the *mental* empire of Oxford
was said to be complete!'

Next day the two pilgrims called on Newman. They found
him 'seated at a small desk in a comfortable room, stored with
books. He is a dark, middle-aged, middle-sized man, with
lanky black hair and large spectacles, thin, gentlemanly, and
very insinuating.' He had a bad cold, but was persuaded by
Irons to meet them at dinner in the evening at Pusey's house.
'The hour of five found us at Christ Church. When we entered Pusey's sanctum we found him and Harrison, Student
of Christ Church, by the feeble light of bedchamber-candle-
stick candle brooding over the last sheet of Pusey's fifth of
November sermon. Presently an argand lamp threw its mild
lustre over the room, and Newman was announced. Pusey
seemed delighted to see him. He asked me how I liked Oxford.' Russell, with perfect tact, 'discoursed on its superiority
over Cambridge' and the party went in to dinner. The conversation was purely theological, Irons working the twin

[1] Russell's account is given in full in the *Life of Pusey*, i. 405 *et seqq.*

oracles for all that they were worth. Pusey spoke very little; but he made one observation of peculiar interest. 'Auricular confession, he feared, was a grace which had been lost to the Church and could not be restored.' Presently relief from the abounding Irons appeared to Newman, when the little Puseys came running into the room. 'One climbed Newman's knee and hugged him. Newman put his spectacles on him, and next on his sister, and great was the merriment of the Pusey progeny. Newman, it is said, hates ecclesiastical conversations. He writes so much that when in society he seems always inclined to talk on light amusing subjects. He told them a story of an old woman who had a broomstick which would go to the well, draw water, and do many other things for her; how the old woman got tired of the broomstick, and wishing to destroy it broke it in twain, and how, to the old woman's great chagrin and disappointment, *two* live broomsticks grew from the broken parts of the old one! We quitted Christ Church about nine, highly delighted with our visit. It was esteemed the highest honour which could have been paid us.' Pusey sent after them a copy of his sermon.

Russell's account of Newman's conversation at this period of his life needs to be supplemented by others. His powers of general conversation must have been remarkable to have attracted the attention they did, in a society where good conversation has never been allowed to perish. Certainly they were no small part of his power over young men. So much had he changed from the silent tongue-tied youth whom Whately had licked into shape. But it was not, apparently, a *reportable* conversation. He was not the manufacturer of *bons mots*, nor the enunciator of paradoxes, nor the *raconteur*, nor the pursuer of original fantasies, nor the deliverer of profundities. He tells us that he used irony, and enjoyed leading tiresome men into morasses. But, apart from this, and apart from the stimulating companionship of friends like Hurrell Froude or Rogers, the great virtue of his talk would seem to have been its easy unaffected sincerity. Miss Mitford describes how a young and earnest but not specially brilliant lad of her acquaintance was recommended to Newman's notice, and was invited by him to breakfast once a week. Asked what they talked about, the boy answered 'Everything'. The one subject never mentioned was Tractarianism. 'Conversation flowing continuously' James Mozley reported of Newman's first weekly *soirée* 'and every one at his ease. Newman can manage a thing of this kind better than Pusey. We talked on a variety of subjects.' But at times the fire kindled, and Newman 'spake with his tongue'. When this happened the hearer never forgot the occasion, though he could never repeat what was said. 'In a few words,' said one 'spoken without any effort, as if only the outcome of his habitual train of thought, he took one out of the world one lived in, into another and a higher region.' Sam Wilberforce, in 1836, reported such an experience. He had had some very long conversations with Newman on religious topics. 'And it was really most sublime, as an exhibition of human intellect, when in parts of our discussions Newman kindled and poured forth a sort of magisterial announcement in which Scripture, Christian antiquity deeply studied and thoroughly imbibed, humility, veneration, love of truth, and the highest glow of poetical feeling, all impressed their own pictures on his conversation.' The reporter is not very skilful, but the nature of the impression made upon him is clear enough.

The best account of Newman as he appeared to the young men in the heyday of his power is given by J. A. Froude in one of his *Letters on the Oxford Counter-Reformation*:

'With us undergraduates Newman, of course, did not enter on such important questions [i.e. theological questions], although they were in the air, and we talked about them among ourselves. He, when we met him, spoke to us about subjects of the day, of literature, of public persons and incidents, of everything which was generally interesting. He seemed always to be better informed on common topics of conversation than anyone else who was present. He was never condescending with us, never didactic or authoritative; but what he said carried conviction along with it. . . . Perhaps his supreme merit as a talker was that he never tried to be witty or to say striking things. Ironical he could be, but not ill-natured. Not a malicious anecdote was ever heard from him. Prosy he could not be. He was lightness itself—the lightness of elastic strength—and he was interesting because he never talked for talking's sake, but because he had something real to say.

'Thus it was that we, who had never seen such another man and to whom he appeared, perhaps, at special advantage in contrast with the normal college don, came to regard Newman with the affection of pupils (though pupils, strictly speaking, he had none) for an idolised master. The simplest word which dropped from him was treasured as if it had been an intellectual diamond. For hundreds of young men *Credo in Newmannum* was the genuine symbol of faith.'

But there were occasions, when the virtue went out of him, and he knew it. He was never at ease in unsympathetic society —in society with a different scale of values to his own. He described once in a letter to Rogers how he had come down to Oxford in company with Lord Norreys and a party of Conservative statesmen 'and managed by pure fate to appear the dullest and ignorantest of bookworms. I am sure they must have thought me so. I did not know whether to be amused or disgusted at myself. I sometimes have stupid fits. They knew who I was, and seemed curious about me. My *coup de grâce* on Lord Norrey's patience was mistaking Lord Stormont for Lord Stourton. I wish you had been by . . . My breast is full of a good joke unshared.'

A good joke? Perhaps. At any rate he was determined to treat it so, though it took him back uncomfortably to his *gauche* youth and revived that distressing sense of hollowness

which so often afflicted him. He was not a very good joker,
whether at his own expense or another's, though he sometimes
smiled ruefully at the gap between his achievements and h'
pretensions. A more strongly developed sense of humour
would have saved him from a vast deal of suffering. But then
he would not have been Newman—could never have written
the *Apologia*. What is humour, after all, but a means of coming
to terms with our own imperfections and with the imperfections of others? Newman's whole strength lay in his refusal to
come to terms with imperfection. If he jested, he jested
against it, not *upon* it; in the way of irony rather than humour.
Even of this it is not easy to find instances. Of the lukewarm
Tyler, who had annoyed him by making no use of his sermons in a series of popular volumes, he writes: 'He is dying
for love of the Church, and most seraphic.' The phrase is a
cover for his own irritation. There is often an engaging
dexterity in his letters, which has almost the look of humour.
But the thought behind the expression is never humorous.
The nearest he ever comes to humour is in a certain whimsi-
cality, as when he used letters of the Greek alphabet to distinguish the different contributors to the *Lyra Apostolica*, and
allotted the letter alpha to Bowden; so that Bowden became
'Alpha Lyrae', in memory of the days when they watched the
heavens from the top of Trinity tower and Bowden was 'great
upon' the star which goes by that name.

Perhaps there was another obstacle to humour in his composition—his extreme sensitiveness. In some men humour
exists side by side with emotional receptivity, and is the condition which makes deep feeling tolerable to them. But Newman
sought feeling, and was unhappiest when it was denied to
him. To make fun of it in himself or others was impossible to
him. Irony was one form of self-protection. But he had
another, well described by one of his most intimate friends.
Lord Blachford (the Rogers of this earlier time) recalled how
in 1838 he and Newman were divided by 'not quarrel, not

exactly difference, but a kind of stern alienation for a fortnight, ending in tender reconciliation'. The cause of the tension was a difference of opinion over the question of publishing the Breviary (not Newman's pamphlet, but the Breviary itself). Rogers was against publication. 'This made me a disagreeable confidant to him, and this again he took as very unkind, and showed it in a certain flinty way which he had at command on great emergencies. But then, you occasionally saw what this flintiness cost him. And when you came to frank explanation, there came from the rock a gush of overpowering tenderness.'

Such was Newman at his zenith, and at the zenith of the Movement, which he dated himself at June 1838. From that time onwards its fortunes began to change, and the change synchronized with his own loss of confidence in its principles.

Even before that time, and apart from Arnold's attack, there had been signs and portents. The sky was not clear. The summer's cloud of the Romanist controversy was increasing and darkening. Towards the end of 1837 Bagot, the Bishop of Oxford, took alarm at the reports which were constantly being carried to him of strange practices in the heart of his own diocese—needless bowings, unusual attitudes, crosses worn over surplices, and the like. Pusey did his best to put the Bishop's mind at rest, but the atmosphere of Cuddesdon, though kind, continued a little heavy. Pusey's action in taking into his own house four young Bachelors of Arts, engaged in theological study, giving them food and lodging and the run of his library, was some encouragement to malicious gossip about proselytizing. In 1838 he was obliged to abandon this plan on account of his wife's health. He and Newman took a house in St. Aldate's and put it to a similar purpose. Amongst the occupants of this *coenobitium* (as Newman named it) were James Mozley and Mark Pattison. The establishment was not a success, and was abandoned after a couple of years. But if Newman and his friends referred to the inmates as 'young monks', what was the language of their enemies?

Another interruption to the easy flow of the new doctrines was the publication of Tract 80, which appeared in 1837. This was the essay *On Reserve in communicating Religious Knowledge* by Isaac Williams, which created so great a storm. The author was neither a profound thinker nor a lucid stylist, and though it must be supposed that he had a purpose in writing his essay it is extremely difficult to discover what the purpose was. Sir Leslie Stephen's pencilled comment on the back of his copy[1] runs: 'An interesting essay—though with some damned nonsense and questionable applications. The thought really confused. If he would only say clearly what he means by "reserve" and when it is a duty, he would not slide into an apology for lying.' Dean Church, on the other hand, considered it 'a beautiful and suggestive essay, full of deep and original thoughts', but believed its publication to have been very unfortunate. The conclusion was drawn, on all sides, that the Tractarians could not be taken to mean just what they said. Like the Jesuits they kept their secret aims and doctrines out of sight.

It was, however, the publication of Hurrell Froude's *Remains* at the beginning of 1838 which first supplied the critics of the Movement with a really easy and effective target. The *Remains* appeared in two volumes; and two more volumes of sermons and papers were published later. But it was in the first volume of the four that the deadliest ammunition was to be found. It contained the Private Journal, the Occasional Thoughts, the Letters to Friends, and the Sayings in Conversation. Keble wrote the anonymous preface.

These papers had come by degrees into Newman's possession—the Private Journal not until eighteen months after Hurrell's death. He was deeply impressed by the Journal, of which even he had known nothing—so secret was Hurrell's

[1] In the London Library.

inner life—and by the account of his fastings and minute
faults and temptations. 'Does it not seem as if Providence was
putting things into our hands for something special?' he
wrote excitedly to Rogers. As publication approached he became less confident. There would be a flood of criticism, from
all quarters. Even friends would say ' "What *could* he mean by
putting this in? What is the use of that? How silly this! How
trifling that! What is it to the world if so and so? How injudicious! He is cutting his own throat." But *on the whole* I
trust it will present, as far as it goes, a picture of a mind; and
that being gained as the *scope*, the details may be left to take
their chance.'

Certainly the volume presented a picture of a mind. But
Newman and Keble badly miscalculated its tactical effect.
We may be thankful for the miscalculation, which gave us one
of the most interesting psychological documents ever published. But how could the editors have supposed that Froude's
diary would not seem, even to many of his friends, the product
of a most un-English morbidity rather than the portrait of a
young man 'secretly training, as in God's presence, in that
discipline which shuns the light of the world'? They hung
their friend's heart on a tree to be riddled by the arrows of
contemptuous criticism. How could they have imagined,
again, that Froude's violent invective against the Reformers,
his silly tirades against Milton, his mixture of religion with
devotion to King Charles the Martyr, his uneasy awareness of
Rome, could fail to put heart into their enemies and to make
the half-way men shake their heads? Was *this* the real basis of
the new doctrine? Lord Morpeth in the House of Commons
was moved to denounce a set of damnable and detestable
heretics of late sprung up in Oxford, mentioning Mr. Newman by name as the editor of the *Remains*.

CHAPTER X

THE CATACLYSM

I. EARTH TREMORS

In August 1838 the Bishop of Oxford delivered a charge to his clergy, Newman attending. The editor of the Tracts came thoughtfully back to his rooms in Oriel, and sat down to report to Keble. The Bishop had not been very kind. As far as observances went, he had no great fault to find with the Apostolicals. Charges had been made of Romanist practices. He was glad to say that investigation had revealed only a single instance—the addition of a certain clerical vestment (this was a cross-embroidered 'scarf' worn by a hothead at Magdalen)—and this had been discontinued. There was (he implied) no harm in turning to the East; fasting and the observation of saints' days were equally unobjectionable. Over doctrine he was a little uneasy. The Tracts for the Times contained much that was most opportune and serviceable. But some of the expressions used seemed to him injudicious. He feared more for the disciples than for the masters. He conjured the latter to beware of leading others into error, which they themselves were sufficiently instructed to avoid.

Altogether, one might have thought, a discreet enough episcopal pronouncement. A word of caution to the wise, uttered in the friendliest spirit, but no more. Yet Newman was perturbed. There was more behind this than met the ear. Did it not fling an indefinite suspicion over the Tracts, which their general orthodoxy did not deserve? Why should the Bishop have said these things in public, without speaking first to the editor in private? He asked Keble these questions

Sitting on in his rooms, after the letter had gone, he became more and more uncomfortable. Something must be
done, and done quickly. He wrote a second letter to Keble,
sending it by the night coach, since 'despatch will be requisite
if I adopt the following plan.' The plan was nothing less than
to offer, through the Archdeacon, to withdraw any Tract
which the Bishop considered unsafe, except Pusey's Tracts on
Baptism over which he had no control, and a few others
which were not his property. Even these he would, if the
Bishop wished, exclude from the series. 'By doing this I think
I set myself right with him. I really cannot go on publishing
with this censure upon the Tracts. And, if he ordered some to
be suppressed, the *example and precedent* [i.e. of ecclesiastical
discipline] I am sure would be worth ten times the value of
the Tracts suppressed. Unless you think this quixotic, I am
disposed very much to do it.' Even while he read the letter
over, his resolution hardened, and he added a postscript.
'Since writing this, the idea so grows on me of the absolute
impossibility of going on (consistently) with the Tracts, with
the Bishop saying that parts are dangerous, that if I do not
write as above to him, I certainly *must* cease them.'

Keble replied that he entirely agreed in this proposed
course of action, and had come to the same view before he
received Newman's letter. He had already had some account
of the Bishop's charge. (That part of it which referred to the
Tracts had been reported in the *Oxford Herald*.) Accordingly
Newman wrote to the Archdeacon an even more definite
letter than he had originally contemplated. He proposed to
stop the Tracts, and withdraw the existing ones from circulation, unless the Archdeacon could find out privately from the
Bishop what particular Tracts he disapproved of. These he
would at once suppress. And while he waited for the Archdeacon's reply he sent a long account of the whole affair to
Bowden. What the Bishop had actually said was, he admitted,
'very slight indeed, but a Bishop's lightest word, *ex cathedra*,

is heavy.' Except for the reference to the Tracts, the charge
was all that they could wish—'strongly in favour of observing
the Rubric, of recurring to Antiquity, of Saints' days' and so
forth, 'exceedingly strong and bold'. But the attack on the
Tracts—'well, my dear Bowden, has not this come suddenly
and taken away your breath? It nearly has mine. But I do not
think I can be wrong, and I think good may come of it . . .
the precedent will be very good; and it will make people see
we are sincere and not ambitious.'

The Archdeacon disclaimed all responsibility. He had not
been consulted about the charge. It would be better for Newman to leave him out and write direct to the Bishop. So
Newman wrote 'merely asking whether I should call or write
to him.' Nothing could have been kinder or more sympathetic
than the Bishop's reply. He urged Newman to wait until the
charge was printed. He had not at all wished to censure the
Tracts, but only to sound a note of warning. The withdrawal
of the Tracts would make him seem to have said more than
he meant, and therefore be unfair to him.

Newman answered that he would certainly wait till the
charge came out; but that the Bishop's word was his rule,
and he feared lest the world and his opponents should see him
in the false position of being in opposition to his Bishop. He
entreated his Lordship to believe that he would find real
pleasure in submitting himself to his Lordship's expressed
judgment. At the same time he wrote to Pusey. A week had
passed since the delivery of the charge, and Pusey as yet
knew nothing of what was in the wind. He was at Weymouth,
in deep anxiety about his wife's illness. But perhaps the real
reason why Newman did not at once expose his mind to
Pusey, as he did to Keble and Bowden, was that instinct told
him Pusey might take a different view. And in fact Pusey
could not at all make out why Newman should be so upset.
He did not share, did not even understand, Newman's
peculiar view of the relation in which he stood to his Bishop.

'I loved to act in the sight of my Bishop,' wrote Newman in the *Apologia* 'as if I was, as it were, in the sight of God. . . . I desired to please him personally. . . . I considered myself simply as the servant and instrument of my Bishop. I did not care much for the Bench of Bishops, except as they might be the voice of my Church; nor should I have cared much for a Provincial Council; nor for a Diocesan Synod presided over by my Bishop; all these matters seemed to me to be *jure ecclesiastico*, but what to me was *jure divino* was the voice of my Bishop in his own person. My own Bishop was my Pope; I knew no other; the successor of the Apostles, the Vicar of Christ. This was but a practical exhibition of the Anglican theory of Church Government, as I had already drawn it out myself, after various Anglican Divines.' But it may be doubted whether he would have drawn the theory out to such an extreme point, unless Bishop Bagot's personality had been such as to inspire him with a 'special affection'.

Pusey, not holding any such view, felt a sense (unusual with him) of baffled despair. But one thing was clear to him —the Tracts must not be withdrawn. It would be interpreted everywhere as an abandonment of their cause. It would be a blow from which he would never live to see things recover. It would terribly embarrass the Bishop. (Was Newman, one cannot help wondering, entirely guiltless of a wish to embarrass the Bishop?) His own Tracts could not possibly be excepted; they had been the most severely criticized of all. Would Newman not let him act as mediator on his return to Oxford?

To this proposal Newman could not say no. But he was distressed at his friend's lack of understanding, and at once conjured up a pathetic picture of his own isolation. 'I do not think you enter into my situation' he wrote, in a mood of almost hysterical exaggeration, 'nor can anyone. I have for several years been working against all sorts of opposition, and with hardly a friendly voice. Consider how few persons have

said a word in favour of me. . . . My sole comfort has been
that my Bishop has not spoken against me; in a certain sense
I can depend and lean, as it were, on him. Yet, I say it
sorrowfully, though you are the only person I say it to, he has
never been my *friend*—he has never supported me. His
letting me dedicate that book to him was the only thing he has
done for me, and very grateful I felt. I can truly say that I
would do anything to serve him. Sometimes, when I have
stood by as he put on his robes, I felt as if it would be such a
relief if I could have fallen at his feet and kissed them . . . yet
he has shown me, *as* me, no favour, unless being made Rural
Dean was such, which under the circumstances I do not think
was much.' Clearly the over-confidence of the last six years
was beginning to exact its inevitable penalty.

By degrees the sudden conflagration quietly fizzled out.
Nobody but Keble supported Newman's view, with a quotation from Virgil which brought tears into his eyes. Pusey,
Bowden, even Thomas Keble were all against him. The
Bishop was anxious to soothe. Pusey mediated. In the end the
charge was published with a note expressly disclaiming any
'general censure upon the Tracts for the Times'.

But Newman had sustained a shock, not entirely attribut-
able to the apparent external cause. Earthquakes, they say,
happen along deep-seated geological faults. Newman's per-
turbation over Bishop Bagot's mild remarks was—if the
analogy is not too fanciful—related to a similar dislocation in
his innermost self. It left him in a more than usually sensitive
condition. And his discomfort was increased by a growing
sense that he was not fully trusted by his friends. Already,
earlier in the year, he had stumbled into an uncomfortable
encounter with Thomas Keble. He had unwittingly credited
that stern man, in a pamphlet war with Dr. Fausset, the Lady
Margaret Professor of Divinity, with holding that the Pope
was *the* Antichrist. It is not quite clear what the Vicar of
Bisley actually held the Pope to be; but apparently he did not

go to this extreme. Isaac Williams hinted to Newman that all was not well at Bisley, and Newman wrote to apologize. Thomas Keble answered that he did not wish to argue the matter and that he heartily wished Newman would go out of Oxford somewhere or other for a time, and forget Fausset. Newman was much hurt by the unexpected tone of this letter; and matters were not improved when he was sharply reprimanded for printing a Tract which Thomas Keble had sent him, as he supposed, for that very purpose.

This was the prelude to worse trouble. The Tract about the Roman Breviary had frightened Newman's own friends. Now, they learned, he was at work with his young men on a complete translation of its four volumes. Some of it was already in type. Sir George Prevost, Isaac Williams's brother-in-law, had been taking counsel with Thomas Keble and another. He found them no less alarmed than himself, and despatched a 'needlessly abrupt' letter to Newman, offering to pay the expenses of stopping the undertaking, and implying that Newman's rashness had already alienated many who used to sympathize with the party.

The editor of the Tracts sent Prevost a sharp reply, and plunged into an agitated correspondence with Keble. He overflowed with a bitter sense of grievance. He put himself into Keble's hands, would do whatever Keble suggested, make any submission Keble required. He could not help being himself—having certain opinions and a certain way of expressing them. But even in the field of self-expression he would surrender to Keble's judgment. If Keble would tell him what not to do, he would not do it. He would stop writing, stop giving weekly parties, stop anything and everything. That being understood, he asked for some little confidence in him in return. Conscious as he was that everything he did was imperfect, he would soon be driven by this appearance of suspicion, jealousy and discontent to lose heart altogether. Was such conduct towards him kind? Was it feeling? At this rate he

would soon be silenced, whether his critics wished it or not.
'If such a result takes place,' he concluded a not too dignified
letter 'if persons force me by their criticisms into that state of
disgust which the steady contemplation of his own doings is
sure to create in any serious man, they will have done a work
which may cause them some sorrow, perhaps some self-
reproach.'

Keble, always nervous at being asked to deliver a judgment, put himself into communication with his brother. It
seemed that Bisley wished for some supervision to be exercised over the Apostolic propaganda. What did Newman
think? Newman had no objection, in principle, to the proposed 'Decemvirate of Revision', but who were the revisers
to be? Would Keble's brother allow more than one or two out
of all their friends? How could time be found? Were all the
articles in the *British Critic* to have a second reviser after
Newman himself? This was 'virtually enjoining silence, which
if it is to be done had better be done openly.'

The triangular correspondence continued—Keble an uneasy shuttlecock between the principal contestants. Bisley
claimed to speak for the country clergy. Newman retorted
that he naturally wrote for those he knew—'the generation
lay or clerical rising into active life, particularly at Oxford.'
At Oxford, if one spoke at all—and it might be better *not* to
speak—'one must be prepared to pursue questions and to
admit or deny inferences.' On the whole it would probably be
better for him to give up the Tracts, the *British Critic*, and St.
Mary's. He could then devote himself entirely to the Fathers.
Of course, if he did so, things would begin to go wrong;
and he would be blamed 'by those who now, without knowing it, are certainly going the way to bring it about.' The
Kebles took umbrage at the implied depreciation of the
country clergy and, when this red herring had been disposed
of, they seem to have put forward a proposal that the Tracts
should in future be revised by two nominees of Thomas

Keble's. Newman professed himself willing, but asked who
the nominees were to be. 'Isaac Williams of course is one; is
Prevost the other?' The answer, if any, is not recorded in the
published correspondence; and the proposal, to all appearance, died a natural death. But again Newman's confidence
in himself had been severely shaken. How severely, he concealed from his intimates with the 'flinty' manner, described
by Lord Blachford.

Nevertheless, when he looked back to this time in later
years he had forgotten its vexations. 'In the spring of 1839' he
wrote in the *Apologia* 'my position in the Anglican Church was
at its height. I had supreme confidence in my controversial
status, and I had a great and still growing success in recom-
mending it to others.' Perhaps this recollection was somewhat
coloured for dramatic purposes. Perhaps he had passed that
high point several months earlier, and was now upon the
actual descent. Still, by contrast with the disasters and the
headlong plunge into doubt which were so near at hand, he
was still upon the heights. The sunlight of the afternoon
seemed as bright as that of the middle day, compared with the
darkness of the long night, 'in which the stars of this lower
heaven were one by one going out.'

The year behind him had been a year of success. Its degree
was reflected in the rapidly increasing popularity of the
Tracts. Scorned and rejected of publishers in the beginning,
more than sixty thousand had been sold in the twelve months.
They were selling in January of the new year, he told Rogers,
faster than they could be printed. His own new volume of
sermons went quickly into a second edition. The *British Critic*
was flourishing. The April issue contained a long article by
Newman himself on the *State of Religious Parties*. Liberalism,
he concluded, was too cold a principle to prevail with the
multitude. Evangelicalism did but occupy the space between
contending powers, Catholic Truth and Rationalism. 'Then
indeed' he foretold in a magnificently characteristic sentence

'will be the stern encounter, when two real and living principles, simple, entire, and consistent, one in the Church, the
other out of it, at length rush upon each other, contending
not for names and words, or half-views, but for elementary
notions and distinctive moral characters.' Either the Church
of England must renew herself in the principles of the
Apostolical party, or she must leave the field to Rome. The
misty compromises of the typical Establishment men (in
Apostolical slang the 'Z's')[1] would be useless in that day. And
yet, he complained in phrases of admirable irony, 'this is what
the Church is said to want, not party men, but sensible, tem-
perate, sober, well-judging persons, to guide it through the
channel of no-meaning, between the Scylla and Charybdis
of Aye and No.'

So long as the Apostolical guns had such ammunition as
this to fire, what could stand against them? But no such shot
was ever to be fired again. These, said Newman in a signi-
ficantly ambiguous phrase, were 'the last words which I ever
spoke as an Anglican to Anglicans.' Even as he wrote them,
he was in truth winding up his accounts with the Movement,
little dreaming that so it was.

The alarming spread of the new High Church principles,
and the high tone now being adopted by their champions,
stimulated the enemy to come out of his entrenchments and
risk an engagement more or less in the open. The ground was
cleverly chosen, and the engagement ended in a certain dis-
comfiture for the Tractarians. The architect of victory was a
renegade, the Rev. C. P. Golightly.

Golightly had been one of Newman's early pupils at Oriel;
so intimate with him, that Henry Wilberforce declared himself jealous of the ground he was making in their adored
tutor's acquaintance. But he was not of the stuff out of which
disciples are made. 'There was a certain humorous oddity in

[1] X=Evangelical, Y=Apostolical, Z=Establishment. I think Froude
invented these symbols.

Mr. Golightly' said Miss Anne Mozley 'which blinded his friends to the possibilities of bitterness that lay beneath.' He was the kind of man who must have his own opinions and cannot take them from another or from a school, and he seems to have achieved this not by original thinking but by appropriating what pleased him here and there. Having private means, he had no need to please anyone but himself; that he succeeded in doing so gave him a very good opinion of his own judgment, and a very poor opinion of those with whom he came into collision. At the start of the Movement he enrolled himself amongst its supporters, subscribed £50 towards the Tracts (the money was later returned to him), and sent Newman a letter of faintly supercilious advice. Then, in 1835, Newman, unwarily taking the advice of Tom Mozley, offered him the curacy of Littlemore when the new church should be completed. To do Golightly justice, he warned Newman that his preaching might not be to the taste of Mrs. Newman and her daughters. Would it not be wise, he suggested, if Newman would look through two or three of his sermons before he confirmed the offer? It would be unfortunate if their religious sentiments proved incompatible. Newman thought there was no risk of that. And then Pusey's Tract on Baptism came out, and Golightly preached in Oxford violently against it. What, after that, could Newman do but put an end to the prospective engagement? 'This must have been' he noted 'in the spring of 1836. He never got over it. We were never friends again.' A little later Pusey, somewhat unwisely, hearing that Golightly was talking freely against his old friends, wrote and told him to behave himself better. Golightly was not the man to accept such a rebuke. From this time onward he became a bitter and relentless enemy both of Pusey and of Newman.

Golightly's sense of humour must have been agreeably tickled when his great idea came suddenly into his head. Why should there not be, in Oxford, a memorial to the three

great martyrs of the English Reformation, Cranmer, Ridley
and Latimer? Cranmer and Latimer were Oxford men;
Ridley, a Cambridge man, died at Oxford. The memorial
might be erected on the very spot where all three were
burned at the stake. The proposal was bound to prove irresistible. The martyrs had been 'in a manner canonized' in the
Church for the last three hundred years. Nobody would dare
to say no. In the first flush of their enthusiasm Golightly and
his friends talked of a church of the Martyrs. But this would be
to offer the Puseyites and the Newmanites too good a ground
of objection. The martyred Reformers were not, after all,
Saints. A memorial would serve the purpose Golightly had in
view just as well as a church—even better. It would be a very
nasty pill indeed for the editors of Froude's *Remains* to swallow. If they and their friends subscribed to the memorial they
would be making hay of their own principles; if they stood
aloof they would cover themselves with odium. Some would
come in; some would stand out. The party would be cleaved
in two, and become a laughing-stock to the University.

And so—or very nearly so—it proved. The subscription was
successful. The Martyrs' Memorial stands now, a pious eye-
sore, preserving the legacy of ancient wrongs. The Tractarians *were* embarrassed; Keble and Newman remaining
rigidly aloof, while lesser men fell dumbly into the trap. Even
Pusey was nearly caught. Assisted by his friends he climbed
out on the top of a lengthy correspondence with the Bishop of
Oxford. He tried to transform the scheme into a proposal to
build a church to the honour of the Holy Trinity, with a
carefully worded inscription about the Reformation to which
nobody could take exception. In this attempt he had the
guarded approval of his two associates. The committee of
the memorial were not, however, so easily baulked. Pusey,
therefore, was compelled to stand aside. But at the Bishop of
Oxford's suggestion (for the Bishop knew well what the real
object of the memorial was) he composed an open Letter to

the Bishop, in the form of an octavo book of 239 pages, designed to exculpate the Tractarian Movement from the charge of Romanism. It was, according to his biographer, one of his happiest efforts, and reached a fourth edition in twelve months. Golightly's triumph was not as complete as it looked.

2. PUSEY IN PROFUNDIS

No one could dare, just now, to point the finger of scorn at Pusey, for both his wife and his son were under the shadow of death. His third child, Katherine, had died in 1832. There were left the two children—Philip and Lucy, who were on such intimate terms with the great Mr. Newman, and the youngest little girl, Mary. Whatever might be believed to the contrary, there was no grim barrier between Pusey and his children. The malicious said that he used to punish them by holding their fingers in the candle for a foretaste of hell-fire. In fact he never administered even the mildest form of punishment. The nearest approach to a definite rebuke that Philip could remember was that once, when his father found him reading a novel on a Sunday, he pulled his ear and said, 'Oh, Phil, you heathen!' Tuckwell, who tells this anecdote and knew the family well, follows it with an amusing illustration of his mildness. Pusey happened to sit next to a talkative lady in an omnibus, who informed him that Dr. Pusey was in the habit of sacrificing a lamb every Friday. 'My dear Madam,' he said 'I am Dr. Pusey, and I assure you I do not know how to kill a lamb.'

Naturally the children were brought up to be religious. When Mrs. Pusey was away, Pusey himself saw to it that they said their prayers properly, morning and evening. And Philip's own childish ambition was to succeed his friend, Mr. Newman, as Vicar of St. Mary's. But there was nothing of sternness in his relations with them. He confessed that he was a poor hand at joining in their games. But, when his wife was away, he liked to have them in his study, while he was working; and his letters show how deeply he loved them.

Pusey had been married some six or seven years when his wife's health began to break down. Her marriage had changed her completely. She had thrown herself without reserve into his pursuits and his way of thinking—accepting him and John (i.e. Newman) as the oracles of religious truth, spending long hours collating manuscripts, toiling at her own education and that of her children, nursing her husband in his frequent illnesses, and devoting all her spare time to religious and charitable exercises. It is not surprising that so much rigorous self-discipline laid her open to the common scourge of those days—consumption. The last five years of her life were years of constant physical pain and weakness. To this trial another was added. Philip, now a promising little boy of seven, fell dangerously ill. It was thought that he could not live; and when, against hope, he began gradually to recover, it became clear that he would be a cripple and an invalid for the rest of his life. In the event he lived to be nearly fifty. It would be hard to find a more pathetic letter than that which Pusey wrote to his wife, upon receiving the doctor's report. 'And now, dearest wife, this is a sorrowful letter; and it is one trouble which you have from casting in your lot with me, that our children's lives are precarious at best; yet many a mother might, if she knew the real state of things, gladly have our sickly, and if it please and when it pleases God, our dying or dead son, before their living one.'

In the summer of that year (1838) the strain upon Pusey relaxed a little. Mrs. Pusey seemed a little stronger; and Philip's condition was improving 'though his more than ever stunted and aged form shows how deeply the disease has laid hold on him.' But in the autumn—just about the time when the Bishop of Oxford's charge was published—the news was broken to Pusey that his wife had only a few months to live.

He could not bring himself to believe that it was really true. And when, in May 1839, his last obstinate hopes were extinguished, he could not think of the approaching blow except as a punishment for his sins. His friends did their best to reason gently with him. 'It is nothing' said Newman 'out of God's usual dealings.' 'I want you' wrote Keble 'to be on your guard against *bitter* self-reproach.' He answered evasively that his danger did not lie that way. 'I much more fear that I should not act up to the extent of this visitation, than that I should feel it too bitterly. I dread my own love of employment, if I have strength given me: I dread becoming again what I was before, and yet probably I do not dread it enough.'

The end came on May 26, 1839. When it was over, his mother 'against his first wish' sent for Newman. 'It was like the visit of an angel' he confessed to Keble. And a little later he wrote touchingly to Newman. 'My dearest Friend, God bless and reward you for all your love and tender kindness towards us. I received day by day my share of it, with little acknowledgment, for words fail one, and one is stopped by a sort of αἰδώς from thanking to the face for great kindness. Your first visit . . . was to me like that of an angel sent from God: I shrank from it, beforehand, or from seeing any human face. . . . It seems as though it had changed, in a degree, the character of my subsequent life.'

In truth, not Newman's ministrations, nor any other agency, were able to prevent his heart from feeding on its sorrow. His whole life had been centred upon his passion. He had tried, perhaps, to subordinate this earthly love to the love of God. Intellectually he could do so; the one existed in the other; there was no need for conflict. But, if conflict there had been, which would have come first? Years afterwards, Tuckwell relates, 'a common friend was sacrificing an important sphere of work in order to seek with his delicate wife a warmer climate, and I asked him [Pusey]—no doubt a priggish query—if the abandonment were justifiable on the highest grounds. "Justifiable?" he said, "I would have given up everything and gone anywhere, but—"; his voice shook, the aposiopesis remained unfilled.'

The effect upon Pusey's subsequent life was indeed profound. The memory of his loss was never far from the surface of his mind. When he walked across the great quadrangle to the Cathedral he would never lift his eyes from the ground, for fear lest he should see again the shroud on the coffin fluttering in the wind. He never removed the crape band from his hat; wore always a crape scarf over his surplice. He would not enter the drawing-room of his house. He withdrew completely from society of every kind, refusing even to accept invitations to dine in the chapter house or the hall of his own college. His personal appearance became a matter of entire indifference to him. His boots went unbuttoned, his chin unshaved, his hair and his collar unbrushed. These things were symptoms of an inner misery, which never left him. He had loved his darling, he loved her still, better than God; and he attempted to drown his consciousness of this terrible fact by an abasement of himself before God, far more extreme than the self-abasement of Keble or Newman or even of Hurrell Froude.

Whether, in his exploration of these depths, he is to be called a pervert or a saint is a matter for every reader's private judgment. The materials for such a judgment will be found in his biography.[1] It was in 1846, the year after Newman's secession, that he persuaded Keble—sorely against Keble's will and better judgment—to become his confessor and to prescribe him a rule of penitential discipline. He conceived that his wife had been taken from him as a punishment for his sins. Ever since her death he had seen himself 'scarred all over and seamed with sin, so that I am a monster to myself.' In

---

[1] *Life of Pusey*, by H. P. Liddon, D.D., vol. iii. chapter 4, 'Penitence and Confession'.

the event, he drew up his own set of rules; all that he needed from Keble was the semblance of an authoritative command to observe them. Keble uncomfortably complied. The rules were long and detailed. They prescribed the wearing of hair-cloth, the use of a hard chair and a hard bed, the disuse of gloves, abstinence from wine and beer and from food, except what was required for health. If they did not prescribe flagellation, it was only because he was afraid of the physical consequences. 'I think' he wrote to Keble 'I should like to be bid to use the discipline. I cannot even smite on my breast much because the pressure on my lungs seemed bad.' In eating he was to masticate his food slowly and penitentially 'making a secret confession of unworthiness to use God's creatures, before every meal'. At dinner he must drink cold water 'as only fit to be where there is not a drop "to cool this flame".' When he looked at the fire he must see in it 'the type of hell'. Whenever he caught anyone's eyes, or saw a child or a poor person or anybody 'very degraded', he must make a mental act of being their inferior; and this act of internal humiliation he must specially perform when undergraduates and college servants saluted him. Out walking he must keep his eyes on the ground (except that he might observe the beauties of nature), associating himself mentally with the publican. Nothing was to be looked at out of curiosity. In conversation he must never jest (except when with children), never interrupt another speaker, never go on speaking if another interrupted him. In confession he was to 'hear all the very worst confessions, very penitentially, as worse myself'. In daily prayer he was to ask for trouble and for sharp bodily pain and for σεμνότης.[1]

Was it strange that when Newman met Pusey at Keble's house after twenty years of this discipline he found him sadly changed? 'Indeed' he reported to Father St. John that evening 'the alteration in him startled, I will add pained and

[1] 1 Tim. iii. 4. The word is translated 'gravity' in the A.V.

EDWARD BOUVERIE PUSEY
From the drawing by George Richmond
in the National Portrait Gallery

grieved, me. . . . I recollect him short and small, with a round head and smallish features, flaxen curly hair; huddled up together from his shoulders downward, and walking fast. This as a young man; but comparing him even as he was when I had last seen him in 1846, when he was slow in his motions and staid in his figure, there was a wonderful change in him. His head and features are half as large again; his chest is very broad, and he is altogether large, and (don't say all this to anyone) he has a strange condescending way when he speaks.' The prayer for σεμνότης had been all too plainly answered.

It is interesting to compare this description of Pusey in 1865 with an earlier description from the same pen. 'Pusey is returned' Newman wrote to Bowden in the autumn after Mrs. Pusey's death 'and in appearance much better. It is no exaggeration to say he is a Father in the face and aspect. He has been preaching to breathless congregations at Exeter and Brighton. Ladies have been sitting on the pulpit steps, and sentimental paragraphs have appeared in the papers—in the Globe! Fancy!' The slight figure had begun to expand some time before this. In 1836 Newman read a malicious description of a typical High Churchman in the Standard ('half prig, half dandy, perfumed and powdered, and a little corpulent') and his thoughts 'at once went to Pusey, as answering every point of it, especially the corpulence (!)'. After his wife's death his physical appearance degenerated rapidly. In 1841 his mother, then in her seventieth year, observed that he looked wretched: 'with his emaciated face, he looked older than the clergyman of Holton, who is near my age and with a lined face, only that Edward is not bald.' But this was just after the shock of Tract 90.

Long before Pusey began to confess to Keble, he had become the confessor of others. During the second period of the Oxford Movement—between 1840 and 1845—the High Church party revived the practice of auricular confession— that grace which he had once supposed to be lost for ever. An

article upon the subject appeared in the *British Critic* early in
April 1843. To confess to Dr. Pusey became something very
like a fashion. For the most part his penitents were women.
'Flys came to the door' says Tuckwell with genial cynicism
'from which descended ladies, Una-like in wimple and black
stole, "as one that wily mourned", obtained their interview
and went away.' But men came, as well as women. 'I once
and once only' admitted Mark Pattison 'got so low by fostering a morbid state of conscience as to go to confession to
Dr. Pusey. Years afterwards it came to my knowledge that
Pusey had told a fact about myself, which he got from me on
that occasion, to a friend of his, who employed it to annoy
me.' The habit of hearing confessions seemed to have a bad
effect on Dr. Pusey. The curiosity which he tried to repress in
the ordinary affairs of life broke out in an almost morbid
interest in the spiritual ailments of others. He would cross-
question all manner of people about the state of their souls,
their inmost wishes, habits, intentions. Only the slow, sweet,
disarming smile, by which the ascetic sternness of his face was
surprisingly relieved, seemed somehow to deprive the questions of offensiveness.

Whatever judgment may be passed on the type of religion
which dictated that crushing discipline, it was at any rate no
intellectual or aesthetic formula. Aestheticism indeed was
conspicuously absent from his world. He had a certain liking
for richness in ecclesiastical costume. He confessed to Bishop
Bagot that he thought the ornaments in use in Edward VI's
time were much handsomer than those of his own time;
'especially' he said 'the Bishop's is very beautiful.' Yet such
things were to him valuable, not in themselves, but as
symbols; and he told Russell that he would be sorry to find
himself in a richer dress until the Church were in a happier
state. He was content with the surplice as token of purity, and
the scarf as emblem of Christ's yoke. For the ritualistic pre-
occupation of some of his followers he had an instinctive con-

tempt. As for intellect, he laboured to place the faith on the surest ground of reason he could find; and he employed all the resources of his scholarship on the catharsis of Christian tradition. This was merely the service which his mind was capable of rendering to a faith which he had embraced with his heart. The same was true of Newman. But whereas Newman was repeatedly tortured with the thought that in his intellectual refinements of doctrine he was losing sight of his first and simply felt convictions, Pusey had the power in himself of drawing upon his emotions whenever he needed to do so. In this difference of temperament it is possible to perceive one cause of the difference in their two careers. For Newman the struggle between intellect and feeling for priority of place necessitated submission to a paramount arbitrator, such as he could only discover in the Roman system. For Pusey no such problem existed.

The emotional nature of his religious life is exhibited most clearly in the manual of *Private Prayers* published after his death, and composed for his own use between 1850 and 1860. It was a book calculated to drive young men, of different temperament, into a premature disgust with all religion. The source of these prayers was a book of German devotions, after the Moravian model, by J. M. Horst, which he translated and adapted to the use of the English Church, in 1845-1847, under the title *Paradise of the Christian Soul, enriched with the Choicest Delights of Varied Piety*. An imaginative reproduction by the devotee of the details of Christ's passion and agony was the basis of this devotional system. The phraseology of the title is unpleasantly like the titles of books in that class of literature described in booksellers' catalogues as *facetiae*.

As a preacher Pusey exercised an influence second only to that of Newman himself. He had no oratorical graces. The matter of his sermons was dry, strained, dogmatic; the delivery harsh and unmusical. He could never learn to manage his voice. These defects were outweighed by the intense uncompromising earnestness of the preacher, his authoritative conviction of the supreme importance of his message. And they added a particular force to moments when his argument became disconcertingly alive and probed, with an uncanny assurance, into the most sensitive recesses of the listener's conscience. Two instances of his power are recorded, one by Tom Mozley, the other by his brother James. Tom was present when Pusey preached in the Cathedral on the text, 'For it is impossible for those who were once enlightened . . . if they shall fall away, to renew them again unto repentance.'[1] Here is his account of the impression he received. 'Every corner of the church was filled. One might have heard a pin drop, as they say. Every word told. The keynote was the word "irreparable", pronounced every now and then with the force of a judgment. Not a soul could have left that church without deep and painful feelings.' Stunned, as he said, for the time, he recovered his critical faculty afterwards. 'The word irreparable, with which Pusey every now and then smote the listening crowd, as with a scourge, is both the argument of the sermon and the reply to it.' All sin, he thought, is obviously irreparable; this is a natural fact, not a revealed truth. Pusey, in short, had overstated his case. But the impression of awfulness remained.

The other sermon, at which James Mozley was present, was the first which Pusey preached after his wife's death. In the middle of some quite normal observations on the vanity of human life he touched upon the increase of undergraduate luxury. And then, suddenly, dropping his voice almost to a whisper, amidst a breathless silence, he asked if other members of the University, in a higher station, could not adopt a greater simplicity of life. The shaft was aimed—and the aim was the more deadly because there was no malice behind it— at the Heads of Houses. The effect caused by the sudden drop of voice was electrical. But it was not a rhetorical device.

[1] Hebrews vi. 4-6.

EDWARD BOUVERIE PUSEY
*From the painting after Miss R. Corder
in the possession of Keble College*

Pusey had simply 'meant the undergraduates not to hear, as
he told Newman with the utmost simplicity after. It was to
have been a sort of an aside from the preacher in the pulpit
to the Vice-Chancellor over the way. The Master of Balliol
was seen to march out of church afterwards with every air of
offended dignity.... The Heads were looking serene and composed, when, all on a sudden comes this highly practical turn
to the subject.'

Such was Pusey, in the days of his ascendancy, in the late
'thirties, the 'forties, the early 'fifties. Later, as the tide of
secular education inundated and transformed Oxford, that
mysterious empire dwindled, in his own lifetime, into an all
but incredible legend.

3. THE FATAL SUMMER

'The Long Vacation of 1839 began early. There had been
a great many visitors to Oxford from Easter to Commemoration; and Dr. Pusey and myself had attracted attention, more,
I think, than in any former year. I had put away the controversy with Rome for more than two years. . . . I was returning, for the Vacation, to the course of reading which I
had many years before chosen as especially my own. I have
no reason to suppose that the thoughts of Rome came across
my mind at all. About the middle of June I began to study
and master the history of the Monophysites. I was absorbed
in the doctrinal question. This was from about June 13 to
August 30. It was during the course of this reading that for
the first time a doubt came upon me of the tenableness of
Anglicanism.'[1]

A momentary glimpse of Newman and Keble as they
appeared to a pair of critical feminine eyes on this very day,
June 13 1839, occurs in a letter describing the festivities of
Commemoration week. It was the year when Wordsworth and

---

[1] *Apologia*, Part V.

Sir John Herschel were given honorary degrees, and Oxford—as Newman remembered—was full of visitors. The day after the ceremony Frank Faber of Magdalen, a friend of the poet's and of Newman's, gave 'a grand breakfast party', to which Newman, Keble and others were invited to meet Wordsworth. Frank Faber's brother, Frederic, the future hymn-writer and head of the Brompton Oratory, and several ladies were present. Wordsworth was, of course, the lion of the gathering. The eyes of all the female guests were upon him, and their ears strained to catch what little they could hear of his conversation. In comparison with him the author of *The Christian Year* and the editor of *Tracts for the Times* seemed very unimpressive, and the letter-writer dismissed them in a sentence: 'Newman was there and Mr. and Mrs. John Keble—the latter a pretty shewy person—he is a poor-looking pinched-up person—so is Newman.'[1]

These distractions over, Newman settled down to the course of reading he had designed for the months of the summer vacation. The *History of the Arians* and the edition of Dionysius of Alexandria had hitherto concentrated his attention mainly upon that period of early Church history which culminated in the first of the Oecumenical Councils—the First Council of Nicaea in A.D. 325, at which the Arian heresy was condemned. His Dionysius was nearly finished. He was free to explore the later history. And as he travelled upwards through the centuries he found his curiosity fastening itself upon the fourth of the great Councils—the Council of Chalcedon in A.D. 451.

By his own account of the matter, he little knew what Chalcedon would do to him; and all his letters and memor-

[1] From a family letter in the writer's possession. It is fair to add that neither Frank nor Fred Faber would have subscribed to this opinion. Frank's account of the party says that Keble was 'very pleasant and full of animation'. He sat opposite to Wordsworth. Newman was at the other end of the table. But the lady's description confirms the evidence of other contemporaries—namely that, at first sight, Newman's appearance was disappointing.

anda bear his story out. Yet it seems strange that he should
have gone straight to Chalcedon for his vacation reading,
passing by the Councils of Constantinople and Ephesus. It is
quite clear that this is what he did; for writing to Rogers in
July he says, 'now that I am in the Monophysite controversy,
I think I shall read through it, and then back to the Nes-
torian.' Surely some secret anticipation of what he was going
to encounter, and a secret desire to encounter it, not allowed
to rise above the threshold of consciousness, must have determined his choice?

The reader who has no knowledge of heresies and councils
cannot follow the action of Newman's mind at this decisive
point of his career unless he is willing to accept a little superficial instruction. If he will endure for a few pages I will do my
best to provide him with the essential facts. As we are not
concerned either to approve or to condemn doctrine, they can
be very simply set out.

The Arians had held that the Son was created by the
Father, from whom he was totally and essentially distinct,
and to whom he was inferior. In condemning this heresy the
Council of Nicaea (A.D. 325) decided that the Son was of the
same essence as the Father, though a distinct person. But the
Arians had not held that the Son, incarnate in the Christ,
was an ordinary human being. In their view he had worn
human shape, but not possessed a human nature. This view,
also, the Council condemned. The Son was both God and
Man.

Towards the end of the fourth century a new heresy arose.
How—asked Apollinaris, the Bishop of Laodicea—could
Christ be a man, like other men, if he was also God? Apollinaris and his followers had no wish to belittle the divinity of
the Son. They tried, therefore, to make the decision of the
Council of Nicaea more intelligible by explaining that the soul
of the human Christ was not an ordinary human soul, but the
divine principle, the Logos, the Word. Chief amongst those

who withstood the Apollinarian theory was the Bishop of Constantinople, Nestorius. At a second Council, held at Constantinople in 381 A.D., the Church decided against the Apollinarians and insisted on the truly human nature of the incarnate Son of God.

It was now the turn of Nestorius himself to fall into the pit of heresy that he had dug for another. The Apollinarians, by their denial of ordinary humanity to Christ, had been able to exalt Mary with the title 'Mother of God'. Nestorius conceived that if Christ was fully Man, as well as fully God, his human mother was but the mother of his manhood and therefore not entitled to the divine or semi-divine honour which the title implied. A third Council, held at Ephesus in A.D. 431, convicted the Nestorians of heresy and allowed that the mother of Jesus was rightly named the mother of God, since his human and divine natures were indivisible.

But the chain of reckless speculation upon the nature of Christ had still other links to unfold. Scarcely had Nestorius followed the way of Apollinaris when the aged abbot of a monastery in Constantinople, named Eutyches, whether presuming upon the fact that his godson was the favourite eunuch of the Emperor Theodosius II and a close friend of Dioscorus, the infamous Bishop of Alexandria, or simply trusting to the licence of old age, allowed himself, in a denunciation of the shattered Nestorians, to assert that the nature of Christ was single and divine. At once Byzantium was in an uproar. The Bishop, Flavian, convened a domestic synod. Eutyches was condemned. The Emperor took up his cause and summoned a General Council of the Church. At this point Leo, Bishop of Rome (not yet known to Christendom as the Pope, although the title is given to him by Newman and by modern usage) entered the arena. His primacy was already an accepted fact. The Council of Constantinople, besides condemning Apollinaris, had claimed for the See of Byzantium merely the second place, after the See of Rome.

Even this claim was denied by Rome for the next eight centuries. Both Eutyches and the Emperor appealed to Leo, who
wrote 'somewhat sharply'[1] to Flavian, the Bishop of Constantinople, for further information. Receiving Flavian's report
Leo indited an official condemnation of Eutyches, promul-
gating once more the doctrine of the Two Natures, adopted at
the Council of Constantinople. This document became known
as the Tome of St. Leo. He also agreed, though reluctantly,
to the holding of a General Council.

The Council met at Ephesus. It was packed by the supporters of Eutyches, and dominated by Dioscorus, Bishop of
Alexandria, who used the occasion to assert the power of his
own See against the rival Sees of Rome and Byzantium. The
heretic was acquitted. Flavian was insulted, with physical
violence, by Dioscorus, and died of his injuries. The Roman
delegates, having recorded their disgust with the proceedings,
hardly escaped with their lives. The Council, though it had
been convened with the consent of Rome, was never recognized as authoritative, whether by the Greek or the Roman
or the Anglican Church. It was stigmatized by Leo as a *latro-
cinium*—a mere band of ruffians. Rome, then, had attempted
to impose her authority on the East, and the attempt
appeared to have failed.

It is to be noted that none of the definitions of the faith
arrived at by these Councils resulted from the initiative of
Rome. They were provoked by controversies arising in the
Greek-speaking East. Her general attitude towards these
Eastern speculations was unsympathetic. Of herself she
would perhaps have avoided the dangerous task of defining a
mystery in logical terms. The temper of the Roman mind was
practical. In the great days of the Republic and the Empire
her men of letters took their philosophy from Greece. The
Greek language was to every educated Roman what the

---

[1] I quote the phrase from the lucid synopsis of the controversy given
in Chapter I of the *Correspondence of Newman with Keble and Others*, edited
at the Birmingham Oratory.

French language has been to a few educated Englishmen—
the language of a more subtle culture. But this was ancient
history. Even before the time of Leo Greek had ceased to be
either spoken or understood in Rome. The controversies of
the East were Greek controversies, stimulated by the elastic
genius of the Greek language for expressing the subtlest forms
of thought. They could not even be understood in Rome until
they had been translated into Latin; and in submitting to the
hard precision of Latin they underwent an inevitable distortion. The pronouncements of the Roman Bishops had again
to be translated from Latin into Greek, before the East could
understand them. And in the actual discussions at the Councils the Roman envoys were commonly reduced to silence by
their ignorance of Greek.

The task of maintaining the purity of the faith under such
conditions was not a simple one; and it was still further complicated by the interferences of the civil power, that is to say
of successive Byzantine Emperors—now on the side of
orthodoxy, now of heresy. But the old practical Roman spirit
triumphed over all these obstacles. The Bishops of Rome
knew the art of biding their time, and of using the jealousy
between Constantinople and Alexandria to increase the tradition of their own supremacy.

Leo had not long to wait. Theodosius was killed by a fall
from his horse; and the new Emperor Marcian at once reversed the policy of his predecessor. A new Council—the
fourth of the Oecumenical series—was summoned to meet at
Chalcedon in A.D. 451. The Tome of St. Leo was read amidst
scenes of enthusiasm. 'Peter' cried the assembled bishops
'has spoken through Leo.' Dioscorus was deposed from the
See of Alexandria on the ground that he had continued the
Council of Ephesus 'without the authority of the Apostolic
See'. And though Eutyches was not formally condemned as a
heretic the Council explicitly affirmed the doctrine of Christ's
two natures, human and divine, indivisible yet distinct,

united in one person. But the Council nearly came to wreck
over the precise wording of the formula in which this doctrine
was to be expressed. A fierce battle raged over a preposition.
The Christ in one person, all could accept; but was the Christ
in two natures or *of* two natures? The Greek-speaking bishops
clung to the preposition 'of'.[1] The Roman delegates insisted
upon 'in'. The difference, Gibbon dryly observes, is one more
easily remembered than understood. But it is not difficult to
see that the Roman formula minimized the risk of further
subtle refinements. 'In' was a definite, unambiguous, word;
'of' or 'out of' might be twisted to mean anything. The
Emperor came down heavily on the side of Leo, and the
Greeks surrendered.

The Council of Chalcedon finally determined Catholic and
Greek Orthodox doctrine of the nature of Christ, and the
doctrine so determined remained the doctrine of the re-
formed Church of England. It is expressed in the Second of
her Thirty-nine Articles, in the words 'so that two whole and
perfect Natures, that is to say, the Godhead and Manhood,
were joined together in one Person, never to be divided,
whereof is one Christ, very God, and very Man.' Though it
would seem that the word 'whereof' perpetuates the Greek
rather than the Roman form of the definition.

After the Council had dispersed, however, a good deal of
dissatisfaction with its decrees became evident in the East.
Subtle as it was, the Greek mind could not easily bring itself
to rest in what seemed to be a self-contradictory statement.
How could the two natures of Christ be thought of as *two* if
they were indivisibly joined? If they were two, then they must
be divisible. Large masses of the Church adopted the heretical
position that the two natures had coalesced into one. The
heretics stated their position in a bewildering variety of ways
—some grouping themselves with Eutyches, the greater part
following a middle way between Eutyches and Chalcedon—

---

[1] The Greek word is ἐκ, which primarily means 'out of'.

but they were all called Monophysites, that is to say, believers in the single nature. The Monophysites flourished
particularly in Egypt and in Syria; they broke away from the
Church and founded communions of their own, which survive to this day in Armenia, Egypt and Abyssinia.

Such, in bare outline, was the chapter of history into which
Newman plunged himself in the summer of 1839, and by
which he was ultimately converted to Rome. Two things
struck him almost at once—'the great power of the Pope (as
great as he claims now almost) and the marvellous interference of the civil power, as great almost as in our kings.'
So he wrote to Rogers on July 12. At the end of July he
talked excitedly about these topics to a friend whom he happened to meet. By the end of August he had finished his
reading and sat back to consider how it had affected his mind.
The more he reflected, the more he saw in the events of the
fourth century an allegory for his own times. 'I saw my face
in that mirror, and I was a Monophysite.' He did not mean
by this vivid phrase that he held the Monophysite heresy—
he held to the Catholic doctrine enshrined in the Anglican
Articles. He meant that he stood in the same relations with
Rome as the Monophysites had stood. He compared his *Via
Media* with theirs, the Protestants with the Eutychians. If
they were in heresy and schism, so was he. 'There was an
awful similitude, more awful because so silent and unim-
passioned, between the dead records of the past and the
feverish chronicle of the present.' The Rome of the fifth
century was the Rome of the nineteenth; her inexorable
resolution had never wavered; his spirit bowed down to it.
The heretics of the fifth century, 'shifting, changeable, reserved, and deceitful, ever courting civil power, and never
agreeing together, except by its aid', were paralleled (in all
but the subject-matter of their heresies) by the Protestants of
the nineteenth; and the civil power, in England no less than
in Byzantium, was still engaged in 'substituting expediency

for faith'. 'What was the use of continuing the controversy, or defending my position, if, after all, I was forging arguments for Arius or Eutyches and turning devil's advocate against the much-enduring Athanasius and the majestic Leo? . . . Sooner may my right hand forget her cunning, and wither outright . . . ere I should do aught but fall at their feet in love and worship, whose image was continually before my eyes, and whose musical words were ever in my ears and on my tongue!'

It is plain that the great revolution of his mind was not brought about by reason, though he claimed that it had been so. He wished, he told a Roman Catholic friend in 1841,'to go by reason, not by feeling'. Yet, when he had finally decided that he must leave the English Church, and tried to put on paper a history of the reasonings which had led him to that point, he could not do them justice. 'The process of argument' he noted 'is like a scaffolding taken down when the building is completed.' He was baffled in the effort of self-explanation by the presence in himself of an obscure motive which his explanations simply left out. Writing in the white heat of recollection he succeeded, in the *Apologia*, in making the process of his conversion one that every sensitive reader could *feel*; but not in making it appear a process of reason. For the obscure motive becomes partially visible in more than one passage of that passionate autobiography. He must, he says, for years have had an habitual notion, though it was latent and had never led him to distrust his convictions, that his mind had not found its ultimate rest, and that in some sense or other he was on journey. He was being impelled on that journey by something in himself which would not let him stand still. And this was not ambition nor a desire for intellectual consistency; it was the search for an absolute spiritual ruler. In Leo's voice he first recognized the veritable accents of power, severe, uncompromising, peremptory.

The first thought which struck him, as he contemplated

the shaking edifice of his own *Via Media*, was that he might escape his difficulties by leaving Oxford. 'You see,' he wrote to Rogers on September 15 'if things were to come to the worst, I should turn Brother of Charity in London—an object, which, *quite* independently of any such perplexities, is growing on me.' The letter, as printed, does not say what the 'perplexities' were; it is a reasonable guess that they related to his new suspicion that the English Church was in a state of schism. A week later he wrote again to Rogers to say that he had just had 'the first real hit from Romanism'. A friend of his (Robert Williams) passing through Oxford showed him an article by Wiseman in the *Dublin Review*. The article compared the Church of England to the Donatists, a powerful section of the Catholic Church in Roman Africa, who seceded from Rome early in the fourth century—'a memorable schism' in Gibbon's words 'which afflicted the provinces of Africa above three hundred years, and was extinguished only with Christianity itself.' The article, coming on top of the misgivings excited in him by the Monophysite history, was like a dose on top of an alterative and gave him a stomachache. (These are his own metaphors.) The coincidence was in itself enough to alarm him. Then there was the strange parallelism of time—just over three hundred years had passed since England had broken with Rome. In the *Apologia* Newman declared that when he read the article he 'did not see much in it.' His letters prove that, on the contrary, he saw a great deal in it. 'I seriously think this a most uncomfortable article on every account' he told Rogers in September; and to Bowden (wintering abroad after the first onset of the illness which was to kill him before Newman reached his goal) he described it, in November, as 'the best thing Dr. Wiseman has put out.'

Little did the well-intentioned Mr. Williams, a strong opponent of Roman pretensions, realize what he was doing when he put the *Dublin Review* into Newman's hands. And

what can have been in his mind when he drew Newman's
particular attention to the majestic phrase of St. Augustine,
quoted in Wiseman's article—*securus judicat orbis terrarum*?
It is an almost untranslatable sentence; perhaps it may be
paraphrased 'the judgment of the whole world cannot be
shaken.' The words rang in Newman's ears. They made
mincemeat (it seemed to him) of his appeal to Antiquity.
Augustine had applied them to the Donatists; Newman drew
out their enigmatic meaning, and applying it to the Church of
England perceived that she was condemned, just as the
Donatists were condemned, by 'the deliberate judgment, in
which the whole Church at length rests and acquiesces', and
in which it has 'an infallible prescription and a final sentence
against such portions of it as protest and secede.' The *Via
Media*, already shaken by Chalcedon, crumbled into dust
beneath his feet.

Such were the two powerful blows which drove him out of
his course. And surely it is clear that their power lay in their
effect, not upon his reason, but upon his emotional imagination. It is not easy to reconcile this with the statement in the
Apologia, conveyed in the following words: 'The question of
the position of the Pope . . . did not come into my thoughts at
all; nor did it, I think I may say, to the end. I doubt whether
I ever distinctly held any of his powers to be *jure divino*, while
I was in the Anglican Church;—not that I saw any difficulty
in the doctrine; not that together with the history of St. Leo
. . . . the idea of his infallibility did not cross my mind, for it
did,—but after all, in my view the controversy did not turn
upon it; it turned upon the Faith and the Church. This was
my issue of the controversy from the beginning to the end.
There was a contrariety of claims between the Roman and
the Anglican religions, and the history of my conversion is
simply the process of working it out to a solution.' And, in an
illustration which he used more than once, he compared the
Anglican conception of a detached and objective Truth to a

Calvary, exhibiting Christ alone on the Cross; while he likened the Roman vision of Truth to the Child in the arms of a Madonna 'lying hid in the bosom of the Church as if one with her, clinging to and (as it were) lost in her embrace'.

But note how the analysis of a rational controversy ends in a highly emotional picture. For this helps to explain how Newman was able, at one and the same time, to do full justice to the emotional processes of his conversion and yet to describe it as though it had been the solution of a logical problem. His intellect justified him; but it took its direction from feeling, and it expressed its conclusions in a simile.

A week or two later, walking in the New Forest with Henry Wilberforce, he unburdened his whole mind. A vista, he said, had been opened before him, and he could not see to the end of it. Perhaps it would all come right when he got back to his rooms and could think it out quietly. But if it did not, what could there be for him to do but go over to Rome? Horror-struck, Henry exclaimed that he would rather see his friend dead. To which Newman replied—instinctively clinging still to the curious idea that going over to Rome would be committing a deadly sin—that he had seriously thought of asking his friends to pray, 'if ever the time should come when he was in serious danger', that he might be taken away before he could commit himself. Long and painful silences punctuated the conversation. It was clear to Henry that the wound was mortal, though he did not realize that it was contagious. And every now and then as his mind rested on one or other aspect of the terrible, but at the same time exhilarating, crisis so suddenly reached in his life, Newman would break the silence with some characteristic reflection. He must produce a satisfactory answer to Dr. Wiseman, or the young hot-heads, like Ward, would be streaming over to Rome. (Ward, he had said prophetically to Rogers, would not let him go to sleep on Wiseman's article.) Again, he said that he could promise one thing—he would never take such a step, unless

Pusey and Keble agreed that he must. And then, again, with a swift change of sentiment, 'I wonder whether such a step would be justifiable if a hundred of us saw it to be their duty to take it with me.'

4. TRACT 90

Looking back on these events Newman, perhaps, under-estimated the length of time during which the impression they made lasted in his mind. It was natural that he should do so; for he lay under the imputation of dishonesty, of having been from at least 1835 a 'concealed Romanist'. Nor was the charge an easy one to parry. Parry it he did, with a contro-versial skill which silenced his calumniators in public, if not in private. But there was enough of truth in it to induce him, all unconsciously, to limit the devastating effect of Chalcedon and Augustine to an impossibly narrow space. 'The heavens had opened and closed again. The thought for the moment had been, "The Church of Rome will be found right after all"; and then it had vanished. My old convictions remained as before.' But, as he himself wrote in the preceding sentence, 'he who has seen a ghost, cannot be as if he had never seen it.'

He returned to Oxford to find the Romanistic tide setting in with an embarrassing fervour. During his absence Jack Morris, an intimate friend of Frederic Faber, had taken the pulpit at St. Mary's. 'What does he do' complained Newman to Bow-den 'on St. Michael's day but preach a sermon, not simply on angels, but on his one subject, for which he has a mono-mania, of fasting; nay, and say that it was a good thing, whereas angels feasted on festivals, to make the brute crea-tion fast on fast days: so I am told. May he (*salvis ossibus suis*) have a fasting horse the next time he goes steeple-chasing.' Not content with this, Morris had delivered another sermon abusing everyone who did not hold the Roman doctrine of the Mass. He was had up before the Vice-Chancellor,

formally admonished, and reported to the Bishop. Newman
disowned him; but he observed that the Vice-Chancellor's
family no longer came to his services.

Then his curate at Littlemore, John Bloxam of Magdalen,
a man old enough to know better, was reported to have
attended a Roman service during the vacation, in the private
chapel at Alton Towers (Lord Shrewsbury's seat), and to have
bowed his head at the Elevation of the Host. Interrogated,
Bloxam explained that he had indeed gone into the gallery of
the chapel every day, and had there said Morning and Evening Prayer by himself. But he had stayed on, kneeling at his
private devotions, during the Roman services which followed.
Newman felt obliged to tell the Bishop what had happened.
A long and distressing correspondence ensued, in which the
Bishop made it clear that he thought the Vicar to blame for
not discouraging such deplorable indiscretions on the part
of his young men. Bloxam was reduced to a state of collapse,
and resigned his curacy soon afterwards.

Newman's mind during 1840 was in a state of division
against itself. He was beaten—not by argument, but by his
own surrender to a vision—and yet he would not admit it.
His only way of dealing with the situation was to throw himself more violently than ever into controversy with the
Romanists. When a Roman Catholic priest named Spencer
came to Oxford in January, Newman categorically refused to
meet him at dinner; but at last Palmer persuaded him to give
Mr. Spencer an interview. 'I wish these R.C. priests had not
so smooth a manner,' he protested to Bowden 'it puts me
out.' To quiet his own uneasiness he wrote to Mr. Spencer and
told him that the voice was Jacob's voice, but the hands were
the hands of Esau. In the *British Critic* of January he published
a reply to Dr. Wiseman which quietened his uneasiness for a
time. Towards the end of the year he attacked the Roman
Church in the same paper with concentrated bitterness. 'We
see its agents,' he said, 'smiling and nodding and ducking to

attract attention, as gipseys make up to truant boys, holding
out tales for the nursery, and pretty pictures, and gilt ginger-
bread, and physic concealed in jam, and sugar-plums for
good children. . . . We Englishmen like manliness, openness,
consistency, truth.' Charles Kingsley could not have done it
better.

Nevertheless he took up with Pusey the suggestion which
Mr. Spencer had called to make. The idea was that Christians everywhere should offer up simultaneous prayer once a
week for the restoration of unity to the Church. After a great
deal of discussion it was resolved to ask for episcopal sanction.
The Bishop of Oxford, approached by Pusey, took refuge (as
usual) with the Archbishop. The Archbishop's reply indi-
cated a certain scepticism about the efficacy of prayer for an
unattainable object; and though he did not definitely say so
his language suggested that the kind of unity desired by Dr.
Pusey and his friends was not the kind of unity desired at
Lambeth. However, Newman drew up a form of prayers
which was used in private by many of the Tractarians.

In March he left Oriel for a time, ignoring his friends'
protests, and went to live at Littlemore. The immediate
reason was that Bloxam had been called away by his father's
illness. But the change of scene and occupation relieved
Newman's mind from the weight which lay upon it. He spent
his time teaching in the school and catechizing the children.
It became the fashion in Oxford to walk over to Littlemore
and watch the great man at his catechizing, 'done with such
spirit, and the children so up to it, answering with the greatest
alacrity'. So much did he enjoy this novel duty that an old
idea of coming to live permanently at Littlemore revived in
his mind. Ought he in that event to resign his Fellowship?
Perhaps he could retain it if he took theological pupils into
his house, which might then be regarded as a sort of Hall
depending on Oriel. Perhaps, too, there would be a movement
in favour of monastic establishments; his house might be then

'obliged to follow the fashion, and conform to a rule of discipline'. He put in this somewhat disingenuous way to Rogers, what he had broached a few days earlier in a more direct way to Pusey. He had, in fact, conceived a definite plan 'of building a monastic house in the place and coming to live in it myself'. He would still continue to preach at St. Mary's. Pusey, though in natural sympathy with the scheme, advised caution. It would not do for Newman to cut himself off from Oxford. What about his Tuesday evenings? What about the Provostship of Oriel, if Hawkins should be promoted? Would it not be wiser to name the house after an English rather than a Roman Saint (St. Gregory had been suggested)? And would it not be better to begin very modestly, with a small house—just two rooms for himself, and accommodation for three or four friends?

On this more modest scale the thing was done. In May he and a group of friends bought nine acres; and Newman wrote to Tom Mozley (who was something of an amateur architect) for hints about building. The land was to be planted with larches and firs; and the nucleus of the intended monastery was a range of stables at the corner of two lanes. This was converted into a group of cells connected by a sort of cloister, with a kitchen and a sizable library. It was not either beautiful or impressive. Mozley thought it depressing; and others called it barnlike. But Newman loved it. By November the planting was done and looked 'very nice'; and his own two rooms were nearly ready for his occupation. In the following March he was evidently living there, for a letter to Bowden on March 5, 1841, is dated from Littlemore.

As the notion of a quasi-monastic life on the edge of Oxford took hold of his mind, he began to consider if he should not resign St. Mary's. At last he wrote to ask Keble's advice. Was he not using St. Mary's for a purpose which did not properly belong to it—neglecting his parishioners in order to influence the University? Then his preaching was not acceptable to the authorities, nor was it (he must confess) 'calculated to defend that system of religion which has been received for 300 years, and of which the Heads of Houses are the legitimate maintainers in this place.' The Heads were right; his influence was undermining things established. 'Ought one' he asked, anticipating the charge which Kingsley was to bring against him, 'to be disgusting the minds of young men with the received religion, in the exercise of a sacred office, yet without a commission, and against the wish of their guides and governors?' Worse, he knew that he was disposing these young men towards Rome. And indeed he was far from sure that he was not in danger himself.

Keble thought that, if he resigned St. Mary's, people would think he was repenting of the movement altogether. The argument was thin; but it served its purpose. Newman decided to retain his living. After all, the English Church might be able to stand a yet greater infusion of Catholic truth. And at least he was championing religion against the great evil of the day—namely, rationalism.

For the rest, the year 1840 went quietly by. It was the calm before the storm. Right views and practices, he reported to Bowden, were spreading strangely. 'Yet I am not the less anxious on that account. Anglicanism has never yet been put to the test whether it will bear life; it may break to pieces in the rush and transport of existence, and die of joy.'

February 21 1841 was Newman's fortieth birthday. 'I never had such dreary thoughts' he said to his sister. Six days later appeared the famous Tract 90, entitled, *Remarks on Certain Passages in the Thirty-nine Articles*. No name was attached to it, but the world knew at once that it was Newman's.

The object of the Tract was 'merely to show that, while our Prayer Book is acknowledged on all hands to be of Catholic origin, our Articles also, the offspring of an uncatholic age, are, through God's good providence, to say the least, not uncatholic, and may be subscribed by those who aim at being Catholic in heart and doctrine.' Thus the Introduction; while the Conclusion pointed out with serious irony that, while the Articles were certainly intended to exclude a Catholic interpretation, equally certainly the intention had miscarried. And, this being so, Catholics were not merely at liberty but obliged to interpret the Articles in a Catholic sense. This conclusion was arrived at by a detailed and extremely ingenious examination of many of the Articles, word by word and sentence by sentence. A single example will indicate the general method. Article XXI declares that General Councils may err, and have sometimes erred. Certainly, agrees Newman, *unless* it is promised by God that they shall not err, as in the case of the Oecumenical Councils. And a highly subtle metaphysical argument applied to Article XXVIII demonstrated that the doctrine of Transubstantiation, as therein condemned, was not the same thing as the doctrine 'of a real super-local presence in the Holy Sacrament'.

The sensation which the Tract produced in Oxford was enormous and all but instantaneous. A week of deceptive silence, and the storm broke. The whole body of Protestant opinion was roused, just as it was roused in a far less consciously religious age by the Revised Prayer Book of 1927. The effective answer on each occasion was the same: 'This is what *you* mean and want; but it is not what *we* mean and want.' And an answer of this kind is final. The whirlpool of Tractarianism had drawn many different sorts of men into its vortex—men of subtle intelligence, warm imagination, devotional temperament, together with some whose qualities would have to be described in less complimentary terms. But it had not caught hold of the typical Englishman; still less had it converted the Heads of Houses. The latter, and the mass of tough ordinary folk, of whom they were the sharpened and polished exemplars, had watched the whole course of the movement with growing antipathy and mistrust. They had said—going by one of those short cuts to wisdom so unjustly closed to cleverer men: 'This means Rome.' They knew very well that if they once embarked upon the sea of dialectic they would be lost; and they had no intention whatever of being lost. They waited for the inevitable *démarche*; and, when it came, they pounced instantly on the unwary skirmisher.

Historians of the Movement have laid much stress on the fact that Newman was condemned without being heard in his self-defence. It is a waste of breath. The Tractarians had not shown themselves anxious to let Dr. Hampden defend himself; they were now hoist with their own petard. Certainly the Heads of Houses behaved clumsily and stupidly. But can anyone seriously maintain that, if Newman had been formally tried for heresy, the verdict of his judges would have been more favourable to him?

The same historians have shown, out of Newman's own mouth, how unexceptionable his motives were. He had been urged to keep his young men straight. The great difficulty was that of subscription to the Articles. It was therefore his simple duty to remove that difficulty if he could. This was all very well. No doubt this was a motive. But was it the only motive, was it even the real motive? Was not the Tract written, actually, for the sake of the 'hazardous experiment—like proving cannon' of trying how much the English Church would bear? Only a few weeks before the Tract was published he was pressing this notion on Keble, and insisting that 'as to the result, viz. whether this process will not approximate the whole English Church, as a body, to Rome, that is nothing to us.' In truth he wrote with a divided mind—half hoping that the Church would tolerate the 'large infusion of Catholic truth', half hoping that she would refuse it. Either way the air would be cleared.

And what, moreover, did he precisely mean by 'Catholic' truth? He no longer knew. In the confident days of the *Via*

Media he meant by it the doctrine of the early Universal Church, before the schism of East and West and the growth of Roman error. But already he had begun to see that the appeal to Antiquity was a doubtful criterion. In what sense were the Councils of Nicaea, Constantinople, Ephesus and Chalcedon true Councils, in which the Council of Trent (A.D. 1545) was not a true Council also?[1] His idea of Catholic truth was now hardly to be distinguished from the pure Roman doctrine defined at Trent. So far had he moved from Hurrell Froude's prejudice against the 'wretched Tridentines'.[2] The Tract, therefore, while it distinguished 'Catholic' from 'Romish' doctrine, distinguished also 'Romish' from 'Tridentine' doctrine. The latter could not have been condemned by the Articles, because the Articles were drawn up before the decrees of the Council. A man might consequently accept the Roman Catholic faith as defined by those decrees, while he repudiated the popular doctrines stigmatized as Romish by the reformers; and this was practically Newman's own position.

First on the warpath was the implacable Golightly. A number of Fellows and Tutors, galvanized by him into activity, met together and resolved on a letter of protest to the editor of the Tracts. Tait, the future Archbishop, drafted it, and was one of the four signatories, whose names were carefully chosen for tactical reasons. This was the famous Letter of the Four Tutors. It complained that the Tract opened the door to 'the most plainly erroneous doctrines and practices of the Church of Rome', and invited the anonymous author to come out into the open. It bore the date of Monday, March 8, and printed copies were being circulated in Oxford next day. Simultaneously Palmer, who had been cool towards Newman ever since the publication of Froude's *Remains*, wrote in the

[1] The wording of this question is taken from the draft of a letter dated in 1844, *Correspondence with Keble*, p. 22. But it is clear from the letter that the question had been in his mind for a 'very long' time.

[2] Tridentine is the adjective—'pertaining to Trent'.

warmest terms to thank him for this *'most valuable'* of all the Tracts, and did his best to counteract the swelling chorus of indignation.

Golightly continued his subterranean campaign. He called on the Vice-Chancellor and persuaded him to submit the Tract to the meeting of the Hebdomadal Board (i.e. the Heads of Houses) on Wednesday, March 10. The Heads were too angry to formulate any coherent resolution, and adjourned to Friday, when they decided, by a majority of nineteen to two, to censure the Tract, and appointed a subcommittee to draft the notice of censure during the week-end. They met again on Monday. Meanwhile Pusey had pointed out to the Provost of Oriel that it would be wiser to wait until Newman had published an explanation, upon which he was hard at work. Hawkins saw the force of this, and proposed delay. But the infuriated Heads would not listen to him. And on Tuesday morning the notice, declaring the principles of Tract 90 to be incompatible with the University Statutes, was published. Next day Newman published his defence in the form of an open letter to Dr. Jelf.

A judicial blunder, without doubt. But would the ultimate course of events have been any different if the Heads had waited for Newman's defence? Pusey believed so, and lamented ever after. But then Pusey, up to the very last moment, remained blind to the irresistible change which was taking place in Newman's religious opinions.

The blow fell somewhat heavily upon Newman himself. The change in his views had not yet fully and consciously worked itself out. He was still too closely bound to the Church to leave her; still unable to stomach what seemed to him the vulgar phenomena of popular Romanism. The claims of all those who looked to him as their teacher were a further brake upon his movements. He bowed his head to the storm, determined to reef his sail and go softly and humbly. In this spirit he wrote to the Vice-Chancellor acknowledging that

he was the author of the Tract, saying that his opinions had
not been shaken by the censure, but confessing that everything he attempted might be done in a better spirit. In the
same spirit he came to a *concordat* with the Bishop of Oxford.
Tract 90 was not to be suppressed. But no further Tracts were
to be published; and Newman was to write a public letter to
the Bishop, acknowledging the Bishop's disapproval of Tract
90. He professed himself satisfied with this bargain—as well he
might be. Tract 90 still existed, and had not even been formally
condemned. Perhaps the infusion of Catholic truth would be
tolerated by the Church, after all. His friends observed that
he had recovered his spirits, and so indeed he protested himself. People would soon see that the Tractarians were 'ducks
in a pond, knocked over but not knocked out'.

5. RETREAT

And now a new champion appeared in the lists. This was
William Ward, a young Fellow and Lecturer of Balliol. A
stout, lively, brilliant young man, not yet thirty, with an in-
satiable appetite for theological argument and a delight in
extreme conclusions, Ward was the *enfant terrible* of Newman's
spiritual family. He was also one of Dr. Arnold's failures. Not
that he was a Rugby boy. On the contrary, he was educated
at Winchester. But he was intimate at Oxford as an undergraduate with several Rugbeians, and he was drawn into the
circle of admiring young men which revolved about the
Doctor. 'Drawn' is perhaps the wrong word. It would be
truer to say that he burst into it. When doubt began to assail
him he dashed down to Rugby and sat up arguing in the
Headmaster's study far into the night. The next day Dr.
Arnold kept his bed in a state of complete exhaustion, while
Ward returned unappeased to Oxford, to transfer his allegiance to Newman. Soon after this he preached for Newman
at Littlemore; his sermon was one of Arnold's sermons, in-

geniously perverted by cunning additions and alterations, which it pleased him to think would have driven Arnold mad, if he could have heard them. After the service he walked back to Balliol with Jowett in the highest spirits, singing songs from the operas the whole way at the top of his fine voice.

This was the man who now plunged into the controversy over Tract 90 with two pamphlets in its defence. The defence was not of the sort which could smooth troubled waters. The Church of England, he said, was decayed and degraded; he spoke of the darkness of Protestant error; he used the language of respect towards Rome; he avowed that the natural meaning of the Articles, where it was plainly Evangelical, presented no stumbling-block to him since he subscribed to them himself 'in a non-natural sense'. This was too much for his Balliol colleagues, who obliged him to resign his lectureships. Ward, nothing abashed, and still remaining on the best of terms with the members of the Balliol common room, turned his attention to the *British Critic*. Tom Mozley had taken over the editorship from Newman. Under his easy-going rule the pages of that hitherto decorous review began to be monopolized by Ward and his equally extreme friend Oakeley. The blood of the moderates ran cold in their veins. Even Newman shuddered; and Mrs. Thomas Mozley's health became seriously affected.

It was all very uncomfortable for Newman. He had made up his mind to 'lie low and say nothing'. He was quite certain this was the right course. But it was not in Ward's nature to lie low; and the worst of it was that Newman could not honestly say that Ward was wrong, only that he was imprudent. Nor would Ward ever leave him alone. His skin was as thick as Newman's was thin. He plagued his leader, much as he had plagued Dr. Arnold; with the difference that Newman was moving in the same direction as himself—only not quite so fast. Events, too, would not leave Newman alone. He tried to settle quietly down to the works of Athanasius. But peace was impossible. The Bishops began to move against him and his friends. In July Winchester refused, in the most pointed manner, to admit Keble's curate to priest's orders. In September Gloucester and Bristol denounced Tract 90 in his charge. In October the appalling news reached Newman that the Archbishop and the Government had fallen in with M. Bunsen's long-cherished scheme of an Anglo-Prussian Bishopric in Jerusalem. The official leaders of the Catholic Church in England holding hands with Lutheran heretics and admitting them, without formal renunciation of their errors, to her communion! This act it was which brought him 'on to the beginning of the end'. Simultaneously came the affair of the Poetry Professorship. Keble's term had expired. Isaac Williams was proposed as his successor. At first no opposition was expected. Then, because Williams was a Tractarian, another candidate appeared on the scene. The election was fought as though it were a religious issue, passions running at their highest, and ended in another Tractarian defeat. In the midst of it Oxford resounded with the news that Mr. Sibthorpe of Magdalen had been to Oscott and come away a Roman Catholic. True, Mr. Sibthorpe was soon disillusioned and was to be seen dining at Magdalen and turning up the whites of his eyes as though nothing whatever had happened. But he was followed by a colleague—Mr. Seager—the gentleman whose embroidered scarf had so much upset the Bishop; and Mr. Seager did not return.

The *coup de grâce* came with the Bishop of Oxford's charge in May 1842. Many other Bishops had followed the example of Winchester, of Gloucester and Bristol. The Bishop of London was reported to have said at 'a dinner-table full of young clergymen' that no power on earth would induce him to ordain any person holding the opinions expressed in Tract 90. And now Newman's own Bishop declared *ex cathedra* that 'although the licence of Calvinistic interpreters had often gone beyond what was attempted in the Ninetieth Tract he could not reconcile himself to a system of interpretation which was so subtle that by it the Articles might be made to mean anything or nothing.' The Bishop had borrowed this unfortunate phrase from his chaplain, who never afterwards forgave himself for it.

The Oxford charge was succeeded by others of a more violent nature. Everywhere, it seemed, the rulers of the Church were doing their best to deny the Movement which put their office so high. The strain on Newman's and Pusey's nerves showed itself (at least this is the most charitable interpretation) in fantastic comments upon the deaths of two particularly hostile Bishops. When Shuttleworth of Chichester died at the beginning of 1842, before delivering his charge, Newman wrote to Pusey that it was a solemn, sobering event. 'I don't think anything has happened in my time which has so struck me.' And when in August Dickinson of Meath died on the very day on which he was to have delivered a charge against the Tracts Pusey agreed with Newman that it was 'awfully strange how two of these Charges were thus withheld. It looks like "Thus far shalt thou go."' If God had killed a few more Bishops, would Newman have been saved for the Church of England?

Death, however, stayed his hand amongst the Bishops and did not visit the enemies of Catholic truth in Oxford. The counter-revolution was having things all its own way. The Provost of Oriel was refusing testimonials to young men of his college, candidates for Holy Orders, who were known sympathizers with the Romanizing party. High Churchmen stood no chance of obtaining Fellowships. Colleges changed their dinner-hour on Sundays to prevent undergraduates from attending the sermon at St. Mary's. Espionage, *agents provocateurs*, ruthless interrogations—all the symptoms of political terrorization, so painfully familiar to readers of modern newspapers—were appearing on the small ecclesiastical stage of Oxford in the early 'forties. The Party was on the run.

The whole academical pack snapped and snarled at their heels.

From this miserable scene, which he described afterwards in his novel *Loss and Gain*, Newman (in February 1842) withdrew permanently to his embryo monastery at Littlemore. He was on his deathbed, as a member of the Anglican Church. But he had scarcely yet admitted this fact to his conscious mind. He thought of the retirement to Littlemore in terms of the Duke of Wellington's despatches. Littlemore was his Torres Vedras. Had he lived a century later, Gallipoli might have provided him with a truer analogy.

For the effect of all these external blows had been supplemented by an internal hemorrhage. Interrupted as his readings in Athanasius had been, the same spectre which had thrilled him so exquisitely in the history of the Monophysite controversy had arisen during the previous summer, even more horrific, out of the vasty deeps of Arianism. How could he have been so blind in those far-off days, when *The History of the Arians* provided him with the foundations of his *Via Media*? For now that he went back over the old familiar ground he 'saw clearly that in the history of Arianism, the pure Arians were the Protestants, the semi-Arians were the Anglicans, and that Rome now was what it was then. The truth lay, not with the *Via Media*, but in what was called "the extreme party".' Athanasius had reopened the breach in his system made by Leo. The sea was pouring in over the fertile levels so painfully reclaimed from Antiquity. The struggle to repair the damage seemed hopeless. Storms and darkness increased the difficulty of the task, which he must, moreover, accomplish alone.

He did what he could, not by attempting to fill in the breach, but by contracting his defences. The improvised theory, which took the place of the *Via Media*, was delivered in four sermons at St. Mary's in December, 1841. It was based upon a comparison between the Church of England and the

Ten Tribes of Israel. Just as Israel rebelled against the House of David and fell into schism and worse than schism, so had England rebelled against the Catholic Church and fallen into schism. But just as the Divine Mercy was not withdrawn from the Ten Tribes, so it had not been withdrawn from the Church of England. The Church had her divines and her saints, even as Israel had the prophets Elijah and Elisha. The prophets had not demanded that Israel, as the price of salvation, should be reconciled with Judah. No more, then, was it to be demanded of the Church of England that she should submit to Rome. She had the Apostolic Succession; she held the Apostolic Creed; she had the 'note of holiness of life'.

For the time being Newman was extremely pleased with this ingenious improvisation. Strongly as he was drawn to Rome—he was freely admitting as much now to his friends— the fear of idolatry held him back. His new theory enabled him to say that it was his duty to remain an Anglican, that he was 'content to be with Moses in the desert, or with Elijah excommunicated from the Temple'. Nevertheless the 'frightful suspicion' was now constantly present to his mind that he might perhaps break down in the event. He said so, at the beginning of 1842, to Robert Wilberforce, now Archdeacon of the East Riding. Wilberforce was never 'so shocked by any communication' and began to regret that he had ever taken up with so uncertain a study as theology.

The new theory, as preached at St. Mary's, and the retirement to Littlemore set the tongues of all the scandalmongers wagging. It was said that Newman and his intimates were already Roman Catholics, that they had been given a special dispensation by the Pope to remain in the Church of England, so as the better to disrupt it. It was said that the Littlemore establishment was a monastery under Roman discipline. Newspaper publicity threw its distorting beams upon the dingy row of converted loose boxes, and revealed dormitory cells, chapel, refectory and cloisters advancing to Gothic perfection. Undergraduates and even Doctors of Divinity spied into the interior, while Heads of Houses walked their horses suspiciously round about. The Warden of Wadham knocked at the door and asked to see the monastery. 'We have no monasteries here' replied Newman and slammed the door in his visitor's face. What then was he doing at Littlemore? Partly, he went up there in order to say his prayers as he thought they ought to be said. It was impossible to do so at Oriel, where the sound of his voice, as he wrestled with his Maker far into the night, was plainly to be heard in the street. Partly he went there to be alone with his own thoughts. But the newspapers were nearer the truth than he would allow. He went there in order to practise, with his friends, a rule of life and a system of devotions framed on the Roman model.

A time-table, dated 1842, shows how the day was spent.[1] He rose before five, and said Matins and Lauds from five to half past six. Breakfast followed, then Prime, then a period of study, with Tierce. At ten he went to morning prayers in the Anglican church. Three hours of study followed, with Sext— there was no mid-day meal. Between two and three there was an hour of recreation, before afternoon prayers in the church. More recreation; another spell of study, with Nones. Then supper at six, lasting half an hour, and followed by an hour of recreation. Two hours of study ended with Vespers and Compline. From a quarter past ten to five was allotted to 'sleep, etc.' The twenty-four hours were divided by this programme as follows: Devotions $4\frac{1}{2}$, study 9, meals 1, recreation $2\frac{3}{4}$, sleep $6\frac{3}{4}$. No talking was allowed except between two and half past seven.

Mark Pattison has preserved for us in his Memoirs his diary of a ten days' visit to Littlemore in 1843. It opens and closes with entries, which show more vividly than pages of description how Newman held the younger generation in thrall, even when his star was dipping to the horizon. Pattison was a

---

[1] *Correspondence of Newman with Keble*, p. 295.

man of thirty, and his Tractarianism was only an interlude
between the crude Evangelicalism of his youth and the
learned polished Agnosticism of his old age. Already he had
begun to despise the mental calibre of the young apostles.
But this was the manner of his diary: 'Newman kinder, but
not perfectly so. Vespers at eight. Compline at nine. How
low, mean, selfish, my mind has been to-day; all my good
seeds vanished; grovelling, sensual, animalish; I am not
indeed worthy to come under this roof.' Again: 'How uncomfortable have I made myself all this evening by a childish
fancy that once got into my head—I could not get out of it—
a weak jealousy of N.'s good opinion. Oh, my God! take from
me this petty pride. . . .' And finally: 'On a review of the
whole time I am thankful for much, much happiness. I felt
lifted more into the world of the spirit than ever before;
thought I had more faith, but how much evil was mixed up
with this in my heart; thought so much of little mortifications,
yet talked as if they were familiar to me; felt so anxious for
N.'s good opinion, and suffered my mind to wander miserably
in prayers.'

6. THE PENULTIMATE STAGE

In February 1843 a paper called the *Conservative Journal*,
under the heading OXFORD AND ROME, published an anonymous *Retractation of Anti-Catholic Statements*. That the writer was
Newman was evident to everybody. Why then had he withheld his name? And what was the reason for the retractation?
His sister wrote discreetly wondering about the history of this
rather mysterious document, which was making a great hub-
bub in the world. He answered that it was making very little
talk in Oxford. There had been letters passing between himself
and Pusey on the subject of this recantation. All he had done,
he insisted, was to unsay his abuse of Rome; he had not said a
word on doctrinal matters. But though Pusey had been un-

easy about Tract 90—defending it rather from love of its author than because he approved its matter; and though he was puzzled and unhappy about the recantation—which looked unmistakably like the prelude to something worse; still he could not think anything wrong which Newman thought it right to do. He saw his friend in a halo of martyrdom. 'I had infinitely rather than the whole world' he wrote 'have all the judgments, harsh speeches, mistrust which have fallen upon you, only that I am not fit for them.'

Pusey's suppressed wish was very quickly granted. On May 14 he preached in the Cathedral, before the University, a sermon upon the Holy Eucharist, in the course of which he used a number of expressions, borrowed from or modelled upon the language of the Fathers, which were supposed by many of his hearers to imply a belief in Transubstantiation and other heretical doctrines. He spoke for example of touching with the lips Christ's cleansing Blood, and his language appeared to suggest that the Sacrament was a perpetual repetition of the sacrifice of Christ upon the Cross. A day or two later the Vice-Chancellor, moved thereto by the Lady Margaret Professor, sent for the sermon. Pusey, characteristically, asked for a delay of two or three days, in order to add references; it disturbed him to think that his judges might, through sheer ignorance, 'condemn e.g. St. Cyril of Alexandria, when they thought they were only condemning me.'

Meanwhile the Vice-Chancellor selected six Doctors to sit in judgment upon the sermon, when it should reach him. These included the Lady Margaret Professor (the delator of the sermon) and the Provost of Oriel. All six were hostile to 'Puseyism', not excepting Jelf, who consented to serve on the Board in spite of the fact that he was Pusey's oldest friend. Jelf seems to have honestly hoped that he might succeed in acting as a brake upon the violence of his colleagues. The hope was not realized. If the condemnations of Hampden and Newman had been open to formal criticism, the pro-

ceedings of the six Doctors and of the Vice-Chancellor himself broke every canon of justice and common sense. First they
condemned the sermon without allowing Pusey to appear in
person to defend it. Next they attempted to make him recant,
under threat of suspension if he did not, having first obtained
from him a promise of absolute secrecy with regard to these
negotiations. Pusey was foolish enough to give this promise,
and was thus entirely cut off from his friends. The recantation was to consist in putting his signature to a document prepared by his judges. Two such documents were prepared;
but after Pusey had pointed out the theological difficulties
which they involved, the six Doctors—alarmed at the prospect of being drawn into a discussion beyond their abilities—
abandoned this course of action and advised the Vice-
Chancellor to suspend Dr. Pusey from preaching within the
University for a period of two years. The decree of suspension
was sent to him privately and not published. When, by
Pusey's dignified protest, it became known that he had been
suspended without a hearing, the Provost of Oriel tried to
suggest that he had, in effect, been given a hearing in the
course of the secret negotiations. Indeed he actually accused
Pusey of dishonesty because he had, in pursuit of his promise,
said nothing whatever about them. Dr. Hawkins's long
struggle with the monster to which his own college had given
birth had made him none too scrupulous about his weapons.

But to suspend Pusey was a very different thing from cen-
suring Tract 90. Not only did Pusey succeed in having the
last word in a further Protest to the Vice-Chancellor. The
sympathies of many who were not Puseyites at all were
entirely with him. Moreover, everybody asked, on what
grounds he had been suspended. What *was* the heretical
doctrine he had been found guilty of expressing? Moderate
men, independent of party, like Frank Faber of Magdalen,
protested 'that the silence of the gentlemen who examined
the sermon is very perplexing to us who may have to preach

at some time or other before the University.' But the oracles
of orthodoxy were dumb. The Vice-Chancellor took refuge
in a silence, which (he asserted) was prescribed to him by the
silence of the University Statutes on the point which Mr.
Faber (and many others) had raised. When a body of distinguished Oxonians, including Mr. Gladstone and Mr.
Justice Coleridge, addressed a letter to the Vice-Chancellor,
protesting that 'when a sermon is adjudged unsound, the
points in which its unsoundness consists should be distinctly
stated', Dr. Wynter refused to receive it and admonished the
signatories 'to have a more careful regard to the oaths by
which they bound themselves upon admission to their respective degrees'. This exhibition of academic folly exposed
the Vice-Chancellor naked to the storm. The newspapers
commented happily on the spectacle of an Oxford Doctor
rebuking a Judge of the High Court for not observing an
oath. Even the Provost of Oriel turned and rent him. The
affair ended in public merriment, a comfortable martyrdom
for Pusey, and a general conviction that the government of
the University of Oxford needed overhauling. Earnest
admirers mourned for Pusey—poor Mrs. Hook, the wife of the
Vicar of Leeds, was found by her husband crying over his
Protest. But there was no necessity for tears. A little unjust
persecution was exactly what the cause most needed.

Newman, from Littlemore, watched his friend's ordeal with
sympathy and gave him some excellent practical advice. But
a tone of detachment crept into his letters. He was wrestling
with a problem of his own—whether the time had not come
to resign his office as Vicar of St. Mary's. It was to Keble, and
not to Pusey, that he turned for advice. 'To whom' he said
pathetically 'would Hurrell go, or wish me to go but to you?'
The summer was filled with this long and painful correspondence.[1] It began, on May 4, with Newman's 'shocking'

[1] Published for the first time in full in the *Correspondence of Newman with
Keble and Others*.

avowal (it was his own epithet) that he considered the Roman
Catholic Communion the Church of the Apostles, England to
be in schism, and 'that what grace is amongst us (which,
through God's mercy, is not little) is extraordinary, and from
the overflowings of His Dispensation.' Keble must have fore-
seen what was coming. But this direct confirmation of his worst
fears was almost more than he could bear. He blamed himself bitterly for having engaged in these high matters with so
little knowledge and preparation. He felt that the responsibility for his 'dearest Newman's' unsettlement lay ultimately
with himself. Gone, utterly, was the old unaffected joyous
exuberance belonging to those glad days 'when master was
the greatest boy of them all.' Gone all the gay classical quips
and humorous rusticities. The Keble of 1843 was a depressed, almost a broken man, pitifully anxious to be of service to his brilliant pupil, pitifully shrinking from the now
inevitable blow.

At the beginning of September Newman had still not finally
made up his mind about St. Mary's. But he was finding it
more and more difficult to hold his young men back. One
impetuous member of the Littlemore community had just
broken his promise to Newman of remaining quiet for three
years and was being received into the Roman Communion.
This seems to have been the conclusive factor. A suspicion of
what was coming was abroad. 'No Newman yesterday' wrote
Frank Faber in a letter dated October 2. 'After the prayers
I had the wickedness to go to the south door to listen if it was
the silver voice. Tones anything but silvery fell on my
tympanum, but I knew them to be Marriott's and so I went
in being sure of a good sermon.' On the 7th Newman wrote
to the Bishop of Oxford for permission to resign St. Mary's.
It was necessary for the formal act of resignation to be performed before a notary at Doctor's Commons. After a sleepless night he took the train to London—it is the first mention
of the railway in his history—on the 18th, returning on the

same day. On the 24th he preached for the last time at St.
Mary's, and on the next day at Littlemore he preached
'No. 604, my last sermon'.[1] A few days later, at St. Mary's, he
took his final farewell of his ministry in the English Church
by celebrating the Holy Communion, together with Pusey.
'Some who were present in the gloom of that early October
morning'—so Dr. Liddon described the scene—'felt that
they were assisting at the funeral of a religious effort which
had failed.'

There could be no doubt now of what was coming. There
was, indeed, no real doubt in Newman's own mind. He was
not yet prepared to make the definite move. He made others
wait, if he could, and waited himself, in a state which he
called *indifferentia*, for a sign or a call from above. The conviction must be allowed time to prove itself beyond all possibility of doubt. The emotional ties to the past must be
allowed time to dissolve. There were moments when he
spoke and wrote as if he were not yet certain. But what could
be more definite than his language to Manning, at this time
Archdeacon of Chichester, when Manning wrote to ask why
he had resigned St. Mary's? 'Because' he said 'I think the
Church of Rome the Catholic Church, and ours not a part of
the Catholic Church, because not in communion with Rome,
and I felt I could not honestly be a teacher in it any longer.'
This was in October 1843. And in November 1844 he assured
Keble 'for three full years I have been in a state of unbroken
certainty.' He put himself entirely on the ground of intellectual certainty. Nevertheless he continued for some time to
draw a distinction between the belief that Rome was the one
true Church, and the corollary (obvious as it would seem
to most people) that he ought to join her. All his feelings and
wishes, he told Jemima, were against change. He was setting
his face absolutely towards the wilderness. He was giving up
friends, popularity, income. All this was true, so far as he

[1] Quoted on page 346.

could judge of himself. But the wilderness has its own secret fascination.

Manning communicated Newman's answers to his letters to Mr. Gladstone. 'I stagger to and fro' wrote the President of the Board of Trade 'like a drunken man, and am at my wit's end.' His first thought was that Newman must have been playing a double part. As the correspondence continued he began, as he thought, to realize the state of Newman's mind and to hope that his secession might be prevented. The hope was inspired by the phrasing of a letter written to Manning on Christmas Eve, in which Newman spoke of remaining 'where I am as long as I can.' Every effort, Gladstone insisted, must be made to bind Newman to the Church by 'cords of silk'. The Bishops must be persuaded to moderate their language. Newman must be warned 'of the immense consequences that may hang upon his movements.' A little flattery —in Gladstonian language 'every manifestation of sympathy and confidence in him, as a man'—might have a useful effect. But the time for cords of silk was over.

The correspondence with Keble and Jemima went on. Letters rained upon Littlemore—letters of abuse, of earnest argument, of passionate pleading, of request for spiritual counsel, letters from strangers, from old schoolfellows, from former pupils, from friends and enemies and perplexed clergymen. They were all answered, at patient length. The life of the little community was of the plainest and most rigorous description. It astonished the Italian priest who stayed there in 1845. 'A Capuchin monastery' he said 'would appear a great palace when compared with Littlemore.' Round Newman were a handful of devotees—St. John, Dalgairns, Bowles, Stanton; others, like Albany Christie, came and went. They were not men of the calibre of his old friends. 'It was a general wonder' according to Mark Pattison 'how Newman himself could be content with' their society. But it was the only kind of society tolerable to his inflamed sensibilities.

When he went down into Oriel he felt himself to be an uneasy *revenant*; the Fellows, the young men, even the college servants eyed him curiously; the very stones had an unwelcoming look. Discussion had become a mere weariness. The rational conflict, such as it had been, was nearly over. He could provide all the intellectual conversation which Littlemore needed, when he took his disciples out walking, going so fast that they could scarcely keep up with him, and talking with his old fascination on every subject, except the one which was in all their minds. In his own study, when he was not answering letters, he was at work on an annotated translation of Athanasius, which was 'very trying' but hardly an exercise for the higher powers of his mind. The other literary work on which he was engaged, as editor of a series of *Lives of the English Saints*, was not, in spite of his anger with Kingsley for deriding it, an undertaking governed by very high critical standards. For the rest he entered cheerfully enough into the simple little jokes of his rather insipid household, writing for example to St. John away on a visit to Norwood that the absent brother's favourite tin canister was in danger and that Bowles had robbed his mother's garden of all her bulbs. Trivialities of this sort were a relief from the intensity of his prayers and the exhausting mechanical labour of translation and letter-writing.

There was only one friend now to whom he talked without reserve, and this was the latest of them all. Ambrose St. John was a fair-haired young curate, with a passion for mountaineering, inclined towards Transubstantiation and the Invocation of Saints, very earnest, very unselfish, very much in need of a hero to worship, neither deeply read nor originally gifted, but sufficiently intelligent and educated to fill the *rôle* of a useful listener. He paid a short visit to Littlemore in June, 1843. The two men were instantly attracted to each other. St. John refused the offer of a curacy in order to return to Littlemore at the end of July. From that time to his death in

1875 he was scarcely ever parted from Newman. It was to him that Newman dedicated the *Apologia* in words of almost passionate tenderness: 'And to you especially, dear Ambrose St. John; whom God gave me, when He took every one else away; who are the link between my old life and my new; who have now for twenty-one years been so devoted to me, so patient, so zealous, so tender; who have let me lean so hard upon you; who have watched me so narrowly; who have never thought of yourself, if I was in question. And in you I gather up and bear in memory those familiar affectionate companions and counsellors, who in Oxford were given to me, one after another, to be my daily solace and relief. . . .' And when, eleven years later, this companion too was taken from him the old man, now seventy-four, threw himself upon the bed where St. John's body lay, and remained there all the night in a passion of overwhelming grief.

In this new friendship, closer and more intimate and lasting than any other, Newman found the support he needed for his adventure into the unknown. He could look nowhere else. Bowden was dying; Hurrell Froude was dead; Rogers had written sadly to say that their intimacy was ended; Henry Wilberforce was hanging back; Pusey was only not divided from him because he was unable to follow the workings of Newman's mind; Keble was a broken reed; Ward and Oakeley and Frederic Faber, in their various ways, an exasperation, rather than a comfort. Even if any of these had been keeping exact step with him, none of them could give the single and entire devotion which St. John humbly offered him. And even if they had offered it, he could not have taken it. From this young ingenuous adorer, so plainly sent to him by God, he could accept what it distressed him to observe in men whom he regarded as his equals or his superiors. When Judge Coleridge proposed a private address to Newman, assuring him of 'gratitude, veneration and love' and Keble told him of it, he was deeply shocked. 'Such words as venera-

tion, love, etc., I really could not bear. I am not used to them.
I have never heard them . . . I really could not bear them.'
No doubt he could not have borne the *words* even from St.
John; but he lived on the reality.

In the uncritical society of Littlemore Newman's puerile
love of supernatural and miraculous stories revived unchecked. Mark Pattison observed this 'lurking fondness for the
miraculous' during his stay. His diary recorded some specimens of the talk at dinner—how St. Macarius stood upright
in his cell for a week without eating anything, but chewed a
palm-leaf out of humility; how St. Goderick stood all night
in the river up to his neck, and frozen; how a blasphemer in
a Leicestershire public-house uttered the common oath,
Strike me blind! and was on the instant taken at his word by
a flash of lightning, but became a Cistercian and recovered his
sight on first receiving the sacrament. It is fair to add that
stories of this kind were current elsewhere than at Littlemore.
Pusey, writing to Newman in July, 1844, related with gloomy
relish how a poor wretched woman who had taken the wafer
into her mouth without the intention of swallowing it was
suddenly seized by a devil, and declared that her soul was
lost—'a most dreadful instance of what you allude to in a
sermon, God's awful avenging of the profanation of the Holy
Eucharist.' Readers of *Loss and Gain* will remember how the
hero, visited by an unctuous dissenting minister and at a loss
how to get rid of him, seized a crucifix and drove him,
slobbering with terror, down the staircase into the street.

The weaker elements in Newman's mind were coming to
the surface. The old ideal of grave stability had gone; a new
ideal of emotional surrender was replacing it. The quality of
his thought was beginning to decline. It had always been
exercised, unhappily for the world, in an unnaturally limited
field. The boundaries were now contracting further; his
powers, used for a prescribed purpose, lost their elasticity.
Only when Kingsley's libel threw him back in imagination

into the days of his greatness was he to give of his best again. 'What I wrote as a Protestant' he lamented on the threshold of his sixtieth year 'had far greater power, force, meaning, success, than my Catholic works, and this troubles me a great deal.'

There was no failure in his powers as a letter-writer. But the egotistical tendency always present in his character increased, in proportion as the desire of self-surrender increased, and began to distort his whole vision, until everything that happened seemed to have happened for his own spiritual good. God, he felt sure, as he explained in a very long letter to Keble, 'repeatedly and variously chastised me and at last to win me from the world He took from me a dear sister.' And then, when he was in Sicily, 'it seemed as if someone were battling to destroy me, and the idea has long been in my mind, though I cannot say when it came on, that my enemy was then attempting to destroy me.' He was saved for some great work. To these and similar ideas he recurred again and again, until it became as clear to his mind as a mathematical conclusion, that he had all along been led towards Rome and that the great work for which he had been saved was not the Movement which had so tragically (he said, later, absurdly) failed, but the conversion of England to Roman Catholicism.

And so he began to prepare Keble and Pusey and the sister with whom he was most in sympathy for what was coming. It was hard to convince Pusey. Words had to be picked for their effect. 'And now my dear Pusey,' he concluded a series of letters in August 1844 'do take in the whole of the case, nor shut your eyes, as you so kindly do continually.' The blow fell on Pusey with far greater force than his own suspension or the loss of his little daughter, Lucy, a few months earlier. 'I do not shut my eyes now' he answered, with a pathetically unusual directness; 'I feel everything I do is hollow, and dread its cracking. . . . I seem as if the waters were gathered

on heaps on either side; yet trust that we are Israel, not
Pharaoh's army, and so that they will not fall.' A few days
later Bowden died, and Pusey knew a flicker of hope. Newman could not see his oldest friend die in such calm confidence of salvation, still less could he see Bowden's children
'finding quite a solace of their pain in the Daily Prayer',
without feeling that the Church of England must, after all,
have something to be said for her still. He was a little thrown
back. Over Bowden's coffin he 'sobbed bitterly, to think that
he left me still dark as to what the way of truth was.' But to
St. John he put the Church no higher than 'a sort of Zoar, a
place of refuge and temporary rest because of the steepness
of the way'. It was not long before he was prepared to resume
the ascent.

There was still one ludicrous incident to be played out
before the curtain fell. The *British Critic* had come to an end
in the autumn of 1843, and the teeming brain of Ward found
itself without an organ of expression. His ideas piled themselves up into a book—a reply to an attack made by Palmer
upon the *British Critic* as Ward and Oakeley had remade it
nearer to their hearts' desire—projected as a pamphlet, but
issuing in a volume of 600 pages, called *The Ideal of a Christian
Church considered in Comparison with Existing Practice*. Ward, in
this work, was not content with maintaining that the English
Church failed to exhibit the true notes of a Church; or that
the Roman Church, on the other hand, exhibited them all.
He rejoiced to find 'the whole cycle of Roman doctrine gradually possessing numbers of English Churchmen'. And he
exulted in the thought that, while he had plainly declared
that in subscribing the Articles he renounced no Roman
doctrine, he had not been visited with any ecclesiastical
rebuke.

Such a challenge could scarcely be ignored. But the retaliation was conceived with a humourless rancour, which would
have made the proceedings into a pure farce if it had not been

for the fact that Newman and Tract 90 were dragged in. Even so, the episode of Ward's *Ideal* is one of the comic events which relieve tragic histories. 'The mischief-makers' Dean Church relates 'were at work, flitting about the official lodgings at Wadham and Oriel.' Conspicuous among them was, no doubt, the busy figure of Golightly, in whose mind the task of annihilating Newmanism had become so much of an obsession, that he trembled to walk the streets at night, lest he might fall into a Tractarian ambush. It was proposed, not only to censure the *Ideal*, and to degrade Ward to the status of an undergraduate, but also to censure the principles of Tract 90, by a formal act of Convocation. The Heads of Houses were delighted with the idea. But Church himself was one of the Proctors. He has given, in his *Oxford Movement*, an account of the proceedings in Convocation, which it would be an impertinence to paraphrase. It is enough to say that the *Ideal* was condemned by a majority of 777 to 386; Ward's degradation to undergraduate status was carried by a majority of 569 to 511; but the motion to censure Tract 90 was vetoed by the Proctors. The motion, said Dean Church, 'was the last act of a long and deliberately pursued course of conduct; and if it was the last, it was because it was the upshot and climax, and neither the University nor anyone else would endure that it should go on any longer.' The proposal was abandoned, and was not revived when the new Proctors took office.

Ten years later Parliament descended upon the University, and took away from the Heads of Houses the oligarchic power they had so foolishly misused. But Parliament also took away not long afterwards from the Church of England the exclusive control she had hitherto exercised over the University. The ultimate victory did not lie with the party, of whom Dean Church became not the least distinguished spokesman.

But this is a consequence not strictly relevant to the story of the Oxford Movement. Nor is the highly absurd picture of the rotund and cheerful Ward wearing a commoner's gown, and receiving the congratulations of his friends outside the Sheldonian Theatre upon the unexpected announcement of his engagement to be married, appropriate to an account of Newman's last agonies. The scene shall end with the passionate defence of the man, with whom he was no longer on terms of intimacy, published by Frederic Rogers five days before the Proctors used their right to veto. The charge of dishonesty, he said, was plainly insinuated by the proposed resolution. Those who had been honoured by Mr. Newman's friendship must say what they felt about such a charge. But it was not easy to find words to say it. 'When they see the person whom they have been accustomed to revere as few men are revered, whose labours, whose greatness, whose tenderness, whose singleness and holiness of purpose, they have been permitted to know intimately . . . called again to account for a matter now long ago accounted for . . . it does become very difficult to speak without sullying what it is a kind of pleasure to feel is *his* cause by using hard words, or betraying it by not using them.'

7. FINALE

The stress of the long inner struggle—not less exhausting because it was largely subconscious; the endless letter-writing; the arduous devotions and meditations; the mean Littlemore diet; the fastings; the lack of sleep; all these causes combined to weaken Newman's physical health. When his favourite physician, Dr. Babington, saw him at the end of Lent in 1844 he was alarmed by his patient's 'shrunk and debilitated' appearance. In September he received a report from Newman which revived his anxiety, and he spoke out sharply. 'It is impossible to avoid the suspicion that, partly by overwork, and partly by deficient nutriment, you are rendering yourself unfit for exertion.' In November Newman went to take Babington's advice 'for my drowsiness and unsteadiness of handwriting'. The doctor advised tonics. But tonics had a way of throwing too much blood to his head. A certain relaxation of the religious discipline seems to have followed. But the lost vigour did not return. 'My days' he lamented 'are gone like a shadow, and I am withered like grass.' At the age of forty-four, in what should have been the prime of his life, he wrote and thought of himself as already an old man.

After the letters to Keble, the correspondence between Newman and his favourite sister Jemima throws the fullest light upon his state of mind. In some ways the letters to Jemima reveal more than the letters to Keble. They show the barrier of reserve between brother and sister, which hid his own longing for sympathy and her longing to give it, broken down at last. This new intimacy dated from a letter from Jemima in November, 1844, in which she confessed how miserable she had been made by some expression of her brother's, implying a lack of sympathy and understanding on her part. 'You must know, dear John, that your slightest act or feeling awakens my interest and anxiety. . . . I could write no letters and ask no questions, and dreaded to be spoken to by anybody I saw. . . . I am afraid I shall not at all have succeeded in justifying myself, because I know reserve and all feelings and habits connected with it are a great fault with me.'

Her brother answered with a burst of painful confidences: 'I have gone through a great deal of pain, and have been very much cut up. The one predominant distress upon me has been this unsettlement of mind I am causing. This is a thing that has haunted me day by day. And for days I have had a literal pain in and about my heart, which I suppose at any moment I could bring on again. The translation of St. Athanasius is, I am glad to say, just coming to an end, and I shall (so be it) relax. I suppose I need it. This has been a very trying year.' He went on to say that his joining the Roman

Church was only a question of time. 'And now what a deal I
have said about myself. I wonder how many I's are in this
letter. . . . I am tired and out of spirits.'

A little later he gave her one of the reasons which delayed
him from taking the final step. 'It is the fear that there is some
secret undetected fault which is the cause of my belief which
keeps me where I am, waiting.' He had not discovered it, he
said naively, nor had Keble, to whom he had submitted a
record, kept for the purpose, of his most intimate thoughts.[1]
'Now, my dear Jemima,' he continued after an anxious discussion of his own position, as one who was no longer in
ignorance of the truth, 'I am sure you will feel that I am not
arguing, but I wish you to understand where I stand, and
what I feel—for my own comfort. I have never wished there
should be any reserve between us—it is most repugnant to my
nature to conceal things . . . it will be a great comfort to me
if you will let me be open with you, and to tell you what the
state of my mind is. Indeed, there can be no exercise of love
between persons without this openness.'

About this time he put aside all other work to write the
Essay on the Development of Doctrine. And as he wrote it, 'while
his eyes were yet dim, and his breast laden, and he could but
employ Reason in the things of Faith', it became clear to his
mind that he must wait no longer. The book cost him incredible pains. Every page of it was rewritten and rewritten
again, while he stood at his high desk for hours, and whole
days, at a time. The disciples watched him growing paler and
thinner, till it seemed to their worshipping gaze that the sunshine was breaking through the almost transparent face.
It was a great task that he was engaged upon—nothing less
than that of justifying Roman 'corruptions' as legitimate
developments of primitive doctrine. With magnificent
rhetoric he turned the very calumnies which men brought

[1] It is greatly to be wished that this journal, if it exists, and others like
it, should be given to the world.

JOHN HENRY NEWMAN
From the water colour drawing by Sir W. C. Ross (1845)
in the possession of Keble College

against Rome into jewels in her crown. The historic past became the historic present. Argument passed into poetry; reason into faith.

In July 1845 Jemima came to pay a last visit to Little-more, lodging in the village for a fortnight, and walking daily with her brother. She found him looking 'just the same'; but perhaps it needed the eye of faith to observe the sun shining through the wasted face. There was no longer any secret about what was coming. Down in Oxford Pusey knew it and brought himself to believe that Newman's case was 'a special dispensation'—for some peculiar purpose of the Almighty's which he was not very well able to define. At Hursley Keble waited anxiously by his wife's sick-bed. In London Mr. Gladstone gloomily reckoned up the terrifying consequences. Golightly rubbed his hands; Wiseman, too, but for a different motive. All over England—incredible as it now seems—there was a kind of thunderous hush. 'The first drops of the storm began to fall.' St. John and Dalgairns, of the Littlemore community, went first. Others were going in other parts of the country. On October 3 Newman wrote to the Provost of Oriel to resign his Fellowship; and on the 6th the Provost replied, accepting the resignation, and expressing the most earnest hope that whatever Newman did he might 'still at least be saved from some of the worst errors of the Church of Rome, such as praying to human Mediators or falling down before images.'

The central figure in this protracted last act of the drama was not uplifted by any sense of deliverance from his weight of misery. A little before the end he walked back from Oxford to Littlemore with Albany Christie. He could not speak. Not a word was uttered the whole way. He clung to his companion's hand, like a man suffering in extremest agony, carrying it to his face and wetting it with his tears.

In the afternoon of October 8 Dalgairns prepared to leave Littlemore in order to meet the Passionist Father

Dominic in Oxford. Father Dominic was to stay the night at Littlemore. As Dalgairns was taking his stick, Newman approached him and said, in a low voice: 'When you see your friend will you tell him that I wish him to receive me into the Church of Christ?' The coach was late in arriving. It was not until eleven o'clock that Father Dominic reached Littlemore in pouring rain. Newman had spent the interval writing to his friends. As the priest sat down by the fire to dry his clothes, Newman entered the room, fell on his knees, and begged to be received into the Church. He made his general confession that night. After it was over, he was so exhausted that he could not walk. St. John and another disciple took him by the arms and helped him, stumbling and half fainting, to his bed.

INDEX

PRINTED IN GREAT BRITAIN
BY ROBERT MACLEHOSE AND CO. LTD.
THE UNIVERSITY PRESS, GLASGOW